To Daniel Copeland
for being the spark behind it all

# - MAP OF -

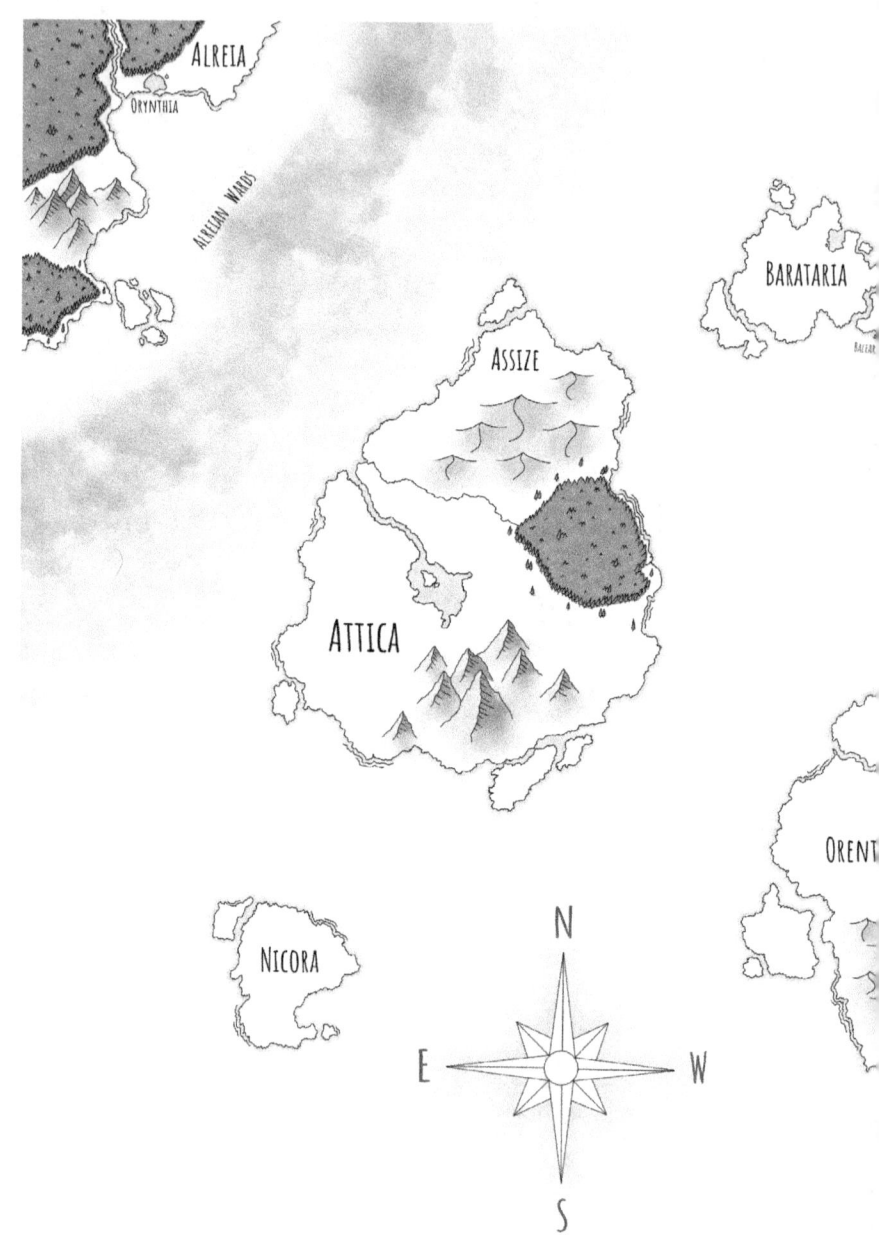

# - THE WORLD -

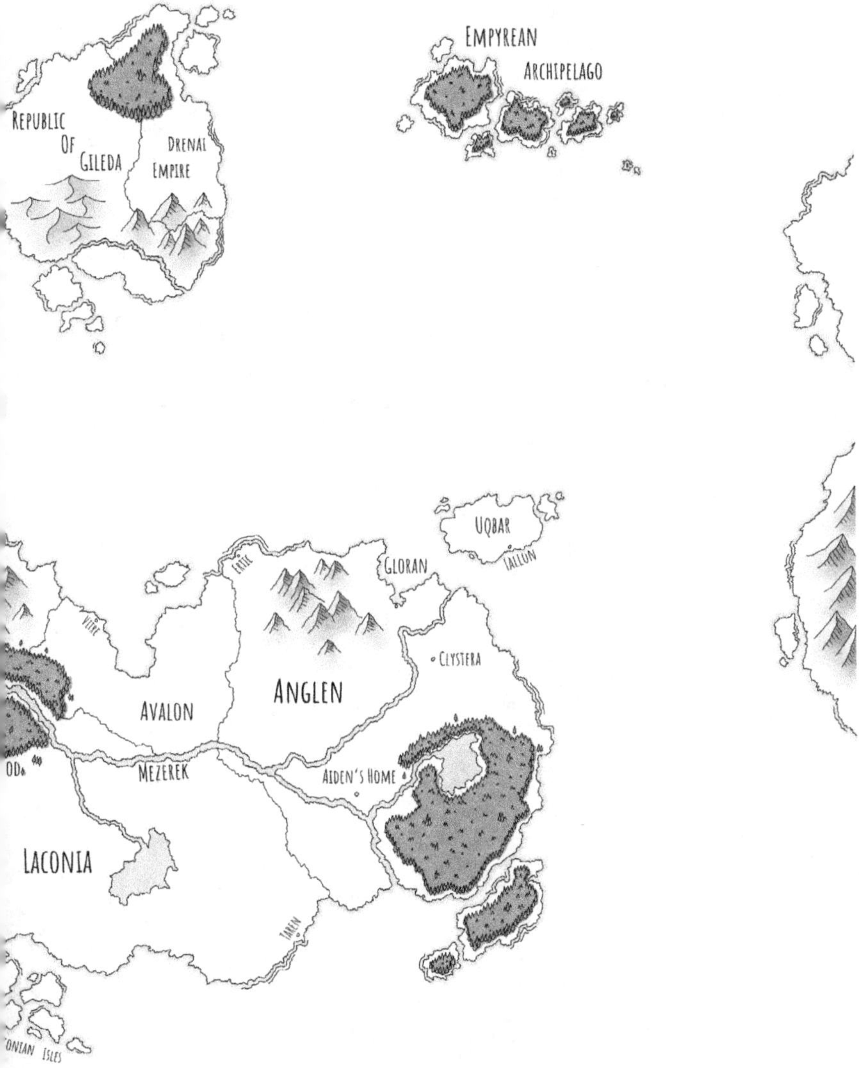

REPUBLIC
OF
GILEDA

DRENAL
EMPIRE

EMPYREAN
ARCHIPELAGO

UQBAR

TALLON

GLORAN

CLYSTERA

ANGLEN

AVALON

MEZEREK

AIDEN'S HOME

OD

LACONIA

ONIAN ISLES

# PROLOGUE

*Thirteen Years Ago*

# CORA & OBERIN

"Cora, we're going to be late," Oberin shouted from the bedroom. Through the open door, he could hear the sounds of Cora making vain efforts to do up the buttons at the back of her dress.

"I can't get...," she was saying as he walked into the room. It was a kind of funny scene that met his eyes: Cora, trying with pitiful skill to force the buttons through the holes while across the room, standing in his cradle holding the bars, the baby watched laughing and jumping slightly.

"Aiden seems to find you funny at least," joked Oberon.

"Ha ha, dickhead. Now come help me get this on, I don't want to miss the opening."

"You do know you're going to have to quit swearing like a sailor someday, or everyone will think our child grew up with pirates."

"In that case," Cora said, not missing a beat, "I think we should get him an eye patch just to get rid of any doubt about his involvement with pirates."

"Our son can barely run, and you're already thinking of how you're going to get him into organized crime," Oberin replied as he walked over to her. She turned her back, pushing aside a length of brown hair and exposing the buttons of her dress. It wasn't a fancy thing, but for this town, she'd be dressed as nicely as any lady there.

"You sure little Aiden's gonna be alright by himself for a few hours...?" Oberin questioned. "You do know he can get out of that cradle whenever he wants, right?"

"He can, but he hasn't quite figured outdoors yet, and anyway, I bet he'll be asleep as soon as we leave." Oberin dropped the point, doing up the last of the buttons and grabbing her hand to twirl her around. She took it, and her skirts flew a little as she spun.

"Do you know who all is going to be there?" Oberin asked.

"Not exactly. Jeb and Sara said they couldn't leave little Rose home alone yet, but they have less faith than we do... Aiden knows not to try to go outside."

"Oh really, the two-year-old knows not to go outside?" Oberin taunted.

"He's nearly three...," Cora said, and paused for a moment. "Do... Do you think we shouldn't leave him, maybe Jeb and Sara?"

But Oberin cut her off. "I'm just messing with you. Of course I think we should go. Aiden will be fine." He touched her shoulders consolingly before walking over to the crib and reaching in, pulled Aiden out, tucking him against his chest as he carried the child over to Cora. She smiled at him, resulting in another long fit of babyish laughter.

Five minutes later, they had both pecked Aiden on the head and were now walking down the street, making their way to the pub.

It was as raucous as any night Cora or Oberin had ever seen when they pushed open the door to escape the bite of the fall cold.

"Opening night, you drunk fuckers!" was the first speech they heard upon entering, supplied by the new owner of the pub, a middle aged man with a thick accent who didn't really need the pub for money but had more than enough to spend and more than enough liking for ale than to warrant his owning a place to drink it.

"Congrats to you too, Ganic, you pint coddling swine!" Cora shouted while grabbing a pint of her own off one of the server's trays.

"Ayyy!" Ganic shouted, hopping down from the table and walking over to them.

"Glad you could make it," he said, clinking mugs with them.

"Looks like we weren't the only ones," Oberin said, taking a pointed look around the room. It was buzzing with activity, every seat taken, and that many people again reveling, standing, or near falling down from drink.

"Agh! Well, ya know how it is, people like a good time, and it ain't often you north folks get ta meet a true south man like me fine self."

"True south man, my ass," Cora said, finishing a swig from her glass.

"Oh, you don't know what you're saying," drawled Ganic. "Down where I'm from it gets so damn cold that the driblets of beer in your beard will freeze. Folks down there won't drink any ale lighter than mud."

"You're having a laugh," Oberin said, not at all minding the story though.

"Not at all, it's where I got this stock, that's why y'all like it so much, most a ya never had good southern ale, also why so many of ya are already on the ground," he finished with a hearty laugh pointing around the room to where multiple people already seemed to have fallen asleep, or passed out was probably more correct, all around the room.

"Now mind ya selves, it's good stuff," he began to turn away back into the crowd of people. "But it'll give you the hangover of ya life if ya ain't careful." He disappeared into the crowd almost instantly.

The two of them sipped at their pints for a minute longer before Cora asked, "Care to take your lady for a dance?" She held out a hand, nodding over to the empty stretch of floor in front of the live musicians.

The night flew by quickly, one dance turning into another, and another turning into group dancing. Spilled drinks, slurred speech, and outlandish tall tales. When they left, it was in the middle of one of the older guests telling a story about a time he visited a cafe in the capital that was made entirely out of glass.

"No, no, I'm not lying, all glass and it went out above the street, so if it'd broken, you'd fall right onto the street below."

"Whatever you say, old man," another said, waving a hand.

Oberin and Cora stood. "I'm 'fraid… we must bid you all adieu," Cora said, slurring her words the slightest bit as she gave them all a mock bow and took Oberin's arm in hers.

The chill outside hit them like a wall the moment they stepped out the door. It had been just after sunset when they'd left their house, the air had still been warm. But the night had stolen any memory of that warmth, and now they clung together for it, short as the walk home was.

Someone yelled, "Friend!"

They both looked round at the shout.

"Over here!"

They looked in the direction of the shout to find a tall man with a cloak partially covering his face and wrapped close around him for warmth.

"Hello?" Cora said, shivering against Oberin. "Is there anything we can do for ya? It's cold as a bitch's tits out here."

The tall man let out a small, deep chuckle."Maybe, I feel like I know you from somewhere… What's your name if you don't mind my asking?"

Cora didn't mind, but it was too cold for this conversation, and her already starting hangover wasn't making her want to stand out here any longer than necessary.

"I'm Cora, this is Oberin." Oberin raised a hand in greeting. "What did you say it was you needed help with again?" Cora asked.

"You say Cora and Oberin. Damn, I could sworn I knew you from somewhere. What was your last name?" the man asked, totally dogging Cora's question.

"Our last name's Windren," replied Oberin. "Now really friend, it's cold, what can we do for ya? We gotta get home, we've got a little one waiting for us."

Something shifted in the man at Oberin's words, shifted in a way that made Oberin uneasy, and he took a subtle step closer to Cora. Cora was about to insist that the man tell them what he needed or they were going to have to leave when two figures stepped up beside the man.

"You've done all I needed you to," the taller man's demeanor had shifted fully now, cold, harsh. He flicked off his hood, revealing a long hilt of a sword. The other two at his sides did the same.

"My client just needed me to confirm who you were."

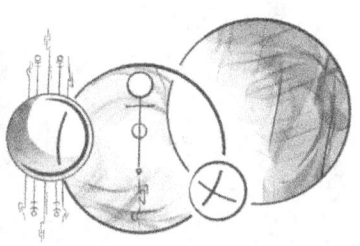

# I

## What One Makes Of The World

# CHAPTER 1

A dog jumped over a crate of apples, just set down by a farmer unloading his new harvest, as an old man followed in pursuit of a menacing dog who had terrorized a cat and since been rampaging in the market with blind joy. Nearby, boys and girls played, and the baker kneaded his dough. A musician played his wonderful violin, the melody so breathtaking that the old man gave up on his chase in favor of simply listening to the melody. And with the music, he betrayed his anger.

He walked back to his home on the other side of the stream and continued his prior quarrel of attempting to re-thread his shoelaces, his ever-withering fingers making the task difficult. Still, even as he dropped the lace, he wasn't so much as annoyed; he'd lived a long life. And in that moment, the old man knew, if his death were to come tomorrow, he would not be sad or angry. His only wish would be to hear the song of his people across the stream, not just the melody of the violin but also the laughing children, the barking dog, the slapping of the baker's dough on his workbench, and most of all the holistic tune of life emanating from the town.

Peace and prosperity, love and life, the great ambition of his life's work, come to fruition.

As the kids played, one boy stopped for a moment, bracing his hands on his knees to catch his breath, and whilst doing so, saw a dog race past, closely followed by a man. He thought the man looked angry at first, his beard only partially obscuring the look of frustration plastered across his face, eyebrows furrowed. But when the man's ears caught the tune of the musician, his expression softened, and the boy could have sworn that he saw a flash of silver in his eye. The boy watched, some curiosity gripping him. The man was not ordinary, at least not like the others of the town. The boy knew at least by sight, if not name, nearly everyone in the town by now, and none of them wore gold-threaded clothes and boots, polished so finely you could see the sun in their reflection. No, there was something off about this man, not bad necessarily, but... off.

When the song ended, the man turned the way he had come and slowly began to walk. Attracted by that strange curiosity the boy couldn't quite place, he followed. Maybe it was the fine clothes, or maybe it was the way the music had caught his attention. The man didn't look back, and the old man's ears, tired with age, it seemed, didn't detect the boy. The man passed over a small but unmistakably expensive bridge, with an engraved keystone, reading, "*KW*". The boy had no idea what it meant. He rarely frequented this side of the town, and in all his years of life here had never bothered to venture into this section of the surrounding woods. The man reached a large house, the largest the boy had ever seen, and walked inside. The boy paused, and, after a moment of hesitation, he crept up to the still-open door. Cautiously peering around the edge, he found the man attempting to lace another fine pair of shoes, these ones dyed a reddish sort of brown. He struggled and dropped the laces. The boy didn't understand why the man couldn't do it. It should only take a moment to weave the thread through the holes. But as the boy pondered this, he stepped back and slipped on the slightly wet mossy stones, thudding as his butt hit the floor.

# Chapter 2

Something hit the ground outside the door, and the old man stood.

"Probably that daft cat," he muttered. He looked around the door to find not a cat but a slightly nervous-looking boy.

Wide-eyed, the boy peered up into his face and began tentatively, "I'm sorry, I didn't mean to spy…"

But the man held up a wrinkled hand."It's okay." He extended that same hand and pulled the boy to his feet. "What's your name?" said the man with surprising gentleness.

"Aiden."

"And where are your parents?"

"I don't have any," said the boy, beginning to shy away. "They died twelve years ago."

"So who's been taking care of you?"

"No one but sometimes the baker lets me wash his dishes for food."

The man didn't respond for a second. "Well, Aiden, my name is William. Would you like to come in and have a bite to eat?"

The boy's face broke into an uncertain grin, and he followed the man inside. The house was wonderful, like nothing Aiden had ever seen. Walls of stone with dark polished wood surrounded the doorways and supported the high sealing. They reached a balcony with a small table and two cushy chairs. William asked him to wait for a moment. Not knowing what to do he sat in one of the chairs. A minute later William returned and said that someone would be up with food shortly.

"So who are you?" Aiden asked, still tentative.

"You need not be worried, I'm King William, ruler of Anglen."

"So what do you do?" Aiden asked he'd heard of Kings. He knew Anglen had one. He knew there were great cities to the north of the kingdom and that the capital was there, but that had always felt so far away, like it was somehow a different world. The man pondered for a moment and then responded.

"I suppose the ultimate goal of my job is to keep Anglen prosperous." William continued to explain, and a moment later, a woman appeared carrying a tray with two plates, both laden with silverware, a small chop of lamb and a small amount of asparagus on both. The woman set down the tray, offering a warm smile, and walked away. They both began to eat.

When Aiden had finished his meal William asked where he lived. Aiden told him of how the butcher allows him to sleep in the meat room so long as he chases away any mice who try to eat the drying meat.

"How old are you?"

"I'm 15, I'll be 16 in May," replied Aiden.

"Young, but enough of a lad to be out and about, though I can't imagine you've always been old enough for that to be a reasonable arrangement."

"That… is probably true," Aiden conceded.

William nodded and offered to walk him back to the village. "It's beginning to get dark. I think it's best if you get back before the light truly fades." They walked together, backtracking Aiden's steps, all the while carrying on a pleasant conversation.

They finally got back to the town. "If you like, you're welcome to come back to my home tomorrow and I can show you more of what I do," offered the King. And with that, the old man bade him a good night and walked away.

# CHAPTER 3

Aiden walked into the butcher shop. "Hi Frank," he quipped.

"Hi there, Aiden," the man called back, not looking up as Aiden walked into the back room and to the small spare cot Frank had given him to sleep on in the meat room, along with a scratchy but still thick wool blanket. As Aiden lay down he thought of his life and his meeting with William. Aiden supposed he was technically homeless. He was allowed to sleep here on a whim, and the kindness of Frank. He had no stable way of getting food, or clothes. Though somehow, he had never felt homeless, since the death of his parents when he indeed had been too young for a self-sufficient life to be at all reasonable. Yet, he'd done it. He couldn't remember them. Either way, they'd gone out one night and had not come back. People thought they had been killed, a crime so rare here that in the uproar he as a small toddler was largely forgotten. But this town was a good one, and through the kindness of some adults in the town, he had been raised. Not as anyone's child, per se, but more like a stray cat. He went around as he pleased, helping people in exchange for food and shelter as the opportunities arose. He had friends and got along quite well with nearly everyone in town. But he wasn't ignorant; he knew that there were bad and cruel people in the world. It was for that reason that he had been so nervous about William earlier that day, though the man had been kind and had emanated a sense of knowledge and warmth. And with that thought, he drifted into sleep.

He woke to the sound of Frank operating the shop,

"Any trouble last night?" Frank knew there hadn't been. There hadn't been a mouse in years, but Aiden didn't have anywhere to sleep so Frank let him sleep in the back room, out of kindness and maybe he was even a little fond of Aiden. Frank chuckled under his breath at this thought as Aiden walked out of the back room.

"Good morning," Aiden said with a yawn. Aiden also knew that there were no mice and that Frank just let him sleep there, but Frank didn't seem to mind and Aiden liked Frank well enough, and the back room.

"Be safe out there," said Frank.

Aiden flashed him a happy if not slightly mischievous grin. When he walked out it was to find some of his best friends Sara, Dante, and Roy playing with a dirty, not quite round ball. None of them were actual strays like him, but still, their parents and the town in general had an unspoken rule of letting the children learn their own lessons. If they got hurt, it was bound to happen sooner or later, and in the twelve years since Aiden's parents' murders there hadn't been any cause for the parents of the town to do otherwise. So this was the routine, do as they like all day and find a place to plop down at night.

"Join us!" they shouted through all their laughter, and he ran to do so.

"You're on my team!" Dante shouted and passed him the ball. They continued to play down one street, then the next, until they got to the main street where, unbeknownst to them in their careless joy, a small group stood, not of their town. These people were clad in black cloaks, two men, one woman, and one girl about Aiden's age.

"I'm open!" Aiden shouted to Dante.

Aiden ran to get the ball Dante sent sailing. Ran, right into one of the men, tall and powerfully built with a long sword poking over his shoulder from under his cloak. The man stumbled. Aiden bent around to offer a word of apology when he caught sight of the man's face, grim with anger and eyes gleaming with a promise of violence. Without a moment's hesitation, in a lazy movement, he struck Aiden on the side of the head so abruptly and hard he was knocked clean off his feet. The girl in the group let out a small noise and the man's attention snapped to her. As fast as an asp he struck her as well, but she didn't waver or stumble as though she was ready for the blow.

His friends ran over and grabbed him, pulling him away and they all ran. When they were all out of breath and panting they stopped."Who were those people?" Sara gasped as the others shook their heads.

"I should go talk to someone," Aiden rasped. "I'll be back later." Not waiting for their responses, he began for the far end of town.

# Chapter 4

William was sitting in the great room of his summer home reading the numerous letters received just that morning, addressed from everyone from noblemen to other Kings to one of the blacksmiths in the town whom he had sent a letter to last night commissioning him to make a sword. This response was likely just the invoice for the project. But another letter caught his eye, a bright red letter from one of his neighboring Lords. The reception of the letter in and of itself wasn't anything unusual, but the red envelope was. Tearing open the letter, he began to read, a feeling of unease growing in his gut with every word his eyes passed over.

*Dear King William*

*I am sending this letter as a warning in the hopes that should they come, you will know the threat they pose and you will be spared any potential ruin they may cause. There is a small band of whom I can only guess are mercenaries based on how they drenched the streets of Taren in blood. My informants tell me it's a band of four: two men, one woman, and a girl. I bid you proceed with caution and would counsel you to attempt to reach a diplomatic end should they do more than pass through. Last my informants heard, they were heading in your direction, I bid you be cautious and hope the best for you.*

*Yours sincerely,*

*King Roland*

The King let loose a long sigh, uttering a silent prayer to the gods that the mercenaries, whomever they are, don't come to Anglen. That they piss off back to whatever backwater they're from and leave his kingdom in peace. He rose and walked to his desk to write a letter to the nearest outpost of guards. Alerting them of the concern and ordering them to increase their patrols, he included the description he'd been given and a warning that they may be more dangerous than the description would suggest. William hadn't had to deal with any kind of violence in his lands under his reign. Gods willing, he had always been grateful for it.

As he continued to ponder this thought, he heard light but slightly frantic footsteps, quiet, but growing louder. A moment later Aiden pushed open the door and stepped in, out of breath and closely followed by Mary, his servant.

"He said it was urgent," Mary stated.

"What is it dear boy?" William asked, alarmed at Aiden's appearance as he stood.

"There were these three people...," he panted, "With swords in the town. They had a girl with them. I bumped into one of them while playing with my friends. He looked at me and hit me."

23

William didn't know why, but at those words, anger flared, but he quickly mastered himself.

"Then, when the girl made a noise, he hit her too. Then came here to tell you…," he said, pausing and looking slightly nervous. In hindsight, Aiden realized that maybe he should not have come. Perhaps William wouldn't care. He was a King after all and probably had better things to do than worry over the trifles of a stray child.

But William sighed and said, "I just received word that a group meeting that description might be passing through."

"Is there any way I can help?" Aiden asked before thinking.

William hesitated. "Perhaps." He paused again. "But you need to understand that in doing so you would be shouldering quite a lot of potential risk."

Aiden's only response was a nod.

"If you could discover their intentions, it would be extremely helpful," suggested William.

"I will," said Aiden, and made to leave, already ready to do what he'd been asked, and a little nervous that it might be impertinent to have come in the first place, at least so abruptly.

"Aiden!" called the King. "If they ask, don't tell them I sent you."

"I won't," Aiden replied and walked out the door.

Aiden figured that he had at least a few days to find out what the group was up to.

William hadn't mentioned a time, not that Aiden had stayed long enough for him to provide a deadline. And so, in the meantime, he went to the bakery and asked Phil, the baker, if there was anything he could do for a scrap of food. An hour later, after cleaning the dishes and helping Phil need some fresh dough, he was given a sandwich and a rich chocolate eclair, both wrapped in a small bit of wax cloth. Phil was a kindly man like Frank. He didn't need Aiden's help, but he had always been good to him and never let him go hungry. Aiden left the bakery with a wave of farewell and made his way back to the meat shop, more tired than he ought to have been. With thoughts of strangers in dark alleys, he went to bed.

The next morning, he awoke a little before sunrise, making an effort to stay unseen until he found Sara. Small town, small world, he figured. Following that line of thinking, someone probably saw where the people went, and with the small world of the town, word of where they went was probably already circulating about.

"Do you know where those people from yesterday are?" Aiden asked Sara.

She raised her brows. "Ricky told me that they went down to that barn with the well."

Aiden knew what she meant; there were few places in the city he didn't recognize from a vague description. And so, he made his way in that direction. When he got to the barn near the river, he crept up to the small ivy-covered window in the back of the structure and crept through. Sure enough, there they were, one leaning against a beam, two sitting and one standing. Small rays of light stabbed through the stale, hay-smelling air, casting the rest of the dark space into an even deeper shadow. He crept in closer, crouched behind a pile of hay, and listened.

"Let's send a message and get out of here," the woman breathed. "I hate this place, it's full of sentimental old fools and children who don't know their places."

"Agreed, but what?" growled the shorter of the men.

"Whatever we want," she said with a vague wave of her arm. "Well, kill a few shop owners the town relies on, leave the bodies, and high tail it," said the woman.

"Who?" asked the taller and more powerfully built man, the one who had hit Aiden. Even now, with supposedly his friends, the man felt mean, his face, the harsh way his hand scratched at his chin. Looking at the way the others looked at him, it seemed he was the leader.

"That merchant, the butcher, and maybe a farmer," snorted the woman.

Aiden's breath caught in his lungs and he made a small noise. Pressing a hand to his mouth, he took a step back.

"That should be enough to send the Kingdom into unrest," the brawny leader hissed. "Then get out of here before anyone knows it was us. When The King claims ownership of the crimes, it'll help show his power and reach."

Aiden looked around the pile again. The scene looked the same but something was off, something was missing. The missing thing only occurred to him as it became obvious what had changed.

"Spying are we?" murmured a silken voice.

Aiden spun around to find the tall, slender woman, with black hair and bared teeth, holding a long, wicked dagger angled so that if he moved, the tip would bury in the arteries of his neck.

"Boys! Look what we have here," she cried, with every indication of cruel pleasure. Grabbing him under the arm, she pulled him over to the others. Pinning his arm behind his back, the woman made him look at them. Aiden didn't fight, it wasn't time for that, not yet at least. He was a trapped animal but not yet a doomed one.

"So what are you doing here?" she purred.

He wouldn't be too scared; that would give him away. But then again, not being scared might do the same. "I just wanted to apologize for running into y-y-you yesterday," he said faking a stutter under the glower the taller man gave him.

"I don't give a damn about your apologies," he snarled. "What did you hear?" His voice dropped an octave for the question.

Aiden didn't answer for a moment. "Something about there being unrest." A partial truth, one he prayed they would believe.

The man stared Aiden down, ripping into him with his gaze. "Go," the man growled and waved a hand indicating to the door.

Aiden didn't need to be told twice. He walked away quickly but not running, but as fast as he could pass off for just being nervous.

# CHAPTER 5

Minutes later Aiden ran straight for the meat shop and burst in yelling for Frank.

"Calm down! What is it?" Frank asked with a concerned look on his face.

Aiden took a few panicked glances around the room before his eye caught on Frank and he burst out, "You need to hide or leave or, at least for a little while." Aiden panted still out of breath

"Now why would I do that?" Frank asked with a jovial smile.

"There are bad people in town right now. They're trying to send us into chaos by killing you and…"

Frank cut him off looking at Aiden with more concern for him than anything he had just said. "Woah, woah, woah, who's trying to kill who?" Frank asked.

"They want to kill you, a merchant and a farmer, I think," A note of pleading now colored Aiden's words.

"Now, Aiden, I'm sure you just misheard someone joking about how they don't like me and those other people. It's nothing to worry about," Frank said, pulling off his apron and tossing it so that the neck loop caught on a hook mounted to the wall behind the counter.

"But…" Aiden started but Frank cut him off again.

"It's nothing, it'll be fine. Come have some dinner my…" Frank was saying, turning back to look at Aiden.

But Aiden ran out of the shop, taking a left up the street, shoes smacking against the hard cobbles of the street, he directed himself for the King's home.

When he got there, Mary let him, less surprised at his state than the first time he'd arrived at the house unannounced. She, however, gave him a strained smile and led him to William, sitting in his study and busy drafting a letter to someone.

Aiden explained as best he could, a task that took considerable time considering the lack of breath Aiden had from the run over.

William said, "I'll get my guards to come up with excuses to get those people out of harm's way." He assured Aiden with his calm but decisive words. "In the meantime, if you are willing to try to keep an eye on them, from afar," he said sternly, emphasizing the last word.

Aiden had conveniently left out the part where the violent strangers thought he may have been spying, worried that William might think it too risky and wouldn't let him help anymore. He took the King's sternness as confirmation.

"Who do you think is trying to kill our people...? I mean, who do you think the King they work for is?" Aiden asked, not knowing whether the question might be out of line or not.

"I can think of a few rulers who have grudges to settle with both me and with our allies. Though I'm not certain that any of them would do this. I will continue to try to uncover things in my own way..." He hesitated for a moment looking uneasy. "You do understand that you don't need to help if you wish not to... And you are free to quit anytime."

"I want to," Aiden supplied with more conviction than he would have expected himself to have. It surprised him a little bit.

"Well, then for what you have already done." The King reached to the side table by the chair he was sitting on, which was one of two around a circular table on the far side of the study from the desk. William grabbed a small bag. "For you," he said, handing over the bag which clanked slightly as Aiden grabbed it. The fabric straining against the weight of whatever was in it.

"What is it?" Aiden asked, starting to feel confused.

"Your payment."

"Payment?"

"You've earned it, 30 silver marks."

"What?!" Aiden gasped in alarm, making to hand the bag back and to stand. He held it out to William like something he might get in trouble just for having.

"Keep it," said the King with an easy smile. "I'm not in the business of unpaid servants."

"But what do I do with it…?"

"Whatever you like, and I have one more thing for you," the King said slowly. "Give me one moment." He left the room and came back a minute later carrying a long package neatly wrapped in brown paper and twine. "For you so long as you promise to be careful and responsible with it," William said sternly.

"I do," Aiden breathed, his curiosity building. William handed it over as Aiden began to carefully unwrap the package.

The King continued, "I do hope you'll come back to learn how to use it with me sometime."

Aiden pulled off the paper to find a sword. Sheathed in its scabbard, it had a burning white handle with a silver inlay of his own name. The guard stretched straight perpendicular to the blade, gleaming, as was the pommel.

"C-Can I take it out?" Aiden asked hesitantly.

William gestured to do so, with even more warmth coming into his expression. Aiden pulled out the blade. It was like pale starlight buffed to a mirror polish. The blade was about an inch and a half wide coming down to a precise point, the fuller beginning just past the guard and ending a few inches back from the tip.

"I commissioned it to be made the day I met you. I do hope you like it. It's called Starlight, or so I am told by its smith." William paused for a breath, "I never had children, and I know I could never take that place for you but... well, if you need anything, I'm here."

Aiden was at a complete and utter loss for words, he carefully replaced the sword in the scabbard causing the blade to wine slightly as he did and set the it on the table before walking over to the old man. There were no tears in Aiden's eyes but he had a sense of a piece being put into place in his life. Like a hole he'd never even asked to be filled now had a mason at its edges, and now that there was, it felt hard to imagine it being empty again. Aiden hugged the old man, and the old man hugged him back. No, Aiden thought, not everything is perfect, but with how much his world changed in the last few days alone, maybe it will be, someday.

"Thank you," whispered Aiden, finding his voice choked up." Tears now began to gleam in his eyes.

William's only response was a wide, warm smile as he grabbed the sword from its place on the table and helped fasten it to Aiden's back, the handle poking over his shoulder, just within reach to grab and draw.

"Which blacksmith made it?" Aiden asked.

"A man by the name of Gardon. He's a traveling smith who comes through these parts now and then. Run along and be careful to get home before it gets dark." The King ushered him out with one more hug.

As Aiden walked back to the meat shop, he decided he was going to buy himself a cloak, and eventually, when he had the money, maybe a knife to match his sword. When he got home, it was to find Frank waiting.

"I've just received a letter from the King asking me to go to a festival in the south for a few weeks. I have agreed. I trust you'll be ok here on your own?" Frank asked before Aiden had a chance to say anything and held out a key.

Aiden took it and said,

"I'm sorry about earlier, you were right, I…"

But Frank cut him off, with a smile that made Aiden sure that Frank wasn't mad at all. "Aiden you don't have to be sorry. I'm honored you care that much 'bout me." He paused, eyes narrowing suspiciously. "What's that on your shoulder?"

"Nothing," Aiden replied.

"Did you steal it?"

"No."

"Then I don't care, just stay out of trouble. I'll see you in a few weeks," Frank replied before he strode out the door.

Aiden walked to the back room and went to bed. He was glad Frank wasn't mad, not that Frank would have kicked him out over it but, still, he didn't want to be on bad terms, with anyone in town really.

The next morning he decided to make good on his decision to buy the cloak. Walking towards the market, he spotted Sara and Roy. He played and talked with them for a few minutes of the sort of idle banter that comes easily to childhood friends before continuing to the market. After a short time wandering the different clothing stalls, he found a vendor selling a wide enough array of styles that he was able to find a black cloak with silver fastenings and a large hood, big enough, he hoped, to cover the hilt of his sword. He wrapped it around himself, feeling the warm fabric brush against his shoulders. He bought it for 10 marks.

When he got back to the meat shop Aiden tried his sword on with his cloak. He'd debated for a moment whether it would be alright to bring the sword into the market, but after seeing Frank's response it seemed a poor decision. But now back at the shop alone, he tried it on again and flipped up the hood. He was able to entirely hide the hilt, and with it down, was able to easily draw the blade.

Some time later he went over to Phil's to work and get some food. He asked Phil if this time he could work extra and get some extra food so he worked with Phil 'til a bit after noon, deciding that he would make his first attempt to find where the foreign group was staying that night.

He hadn't bothered asking any of his friends this time if they knew where those people had gone. He didn't want anybody knowing that he had such a big interest in them. Anyway, he doubted they'd take such big risks in picking a hiding spot this time with how easily he'd found them last time. Wanting to get some rest before night, he went back to the shop. Aiden fell asleep considering what he knew about them and what might help, though he really didn't know anything useful. But that was tomorrow's problem.

# CHAPTER 6

When Aiden awoke, it was dark. He dawned the sword and cloak in silence, watching the pale rays of moon light that illuminated the meat carcasses hanging from the beams of the ceiling. As he slipped out the backdoor disappearing into the shadows, he thought about using the sword. He knew how to use it to some degree at least. A year ago, there had been a knight, Kerstin, who had been stationed in their town, some part of his rising through the ranks of the kingdom. But in the time he was there, he had taken a liking to Aiden, enough so that he offered to teach him how to fight. Kerstin did it as much to have something to do as anything else, but still, it'd worked. By the end of Kerstin's mission, Aiden had become a respectable, if not particularly elegant swordsman.

Either way, he tried to prepare himself mentally for the event of having to use it, though in all likelihood running away would be the better decision. He continued to creep along, the hood mostly managing to cover his face. After a few hours of combing the town for any sign of the group, just when he was beginning to consider calling it, he spotted the shorter of the two men. He began to follow, sticking to the darkest shadows, he kept forty yards behind 'til the man reached a small warehouse and peered around, clearly looking for anyone following. Aiden slunk deeper into the shadows, trying not to move in anyway that might give him away. The man turned back and walked. in, shutting the door quickly behind him.

Aiden assessed his surroundings. Two buildings down from the warehouse there was a barn, old but in good condition and unlocked. Aiden made his way inside, a few horses bristling at his unexpected appearance, stamping their feet. He ignored them and climbed a ladder, got onto the second story, and peered out the window at the end of the building to watch the warehouse. It began to feel like an age watching the building, but perhaps two hours later when his eyelids started to feel heavy and posture gradually deteriorated with drowsiness, the warehouse door opened the slightest bit, so slightly that Aiden at first thought it might be the wind doing it. But it was enough to spark his attention. He watched as the girl who had made the noise at his being struck days ago, stepped out then looked back, seeming more nervous of the people in the building than any outside threat. With one last glance back, she broke into a brisk walk pulling a hood of her own up to cover her face. Aiden slid down the ladder and began to follow her. Walking farther and farther, he began to get more careless with curiosity, and as a result was getting closer and closer. In the market, now dead and empty in the middle of the night, she rounded a corner. When he made to follow, he found the alley empty.

His only warning was the hairs on the back of his neck as he drew the sword and spun around to block the girl's blade as it made a swipe for his ribs. Sparks flew as the blades met hard enough to force Aiden to take a step back. She slashed again, this time for his throat, unrelenting, as he blocked, parried and blocked. He feigned going for the ally, and as she lunged a little too wildly trying to follow him, he grabbed her wrist with his free hand twisting it behind her back before she had the chance to rip it free and make another attempt to kill him. She dropped the sword as he raised his blade to her neck. He held her for a moment, both of them breathing hard for the exertion of the fight.

"If I let you go, promise you won't kill me?" Aiden gasped.

She made to nod but his blade prevented it so she said, "Yes" in a low snarl that really didn't sound like her voice at all.

He lowered his blade and let her arm go. She stepped a few paces away, but didn't run. He squatted down and grabbed her sword, pausing for the span of a second before handing it to he. She snatched it back with a look of surprise at the gesture. He could make out her face now, her hood had fallen back during their fight. She had gold hair, a few freckles here and there, sea green eyes, and if it weren't for the look of, Aiden didn't even know what, painted across her face, she would have been pretty.

"What's your name?" he asked, trying to sound genuine. She could of course attack him again but... She wouldn't, he knew she wouldn't.

"Ava," she said, figuring she owed him that after trying to kill him.

"Why were you sneaking away from your group?"

"My group!" she snapped with a cruel laugh. "They are not my group. They saw that I was good with a sword and pretty and thought they could use me to their advantage. They kidnapped me. And I'm sneaking out because they didn't care to give me food." She stoped glaring at him.

"Do you plan to flee?" he asked gently if not a little curiously.

"Where? To my home is across an ocean? I have nowhere to go other than back to them. That's why I'm not locked up. Even if they would beat me for having left and for having been caught by you, they still know I'll come back, because I have nowhere else to go."

"I'm... so sorry," he breathed, his eyes lining with tears.

She looked like she was about to snap some rude remark but her expression softened after a moment, realizing that he was being genuine. "I know," she said, head bowing.

"I... If you would like... you can stay with me? I have a building I sleep in and a little bit of food..." he trailed off not knowing what he was saying.

She stilled and looked at him suspiciously. "Really?" she said, looking uncertain.

"Only if you'd like to, but it'd be nice to have some company."

"But what about your parents?" she asked."You can't be older than what? Thirteen?" Her tone made it clear she was messing with him.

"I am fifteen actually, and you can't be any older than me."

"Your parents?" the girl asked again,

"They're gone," Aiden admitted dully. "So's the butcher who owns the shop."

"Alright then," she said with a smile. It was a wonderful thing, the smile, it reached her bright sea-colored eyes. She didn't pry about his parents, just took his answer as a fact.

"One last thing," he said in a light voice, "You have to promise not to kill me." Not waiting for her answer, he began to lead her back to the shop.

As they walked back to the butchers shop, Aiden couldn't help asking, "You didn't really think I was thirteen?"

She tried to hide her smile, pretending to examine the wall on one side of the alley as she answered. "You know it's just that baby face of yours," She said, trying to stop a laugh and failing miserably.

" ... Ouch."

# CHAPTER 7

When they arrived, Aiden pulled the thicker of the two blankets off of the cot and handed it to her. "Sorry, but you don't get my bed. We can see if we can find you another tomorrow."

With that, Ava wrapped herself in the blanket and laid her cloak atop the stones of the floor, smiling faintly. She pushed her own sword to rest next to Aiden's under his bed before lying down herself a few feet away. Aiden got in the bed and they fell asleep quickly.

The following morning Aiden woke to the sound of Ava reaching for her sword.

"If you don't want to be noticed, you'd be better off leaving that behind. Not many kids our age carry swords," Aiden said in a groggy voice, yawning and stretching.

"What? You don't bring your sword when you leave here?"

"I only got this sword recently," Aiden yawned again, "But I think you'll blend in pretty well with the other kids in the town without it."

"And what if I need it?"

"In that case, I've always found running like my life depends on it to be a reliable fall back," he said, yawning for a third time.

Ava nodded hesitantly, setting her blade next to Aiden's under the bed again with an unsure look.

"I have some food but if we go over to the bakery I bet Phil will let us help for something fresh."

She nodded more confidently this time and they made their way to the bakery where they found Phil preparing to start the baking for the day. Late as usual, it was never a safe bet to assume that Phil would have food ready before noon but that was made up for by his having the best in town.

"Hi Phil," Aiden said cheerfully. "Any chance Ava could also work for some breakfast?"

"Well, lucky for you, one of my kitchen aides just quit. I could use the help if you think you can make the croissants for today. You've made them with me before, Aiden?"

"Yeah, I think we can do that. Ava?"

She nodded, and Phil didn't ask any questions about her as he led the two of them into the kitchen and set them up at a station where they began making puff pastry.

It quickly became clear that Ava was much better with a sword than a rolling pin. After two hours the croissants were done and ready to be put in the oven. Aiden had done almost all of the process but Ava had tried to help, whether she did was still in question. When the croissants were fully cooked and ready to be eaten, the two of them took the finished croissants to Phil who complimented them and gave them each one of the croissants, a piece of cheese and a sandwich.

"Thanks, Phil," Aiden said with a hearty smile, already taking a bite out of the sandwich.

"Thanks," Ava said politely, a smile tugging at her lips. They ate their meals, keeping the leftovers in a piece of wax cloth Phil had lying around and making their way back to the meat shop.

"I like Phil," Ava said lightly.

"I think everyone does. That's why he doesn't have to open 'til noon and he's still the most popular baker in town."

As they walked back still nibbling on their croissants, Aiden stole himself to say, "We should talk?" It was more of a question than anything else.

She nodded, stiffening slightly and when they got back to the shop Ava sighed. "What would you like to know?" she said, seeming a little uncomfortable.

He paused thinking, "Who are those people who kidnapped you?"

"They're a group of mercenaries hired by the King of Orenth to come to the lands of your King and cause silent anarchy, to weaken them."

Aiden didn't know what to say so he just asked, "Why?"

"Why does any ruler try to take the lands of another?" Ava smirked. "For resources and power. He thinks he might gain something I suppose. I don't actually know the guy and my *friends* aren't exactly forthcoming."

"Ok then, next, who are you, where are you from and where did you learn to fight?" Aiden asked a little more lightly.

"I am Ava Corinth, princess of Attica, and I was forced to learn to fight as a princess and further trained to fight by the mercenaries." She paused, looking unsure if she wanted to continue. After a moment, she said, "I wasn't entirely honest with you when I told you that they took me because I was good with a sword. They took me as part of their mission to destabilize foreign Kingdoms." She paused again. "I have a few questions of my own, " Ava began.

He nodded. The truth was Aiden was an open book. Other than William, he didn't really have anything to hide.

"Where did you learn to fight?" she asked.

"I was taught to fight by a knight who passed through here a year ago."

"Ok." She paused again, thinking for a moment.

"Where did your parents go?" she asked and seemed to realize a moment later that it might have been better to ask a little more gently.

"I don't know," Aiden admitted. "They left one night and were found murdered the next day. I was too young to remember." In truth it really didn't feel all that personal. He hadn't known them and thus had little more love for them than the thought of them.

"I'm sorry," she breathed, and meant it.

But Aiden changed the subject. "Wanna try to find that bed before tonight?" he asked in a lighter tone.

"Yeah, that would be nice," she said with a chuckle.

Now dark outside, they decided it was safe to dawn their swords and cloaks. Aiden wouldn't have but Ava didn't want to walk around with the mercenaries still about. Walking down the cobbled street, Aiden spotted Rose, yet another of the friends he had played with throughout his childhood.

"Hey! Rose, you know if anyone has a bed for sale?"

"I think my uncle was selling one," she yelled back.

"Thanks, catch you later."

"Her uncle is only a few blocks down this street," he said to Ava, turning to the adjacent slightly smaller street.

"Hey, I forgot to ask who owns the shop we're staying in?" Ava wondered.

"It belongs to a man named Frank who lets me sleep there in exchange for helping to watch for pests." Aiden added, "But he's going to be gone for at least a few weeks." They walked a little further down the street.

"Here we are," Aiden said, stepping up to a door and knocking. A moment later a tall thin man with a full but graying beard answered.

"Aiden, it's been a while," said the man. What can I help you with?"

"Rose said you might be selling a bed?"

The man smiled. "I most certainly am. It's not great but it's enough to sleep on. For your friend I assume?"

Aiden nodded in Ava's direction.

"I was hoping to sell it for 20 copper marks but for you, I'd be willing to part with it for 15."

"That's all right," Aiden said with a warm smile reaching into his coin bag and pulling out 7 silver coins. "For you," he said, handing it out.

But the man's eyes narrowed, darting to the bulge poking over Aiden's shoulder and to the fine fastenings on his cloak. "Aiden, have you been taking anything you shouldn't be? I have a hard time believing you got this much money without a job."

"I haven't. I promise," Aiden said, looking straight into the man's eyes.

"Alright then, you don't need to pay me that much."

"No," Aiden said firmly. "You've always been kind to me, and you more than deserve it. You work as hard as anyone I know." It was true the man could be seen all day every day crafting and repairing boats along the river. "And anyway you know me," said Aiden. "I've been living with no money forever, I don't need it for anything."

"Well, in that case, thank you very much. The bed's over this way," he said, leading them into the house. Three minutes later the bed was on the front steps. The man bayed them good night, and as Aiden turned to go he added, "Aiden, if you are getting into any trouble just keep Rose out of it will you?"

"I will," he said with every intention of doing so. With that, he and Ava began to carry the bed back to the shop.

# CHAPTER 8

William sat at his desk contemplating what to do about the damned group that had brought so much trouble into his life. He had just sent a letter to his allies warning them of everything he knew.

He hoped Aiden would come back soon with some information but also just to see the boy and make sure he was okay. The worry that something might have happened to Aiden while trying to do what William had asked him to, had been nagging at him since he sent Aiden out with the mission. That being said though, in all likelihood, Aiden wouldn't be able to find the mercenaries. They were after all professionals and Aiden was, well... not. He wondered what he would do for the boy as payment if he came bearing good information. Perhaps a set of finer garments, or a set of boots, or maybe it was better to just ask him. William shook his head. He had more important things to do than think of how he would pamper Aiden. He needed to discuss the matter with Kerstin, his chief guard and third ranking general whom he had just sent for, asking that he come to William's summer home to discuss some sensitive topics. Kerstin would be arriving any minute now. If he'd been able, William would have made Kerstin first general but tradition demanded that he leave the post to some fat, beer-bellied lord that William seriously didn't think was literate. But that was the way of royal tradition he supposed. As he finished the thought, a knock on the door sounded.

"Come in," welcomed William.

The knight walked in, clad in black leather armor sparingly reinforced with gleaming metal at critical points.

"Please sit, I have much to tell you." When William had finished telling Kerstin everything, save about the boy, he asked,"How big of a threat do you think they pose and how would you counsel me to act?"

The knight paused thinking. "I believe you should continue to attempt to quietly bring a few more guards into town," the knight replied." Meanwhile, have the spies who have gathered this information continue to collect more and hopefully help to fill in the gaps in the picture."

William had always openly asked his guards, generals, and soldiers questions. Though well-versed in diplomatic affairs, he was no commander or general. And so he asked the opinions of those he trusted. Not the fat lord, but the ones whom he thought actually had a clue as to what they were talking about.

From there they dove down the rabbit hole trying to figure out why a foreign king would be seeking to wreak such destruction. Hours later, the captain bayed William good night and strode out the door. The room returned to silence. William realized that it might be a long while before he heard and felt the careless joy and happiness in his lands again. It was a thought that scared him more than any death could.

# CHAPTER 9

The following morning, Aiden woke long before the sun and once again dawned his gear. He set out some of the extra food he had earned working for Phil on the edge of Ava's bed before throwing his own blanket over her. Slipping out the back door with scarcely a sound, he walked back to the warehouse where he had last seen the mercenaries. Arriving at the location, he first climbed back to the perch in the barn. Spotting no signs of activity, he climbed back down the ladder and made his way to the main doors, chained as he expected with the large iron links wrapping around seemingly locked from the inside. Probably a precaution after Ava hadn't come back. Creeping around the side of the building, he spotted a small round window barely a foot across on the second level. He groaned and decided he would first check the rest of the building before resorting to that. He made his way around, finding nothing.

Circling back to the window, he grabbed a horizontal beam, pulling himself atop the first level of the building. He walked across the slate tiles of the roof, trying not to make a noise even as the tiles scratched, and approached the wall that stretched to the top of the roof. He looked up. Four feet above his head lay the bottom of the wooden window frame. Aiden took a step back and leapt for it. He caught the frame with one hand, and fixing his other, he pulled up enough to peer inside. All clear, pulling further he swung one foot over the frame. He had to pull himself through feet first, with how skinny the frame was, and for one horrible moment, he teetered on the edge of falling.

Once inside, he looked around. Deciding it would be safer without the noise, he unfastened his cloak and let it fall to the first-level roof. Continuing, he walked around crates and boxes and other miscellaneous items, finding nothing on the top level. Making for the stairs, he crept down silent as a hare; the steps didn't betray a creak. A victorious and mischievous grin broke across his face as he spotted his quarry. The woman was sleeping on the lone cot, the two men slumped against a pile of hay, cloaks draped over them.

Not wanting to come close without reason, he looked around. Not one foot from the larger man's hand was a satchel, the end of a white scroll of parchment poking out. Stealing himself, he crept over, deciding he might as well go big if he was going to steal from a group of murderers. He grabbed the strap of the bag, lifting it slowly so as not to disturb any of the contents. He slung it over his shoulder, hanging just below his waist. Turning to go, he spotted a gleaming white handled boot knife that seemed to have been made to match his sword. The woman clearly had taken it off to go to sleep. He grabbed that too, pacing back up the stairs and out the window. Feeling he had pushed his luck enough for tonight, he grabbed his cloak and began to pull himself back through the window, this time thankfully not nearly falling. He hopped down from the second level of the building to the grass at the back of the warehouse and began walking in the direction of the shop. He traveled swiftly and took back roads, using a much longer route than he normally would have. Considering what he'd just done, he didn't want to risk it.

Dawn was breaking properly by the time he once again slipped through the back door of the meat room. He found Ava sitting on her cot eating the food he'd left out.

"Where have you been?" Ava asked, noticing his weapons and giving him a knowing smirk. "Spying again?" she said, more of a statement than a question. "Just be careful, they're bad people. You'd rather be dead than if they find..." she broke off, spotting the satchel, which he set down next to the boot knife on his bed.

"You broke into their place!" she said somewhere between a shout and a breathy surprised laugh. "Aiden! What the hell's wrong with you? If they catch you..."

"But they didn't," he teased. "I was sneaky enough to throw another blanket on you before I left.

"OK... but are you sure no one followed you back here?" Ava questioned.

He nodded. "Certain." After a short pause, he said. "Is there any food left?"

"Loads," she replied and then took another bite.

He walked over, taking off his cloak and sitting beside her. She handed him one of the sandwiches and he bit in.

"I was starving," Aiden said in between chewing. "I didn't have breakfast before I left."

After finishing his ham and cheese sandwich, he began again, "I... I have to go speak to William today and tell him what I've learned. You can't tell anyone that though." The last bit sounded a little frantic. He hadn't told her about William but he was pretty sure she'd surmised enough to know he was working on someone's orders.

"I give you my word," she said and he smiled.

"I'll go in a little bit," he said. "I'll tell him you're not a threat and that you're staying with me, ok?"

"Who's William?" she asked curiously.

"The King of Anglen," he said, sounding more proud than there was really reason to be.

"Well, aren't you so popular?" she mocked. Then said, "In the meantime, I saw a deck of cards under the desk in the front, wanna play a game of poker for the last sandwich?"

"You're on," he grinned.

Ten minutes later, Aiden was frowning. It became apparent that Ava was very good at poker and had been doing little more than hustling him. Giggling, she tore the sandwich in half, handing one of the halves to him.

He smiled, saying, "Play a game? That wasn't a game, it was a slaughter." They both laughed,

"You should go talk to the King before it gets too late," urged Ava. "Then we'll have the rest of the day to do whatever we like."

"Ok, what are you gonna do?" Aiden asked refastening his cloak around his shoulders in the other room.

"I was thinking I might go back to the bakery and ask Phil if he needs help with any more basic stuff. We could stockpile a little more food. I don't know about you, but I like to know where my next meal is."

Aiden laughed. "I haven't known where my next meal is ever, but I've always found it. You're right though, that's a good idea."

Aiden put his sword and cloak back on, affixing the boot knife around his ankle and walking out the back door into the alley.

"See you later," Ava called.

"You too."

# CHAPTER 10

As Aiden walked down the alley pulling his cloak over his head and concealing the hilt of his sword, he wondered if William intended to continue to pay him for the spy work. As he thought, he dove down the mental rabbit hole of what he would buy with the money if he was paid. This topic filled his thoughts, as his feet carried him to the King's home. Upon arriving at the door, he hadn't yet decided. Shelving the thought for later, he knocked and Mary answered.

"The King is in his study, upstairs north wing, second door on the left," she said.

Aiden followed the instructions, knocking on the second door.

"Come in," a tired voice answered. Aiden walked in pulling his hood off as he did. "Aiden, I'm glad to see you," William said, his face breaking into a more attentive smile. "Have you news?" William gestured for him to sit at one of the chairs before the desk.

Aiden smiled mischievously and nodded.

"Then come, sit, and tell me all about it." William pushed aside some of the papers on his desk, making room to brace his elbows on the surface.

Aiden sat and began his retelling. "The girl traveling with the group is not one of them. She was kidnapped." He paused and William nodded to continue.

"Three nights ago I spotted the shorter of the men in the group. I tailed him back to the warehouse they were staying in. I watched the warehouse until I saw the girl leave. I started to trail her. At some point she noticed. She tried to kill me at first."

Aiden hadn't been ready to stop but William cut him off. "Are you ok?" he said sharply.

"Yes, I had the sword you gave me," Aiden answered, gesturing to the hilt over his shoulder.

"But you haven't received any training yet!" William protested.

"I... I have."

Williams' brows rose.

Aiden explained, "A year ago a knight was passing through and took a liking to me. He trained me in combat for the months he was here."

"An impressive few months training if you were able to fend off an unknown mercenary so easily."

"That's... not exactly right either," Aiden corrected.

"And how's that?" William asked.

"I only had an instructor for a few months but I've been practicing for about a year now."

"With no weapons? And no one to guide you?" William asked, sounding a little suspicious.

"A few of the town guards like me enough to train with me sometimes, but yeah. But I like fighting with fists more anyway."

"Well, aren't you full of surprises?" William said with a smile and a warm chuckle. "Continue," he said after a moment.

"Well, I found out that those people were keeping her hostage as part of the King of Orenth's plan to destabilize foreign kingdoms. She has a title, but if it's okay with you, I think that's her story to tell?"

"Fair enough, though I would like to hear her side of things," William responded. "Continue."

"Well, now she's staying with me in the shop and doesn't think the group really cares if she runs away, considering her home is across an ocean. But the more important part, last night I went back to the warehouse and snuck in." At this Aiden was cut off again.

"Aiden, you know what kind of people they are. You must be more careful. If they catch you…"

But it was Aiden's turn to cut him off. "But they didn't, and I think you'll like what I've found and… kind of took," he said, pulling the satchel strap over and off his neck. "I haven't looked through it yet. I figured I'd do it with you."

"I'm glad you did, let's see it," the King said gesturing to the table, seeming to have forgotten his worry of a few moments ago.

Aiden held the satchel over the desk, dumping the contents out. Out came the scroll of parchment revealing an unbroken wax seal as well as a small handful of silver coins, seven gold ones, a curved pipe, a small bag of tobacco, an apple, and lastly a golden necklace with a coin-shaped emblem marked with a crossing set of daggers in front of a cloaked figure.

"What do you think this is?" Aiden asked, grabbing the necklace and holding it up.

"I'm not sure," the King replied. "I'll ask around and see if anyone else knows. In the meantime, what is this letter?" William grabbed the letter, carefully broke the seal, and began to read.

To my employed correspondent,

I would like to have you meet the old friend whom I told you of in my last letter. But before you do so I need you to give the local leader my love in hopes that *they are willing to help find a way for you to meet that oh-so-great person I've been trying to mold into a new image of all that we desire.*

*Godspeed my employed correspondent .*
*Sincerely,*
*Your Benefactor*

Aiden sat, staring at the letter in William's hands, mouth slightly open. "Well, what the hell's that supposed to mean?"

William sat staring at the letter, a slight frown creasing his brow. "You're sure this belonged to the group I've been having you keep an eye on?"

"Certain. When I grabbed it, it was less than a foot from the man's hand. I took it along with this," Aiden said, pulling the knife from his boot.

"OK… why the knife? Surely that wasn't the only weapon they had there?" William wondered aloud.

Aiden seemed to shrink a little bit, knowing the answer to the question wasn't as noble as William was expecting. "The knife?" Aiden repeated. "Just because they're bad people, and I wanted it, so I didn't feel so bad about stealing it."

William gave him a small smile. "Very well," he said in a slow resounding voice. "I'm not worried about your small theft from such a group. I am however worried about this letter. I can't imagine it has any good meaning given the group to which it was addressed. But if you like, can we continue to discuss potential meanings?"

Aiden nodded.

"But before we do… your payment, and I have one more thing for you." He once again reached and grabbed a bag slightly bigger than last time. "Forty-five silver pieces and those few gold ones, you've earned," he said with a smile which only grew bigger as Aiden's mouth sagged open. "And one more thing, only if you wish it," he said, pulling out a necklace much like the one from the bag but this one had a silver chain. The silver and gold emblem had the head of a stag on it, in contrast to the blades and hooded figure of the stolen one.

"This is the crest of Anglen. If you accept it, then you are officially a knight, and in your case, a spy for Anglen. Meaning that you work for me. I will knight you, and you will swear an oath to protect Anglen to the best of your abilities... Would you like it?" William asked. He continued, "This is a big deal, your oath will only end when I free you from it."

Aiden paused looking at the necklace, then William. Thoughts bounced back and forth in Aiden's head in the short time he was able to debate before an answer would be expected. First and foremost being why would the King do this? What importance does he have that would make the King want to knight him? Maybe it was dumb, maybe this is all dumb, and he should run away and not get involved in anything like this again. But... To hell with it.

"Yes, I want it."

"Very well then," William said, walking around the desk and setting the necklace over Aiden's head.

"Now for the oath, you will need to make a small cut in your palm."

Aiden reached down and grabbed his boot knife, holding it in his hand he made a small cut in the center of his palm, a small bead of blood pooling.

"Very good, now make a fist and repeat after me", the King ordered. "By the natural magic of this world."

"By the natural magic of this world," Aiden repeated.

"I swear to do everything in my power," William continued.

"I swear to do everything in my power."

"To protect the people and lands of Anglen from harm."

"To protect the people and lands of Anglen from harm," Aiden finished.

A warmth filled the room and a phantom wind blew. For a second, it made Aiden's stomach feel warm, like something in the core of him had changed, or at least felt something odd.

"Hand me your sword," William commanded.

Aiden did so and knelt, assuming he was supposed to.

"With my power I possess as King, I knight you, Sir Aiden Windren," he said as he tapped the blade of the sword on each of Aiden's shoulders. Aiden didn't know how William knew his family name. No one knew his family name except the few people in town who knew his parents, but he supposed that was hardly hard information to find as king. He stood and looked at the King. "Should you ever need access somewhere in Anglen just show that necklace," William explained. "Otherwise, try to keep it hidden."

Aiden nodded, tucking the necklace into his shirt.

"We've done enough for today," sighed William. "We'll discuss the meaning of the letter another time." He paused. "In the meantime, can I trust that you will continue to keep an eye on that group? Should the opportunity arise, I would like to have one of them to question. If you do manage to capture one of them, bring them to the town jail. Show the guards your necklace. They'll let you in and lock the person up. Inform the guards to stay on high alert, then come straight to me. Ok?"

"Ok... thank you," Aiden added, not knowing what to do and decided to bow. The old man chuckled and waved him out casually.

# Chapter 11

Ava had never thought herself capable of having a normal life or even anything close to it for that matter. But as she sat in the backroom of the bakery, she realized that these days, living in the shop with Aiden, were probably the closest thing to one she would ever have. In Attica she had always been bound by her duty to her crown, confined by dresses and good manners, under constant pressure to look and act the right way, always with one eye over her shoulder looking at all the people who didn't like her family.

But here she was half a world away from all that, living with a friend, and for the first time in her life, deciding her own fate. She didn't know if that thrilled or scared her. She also wasn't sure what she wanted to do next, as much as she wanted to flee and just take her chances with the world, and get far, far, away from the mercenaries. She also wanted to stay with Aiden who she could already tell would not abandon this town to the mercenaries, whatever she said. Not that she could blame him for having loyalty. So for now, she would stay and help Aiden. She would do all in her power to save this town. Once that was done, she would ask him what he planned to do. But, if he planned to stay… she wasn't sure she could bring herself to join him. She wanted to see the world, see every town, not just this one. See the rest of the world far from anywhere she might be recognized. But if he planned to travel or even to continue this fight out of this town, then she would join him. If he would have her that is. Have a chance to see the world's joy and even have a person to share it with, someone who from what she could tell would be as good as anyone to travel with.

"Ava, are you almost done kneading the dough?" Phil called from the front desk.

"I think so," she called back.

Phil strode into the room taking one look at the dough and letting out a booming laugh. "Nice one, that's not even close." Shaking his head and laughing under his breath Phil walked back to the front right as Aiden crossed the doorway.

"Hey Phil."

"Good to see you, Aiden, why don't you go help Ava." Aiden walked over and frowned at the dough in a way that said, what have you been doing to that poor stuff?

"How long have you been doing this?"

"Since ten minutes after you left," she said, looking at him annoyed.

"Want, some... help? I have some stuff to tell you anyway," he said, stepping beside her and grabbing half the dough before she could answer.

"What?"

"William made me an official knight. And he gave me a mission." He explained what William had asked him to do.

"So would you?" Ava smirked.

He paused, finishing his half of the dough and grabbing Ava's, she frowned again.

"So, do you want to help?" Aiden asked her. "Catch one of those monsters...?"

She smiled. "Nothing would give me more pleasure. Wanna start looking tonight?"

He nodded, a grin spreading across his face. And, finishing Ava's dough, he called through the doorway to the front of the shop. "The dough's ready."

Phil walked in, thanked them and handed each of them two sandwiches. And a cured sausage between them. "Stay safe," he called as they walked out, mouths full of food. Aiden waved a friendly gesture over his shoulder as they passed the doorway.

On the way back to the shop, they were spotted by Roy and Dante who called over asking them if they wanted to play a two V two. Walking over to join, they set down their food.

"You two versus us," Dante said, passing the ball to Roy. "Walls of the buildings are the goals."

The ally in which they stood was about thirty feet across with the walls to either team's backs. Aiden hung back to defend while Ava walked forward. Roy and Dante did the same. Advancing with the ball, Dante jogged forward, and Ava, with a lazy movement, stole the ball and kicked it against the wall, right past Roy.

Five minutes later they were ten to one, the one being Aiden's fault. Roy and Dante walked over hands up.

"You win. Ava you're amazing," Roy stated. Dante shook Ava's hand muttering something about never having a chance. Aiden and Ava picked up the sandwiches from the crate they'd set them on and headed back to the shop.

"What do you think about me buying a small apartment?" Aiden asked unexpectedly. "I think I have enough now, Then we could have actual beds and it wouldn't smell like drying meat."

She looked at him a little surprised but happy. "That sounds great. I saw an advertisement right down the street from the bakery. But… what do you mean you have enough?" Ava asked. "You said, like yesterday, that you've been broke all your life."

"I have been, up until working for William," Aiden explained." He's been paying me more than I know what to do with."

"So, why are you still working for Phil to get food?"

Aiden looked at her then considered for a moment. "Well, for one, I hadn't thought about it, and for two, Phil said he had that person quit. He could use some help for a few days, and, anyway, Phil has the best food."

"Fair enough. I think it's this way," Ava said and pointed down another street.

They walked down that way to find a large kind-faced man with a rather large beer-belly sitting in a chair next to the advertisement.

"Excuse me?" Ava said. "Are you the one renting out the apartment?"

He smiled enthusiastically, standing. "Why, yes I am. Are you two looking to rent it?" he asked.

"I think so," Aiden said, uncertain about how to work out renting an apartment. He'd seen the man around town before but didn't know his name. From what Aiden had heard, he was a good guy but had a tendency to get a little too drunk and start hugging strangers, which, if it were anywhere else, might have been bad but here the town seemed to have accepted him more as a occasional amusement.

"How much does it cost?" Aiden asked pulling out six of the gold coins.

The man's brows rose and he gave a warm smile. "Well, well, I'd reckon that'll rent it for a year. Those are some pretty pennies right, aren't they? It's a small place, but cosy. Come along I'll show ya," he said in a fun, jovial accent Aiden couldn't quite place. He gestured for them to follow him into the building. Reaching a door, he led them into a small room with a large bed, a small fireplace, a few mostly bare bookshelves, a dresser, a kitchenette, and another door leading to a tiny bathroom. The place smelled like scented candles, like too many of them if Aiden was honest, but that was easily enough fixed with an open window. Aiden spotted a few scattered about the apartment.

The man continued, "It comes with access to the Friday night buffet, 'well as happy hour and music night on Thursdays down the pub," he laughed. He pointed in the direction of the street they'd come down. "And it's an extra 17 silver pieces for insurance."

He finished and Ava asked, "Any rules we should know about?"

"We only ask that you keep the noise down after eight and that you use the fireplace safely. Other than that you're right enough to do what you like, certainly for watcha offered to pay."

Ava was beaming. "What do you think Aiden?"

Aiden turned to the man. "I… have one request, if anyone asks if we live here could you tell them we don't?"

"Sure thing," the man responded.

"Then, we'll take it," he said, handing over the gold coins and 17 silver ones.

"Thank ya very much," the man said, grabbing the coins and handing Aiden a pair of keys. The man pulled out a piece of paper. "You'll just have to sign there at the bottom and it's officially yours."

Aiden grabbed the piece of paper. The man handed him a small pen. Ava stepped in front of him turning her back for him to write against. Holding the paper against her back, Aiden signed the bottom line, his signature looking less than legible.

"I'll let you get settled in, just ask if you need anything. Me name's Ganic. You're the Windren kid though aren't ya?" he asked, gesturing to Aiden.

Aiden made a confused expression."I am, but…" He was trailing off when Ganic answered his unfinished question.

"I used to be friendly with ya parents is all. Didn't know em well but they were good enough people. Anyways, whatta ya say your names were?"

"I'm Aiden and this is Ava."

The man nodded to both of them and stepped out politely, a lumbering mass of easy smiles and a faint scent of sweet hard cider.

It took them the better part of two hours to make the two trips taking all of their normal stuff and a second time with swords and cloaks entering the apartment through the back door hoping no one saw them or at least couldn't tell they were the same people. Getting back, Aiden took off Starlight and his cloak, setting the sword against the wall and the cloak in a drawer of the dresser. Ava did the same and they plopped down on the bed, which felt massive compared to anything he'd had in the past. It occurred to Aiden that he said only earlier that day that they would have proper beds to sleep in and also that he'd just bought an apartment that can only fit one bed.

He was debating what to say on this topic when Ava asked, "How much money do you have?"

"More than I need," Aiden replied. "Why, do you need to buy something?"

"I'd like to have a bow, given what we're doing."

Aiden reached into the coin purse pulling out 25 silver pieces, more than enough to buy two bows, and handed them to Ava. "Go to the market and get one," he offered.

Ava smiled, took the coins, and left. She came back half an hour later, holding a fine yew bow recurved with thin leather wrapping up it in a lattice pattern. She also had a matching quiver and a little over four dozen arrows.

"I got something for you." She smiled and he sat up straight.

"And what is that?" Aiden asked.

She walked over, arm behind her back. She pulled her arm around and handed him a book. The title read *From Blood to Water.*

"It was one of my favorites in Attica. I saw it and figured you might enjoy it too."

"Thank you," Aiden said, standing and grabbing the book, he looked at the cover.

"I've never had a book. Frank let me read his but…" he trailed off. "I love it," he said as he hugged Ava.

She was surprised at how much it meant to him. She hugged him back, noticing the muscles of his chest, though she tried not to.

It surprised him slightly that she hugged him back, but then again she had just bought him a gift. He pulled away, wiping his eyes. They stood like that for a few moments in which Ava set her new bow and quiver against the wall next to Aiden's sword.

Aiden asked, expression hardening slightly, "Who do you think we should try to capture from the group? You spent a lot of time with them, any idea who might be the easiest to catch off guard?"

She paused thinking for a moment. "Definitely the shorter man. He's pretty careless. In fact, he's probably at a bar right now."

"Ok, you think we wait 'til dark then go find him?" Aiden suggested.

Ava nodded.

"Then, I have some time to read my new book," he said with a smile, grabbing the book and hopping down on the bed. Aiden examined the title for a brief second before flicking to the first page. He was still expecting her to say something about the single bed but it didn't seem to matter to her as she plopped down on the other side with one of the few leftover books from the shelves on the other side and began to read beside him.

# CHAPTER 12

With darkness fast approaching, Aiden set down his book, slid off the bed, and grabbed his sword and cloak. Ava grabbed her cloak, sword and bow in kind.

"Ready?" Aiden whispered.

Ava nodded and stepped out the back door. Prowling down the back streets silent as wraiths, they stuck to the shadows. On Ava's recommendation, they checked the bars first. They tried the pub on their street first, but as Aiden expected he wasn't there. The place was well known for being a slightly boisterous place for dancing and reveling and not particularly welcoming to people unwilling to have a good time. They did, however, spot the shorter man at one of the less reputable bars. They caught sight of him through a dirty window, talking with a woman clad in nothing but a magenta robe.

"Let's find a spot to watch," Ava breathed, pointing to a neighboring flat roofed building. After climbing atop it, they waited. It was nearly midnight before the man stood from his seat, swaying the slightest bit, as he shoved open the grubby old blackened door and began down the street. They climbed down and started to follow him.

"I'll wrap around the front and distract him," Ava whispered, darting down an alley. A minute later she stepped out, bow drawn standing not twenty feet in front of the man.

She snarled, "Move an inch and this goes in between your eyes."

The man couldn't tell who she was through her hood. But he had stopped. Snapping to soberness, he stared her down. As he reached for the hilt of his blade, Aiden drew his own, stepping behind the man in a quick tense motion he held it to the man's neck. The man went still as death, any hint of drink gone.

"On your knees," Aiden whispered with deadly calm as the man snarled wordlessly in return. Not daring to turn and look at Aiden, he glared at Ava. As he began to kneel, Aiden raised the hilt of his sword quickly, slamming it down onto the man's head. He fell to the ground, unconscious.

Ava walked over, bow still drawn, as Aiden pulled out two pieces of rope. Only once the man's hands and feet were tied did Ava lower her bow, fastening it over her head and shoulders. She grabbed the man's feet as the two of them carried him the four blocks to the town jail, which was located here no doubt because of the number of disreputable establishments nearby.

As they arrived the guards drew their swords at the sight of them, but quickly put the weapons back as Aiden pulled the necklace from under his shirt. He struggled not to drop the man's upper body from the one hand that held him.

"We need a cell to put this man in," Ava said to the nearest guard, an old man who looked slightly shocked as Aiden and Ava pulled off their hoods revealing how young they were. But the man said nothing as he led them to a large cell with a set of manacles fixed to the wall. Binding their prisoner in them, they asked the guard to get a set for his feet. The guard looked uncertain about the request but hurried away, coming back moments later with a second set.

After fixing them in place, Aiden said, "Put all the guards on high alert. There's a chance that others will come looking for this man. Treat all of them as enemies."

Aiden was about to say that they needed to leave, but Ava asked, "Do you have any sedatives? It'd be good to keep him asleep."

The guard only nodded, coming back with a bottle and saying, "I will alert the others and administer this", showing them the bottle.

Aiden nodded. Then, he and Ava strode out, without another word to the guards. The king's men were looking a little troubled at what just happened and were all giving Ava a wide berth.

They made their way to William's home quickly and knocked. Mary answered, looking tired, but seeming to awaken. She stepped back for the two of them to enter.

"The King is asleep at..." Mary tried to explain.

But Aiden cut her off. "He's expecting me," he said, once again showing the necklace. Mary seemed to understand the situation. Without another word, she turned on her heel, and led the way. They followed, Ava shutting the door.

Coming to an oak door, Mary knocked and opened it partially. "William?" Mary breathed.

"What is it?" said the old man as he sat up slowly, a tired looking outline in the darkness.

"It's me," Aiden answered a little more sharply than he'd intended, taking off his hood. He was starting to feel, for the first time, the gravity of everything that he'd been doing.

"I've done what you asked me to," Aiden explained.

William gave him a gratifying but hard look. "Very good, give me one moment and we can go."

They exited the room, Mary shutting the door. She nodded to both of them and walked away. A minute later William exited the room wearing a cloak of his own. Aiden led the way, Ava and William behind.

As they crossed the stone bridge, William finally asked softly, "You must be Miss Ava?"

Ava just nodded.

"I'm glad to see you're not in the hands of those people any longer," the King offered.

"As am I," Ava replied.

They fell into silence, passing their new apartment on the way to the jail.

"We had the guards give the man a sedative. Ava thought it would be better to have him asleep before we interrogate him," Aiden said.

"Well done. I have a feeling we'll need all the help we can get in persuading him to talk."

Minutes later, they arrived at the jail. Aiden once again flashed the necklace. The guards straightened upon spotting William, looks of even more uncertainty crossing their faces.

Aiden led them to the cell where he found the same old guard. "Any... problems?" Aiden asked.

"None," the guard breathed, clearly stressed. "I gave him the sedative. He should be awake in about half an hour."

"It won't take that long," Ava said in a near growl.

Aiden held out a hand and the guard handed the key over. Aiden opened the cell, and they walked in.

The King asked, "How do you suggest we wake him?" He was looking to Ava. She flashed a cruel smile and walked over to him, raising a fist and slamming it into the man's face. William looked surprised but quickly gathered himself.

The man thrashed as he woke. Finally, seeing the three of them and spotting Ava, now hoodless, he spat blood on the floor growling, "It was you with the bow." He paused for a breath. "I'll kill you, bitch!" He spat. "And, I take it, it was you with the sword!" he exclaimed, shifting his attention to Aiden.

Aiden nodded.

Looking to the King, the man hissed, "And I suppose this was on your orders, old man?"

William nodded.

"Then to what do I owe you the pleasure, pieces of human filth?" he asked with too much swagger for Aiden's liking.

But it was William who spoke, "We'll be asking the questions. And, I think you my..."

Aiden assumed William had been about to say "friend" but realized the fault in the expression.

"... Well, prisoner, are the only one here in a state of filth," William retorted.

"I ain't answering shit for you!" the prisoner flung the words at William.

Ava quickly drew her sword as Aiden grabbed the knife from his boot. He walked over, and holding it toward the man, he whispered, "What was that?" It was feeling more and more real to Aiden now that this man had intended to kill Frank, that this man had wanted to destroy the town, Aiden's town.

"Why are you and your comrades here?" William asked in an iron hard voice.

"To fuck up your little shit hole of a town! What the hell'd you think we were here for?" growled the prisoner.

"And what else?" William pressed.

"We thought we were going to be told to kill you," the man threatened.

A light sparked in Aiden's memory. The letter, that's what it had meant. William seemed to have realized it too. The King went deadly still.

"Who are you?" Aiden asked.

"I don't answer to boys!" laughed the man.

But Aiden stepped forward and dug the knife against the man's cheek.

A trickle of blood ran down the man's face as he said, "My name," he paused, "Is Locken."

"And who are the other two people you've been with?" Aiden continued.

Locken glared at Aiden, promising violence in his eyes, but answered through his teeth, "The man's name's Bjorn. He's the leader, and the woman's name is Vorpal. Mean bitch if I've ever met one."

There was a pause, then William held up the small necklace emblazoned with the crossing daggers and figure. "What is this?" he questioned.

The man's eyes snapped to Ava. "You, it was you who stole the bag!"

But Aiden dug the knife in harder and the man flinched. "That would be me; But I'm starting to wish I slit your throat instead."

Locken snarled eyes on Aiden. "You'll die for this, you know that. They'll kill you or our client will."

"Maybe," Aiden said, unfazed by the threat.

But the man continued, "It's the crest of the assassins' guild."

They all paused and William asked, "What is the King of Orenth planning?"

Locken continued sneering as he answered, "To destabilize these lands before invading, and when he does, it'll make the death we gave your family…"

But he was cut off as Ava had lowered her sword, pressing it against the man's groin. She breathed in a voice of deadly calm, "One more word, and you don't want to think of what'll happen next." She whispered, barely audible, pressing the sword tip still harder. He hissed in pain and she withdrew the blade.

"Are you three the only people the King of Orenth has in these lands?" William continued.

"That I know of. We would have been more than enough. I would have killed both of you tonight, had the two of you not snuck up on me drunk!" Locken said, beginning to shout, rage making him dumb and blind. "And now," he continued, "Me and the others will kill everyone you pigs care about." He paused. "Just like how we cut down your parents and left them to die in the street… Aiden Windren, boy of nothing and no one!" Locken taunted. "We flipped your life on its head, and you were none the wiser. Well, now you know, just in time for us to do it again…"

# Chapter 13

Aiden's head went blank, a buzzing filling his ears.

"You should have heard their screa..."

But Aiden had pulled the blade down, raking it across the man's throat without thinking. The man thrashed, then slumped, as warm, red, reeking blood covered him. The room went silent, even the distant sounds of the guards and streets halted.

"Aiden!?" William breathed, not in reprimand but in consolation and shock.

But Aiden stood sharply, the buzzing growing louder.

"Aiden!" Ava cried sharply as though she knew every thought thundering through his head.

He sheathed his sword slowly, not knowing what he was going to do yet. He still didn't know, but he had an idea, and that was enough. He ran, bolting straight for the warehouse. He'd cleared the prison before anyone had a chance to stop him. Ava chased after him and caught him barely two blocks down. She tackled him, pinning him to the ground as he thrashed.

She shouted, drowning out the buzzing, bringing him back to his own head. "If you need to do this, then do it smart!" Ava yelled, begging him to stop and think.

He kept thrashing, tears trickling down his face, but she held him firm, pressing what small weight she had against him with surprising force. "I'll help you!" Ava gasped. "But you have to agree to do it my way!"

William ran toward them from the jail, a guard at either of his sides.

"Aiden!! If we are going to do this, we have to go!" Ava shouted. "William and two guards are coming!"

He stopped thrashing. Looking at her, he paused for a moment, a moment that held a lot more than that time in it. He didn't care about his parents, or at least hadn't. It had always just been a reality that they were gone and that was just something that he had to deal with. But knowing that he could have had them, that life could have been easier, that he could have had someone there at his side helping him through life all this time. That all of that could have been his, if some person, some stain on human existence, had not taken it away. It brought a rage that he couldn't quite control, even as he tried as he fought to do so. He couldn't control it, but... maybe he could delay it a bit. He looked up at Ava and nodded.

She released him instantly, sliding off him, and they both jumped to their feet. They ran, losing William quickly, and the guards who refused to leave their King's side.

"When we get there, you draw them out. I'll deal with Vorpal," Ava said, panting through her words. She pulled her bow from her shoulder. "You get Bjorn," she ordered.

Aiden nodded in response.

Ava broke off, getting close to the warehouse and slipping into the dark shadows of the barn.

Aiden walked up to the front doors and slammed the pommel of his sword into the wood, leaving a dent. "I know you're in there, you pieces of shit!!" He stepped back, slid into the shadow at the side of the warehouse and waited. The buzzing had stopped, only silence in his head now.

A minute later the door opened, the chain falling to the ground with dull clanks. Out stepped a man no longer veiled in his cloak, his full size and muscular build was apparent, and considerable. He had at least a foot on Aiden and half again in weight. He carried a long, great sword in one hand, letting the tip hover just a little bit above the ground. He was followed by the woman clad in black fabric, holding a pair of long, wicked daggers.

Taking a final breath, silencing every emotion, every thought, he stepped out. Their eyes snapped to him.

"It's been a while, hasn't it, or, I guess we haven't met but I'm told you knew my parents," Aiden said too calmly, his own voice surprised him.

The woman hissed, "And who are yo…"

But she was cut off by the man who growled, "So you're that boy."

"What boy?" the woman asked.

"He was the son of the couple we killed thirteen years ago. Right here in this town. We always figured you'd die on the streets, but look at you now. Come to take your revenge for your parents?" he crooned, already seeming to have sized Aiden up as no threat at all.

"Yes, it's me," Aiden said, taking his cloak off and letting it fall to the ground.

"How'd you find out?" the man asked.

"That's a funny story, actually," Aiden said, with a nasty chuckle. "Locken and I had a little chat."

The two mercenaries straightened.

"He told me all about you, Bjorn and Vorpal, about how you killed my parents and others, about who you work for and why."

"What have you done with him!?" Vorpal demanded.

"Well, first I knocked him out," Aiden said tapping his chin in an act of struggling to remember. He was enjoying this. It was awful. He knew it was awful to enjoy this but he couldn't help it, seeing these people in distress, it made some cold deep part of him smile.

"Then, I chained him up, and what did I do then?" Aiden began to pace. "Oh, I know, I dragged my knife through his filthy worthless throat." Aiden stopped pacing, facing the two.

They glared eyes promising every intent to kill. "You're a dead boy," Bjorn growled. He broke into a sprint toward Aiden, holding the great sword with both hands.

Aiden shouted, "NOW!!" As the word left his mouth, the two wheeled around looking for who he had signaled, right in time to see Ava loose an arrow. Vorpal had only enough time to move her throat out of the way. Still the arrow struck her shoulder, knocking her off balance as Ava rushed at her. At the same time, Aiden rushed at Bjorn still facing the wrong direction. Needing to defend, Bjorn was forced to turn back to Aiden, leaving the now injured Vorpal to Ava. Aiden slashed for Bjorn's stomach, scratching his shirt as he jumped back. Aiden swung again, for his knee this time, but was blocked by the vast blade of the great sword. Bjorn smiled as he swung the massive blade down upon Aiden who raised his sword to block, but it did little against the might of the man as the blade forced through the block and bit into Aiden's shoulder, a blow that, unblocked, would have cleaved him in half. Aiden threw off the blade with a desperate lurch, pain shattering through his body as a scream broke the air. The scream was not Aiden's, but the shrill cry of pain still knocked the breath from him. He turned to watch as Vorpal plunged a dagger through Ava's thigh. In a burst of rage, Aiden threw the man off, slashing the back of Bjorn's knee. The man fell instantly.

Aiden rushed for Vorpal, but she was too far away for his sword. He reached to the hilt of his boot knife, pulling it out and angling it to throw. He missed where he'd intended, but the blade still hit against the back of the woman's leg, making her dip, right as Aiden reached her and brought up his sword. There was a flash of silver, a cracking noise, and blood sprayed as the woman's head rolled.

Aiden dropped to his knees next to Ava who whispered, "He's getting away!"

Aiden didn't move.

"Get him!" Ava pressed, "For both of us."

He hesitated, but nodded, grabbing her bow, and ran after Bjorn. Aiden raised the bow, loosing an arrow. It soared, hitting Bjorn in the side of his lower back, causing the man to crash to the ground. Getting to him, Aiden knocked the sword away, holding his own with the tip to the man's neck. Grabbing Bjorn's hair, Aiden wrenched his head back and looked into his eyes, "Why! Why did our parents have to die? Were they just unlucky? Did they offend you? Were they some target of your King?" Aiden questioned him in a desperate cry.

Bjorn laughed. It was a terrible noise, booming sneering, condescending, all at once. "They were killed," he said slowly, "Because they posed a threat."

"Threat?!" Aiden shouted. "How could they have been a threat?!"

Bjorn laughed again. "Because, oh so arrogant one, the blood pumping in their veins, and yours, was and is of magic," he said in nearly a whisper. Then fear flashed across Bjorn's face for the first time, as though he was slightly scared of what he'd just said.

Aiden's head went quiet again. It took him a few moments before he could speak again. "Magic died a thousand years ago, it's nothing more than legend."

"Perhaps, but legends do have a way of coming true," Bjorn taunted. Without warning he grabbed Aiden's sword by the blade and pulled it not away, but right through his own throat.

Aiden's head began to go buzz again with the shock of what happened. But he was snapped back by a sobbing, far off gasp. Looking up, he spotted Ava, still on the ground. He ran to her, sliding to his knees. He pressed his hand against the deep wound in her upper thigh and his other against the one in her side, trying to stop the bleeding. But he could tell there was something wrong, very wrong; already he saw a tinge of yellow around the wounds where her clothing had torn to expose the uncut flesh. And, she was too pale.

She mouthed something and he leaned in to hear what it was. "Poison," she whispered right before fainting.

Aiden scrambled for Vorpal's dead body, ripping open the pockets of her suit until he found a small unmarked bottle in an inner pocket. Praying it was the antidote and not some awful concoction, he brought it to Ava's lips, pouring it in her mouth and sitting her up to let the liquid trickle down her throat. He sat there holding her in his lap. Fear was coursing through him now, fear and regret and too many different emotions to comprehend. Hands against her wounds, paying no mind to his own, he sat praying to every god he didn't know, for them to have mercy.

# II

## All Ends Turn Into Beginnings

# Chapter 14

Ava didn't know where she was. She was lying down, there was an aching pain in her side.

She could smell something sweet and smoky. Opening her eyes, she found Aiden at the other end of the apartment busy at the stove. She was lying in the bed, looking down to survey herself. She found herself in the same underclothes she'd been wearing. There were bright bandages wrapped around her leg and stomach, tied into a neat knot at each. Trying to lean up, the bed creaked slightly, and Aiden wheeled around, covering the room in three strides.

"Help me sit up," she whispered in a raspy voice. He did so, grabbing her upper arm in one hand and the other on her back as he leaned her up and then back against the headboard.

"What happened?" Ava asked.

His face was soft as he explained, "When we went to kill Vorpal and Bjorn, Vorpal cut you in the fight. I tried to… When I got to you, but you told me to go after Bjorn, and when I got back… You were already pale. You stayed conscious long enough to say 'poison'." He paused. "I found a bottle in Vorpal's suit. I thought it was the antidote, so I gave it to you. I… I thought you were…" A tear now trickling off his face, it fell, landing on her arm. She reached up touching his face, wiping away the second as he continued. "I made you go…" he whispered.

Ava didn't know what to say for a moment. "You didn't make me do anything. I wanted to go, and it was Vorpal who almost killed me, not you." She paused, a frown creasing her brow she asked, "What happened to Vorpal? Did she… get away?"

Aiden's face hardened slightly. "She's missing a head," he smirked.

Ava grinned. "For me, I'm honored," she said off hand.

He looked up, peering into her face, and smiled a grateful, slightly jovial smile.

"What happened isn't your fault," she said a little more firmly. She looked past him to survey the apartment. There were paintings on a few walls and a scented candle sitting on a new bed stand. "How long have I been asleep?" Ava asked slowly.

He paused a moment before answering. "A week," he replied, readying himself for her reaction.

"What!?" Ava barked, making to sit up straighter but wincing as her wound stretched. Aiden held a hand to her back again.

"I've been asleep for a week?" She asked again, not entirely convinced.

He nodded.

"Are these the same clothes?!" was her next question when she noticed how bad she smelled.

He nodded. "I... didn't think you'd want me to change them. I only took off what I had to, to change the bandages," he said tentatively, worried she might be upset. That didn't seem to be the case though. as she ordered him.

"I need to change. Help me up," she ordered him. She slung an arm around his shoulders as he picked her up. Aiden put his arm at her waist to keep her steady even as she swayed. She staggered to the dresser, opening the top drawer and grabbing a set of undergarments. She told him to sit her on the bed, so he did so.

"Turn around," Ava commanded. Double checking that he had, she removed her bra and underwear, swapping them for the new ones. She spotted a large shirt on the chair. "Hand me that." Grabbing the shirt, Aiden handed it to her. She pulled it over her head. It fell below the wound in her leg. The shirt smelled like Aiden. Shaking her head slightly, she tried to ignore that thought.

"Do we have food?" Ava asked.

He nodded, "I just made eggs and bacon."

She smiled. "Help me to the table." As he did, she asked. "What about William…? Is he angry?"

Aiden shook his head, grabbing her a plate of food. "No, he said he understands why we did it. He thanked us for freeing this town of their filth."

She nodded.

"He asked me to tell you, that if you wish," he paused for a beat, "he'd love to knight you as a spy of Anglen like me." She looked up at him, surprised. He continued, "He doesn't expect your answer right away." There was a pause.

"I'll… think about it," she sighed.

As they ate, Aiden informed her of everything that had happened since the fight. How William had paid, not just Aiden, but the both of them. Grabbing a bag he handed it to her.

"Twenty gold pieces, courtesy of William. He was terrified when he heard what had happened."

She marveled at the bag, grabbing it and feeling the weight. "I could go anywhere with this… we could," she pondered.

He nodded. "Let's just focus on getting you healed for now," Aiden suggested. "And when you feel better, William wants to speak with both of us. Then… the world is ours."

They finished eating breakfast, and Aiden helped carry Ava to the bed. "I have to go to the market," he explained. "I'm going to buy you a crutch and get some more medicine."

"Ok," she said, looking back over her shoulder, lying down on the bed.

A minute later Aiden walked out the back door. He slung his sword across his back, and decided to leave his cloak. In all the uproar of the town, he'd decided he didn't much care if people knew what had happened or that he and Ava had done it. There were no more threats in the town, and he felt it was reasonably safe to let people know.

Twenty-five minutes later, Aiden returned, holding a pine crutch and a small bag of items. He smiled at Ava. Walking over and beginning to untie the bandage around her leg, he opened a small tin and spread the white salve across the wound. It was cool and smooth. He tied a new bandage and pulled out another small bag of herbs.

"The healer at the market told me to have you eat two bundles a day. It should help with the pain," he offered.

Grabbing one of the tiny bundles, she plopped it in her mouth and swallowed. "It tastes like rotting grass," she said, making a face.

"Thank goodness I don't have to eat it then," Aiden joked as he moved on to the second wound, pulling up her shirt just enough to expose the bandages and doing the same as with the first.

Ava's condition improved drastically over the next few days. Since she was now able to eat, drink, and take the herbs, her rate of recovery increased. Aiden continued to change the bandages, prepare her meals, and tried to help her with everything. Eventually, however, she told him he was fussing too much. She wanted to go talk to William. Aiden agreed grudgingly. And, so the next day, taking much longer than usual, they made their way across the stone bridge and knocked on the great oak front door.

They were greeted by Mary who gave them a warm smile. "He'll be happy to see you," she said, leading the way to the great room where William sat.

He did indeed seem happy. "Come, sit. I'm glad you're here, and well enough to walk over," he said looking at Ava. "Please sit, I have a proposition." As they did so, Aiden helped Ava onto the couch. William continued, "I assume Aiden has conveyed my proposition?"

She nodded. "I have a few questions, if that's ok?"

"Of course," William said, gesturing for her to go on.

Ava did. "If I were to agree to serve you as Aiden does, would we be forced to work separately?"

William smiled. "If you would like to continue to work together, you may. I swear that I will make no effort to separate you."

Ava nodded. "And would you keep us in this town or would our missions take us... farther?"

Aiden gave a slightly surprised look at the question

"Yes, I am quite sure that you will be taken beyond these lands," William said giving her a knowing smile. "Should you agree, I already have a mission in mind that would take you across the continent." Ava smiled, and William continued, "I have a feeling that your missions will take you many places, places that, beyond accomplishing your missions, I hope you'll take the time to explore and enjoy.

She flashed a grin at Aiden who returned it. "In that case... I'll do it."

# CHAPTER 15

"Well, then, Aiden?" William said, holding out a hand. Aiden drew his sword and handed it to the King. They went through the same steps as when William had knighted Aiden. Ava flinched slightly as she cut her palm. Finishing, William handed the sword back to Aiden.

"Now that you're both knights of Anglen," William began, "I would like you to go beyond to seek any information you can in regards to the mission that Locken, Vorpal, and Bjorn were sent to do. I would like to know the King of Orenth's motives and his intentions going forward." William paused, and they nodded. "When you find something, send a letter back to me detailing what you have found and what you think the best course of action is."

They were all silent for a moment. "Do you have any tips on where to start?" Aiden asked.

"I would suggest the Port of Gloren. It's a key port, and I'd bet there'll be someone there with information involving our quarry." Picking up yet another bag of coins he said, "For the expenses you are sure to face on your travels."

Aiden took the bag.

"There are horses for you when you are ready to depart," William explained. "They'll be your horses for future missions as well." He paused for a heartbeat and looked at Ava more sternly. "I want you fully healed before you depart. Do you understand?"

She made a sheepish noise of agreement.

"Do so quietly. I don't want word of what you're doing to spread," William admonished. "Now go rest. Leave when you are ready and send the letters to the town cobbler. He'll give them to me." They both stood, bowing even as William waved a hand telling them not to bother, and to let themselves out.

The next three weeks were spent preparing and recovering. Aiden's shoulder had healed, so had Ava's thigh, and though her stomach was tender, it was nearly healed. Aiden used the money for the trip to buy them food, a pack each and two bed rolls.

The following day, Ava confronted Aiden, "I'm well enough for us to begin."

"Are you sure?" he asked, staring unsurely into her eyes.

She nodded, trying not to betray any hint that she was still in a little bit of pain.

He continued, "Then we can leave tonight."

They fastened their bags on the two horses Willam had given them. Aiden's was a strong, snow white mare, and Ava's a smaller, midnight black stallion. Pulling onto the horses, they tugged their cloaks over their faces and trotted out along the main road of the town.

An hour later, now deep in the countryside of Anglen, Ava said, "I... I think I'm going to name him Raith."

"Like the monster?" Aiden laughed.

Ava stuck out her tongue. "No, like *the shadow that carries a promise of death,*" she shot back, falling silent.

"So... like the monster," Aiden said grinning.

Ava stuck out her tongue again. A moment later, she asked, "What will you name yours?"

Aiden thought for a moment.

"Well?" she pressed.

"I think I'll name him... Spark."

She laughed.

"What?" Aiden chuckled.

"Nothing," Ava sighed, "Except for that being the most boring name I've ever heard."

"It's still better than Raith, *shadow of death*," he teased back.

"Asshole," Ava muttered, rolling her eyes. She looked up to the darkening sky. "We should find a spot to camp. We have three days to go 'til Gloran either way."

He nodded, and twenty minutes later they were atop a small hill adorned by a single tree, next to which they made camp.

The next morning, Ava awoke to the sound of Aiden's low rumbling snore. With the sun already up, she abandoned sleep and decided to go try to find food. They had a small reserve, but it would dwindle quickly if they relied only on it. Slinging her quiver and bow around her shoulder, she made her way down the hill and into the thicker woods. Steps near silent on the moss-covered ground, she made slow and deliberate movements. After thirty minutes of finding nothing more than worms, she abandoned the attempt and made back for the camp.

As she neared the tree line at the bottom of the hill, she paused, a victorious smile on her face as a grouse crossed her path. Kneeling lower, she took aim, breathed once, twice, when a yell broke the air. Startled, she loosed the arrow, missing the bird by feet. But all her attention had shifted to the sound of the cry coming from atop the hill. She ran in the direction of the scream. As she broke the tree line, she peered up the hill, her breath catching as she spotted two men, one holding a hunting knife to Aiden's throat. Collecting herself, she thought. She needed to think. She took a deep breath, another, and circled to the steeper side of the hill. Ava climbed, reached the top, and pressed against the backside of the lone tree, not fifteen feet from the nearer of the men. She notched an arrow.

"Where's your partner?" one of the men asked.

"She left last night and won't be coming back," Aiden snarled. Ava felt a small wave of affection at Aiden's attempt to save her.

"I don't believe you," the man said with a sardonic bark.

Breathing once again, Ava spun out from behind the tree, loosing the arrow straight through the arm of the man holding the knife. He cried out in pain, dropping the knife. Ava notched another arrow, stopping the second man cold, as he started for her, the arrow aimed between his eyes.

"Are you ok?" she asked Aiden.

Aiden nodded and drew his sword from under his bed roll. He hadn't been able to draw it with the man's knife to his throat; he now held the tip to the injured man's chest.

"Who are you?" Ava snarled, venom tainting the words.

"We're hunters," the second man said, a note of plea and panic clear in his voice "We didn't want you dead. We just didn't want anyone hunting our land. It's been hard getting enough food since those three came through the village."

Aiden's eyes narrowed. He asked, "Were there two men, one taller than the other, and a woman all dressed in black?"

The first man nodded, both of the men's eyes widening. "How did you...?"

"They're dead," Ava interrupted." We killed them five weeks ago."

"But... how? They ravaged our village before they fled. The messengers never even got a chance to warn Clystera," the younger of the men explained.

Ava growled, "I think you'll find that when you fight us conscious, we're much more formidable."

The man raised his hands backing away. "I'm sorry I... I didn't..."

But Aiden cut him off, "We won't... or at least, I won't, hurt you any further," he said glancing to Ava who dipped her chin in agreement, though he didn't get the impression she particularly wanted to play nice.

"But you have to promise us you won't breathe a word of this encounter," Aiden commanded.

Both men nodded vigorously, hands on their hearts.

# CHAPTER 16

Ava and Aiden lowered their weapons. Ava's face softened. "I'm... sorry," she said, looking at the injured man and walking to him. "This might hurt," she warned, grabbing the arrow still lodged through his forearm, and broke it with a crack. The man grunted, and grunted again when Ava pulled out the remaining half of the arrow. Aiden grabbed a tin and a bandage from his bag, and handed it to Ava who spread the salve on both the entry and exit wound, wrapping his arm in the bandage and tying a neat knot.

Aiden said to the other man, "You are free to leave, but if you're willing, we do have some questions."

"Whatever we can do to help. You've spared us and did our home a great service in getting rid of those murderers," the older of the men offered.

Ava cut in, "Do you know where they came here from?"

The second man answered, "Rumor had it that they were in Gloren for a while. I think they caused a bit of a stir."

"Gloren's a big place. You have any idea where?" Aiden asked. In truth, he knew almost nothing about Gloran, only that it lay on the far northern side of the Kingdom and was a big port city, but, still knowing more couldn't hurt.

"I don't, but I have a friend named Arlin in the port," the hunter replied quickly. "I bet he'll know. Show him this," he said, handing over a wolf tooth bracelet. "He'll help you."

Aiden thanked him for the bracelet and asked, "What are your names?"

The injured man answered, "I'm Bran and this," he gestured to the younger man, "And this is Ryder."

"I'm Ava and this is Aiden," Ava offered back. They continued to inquire about the village which had been ruffed up by the attack but seemed to be putting itself back together. The men left after sharing a quick breakfast. Ava and Aiden continued along the road, and the next two days went much more smoothly. They even stopped at a bar one night, cloaked with their weapons hidden. Ava, always the white knight, had broken a bottle over a man's head and thrown him face first into one of the support beams for harassing a barmaid. They left quickly from the encounter before things could get out of hand and made camp a few miles away.

# Chapter 17

Aiden had been considering almost daily how he was going to tell Ava about what Bjorn had whispered to him, just before he'd pulled Aiden's blade through his own neck. But not telling her wasn't an option either, and the longer he waited, the worse he felt.

And, so he blurted out, "Bjorn said I have magic." He paused as Ava halted, turning to look at him, mouth slightly open. "Or he said there was magic in my parents' blood, and mine."

Ava just stared. They stood in silence for a moment.

"Could you say something?" Aiden asked.

Ava swallowed and finally asked, "Are you sure?"

"Those were his last words," Aiden said unsurely.

"Do you know what kind of magic?"

He shook his head, waiting for her to lose it.

"Well, when we get to Gloran, we'll see what we can find out," she said lightly, almost cheerfully.

"What?" He didn't move. "You still want to stay with me?" he asked, surprised.

"Through thick and thin, bandits and murders, and yes, magic," Ava retorted confidently.

She reached for his hand, politely holding it in hers, and grabbed his chin in her thumb and forefinger, lifting his gaze slightly. He stared into her tropical eyes and she into his golden bronze ones. She was close enough to smell him. He smelled of sweet smoke and aspen. She breathed it in. The breath went tight in her lungs as she leaned in closer, standing on her tippy toes, and brushed a kiss to his lips. She pulled back slightly once again looking into his face for a reaction.

But he just slowly swept a hand around her waist, the other brushing against her cheek, and stood there. Ava stood back on her tippy toes.

When they got to the horses, they decided to continue for at least a short while longer, eventually stopping at a small beach along a creek, walled from the road by willows. Aiden tied the horses, unpacking their bed rolls and making a fire ring while Ava tied a thin cord to the tail of an arrow. She took up a place at the edge of the stream. There were fish swimming by, each fighting their own battle up the stream. They would fight and fight for the span of a few feet, then take refuge in an eddy to rest for a few moments. These were the fish she took aim at, the ones hiding in the eddies. They were moving more slowly. Ava had never actually done this before, but she'd read about it, read enough to know that the water distorted the image of where exactly the fish were and that if she wanted to hit them, then she would have to account for this. Eight minutes later, she had five fish and began to walk back to where Aiden was lighting the fire. She took a small knife from his pack and cleaned and gutted the fish before butterflying them on small, wet willow twigs. Once Aiden had the fire going strongly enough, she rigged the branches over the flames and sat beside him. He gave her a small smile and held out an arm, inviting her to join him in the bedroll he'd wrapped himself in to protect from the chilly bite of the wind.

"We'll be in Gloran tomorrow," Ava reminded him.

"I know," Aiden replied. "It'll be dangerous?"

"I'd be disappointed if it wasn't," she giggled, lightly resting her head on his shoulder. "With thrilling tales of death and glory," she said in a mocking voice.

"With sea beasts and crime lords, no doubt," he said, matching her tone.

Aiden grabbed the now cooked fish. It wasn't good, but not having had a chance to eat at the bar, it tasted like heaven. They finished, both a little stuffed, and slumped to the side, still wrapped in the bed roll where Ava fell asleep in Aiden's arms.

Aiden thought of how in the past few months he had gone from being little more than totally alone to having someone he would walk over hot coals and fight the very gods to protect. It was rash to feel so strongly so quickly, but he'd also always imagined that he'd never live to twenty-five. Making rash decisions seemed at least a little more reasonable. He wrapped Ava in his arms a little tighter and drifted into the blank abyss of sleep.

Ava awoke to the sound and warm caress of Aiden's long, deep breathing against her ear. Feeling warm and cozy wrapped in the bed roll, she frowned, annoyed that she'd woken at all, so she shut her eyes against the light of dawn and shimmed further into his warmth.

"We really should get up," Aiden breathed.

"No," she said plainly, pushing into him and slinking under the covers. Aiden laughed softly. But he wrapped his arms around her and pulling her with him, rolled onto his back, out from under the covers, her face now lying against his chest.

"Bastard," she murmured, not yet committing to getting up.

It took Aiden the better part of fifteen minutes to coax her into getting up, in which time he packed the horses and cooked the remaining fish from last night's dinner, eating half, and finally persuading her to get up with the second half. Mounting their horses, they made their way back to the main road and followed it to Gloran, Ava still eating her fish and frowning not having entirely forgiven him for making her get up.

But as they crossed under the massive iron gate of Gloran, she was glad he had. They made their way through the city, stopping at a bar. Again, Ava started a scuffle. Well, brawl was a better term to describe what happened, this time because one of the drunken men had spilled ale on her, which she wouldn't have paid any mind to had the man not called her a *careless lass*. At which point she spun around and buried her fist in the man's nose. Aiden walked to the bar flashing the bar keep, a "I'm sorry about my friend," sort of look as she slammed the drunkard's head into the bar, shaking the whole tavern. Throwing a gold coin down in front of the bartender, Aiden walked over, tripping yet another man running for Ava, who seemed to be rather enjoying herself even as one of the men slammed a fist into her jaw. Neither of them bothered to draw weapons. They didn't need them, and if they used them they'd risk turning this into a whole other kind of fight. So they continued to fight the men, all of whom were at least double Ava's size. But the men, drunk and uncoordinated, were making for little more than entertainment. Aiden and Ava beat their way through them, fighting 'til each and every one of the men lay on the ground. Most of the ones Ava fought were still writhing on the ground, holding their groin, as the shocked and amused crowd broke into applause. Aiden hadn't noticed everyone watching them until it was over, but the rest of the tavern it seemed had halted their reveling to watch the spectacle. Ava noticed this as well, and not able to stop herself, she bowed. Aiden followed suit. Even the barman waved and chuckled as they walked out.

Untying their horses and finally arriving at the main part of the port, they asked around and it wasn't five minutes 'til they found out that Arlin, the man whom Ryder had mentioned, was the captain of the most notorious ship in the port called the Sea Storm. It was at the end of a long wooden subsection of the main dock, flanked by only a few other ships, all of which seemed to be vessels of similar quality. They climbed aboard and made for the helm, and the man standing at the wheel, who by all appearances had to be Arlin. Before they could approach him, they were stopped by a large and unfriendly-looking man who stepped into their path.

"The hell you think you're doing on this ship?" the man asked, sneering and stepping rudely close to Ava who was standing in front of Aiden. Aiden cut in, not wanting Ava to beat the man to a pulp while they were surrounded by his fellows.

"We're here to speak with the captain. We were sent by a friend of his," explained Aiden.

"Like hell you are. Scram!" The man bellowed.

Aiden started but Ava crooned, "Take us to him, or we'll take you to him."

The man began to draw a sword. Well, isn't this just a great way to get help," Aiden couldn't help thinking to himself.

The man finished drawing his rusty and beaten sword, but before it was out of its sheath, Ava slid a hidden dagger from under her sleeve. With a flash of steel, she cut the piece of rope fixing the man's pants in place. Yelling in rage, he brought his blade down toward Ava who sidestepped it with ease. As the man tripped on his fallen pants, his blade sunk into the wood of the deck.

Others were coming for them now. Aiden reluctantly realized that they might have to fight their way off the ship, and in turn the city. He had begun to shrug off his cloak when a young, but strong voice yelled out.

"Stop!!" All the men went still as a man no older than twenty-five, red beard braided into a fine ring, walked down from the helm of the ship. He'd seemed older before but now his age was apparent.

Walking over to them, he asked curiously, "Well, who are you fine people... who have managed to strip my crew of their pants, it seems?" He finished glancing at his man on the ground and stifled a laugh.

Aiden cut in. "We're really sorry about that," he said with a pointed glance to Ava.

"Ava got a little carried away. She has a bit of a wicked sense of humor," Aiden was saying but the man waved away his apology.

"You're all good. Zach here probably deserved it," the captain said to the man now standing in his shirt and undershorts, who Aiden could have sworn a grinned. "So what might I do for ya?"

"We were sent by a friend of yours," he said, "to give you this." Aiden reached into his bag looking for the bracelet but found nothing. Ava, who must have taken it from his bag, unfastened it from her wrist and handed it to the captain.

He grabbed it, a smile breaking across his face as he took it. "Ryder sent you, I take it. How's he doing after that attack?"

"The town is still rebuilding, but it seemed to be getting better," Aiden began. "But actually, we're here because we're looking for information. Ryder thought you might be able to help us?"

The man continued to smile. "Anything for friends of Ryder."

"Great!" Aiden said, choosing not to mention the circumstances of their meeting Ryder. "Is there any chance we could talk somewhere more private?"

"Of course," the captain replied and led them to a door. They found a well-furnished office smelling of sweet wine. He walked around the desk and plopped into a chair that looked like it might once have been made of fine leather, with beaded rivets holding the cushion into tight plumps. But that was once, and it now looked more like tatters of leather over padding.

"Please sit," the captain said, gesturing to the two finely carved chairs. "I suppose I should introduce myself. My name's Arlin, Captain of the Sea Storm. And you?"

Ava had turned sideways in her chair, legs dangling over the armrest. Aiden coughed pointedly, and Ava just waved for him to do it, now inspecting her fingernails. "I'm Aiden and this is Ava. We're knights," he said, gesturing to Ava and looking annoyed.

Arlin gave them a slightly confused smile. "Knights? You two can't be older than… what seventeen?"

"We're both sixteen, actually, but maybe that just makes us better spies," suggested Aiden.

"Fair enough. So what information do you want?"

Aiden paused, debating how best to word it, when Ava twisted, putting her feet on the floor facing Arlin, and broke in.

"There was a band of mercenaries that passed through here a few months ago, the same ones that destroyed Ryder's village." She paused. "We would like to know anything you can tell us about their employer."

Arlin's face had hardened a little. "Yes, they did. They burnt a good bit of the harbor and killed a few dozen people… but what reason do I have to tell you anything?"

Aiden straightened a bit, "We… can pay you?"

Arlin smirked. "I don't need gold…" Arlin began, "But, if you were to help me destroy a small fleet of Orinthian ships that have been making trade hard for this port, I could be persuaded to tell you." He paused, looking intently at the two of them. "And I'd hazard a guess that the commander of the fleet might have even more information than I."

Aiden looked to Ava who lowered her chin in agreement. "We'll help on the condition that we capture the commander... and destroy the fleet without civilian casualties."

Arlin's smile turned a little wicked as it broadened. "Then it looks like we have a deal." He reached for a map laying it across the desk. "The fleet is docked in Tallon on Uqbar. It's about a day and a half sail from here. My connections tell me they have three ships all stocked with black powder."

"So we blow the ships to hell," Ava chimed in.

"Exactly," Arlin agreed. "But we'll have to do so quietly and only after getting the commander."

"So how do you suppose we get the commander?" Aiden asked.

"He's an arrogant prick, he'll be easy to trick into leaving his men."

"I can do it," Ava added. "I'll get the commander."

"Sounds like a plan," Arlin agreed, tightening his beard ring. "Aiden and I will blow up the ships, and you get the commander. We'll leave at noon tomorrow. That way we'll get there at nightfall. You guys good with that?" Arlin asked, looking between them.

They nodded, standing. "See you then," Ava purred. They both walked out, still smiling.

# Chapter 18

Leaving the ship, they made their way down the street.

"This way," Ava breathed, in hardly more than a whisper, and darted down a side street. Three minutes later, they were on quite back road that had it not been well lit and clean, would have been the sort of place Aiden would have avoided. Ava halted abruptly, turning to face a door. "Hold these," she said, pulling off her cloak and all her weapons, short of the knife, which he knew she kept strapped to her arm, hidden beneath her sleeve. "Wait here," she ordered and stepped inside.

Ava entered the shop, which she had discovered earlier that day by impersonating a scholar. She strode over to the desk where she found an older woman wearing a simple blouse and black pants.

"Is there anything I might do for you?" the woman asked kindly.

"There might be," Ava said in a formal voice, holding her hands and placing her feet close together. "Is there any chance you have any history books on ancient magic?"

"Magic!?" the woman exclaimed, looking shocked. "Why, that is an old subject, and an unusual one."

"I know," Ava breathed, faking exasperation. "I'm helping Doctor Arnlmen in his studies of the ancient world and how it has affected the world as we see it today," she finished slowly, hoping that the woman wouldn't think twice about the made up doctor.

"I see…" the woman said, frowning and holding her chin in thought. "I think there might be one back here, come." She walked into the back room, Ava following. Every inch of the room was filled with books and boxes, presumably full of books, some on shelves others in precarious stacks. The shop owner stopped at a small dust-covered box, blowing off the dust. The words in the box read, "*MISC Magic*". *The woman* opened it and pulled out the books. "What type of book are you looking for?" the woman asked and bent over the box to look.

Ava responded. "Ideally, something not only explaining what the different types of magic are, but also how they were identified and used."

"Well, that's very specific. I doubt we'll have all that but perhaps..." She pulled a large leather-bound volume from the box. The title read, "Magic and Where It Comes From". "I think this'll be the best we have. There were few books ever written on how the ancients did it, even fewer exist now."

"I understand," Ava breathed, shaking her head slightly. They walked back to the desk where Ava bought the book for 20 silver pieces.

"Good night dear, stay safe," the shopkeeper offered, looking at Ava with concern.

Ava waved a hand in farewell, walking out the door.

When Ava returned to the street, she was holding a large leather-bound book. "So what was that?" Aiden asked, eyeing the book.

"This is the first step towards figuring out your magic."

"How did you know about this shop?" Aiden wondered.

Walking down the street, she answered. "Because, before that guy at the bar so rudely started the fight..."

Aiden cut her off laughing, "When *HE* started the fight?"

She just pushed Aiden into a puddle and continued. "Before he started the fight, I was talking to a scholar who recommended I come here to find a book on magic," she finished, chin in the air.

"Nicely done," he conceded.

They returned to their horses and booked a room at an inn. A gruff-faced but kind old man gave them the key and informed them that there would be a small breakfast at seven in the morning. Aiden unlocked their room. Both wasted no time in jumping into bed, as tired as they were. Ava managed to take up most of the bed, small as she was.

The next morning, Aiden awoke to Ava slamming a pillow in his face, laughing heartily at his shocked start.

"Payback," she said sweetly.

He groaned, opening an eye and flashing her a rude gesture.

She just stuck out her tongue and told him, "I want to go get breakfast at a cafe. I haven't had a coffee in weeks, and I want a croissant."

Aiden gave a fake pointed snore. Grabbing his hand, she tried to pull him out of bed, but he just gripped her wrist, and yanked her off her feet and back into the bed.

"Asshole," she muttered, pushing him.

Five minutes later they were walking down the street to a cafe. Ava haven squashed Aiden's small protests that they could just eat the free breakfast at the inn.

After giving their order to a young man, they took a seat at the small bar overlooking the bay, where the Sea Storm was being loaded.

Ava drank her coffee smiling. "You know, I think we should just give this up and make coffee for a living."

He laughed. When Ava had finished her coffee they went back to the inn.

"Well, I suppose now's as good a time as any to start reading," she said and plopped down on the bed with the book she had purchased. "I'll tell you if I find anything."

Nodding, he grabbed the book she had given him, *From Blood to Water* from his bag and plopped down next to her. Twenty minutes later, Ava turned to look at him. "According to this, the main branches of magic are 'Mind Magic', meaning that the wielder can read and invade the thoughts and minds of others and, in some rare cases, control them. Then, there's 'Elemental Magic'," she continued, tracing a finger down the page as she read it off. "Where the wielder can control a single element,… fire, wind, earth." She gestured to the page and continued, "Then with 'Physical Magic', the person can make things move, like the air is an extension of their hands. It says that one's weaker than the others, more of a party trick compared to the last ones. And lastly, it just says, 'Raw Power'."

She read aloud, eyes narrowing on the page:

BY FAR THE RAREST OF THE MAGICAL GIFTS, THE FORM OF MAGIC KNOWN AS RAW POWER TAKES NEITHER FORM NOR HAS IT EVER PROVEN TO HAVE LIMITS. RAW POWER IS UNLIKE OTHER FORMS OF MAGIC THAT ARE DEPLETED AS THEY ARE USED, AFTER WHICH THE WIELDER MUST THEN REST TO RECOVER THEIR GIFTS. WIELDERS OF RAW POWER HAVE NO KNOWN LIMIT TO THE FORCE THEY CAN UNLEASH. THOUGH THE MOST POWERFUL OF THE BRANCHES OF MAGIC, IT IS ALSO THE MOST VOLATILE. IT CAN NEITHER BE CONTAINED NOR BLOCKED. IT IS SYNTHESIZED IN THE FORM OF EITHER LIGHT OR DARKNESS, BOTH SAID TO BE COMPLETE IN THEIR EFFECT, EITHER THE LIGHT OF THE STARS THEMSELVES, OR THE DARKNESS BETWEEN THEM.

"Damn!" Aiden laughed, as Ava flicked the page and continued.

THERE HAVE ONLY BEEN TWO KNOWN WIELDERS OF RAW POWER IN HISTORY. IT IS SAID TO BE THE POWERS GIVEN TO THE DESCENDANTS OF GODS.

"It sounds to me like that last one is more of a myth," Aiden said.

"For real? The darkness between stars... given to two people in history? What kind of bullshit is that?" she huffed. "But, it's getting close to noon. We should get going. Arlin won't like it if we're late."

Getting down to the reception area of the inn, Aiden asked the man working to tend to Raith and Spark, flipping him a silver coin and following Ava outside.

"Good to see you two," Arlin called, as they climbed aboard, right as the man Ava had humiliated the previous day untied the ship from the dock.

"Let's get going, then we'll discuss the plan further," Arlin ordered.

Each crew member grabbed an oar and began to row. Aiden and Ava glanced at each other for a heartbeat, then joined, seeing nothing else to do.

Once they had cleared the harbor, Arlin yelled to the crew, "Stop rowing and raise the sail!"

They did so at once, dropping the sail as air filled it and the ship lurched slightly, the wind pulling them along.

"This way." Arlin said, waving a hand and leading Ava and Aiden back into the office.

After a few hours of planning and a small and quickly quashed objection from Aiden, it had been decided that Ava would pose as a romantically interested girl to the captain, who she would invite to go somewhere more private outside the camp. Meanwhile, Aiden, Arlin and Arlin's first mate, Zach, would swim to the backsides of the ships, out of view of the soldiers, sneak on, set fuses in the gunpowder, and then sneak back into the water. Hopefully, in all the uproar, would allow Ava to knock out the commander and drag him down to the beach. Arlin's men would be waiting for her there to bring the captain back to their ship where they would regroup.

After the meeting, a crew member led them to a small cabin below deck. The room was small but well-kept and warm. Lying down, they both quickly fell asleep.

# Chapter 19

"Get up you two! We'll be there in half an hour. Be on deck in five minutes!" someone shouted on the other side of their cabin door.

Ava rolled over, facing Aiden. "You ready for this?" she asked.

"Ready as I'll ever be…" he said, trailing off as he stared into her face.

Tropical eyes soft and warm, she was smiling faintly. "What is it?" she asked.

"Nothing… It's just that we won't be fighting together, and… Just promise you'll be safe?"

Her face turned softer. "I will." She said the words slowly and deliberately, pausing, then brushing him a kiss. "Now you promise me."

"I promise," he said, matching her deliberateness.

They arrived on deck clad in cloaks, Aiden in dark clothing, and Ava in a knee-length dress she'd managed to swindle from a vendor before they'd left Gloran. They found Arlin dressed similarly to Aiden, Sword strapped to his back, along with a bow and a quiver of arrows. Ava had brought no weapons other than a long slender dagger she had strapped to her upper thigh, just short enough to hide beneath the hem of her skirt.

"It's time," Arlin growled as a savage smile spread across his face. "Today these bastards pay for the lives of those they killed in Gloran."

They nodded.

"Stay safe," Ava breathed, kissing Aiden on the cheek.

"You too," he beckoned.

Ava darted off the boat, jumping down and landing on her feet in the sand. She turned to head down the coast and disappeared into the darkness, towards the town playing host to the crew of the enemy fleet.

On silent feet, Aiden, Arlin, and the first mate got into a small row boat. Aiden threw his cloak back onto the ship; if they were swimming all it would serve to do is slow him down anyway. They began to row in silence. They rowed for an hour. Slowed down by their necessity for quiet, they finally got close to the ships whose commander Ava should already have lured away. She was now likely just waiting for the commotion of the exploding ships to incapacitate him.

Silent as the beasts of the sea below them, they anchored the small boat about a hundred yards away and began to swim, branching away from each other fifty yards from the boats. Each went on their own, Arlin on the left, the mate on the right, and Aiden in the middle just as they had planned. Getting to the ship, Aiden grabbed the small ladder built onto its side. Poking his head over the deck, he spotted one guard just as Arlin's spy had described. The man sat atop the helm, leaning against the wheel, picking his nails with a short knife. Aiden silently heaved himself over the rail, hurrying to the wall leading up to the helm. Glancing to see that the guard was still occupied, he moved, sprinting up the steps on light feet. The guard only had time to turn before Aiden slammed an open hand into the man's throat, wrapping his arm around it as the man began to fall. Aiden lowered the man to the ground as he squeezed, holding the position for another moment until the man passed out. Aiden slung him over a shoulder, carrying him swiftly to the dock and setting him there, as they had planned to do with any guards.

Getting back to the main deck, he opened a door near the helm and ran down the stairs to find a table of soldiers playing cards and drinking.

They looked up at his sudden appearance. "Who?!" one of the men began in shock as they all drew their swords.

"Please don't," Aiden pleaded. This was exactly what he didn't want to do right now. The longer he was delayed, the longer Ava would have to spend with the commander. "This will end badly," Aiden added, one last attempt to stop this before it starts.

"What did you do with Erick?!" one of the men asked, looking as though any answer would result in violence.

"He's okay, just unconscious. I…"

But another man yelled, "Bullshit!" and charged.

Aiden drew Starlight, its blade glinting in the candlelight. Blocking with ease, he tripped the man as another swung for his head. Blocking the blow, he slammed his elbow into the man's jaw with a crack that knocked him out cold. As the first man began to rise, Aiden slammed his knee into the man's lowered head. The final man swayed slightly as he ran. Aiden tackled him before he could turn. They hit the ground, the side of Aiden's head hitting the floorboards with a sharp noise. The man scrambled atop him and started raining fists down. Aiden raised his arms to block the blows. Forcing his hips up, he threw the man off, sending him against the side of the table. Aiden scrambled over on his hands and knees, locking his arm around the man's neck and legs around his middle. The man writhed as Aiden held him. Squeezing still harder, Aiden felt the crack of a rib under his leg. The man let out a sound, stifled by Aiden's arm, and passed out.

Aiden lay back on the floor for a moment, taking deep breaths. He'd had the wind knocked from him when he hit the ground. He swore softly to the still-open room. Rising, he took the men's bodies to join that of the first. Aiden discarded the last of them and ran back below deck. He was behind schedule; the fuse should already have been lit. Finding the gunpowder, he poked the long fuse into the barrel, making sure it didn't bump against the floor or barrel. He pulled the knife from his boot and slashed it through the fuse, cutting off a third of it. Grabbing the lantern by which the men had been playing cards, he lit the fuse. Then, he ran above deck and, without hesitation, dove off the back side of the ship. He spotted the mate ahead of him in the water.

Arlin had already gotten to the boat. "What took you so long?" Arlin asked, helping to pull him aboard.

"I took out the one guard before he knew I was there. Then I ran downstairs... to find a group of three more playing cards," he said, clearly unamused and unhappy.

"Shit... Sorry my spies hadn't seen any but the one guard aboard."

"It's fine," Aiden replied, grabbing an ore. "They probably just went on the ship to play cards."

BOOM!! Lights flashed behind them as the ships were blown into little more than smoldering scraps of wood.

"It's all on Ava now," Zach breathed, glancing at the camp.

# Chapter 20

She stepped into the camp, hands held neatly in front of her as she walked, no one thinking to stop the pretty girl. It took her all of five minutes to find the commander, a medium-sized man wearing fine clothes and a rapier that looked as though it had never been used strapped to his hip. Walking over to the group he sat with, one of whom whistled at her arrival, she flashed a warm and slightly naughty smile at the group, then the captain, whom she sat next to.

"Well, hello, is there anything I can help you with?" the captain asked, looking pleased at her arrival. The man wasn't handsome. He had a slightly mousey face and brown, near-black eyes now glazed with a hungry look that made Ava want to vomit.

She schooled her face into a warm, simpering grin and said, "You men looked a little lonely over here. I thought I might come to give some company."

The commander grinned, edging slightly closer to where Ava sat and said, "You could come keep me company back at my tent."

"At your tent, in the middle of this camp?" She gave a fake giggle. "No, but I wouldn't mind keeping you company somewhere a little more private."

The man's hideous smile widened. "Well, go on," he breathed conspiratorially.

"There's a small inn outside of Tallon," she offered.

"Well, in that case, it sounds like we better go there," the commander said in mock urgency.

"I'm afraid we must leave you," he announced to the rest of the men in the group, all of whom nodded, matching his hideous smile. The commander led the way through the camp, his men staring and whistling as they passed. She hoped that the timing would work out as they had planned. If they were on time, then she should have about ten minutes 'til the explosion.

They neared the small inn when the commander began, "I already have a room booked. I'm friendly with the owners, you see."

She had no doubt he had the room booked just for occasions like this. And gods did that only maker her wish for the boom to come sooner so she could be done speaking with the piece of shit.

"Lead the way dear," he said, stepping to the side gesturing for her to lead.

She did so as the inn came into sight and... BOOM!!

"What the...!" the commander started, wheeling around.

Looking back, Ava saw the glow of the explosion as the first of the ships was blown to pieces. Ava struck. With the commander's back turned, she wrapped an arm around his neck, linking it with her other before he could react. Pulling backward, the commander stumbled, and they fell to the ground. The commander struggled, even as his movements slowed and eventually stopped. After holding him for a moment longer, she released him, knowing she had only moments 'til people came looking for him.

Ava hauled the man over her shoulder. She slumped under his weight but made her way the short distance north to the beach where Arlin's men would be waiting for her. She groaned as she hauled him along over the logs and rock of the mellow hillside. Seeing the sand of the beach and the flicker of a torch, she called out. Three men came running up to meet her, taking the unconscious commander and holding him between them. All three looked at the man as though he was something disgusting that could contaminate them. Arlin had talked about this man as though he hated him and that opinion seemed to be shared by his men.

Jogging alongside them, she spotted the small row boat. Aiden, Arlin, and the mate were aboard it as they neared the ship and climbed aboard. Ava heard shouts behind. Looking back, she saw a group of fifteen or more of the soldiers chasing after them, holding torches, one already drawing a bow. The arrow soared, clipping the thigh of one of the men carrying the commander. The third man took his place. Ava held the arm of the injured man around her shoulders and pulled him along. Twenty yards to the dock, another arrow wised by, this one's tip flaming and going out with a sizzle in the sand beside them. Ten yards... the shouts were growing closer. More arrows flew but not from the soldiers. They came from the men aboard the Sea Storm. As the arrows hit their marks, the soldiers fell back, carrying injured men of their own. Ava and the three others hauled the commander, then themselves, over the side of the Sea Storm, the soldiers cursing at them in the distance.

"We have to hurry!" Arlin shouted, all stealth forgotten, heaving the commander against the mast and tying his hands around it with almost brutal force.

The deck was a madhouse as Ava found Aiden still spooked, nose bleeding and cheek beginning to shine with a bruise. She wrapped her arms around him, holding him tight and shouting over the noise of the ship, "Are you hurt?!"

"No!" Aiden yelled back.

Arlin ran past. "Could you two love birds stop hugging and help us get out of here?!"

It was pandemonium when they broke apart. Ava ran for one of the benches, Aiden for another, as they began to row. Looking back, Ava realized the soldiers hadn't fled; they had called for reinforcements. There were now hundreds of men roaring along the beach, getting nearer and nearer as Arlin dropped the sail. The boat lurched violently. They were still too close to the dock and reef to raise the sails safely. But still, the boat heaved away, gaining speed as the first of the army's arrows hit its side.

Arlin was at the helm, shouting orders, grim-faced and cool-headed, every bit the captain acclaimed by Ryder. As arrows rained down, the men ducked against the walls at the side of the ship, hearing the thuds of arrows sinking into the opposite side of the wall. The thudding ceased, replaced with sharp splashes as the arrows met water. They'd escaped, out of range of the archers, and the enemy having no boats with which to pursue. Ava let loose a sigh, standing still for a moment before calmly walking to Aiden.

# Chapter 21

The ride home on the boat was long. The crew wasn't bothering to man the ship any more than was necessary. Three of the men had been hit by glancing arrows and were now below deck being treated. Ava treated Aiden's injuries herself. None of the injuries were consequential, but they looked bad. His nose and cheek were shining a deep purple fringed in yellow, and he was walking with a slight limp.

The next morning after the attack, Ava and Aiden met Arlin in his office to discuss what to do next.

"I'm glad to see the two of you doing so well."

"As are we," Aiden responded.

Ava grimaced, "I would have preferred if you could have done it without breaking Aiden's face. I happened to like it the way it was," Ava said coldly.

Arlin chuckled slightly. "I'm sorry, it wasn't my plan for any of us to get hurt."

Aiden flashed a joking smile, partially because of Ava's compliment.

"Neither did we," Ava continued in a lighter tone.

"So, about the information you said you have?" Aiden asked.

Arlin smiled. "Of course, as promised, I'll tell you everything I know."

Aiden nodded and he and Ava sat.

"When the group came through, they trashed the docks, lighting most of the port on fire as they went," Arlin explained. "They also left a message written in blood. It was painted on the front wall of the theater. It read:

THE DARK POWER OF OUR KING WILL STORM THE WORLD, WREATHING IT IN SHADOW UNTIL THE WORLD CAN BE MADE ANEW.

Aiden went still, not daring to breathe too loudly as his memory was ripped back to Ava reading the book before they left. Based on her expression of fear and comprehension, she'd realized it too.

But Arlin continued, "Or so I am told... the city guard washed away the message before word could get out of what it said. I only know this much from the contacts I have in Gloran," he finished looking a little tenuous. "I ask that you don't tell anyone I gave you this information."

They both nodded sharply and Aiden asked, "What can you tell us of the meaning of the message?"

"Nothing, only that it was written in blood and the group fled the city before they could be caught. Load of rubbish if you ask me, just meant to scare people. But it might give you a clue who they work for. It's not exactly your most normal threat."

"Do you have any idea who might know more?" Ava pressed.

"Not for certain, but I'd bet 10 gold pieces that an unwilling commander will have something to say for the right reason." A truly savage smile crossed Arlin's face at his words, Ava partially matching it.

"Shall we go pay him a visit then?" Aiden asked, rubbing his hands together.

"I believe we should," Ava purred.

The commander had been moved to the brig as soon as they had gotten to sea. Walking down the stairs, they found him still unconscious, shackles bound above him and his head slumped against his arm. There still were purple bruises where Arlin had tied his wrists around the mast. Walking into the cell, Arlin grabbed a pail of dirty brown water, clearly used to wash the brig floor, and flung it at him, bucket and all. The commander awoke with a jerk as it hit his face and chest, soaking him.

He began to wrench against the chains until Ava purred in a voice of violent calm, "Well, commander it appears our night together will have to be rescheduled."

The man observed her no longer wearing the dress, and back in her usual brown pants and white shirt tucked into her waistband, bow quiver and hilt all visible over her shoulders. He seemed to comprehend who the girl had been and what had happened.

"So, captain," Arlin crooned a little sadistically, sitting on the bench beside the commander and splaying his legs before him. "We would love for you to tell us everything you know about your King's plans."

There was a pause and the commander let loose a barking snarl of a laugh. "Over my dead body will I tell you pirates anything."

Arlin smiled. "I was hoping you'd say that. You see… one of the ships you sank was my little sister's."

Aiden's mouth dropped open. Arlin hadn't shown a single sign of sorrow. But, looking at him now, there was a thin glint of silver at the corners of his eyes.

But his words were as cold as the snowy mountains of the far south, as he continued, "So, you are going to tell me everything you know. Then, maybe, just maybe, I'll let you choose how you die."

The commander swallowed slowly, seeming to feel the wrath emanating from Arlin as he pulled a small dirty knife from his boot. "I… I won't tell you…" but Arlin plunged the knife into the man's leg. He screamed in pain and fear, and fear of pain to come. "The King of Orenth is assembling forces. They're gathering in the mountains."

"Where?! What mountains?" Ava demanded, trying to capitalize on the moment.

"I don't know. I just over-heard it from my superiors. Please…!"

"What do you know of the message his men left in Gloran?" Aiden asked.

"The message was just a threat to terrify the people," the commander explained with a grimace.

Aiden took a slow breath and continued, "Does the King really have the dark power the message said?"

The commander seemed to go partially still. "I… I don't know for sure… but there are rumors." He said the last part in barely more than a whispered whimper.

"Rumors of what?" Aiden questioned, matching Arlin's calm, even as Arlin flipped the knife in his hand.

"They say he controls darkness. They say it's like all the light of the world vanishes in his presence!"

Aiden could feel a weight growing in his stomach as words caught in his throat.

It was Ava who stepped to his side and said, "What does he plan to do? What is his end goal?"

The commander shook his head. "I don't know."

"Well, what do you think? If you *had* to guess!" Ava hissed, emphasizing the word and making it clear he did in fact have to guess.

The exasperated commander blurted, "He plans to conquer as much as he can! I think he wants to build an empire!"

Feeling that they had all the information the man could offer, Arlin growled, "Why don't you two go upstairs." His tone left no room for argument.

The man turned pleading eyes to them. "Please!! Don't leave me...!" he whimpered.

Ava whispered in Aiden's ear, "We have no right to interfere." She then spoke to the man, "For the things you have done and those you have hurt, Arlin will be your reckoning." And they walked out.

The screams hit them before they reached the deck. Aiden shuttered and Ava grabbed his hand. "It wasn't our place to intervene," she said.

He nodded vaguely. "I know, but..." he trailed off and Ava let it drop.

They made their way to their cabin. By dawn, the commander's body was strapped against the hull of the boat, barely more than tatters against the waves.

# CHAPTER 22

"We better send a letter to William," Ava suggested. "He'll want to know what we've found out."

Aiden nodded, climbing into their bed at the inn. Leaning against the headboard, he grabbed the book Ava had given him. He held it in his lap but didn't open it. "Are we good people?" Aiden asked softly.

Ava turned to him quickly. "What?!"

"I mean, I killed the invaders back home. Then, I maimed the guards and destroyed their ships. And... and the commander just..."

But Ava cut him off and sat down next to him. "What happened to the commander isn't our fault. What happened to him was of his own doing. Those people back home meant to kill you and our friends, and they kidnapped me and helped murder my family." She continued a little more harshly, "And the ships were being used to wreck other civilian ships and leave the people to drown at sea."

Aiden didn't answer. He just looked at Ava, still feeling unsure.

"And all the smaller fights we've been in have either been started by other people or me. Not you. You haven't hurt anyone without reason," Ava urged.

He nodded, leaning his head against her shoulder.

Ava waited for a moment. "Should I write a letter to William?" she asked.

"Yeah, maybe," Aiden agreed. "But just tell him the commander... died."

Ava gripped his hand tightly and stood. Walking over to the desk in their room, she sat, pulled a roll of parchment from her bag and set it on the desk. She reached into a drawer, grabbed ink and a quill and began to write. When she'd finished, she blew on the paper, drying the still shining ink. She handed it to Aiden who skimmed it, eyes darting back and forth across the page.

He looked up, brows arched high. "You just wrote this?"

She nodded.

"You're an impressive writer," Aiden said in an expression of slight surprise.

Ava smiled and bent over in a deep mock bow. "Courtesy of the formal education of the Attican Palace."

Aiden laughed softly, Ava matching the noise. "I'll send the letter," he said, standing and taking it from her.

"Wait, I need to seal it," she said. He held it as she dripped wax over the seam in the scroll and pressed the blank seal into it.

Aiden left the inn and walked down the street. He had left his sword and cloak, opting for his normal clothing and only carrying his boot knife. Arriving at the messenger office, the crest of their guild flashing above the door, he walked in to find a tall, skinny boy no older than he working behind a desk.

"Anything I can help ya with?" the boy asked lightly.

"Yeah, I was hoping I could send a letter," Aiden replied.

The boy smiled and five minutes later the letter was ready for delivery. Aiden even spent the three extra silver pieces to have it delivered the next day.

Aiden returned to the inn and walked into their room. He felt a bit refreshed and began, "Well, we should have at least two days before we get our next instructions on..." but he trailed off, seeing Ava once again sitting on the bed and reading the magic book.

"Anything new?" he asked

"Nothing about the dark power, and all the information on raw power is really vague. But there's some interesting stuff about the other powers. It sounds like even though they aren't nearly as powerful, they're more useful. This says that with practice they can be used on command to do all kinds of things."

"Like?"

"This says that some people can use the different gifts to heal people. Some can use it to fight. Others can use it for normal things." Ava ran her finger along the page and read:

In many cases, wielders of elemental magic can form the element they control into the form of whatever they visualize. This can be done by using one's will to conform the power. All forms of magic, save raw power, are formed using one's will.

Aiden walked over to the bed, lying across it and looking at the ceiling. "So what does it say about how to know if someone has magic?"

She flipped a few pages, biting her lip in concentration. "It... it says here that it depends slightly on the form of magic. But in almost all cases, it first makes itself apparent in extreme circumstances."

"Like?" Aiden wondered.

"Things like battle, or it says 'NECESSITY'." She paused, and then asked, "Do you want to go see if there are any good places to go get dinner around here?"

"Sure," he agreed. "What do you want to eat?"

She frowned slightly as she pulled her cloak on, choosing to leave her weapons behind. "I think we should treat ourselves. What about that steak house we saw on the way into town last week?"

"The one that was charging 20 silver pieces per person?"

"Yeah," Ava replied with a smile.

Aiden pulled his cloak on, looking at her with raised brows.

"I mean, it's really a business expense if you think about it," she continued with pursed lips.

Aiden shook his head but smiled all the same as he followed her out the inn door.

The city was calm in the late afternoon. They walked up the main street and peered into all sorts of shops. As the main port city on the west side of the continent, it was obvious that many of the wares weren't from Anglen.

"Oh! In here," Ava said, darting into a small shop. Most of its accents were painted blue. The windows were full of ornate weapons, all engraved with different floral markings. The doorbell rang as he entered after her.

"Welcome in," a kind voice called from the back of the shop.

Ava was standing before a large rack of extremely ornately engraved bows. As he stepped beside her she breathed, "These are all from Attica." Tears were lining her eyes as she said it. "They must have been brought here before Attica fell." She shook slightly.

Aiden rested a hand on her back and said, "We'll find the people responsible for what happened there, and whatever you wish to do then, I'll stand with you."

She finally tore her eyes from the bows, looking at him with a weak smile.

"Through thick and thin, magic and fallen kingdoms," Aiden offered with an earnest look.

Ava let loose a small laugh. "We'd better go get dinner," she said, taking one last look at the top bow, a powerful recurved bow, gleaming as bright as the pommel of his own sword, and shining with the silver floral inlay of her kingdom. At last, tearing her eyes away from the weapon, they left the shop.

When they got to the restaurant, the hostess blocked their entry. She was a tall woman wearing a red silk dress and gold jewelry. She took one look at them in their black cloaks and slightly dirty clothes and hissed, "We don't serve children, or riffraff." She stared at them over the check-in desk, sneering slightly. Ava opened her mouth to argue, but the woman cut her off. "Now go away or I'll have you thrown out, girl."

Anger rose in Aiden as Ava's face colored. He said quietly to the woman, "Talk to her like that again, and you'll need more than staff to throw us out."

Realizing the threat, the woman rolled her shoulders back and hissed, "Last chance, leave!" Her body was steady and tall but her words shook as she spoke.

It was Ava who stepped forward, Aiden raising his hands as he said grinning, "I warned you, this one's on you." He stepped back leaving Ava to deal with the woman.

Ava walked right up to the desk, reaching over it and grabbing the front of the woman's dress and pulling her in. "Go get your manager," Ava snarled, letting the woman go.

The hostess ran off, at least as best she could given the dress. She came back a moment later three men flanking her.

One of the men inquired, "Are you two causing trouble?

"No," Aiden replied for her.

"We only wanted to be seated. Your hostess denied us service without a reason and threatened to have us thrown out."

The man now in front glared at Aiden.

"We're happy to pay," Aiden explained. "So I don't see what the problem is."

"I don't care. You leave or I'll beat you 'til you need a wagon to go home," the man snarled.

Aiden shook his head, tutting in mock defeat. "You see, my friend wants to eat here. We've had a long couple of weeks. So, how's about a deal? You can call your biggest man, and if they can pin Ava here..." he gestured to her, "... Then we'll leave."

Ava, in all her mischievous intent, gave them an innocent smile.

The front man smiled back. "OK, you have a deal, on one condition. You have to fight him in our pit in the middle of the restaurant. If you win, you can eat here as much as you like, for free," he said looking Ava up and down.

"Deal!" they both replied in unison.

They were led into the center of the restaurant by the group, where, sure enough, there was a large pit about twenty feet in diameter and ten deep, the bottom filled with sand. One of the three men stalked off down a side passage. Most of the restaurant was looking at them now, seemingly confused at what was happening.

Aiden leaned in close to Ava and whispered in her ear, "Just let me know if you want help."

But she only gave him a feral smile and took off her cloak, then the baggy shirt, leaving her in the slim leather breastplate she wore beneath. A minute later, the man came back, followed by one of the biggest men Aiden had ever seen. He was at least seven feet tall and shirtless. It was easy to see why the man had been so confident. But Ava just kept grinning as she hopped down into the pit.

The man whom they had spoken with stepped right next to the pit and announced to the room, "Welcome one and all! Tonight, we have a special treat!" He paused, allowing for dramatic effect. "Ava," he said, gesturing to her down in the pit, "Has challenged our champion, Draxon."

Some of the guests were looking shocked and a little disgusted at the idea of the fight, but most of the regulars seemed thrilled. Draxon jumped down into the pit opposite Ava.

The man continued, "They will fight using fists alone. Whoever can pin the other to the ground first is the winner and will be given full access to the restaurant." He smiled to Aiden. "Viewers place your bets, and... begin!!"

Draxon lunged for Ava, fist raised, but Ava sidestepped him, placing a hand on the back of his neck and forcing his head down. The man crashed, tumbling on the ground and slamming into the wall. The impact shook the floor a little as Ava raised her arms, gesturing for the crowd to cheer. Those in the crowd who were initially hesitant to watch seemed to warm to the fight. The man who had announced was now tight-lipped. Draxon rose, shaking his head from the impact. Before he had time to collect himself, Ava jumped for him, slamming her fist up into his jaw as her foot swept his legs. His back slammed to the ground. She stepped over him, grabbing his hair to lift his head, only to slam it back to the floor with an elbow. The restaurant was silent in shock as she stood over him, his back to the ground and unconscious. Everyone was quiet.

Aiden stepped to the side of the ring and said to the room at large, "Well, it seems we have our victor!"

Slowly at first the crowd began to clap. Then there was a roar as the whole restaurant joined.

Aiden turned back to the first man they had spoken with, who he was quite sure now was the owner. The man's mouth was open as he looked down at Draxon, still unconscious in the pit.

Ava climbed out as the owner said, "I'm a man of my word. Allow me to take you to your seats and take your orders."

Aiden had expected him to be livid, and even throw them out, but he only seemed to respect them more. They followed him to the second story of the restaurant, seating them next to a large window through which they could see all the way down the hill to Gloran and right out to the sea. The man took their order of lobster and scallops with alfredo. Ava wiped the slight bit of blood off her forearm with the napkin. The food came ten minutes later, and they ate. The meal was delicious, second only to Phil's baking back home.

When they had finished the owner came back. "I would like to apologize for my staff's behavior as well as my own earlier this evening."

But Ava just waved a hand, still dabbing her mouth with the napkin, and said, "I had a good time... but talk to me like that again and it'll be you in the pit."

The man smiled, raising his hands in defeat and nodding. "Well, the two of you are welcome here anytime. If you ever want to fight again, just let me know," he finished, smiling.

"Will do," Aiden replied as they stood shaking the man's hand and walking back downstairs. They found Draxon sitting at the bar, an ice bag pressed to the side of his face.

Ava walked over to him. "Hey, you good?" she asked.

Draxon turned in his seat, spotting her as he stood, and to their surprise, smiled. "Yeah, it's been a while since anyone put me in my place like that. Maybe we'll have a rematch someday."

Ava gave a sly smile. "Maybe."

"If you ever want a big friend, look me up… Draxon Warwick," he finished, reaching a hand out to Ava who shook it.

"We will. Take care of yourself," Ava replied and Draxon nodded.

She and Aiden turned and walked out the door. Ava flipped off the hostess as they walked by. When they got back to the inn, Ava ripped off her dirty outer clothing and plopped right into bed. Aiden only grabbed his money bag from his pack and strapped his sword to his back.

"What are you doing?" Ava wondered.

"I'll be back in just a bit," he answered.

She was still looking at him suspiciously.

"I'm not gonna do anything dangerous," Aiden scoffed. "You can go to bed."

She frowned at him, but pulled the blanket over herself and rested her head on the pillow.

Slipping out the door, he made his way back down the street from which they'd just come. Arriving at the Attican weapon store, he opened the door and walked over to the wall of bows. Aiden grabbed the ornate white one on top that Ava had stared at and brought it back to the counter where he found the same young woman passed out on the desk. Aiden gave a soft but pointed cough.

The woman awoke with a start, rubbing her eyes and muttering an apology. "What can I help you with?" she asked kindly.

Aiden set the bow on the desk and asked, "How much does this cost?"

The woman stared at the weapon, seemingly alarmed that he had taken it off its perch. "This… this bow belonged to the dead queen of Attica, Queen Ariea Corinth."

Aiden's chest tightened, realizing what seeing the bow must have meant to Ava.

But the woman continued, "It belonged to her mother before her and would have belonged to the princess one day. It's called The Bow of Starin."

"OK, how much to buy it, and get a small engraving on it?" Aiden asked.

"You want to engrave it?!" she replied, outraged.

"Yes, I want it to say 'Through thick and thin and anything else'."

"The bow costs 20 gold pieces and..."

"Twenty gold pieces?" he interrupted

"Yes, it's an ancient bow of a lost kingdom. And we'll say another five for the engraving."

Aiden frowned slightly but dipped his chin in agreement and grabbed his coin bag. Pulling out the coins, he counted them, then set them on the desk. The woman then counted them again.

"Very well," she said, "But are you sure you want me to engrave it?"

"Certain," he responded.

"OK," and with that the woman walked into the back room shaking her head as she looked down at the bow. She came back twenty minutes later holding the bow, which now had the words he'd asked for engraved and inlaid with the same silver as the rest of the bow. She handed it to him.

"Take care of it," she breathed, a hint of sadness in her voice.

"I will." He walked out the door.

# CHAPTER 23

Arriving back at the inn, Aiden slipped in the front and found Ava asleep. He hid the bow in the bottom drawer of the dresser, setting his spare clothes on top of it. He peeled off his outer layer of clothing and slid into the bed beside her.

The next morning, Aiden awoke to Ava entering the room with a small letter in her hand.

"What's that?" he asked.

"It's our new orders from William." She sat on the bed beside him and carefully snapped the stag-emblazoned wax seal.

"That was fast," Aiden said in shock. He leaned in to read over her shoulder.

*Dear AW & AC*

*I have received the information you sent to me, and if you are agreeable, I would like you to travel to the lands of the one who you believe has poor intentions. Try to find any evidence of that power and how it might be fought. Stay out of sight and use fake names. When you are done, please come to my home in Clystera.*

*Your friend KW*

"Well, it sounds like we're going on an adventure," Ava said as Aiden grinned at her. "With perilous dangers," she added.

"Well, of course," Aiden mused. "We wouldn't want it to be boring."

"Well, then, we'd better get going," she said, hopping up and striding for her bag. After ten minutes of hurried packing Ava was ready to go.

"Go ahead. I'll meet you downstairs," Aiden suggested.

She nodded and walked out. As she did, Aiden shoved the Bow of Starin into his bag and followed her out.

"How do you think we get there?" he pondered once they were outside.

Ava paused, seeming to consider. "Orenth is on the other side of the continent. Maybe Arlin could take us," she added.

"Arlin, the slightly sadistic one who just helped destroy a band of their ships," Aiden recalled with a sarcastic tone.

She smirked at him. "No harm in asking where he's going next. Maybe he could get us closer at least. And you know you like him."

He shook his head, chuckling, but agreed to ask. They picked up Raith and Spark from the stable at the inn and led them to the port where they found Arlin's crew once again readying the ship. Securing the horses to one of the many tie points of the harbor, they walked aboard.

"Well, look who it is," Arlin called, walking down from the head of the ship. Sweat gleamed on his skin as he grinned. After slapping them on the backs, he asked, "Well, I assume there's a reason you're here, besides seeing my lovely face."

Ava gave a slightly sardonic smile. "As much as we love your face, Arlin…"

Aiden cut in laughing. "We're here to ask where you might be going?"

The captain paused, studying them. "Why?" he asked, looking intrigued.

"Because if it's where we need to go, then we would just love to keep you company," Ava said.

"OK, I'll bite. We intend to work our way along the top bit of the continent for a few weeks over to the Gulf of Avalon, then cut our way north to The Republic of Gileda."

"Well, that works out then," Ava replied. "If you'll have us, we'll join you, at least to the Gulf of Avalon."

Arlin gave a cheerful smile. "I could think of no better company. Who else would I call to sink ships with and humble my crew." They all laughed, walking to the helm.

"We'll set out in three hours," Arlin told them. "You can bring your horses downstairs."

After loading his own horse on the ship, Aiden laughed as Ava cursed at Raith who had refused to get on the boat at all without an apple as compensation. They helped the crew get the last bit of cargo loaded and set sail. The first day they spent mostly on the deck, the sun was warm and the sea breeze smelled of fine salt. Ava rested her head on Aiden's side, enjoying the sun, while Aiden read his book.

One of the larger men on board walked over. "You two," he said in a way of greeting. "What do you say to a two V two sparring match?"

Aiden laid his book on his chest, squinting at the man lazily through the sun.

"Careful there, Zach!" Arlin called from the helm right above. The man, who Aiden now recognized as the first mate and the one Ava had pantsed, just smirked upwards and returned his gaze to them.

Aiden looked down at Ava who squinted up at him. "I'm in if you are?" he said to her.

"Might be fun." She yawned, stretching her arms and standing. Zach looked slightly affronted at the laziness with which they made their decision. "You and two others," Ava yawned.

"You don't think we stand a chance on even footing?" Zach asked.

"No," Ava replied. "I know you don't," she purred.

Zach laughed, "Have it your way, cocky bastards."

Ava stuck out her tongue at him. They walked to the middle of the deck. Zach and two other men took their shirts off, flexing their muscles. Aiden smirked and removed his own, revealing a lean but distinctly muscled body.

"Look at all of you so manly," Ava crooned at all of them. She took off the large, white shirt of Aidens, and now stood in her high cut, skin-tight leather top.

One of the three men whistled. Her eyes snapped to him. "I'm taken, but I'd be happy to pummel you first." The man cracked his neck.

"Well then," Aiden asked, "Shall we begin?"

Before the men had time to finish nodding, Ava ran for them, dropping to her hip and sliding under the attack of the one who had whistled. Aiden tackled Zach who was distracted looking at what Ava was doing.

Ava sprang up inches from the man's exposed back. "Gotcha," she whispered in his ear as she drove her knee up in between his legs. The watching crew groaned and flinched as one.

Aiden, having knocked the wind from Zach, sprung up and stuck his outstretched leg in front of the third man. This sent the man flailing through the air before he could attack Ava. She spun around and seeing the falling man just slapped him across the face with an open hand. He hit the ground with a thud. Ava lightly hopped over the man to Aiden, walking behind him as he dipped slightly and she hopped on his shoulders and sat tall. Ava couldn't help giggling as the stunned crew looked at them.

"Anyone else wanna go?" she laughed to the ship-at-large as a warm joyful smile spread across her face. Still groaning in pain, the three men began to rise.

Zach raised his hands above his head and clapped for them. "You win," he said, shaking his head in amused disbelief.

Ava hopped down from Aiden's shoulders. "You boys don't kill each other for a moment," she quipped, stalking to the base of the helm and calling up to Arlin. "Oy, Arlin, you got any wine? Preferably red."

The captain's laugh was audible. "Just a quick brawl before your fine drink," he joked down at them.

"You know me," she replied.

"There're a few bottles of red in the bottom cabinet of your cabin"

She gave a mock bow and opened the door of the cabin to retrieve the wine.

"Damn, she wasn't joking," Zach breathed, still a little out of breath from being tackled. "You two really can fight."

Aiden smiled and nodded. "I was trained by a knight as a boy and you'll have to ask Ava if you get to know her story.

Zach chuckled and asked, "So how'd you two meet?"

"Ava was being forced to work with some less-than-kind people. I was tailing her when she realized I was there, and she almost split me in half," Aiden explained as Ava came back on deck. She walked over to Aiden who was now sitting with the group leaning against the mast. She sat leaning her own back into his chest with her legs crossed before her on the deck.

"We were just talking about you," Aiden offered.

"Oh yeah?" she responded. "What about?" she asked, leaning forward and grabbing the knife from Aiden's boot.

"About how when we met you tried to kill me," he chuckled.

"Bullshit," she laughed, using the knife to pry the cork from the bottle.

"Don't you break that knife. I stole it," Aiden warned. "The owner almost killed me. It's my knife now," Ava contested. I just let you carry it for me so I can open wine bottles," she said more jokingly as the cork popped free and she took a swig from the bottle. The men around them laughed.

"Whatever, but what would you call the sword I had to block inches from cutting through my ribs?" Aiden jibed.

She smiled innocently at the men, laughing, and replied, "A small misunderstanding."

Aiden just scoffed, but Zach asked, "Who could have almost killed you?" He finished looking at Ava who handed the bottle to Aiden.

"One of the three mercenaries who burned the harbor. She was struck with a poisoned dagger," Aiden answered. Ava ran a finger across the exposed scar on her stomach.

"Gods damn, what ended up happening to them... the mercenaries I mean?" another of the men asked.

"I killed them," Aiden replied bluntly. Everyone was silent for a moment as Aiden swigged from the bottle and handed it off to the man next to him.

"How?" Zach asked, everyone's attention now on Aiden and Ava.

"Those bastards slaughtered half the men who tried to stop them when they attacked Gloran," Ava explained. Aiden shifted slightly, swinging an arm behind his head. Ava continued, "We kidnaped one of the men. We interrogated him until we had everything we needed, then…" Ava trailed off looking over her shoulder to Aiden,

"Then he said something he shouldn't have, and I killed him," Aiden finished. A few of the men shifted, a little uncomfortable at the words.

"And the other two?" Zach pressed.

"We tracked them down and killed them," Aiden replied.

"Well, remind us never to get on your bad sides," one of the men breathed, and they all laughed.

The next few days were spent doing more of the same, talking and drinking. Ava and Aiden sparred on the deck, the other men watching, but none dared to challenge a rematch. Aiden could tell Ava enjoyed this, traveling, doing things one step at a time, not having to follow strict rules. Doing it all with him, having someone to protect and be protected by. Every day they spent in the blaring sun of the sea, both getting more tan by the day. They made a few short stops at different small ports for resupply. They never got off the ship though, spending their days practicing or enjoying the peace and calm.

# CHAPTER 24

At the third stop on the sail west, Ava walked into their cabin, where she found Aiden sitting on the bed reading his book. "Let's go poke around the town tonight while we're docked here," Ava suggested.

Aiden looked up from the book. "OK," he set the book down on the nightstand. "Where would you like to go?"

They began walking down the hall, making for the deck. Aiden called out, "Hey Arlin, Ava and I are going to head into the town for a little bit." Arlin nodded in response, smiling and going back to talking with his first mate.

The dock was small and a little run down, with worn , nearly black planks, and bustling with everyone from merchants to children running around. The town was the same. It had been just a small seaside village until passing ships realized it was a convenient spot to stop and resupply.

"Where should we go?" Aiden asked.

Ava yawned, stretching her arms behind her head as she replied, "Let's go to the market." She looked down a side alley and studied the mass of fine stalls and vendors and crowds of people going about their lives.

"OK, but I'll be back in a second," he said.

She waved a hand in acknowledgment, now looking at a buffet of foreign seafood. Darting into the crowd, Aiden wove his way back to a flower stand they had passed on the way to the heart of the market.

"Anything I can help you with, young sir?" the short, kind-faced old man at the stand asked, looking Aiden up and down.

"I was hoping to get some flowers for someone," he said, feeling a little uncomfortable at the understanding look the man gave him.

"Do you know what type you want?" the shopkeeper asked.

"I was hoping you could help me with that actually," Aiden said.

The man smiled. "I have all sorts. These ones are from Drrenai," he said gesturing to a deep red bouquet. "Or these are native to Laputa, but my personal favorite are these." He spoke softly and gestured to a small bouquet with bright green stems and petals that began in different colors and trailed off into white, seeming to sparkle with crystal dew even in the warm dry breeze of the market. "I don't know where they hail from, but the florist who sold them to me came from the far east. He claimed that the flowers are drawn to magic."

Aiden looked down at the flowers now seeming to pulse under his gaze. "I'll take them," he said looking at the man.

The shopkeeper nodded. "Does ten silver pieces sound OK? Since they're so hard to come by?"

Aiden scoffed, and the man seemed to cower, starting to mutter an apology. He halted as Aiden pulled two gold pieces from his coin bag. "For your magic flowers," he said, holding out the coins.

The old man grabbed the coins, the warm smile once again covering his face. He turned, collecting the flowers and began wrapping the stems in brown paper. He turned back and handed them to Aiden, "For a very lucky lady." Aiden smiled and began walking back toward Ava, the flowers hidden behind his back.

"Aiden, over here," Ava called, spotting him in the alley. Her eyes narrowed slightly as he walked closer and she saw his arms tucked behind him. "What…?"

He quickly pulled the bouquet out from behind him and handed it to her.

She let out a laugh. "You... I love them!" she exclaimed, taking the flowers from him and grabbing his hand. She lifted his hand above her head and spun under his arm.

"The shopkeeper said they find magic," he told her in a skeptical voice.

"Oh, did he?" she breathed, turning and closing the space between them. "They might be better for you then," she whispered, brushing him a kiss. Then, bringing the flowers up to their faces, Ava breathed in their aroma. She shuddered, as her eyes rolled back and she went limp,

Aiden could feel the cold slither of fear wrapping around him as he grabbed her and lowered her to the ground. "Ava?!" He grabbed her shoulders and shook her. "Ava!" The fear tightened its grip as she continued to shudder, eyes still rolled back. Not knowing what else to do, he scooped her into his arms and began to run back to the ship. Screaming at people to get out of the way, he barreled down the crowded street to the docks. The cold slithering tightened around his throat with every step.

"Arlin!!" he cried out when he reached the ship.

The men on the ship looked up. Zach's eyes widened at the sight of Aiden running toward them, Ava in his arms. He turned and ran for the helm as Aiden pulled himself and Ava onto the boat.

Arlin came out flanked by Zach. "What happened?" he asked, brisk and calm.

"I don't know," Aiden replied, his voice cracking. "I got her some flowers and when she smelled them this happened."

Arlin looked her over, still hanging limp and shuddering in Aidens arms. "Bring her," Arlin directed and turned toward the helm. Aiden followed as they came into his office.

"I don't have much in terms of medical supplies," Arlin said over his shoulder, a hint of fear in his voice. He grabbed a brown bottle from a drawer and hurried over to where Aiden had laid Ava across the desk. "This won't get rid of whatever did this, but it'll give her body time to deal with it."

Aiden nodded, cold fear still gripping him as he slipped his hand under her head and leaned her up. Arlin tipped the bottle at her lips. A moment went by. Then she stopped shuddering and her eyes slowly began to close. Aiden's icy fear seemed to loosen the slightest bit as her breathing returned to normal. They all stood at her side for long minutes.

Only after her breathing had returned to normal did Aiden turn to Arlin. "Thank you, my friend. I owe you my life," he said, hugging the man

"I have no need of your life; only of a brother," Arlin replied, hugging back.

# Chapter 25

Ava awoke to a roaring, raging droning sound, like thousands of people screaming. She opened her eyes. She was lying on her back facing the raftered ceiling of their cabin. The noise became painful as she came into full consciousness. Looking around for the source, she found nothing, only Aiden sitting in a chair next to the bed, reading his book. The roaring continued to build and a small scream ripped from her lips. Aiden dropped his book to the floor, turning to her. The sound of the dropping book seemed to snap her back to normality.

"What is it?!" he asked, sharp and loud, as though on a different plane.

"The noise," she whimpered. Her own voice seemed to be in that different plane. A sense of panic started to overwhelm her.

"What noise?" he asked, fear now darkening his face.

Once again, Aiden's voice seemed to snap her back toward normality. The roaring dimmed, Aiden's voice coming into focus.

He continued, "What noise?"

"The roaring..." she cried out.

"There's no roaring," he responded.

But again, the notion of the other plane returned to her, not roaring, not even sound, just thoughts of fear and worry, and some hint of relief. There was still the noise in the background. She had thought it was a roaring sound, but focusing, she made out thoughts, not sound. Hundreds, thousands, of thoughts all coming from above deck.

"Think about something," she told Aiden.

"What? I don't understand."

But before the words left Aiden's mouth she could sense his confusion. "Think of something," she repeated.

"OK?" He frowned a little.

Ava could feel it, his confusion, then a thought. "You're thinking of a bow," she stated.

There was plain shock on his face. "How do you…"

"Know that," she finished for him.

He nodded and she could feel his shock.

"I think… I think I can feel your thoughts, and maybe, emotions," she explained, sounding a little unsure of the last part. Aiden's mouth sagged slightly, and she could feel his thought of Phil's cooking. "Missing Phil?" she asked, and Aiden let out a laugh looking at her wide eyed. "Grab the magic book," she said, sitting up and starting to feel excited.

Aiden scrambled to find the book, also feeling the sense of excitement. He grabbed her bag and rummaged through it. Pulling out the book, he walked back over, sat beside her, and opened the book. Ava snatched it from his hand and could feel his amused annoyance. She flipped through the book to the section on mind magic. Her eyes darted back and forth along the page as she read. Her face evasive. A minute later she looked up from the book.

"And?" he asked.

She looked toward him, face still numb. "It says that some people with mind magic can do all sorts of things."

"Like?" he pressed.

"Like feel and sometimes control others' minds." She paused, then continued, "It also says that the more one uses the power, the more it costs."

"Costs how?" he asked, his heart falling. She could feel his fear starting to return.

"It depends on how you use it," she explained. "If you're only reading and feeling, then it will cause exhaustion. Controlling is worse."

Looking at her, Aiden noticed her slumped posture and tired face. "How do you feel?" he asked.

"Exhausted," she answered. "But I was tired before we left the ship."

She saw the expression of shock cross his face, but only felt a murmur. He took a breath, "You've been asleep for two days."

"What?" Ava responded in confusion.

"You shouldn't be that tired," Aiden offered. "You had plenty of rest."

She sighed, slightly exasperated at the world.

"What does it say about being able to control whether or not you feel the thoughts?" Aiden wondered.

Ava read a bit more and replied, " It just says I have to filter out others' thoughts, from the normal world."

"Do you think you can do that?"

She paused, frowning slightly. She dipped her head and sat like that for a few minutes, occasionally glancing back at the book.

"There," she said, looking up. "Think of something."

Aiden thought of their mission and asked, "Anything?"

She looked to his face, smiling. "Nothing."

"Good, now lie down," he ordered. "I'm gonna get you some soup for dinner." She opened her mouth, starting to object, but he just waved a hand. "Get some rest, " he said. Tomorrow we can do stuff. We still have a week 'til Avalon."

She glared at him but nodded in agreement.

# Chapter 26

"You summoned me? My lord."

William tore his eyes away from the letter, looking to his knight. "Yes, please sit. We have much to talk about."

Kerstin did so, sitting in the chair across the desk. "How may I help?" he asked.

William let loose a long sigh, looking back down to the letter, then back to Kerstin. "This conversation is held in confidence," he said slowly.

"I will tell none," the loyal knight responded, bowing his head.

"Very well," William began. "Let's get to the point then. You know of the group of mercenaries that were killed near my home south of here?"

"Yes, my lord, what of them?"

"They were sent as part of a larger plan, I believe by the King of Orenth." It was quiet for a moment.

"How do you know this?" Kerstin asked.

"I was just sent a letter from a team of spies I recruited near my southern home." William paused. "They believe the King of Orenth is gathering a host somewhere in the Orienthian mountains."

Kerstin didn't know what to say and sat with his mouth slightly open. "What spies?"

"I doubt you know them," William answered. But seeing Kerstin's dismay he explained, "The young girl who was traveling with the group of mercenaries... she was rescued by a boy in the town by the name of Aiden. They have both sworn oaths to me." The King paused, letting this information settle with Kerstin. He continued, "After the ordeal in the village I sent them on a mission to find all they could about the King of Orenth's plans."

The knight's eyes narrowed slightly. "What's the boy's full name?"

William looked confused but replied, "Aiden Windren."

Kerstin's eyes widened, and he let out a laugh. "I trained him when I was stationed there for a few months, just a few years ago."

William smiled in understanding. "Aiden said he was taught by a knight. Now I'm not surprised at his skill, knowing his teacher," William acknowledged. "But back to the point," he said, some of the warmth that had covered his features hardening. "They have informed me that the King of Orenth is trying to assemble more forces and may have already raised an army. They also reported that it has not only been Anglen that has been attacked."

"Where else?" Kerstin asked, once again, shocked.

"Attica fell to Orenth, discreetly on Orenth's part. There have been naval blockades and other attacks by mercenaries throughout the continent." William looked back to the letter. "I would like you to secure defenses across Anglen and ensure that our standing army is in fit form to defend from further mercenaries."

Kerstin nodded. "Anything else?"

"Not for now. I don't want to give any impression that we want a conflict or are expecting one," William explained. "Given the current tensions, such a message could start a conflict on its own. Try to gather more soldiers, discreetly. "

Kerstin nodded, "I will."

William inclined his head. "Very well then, you're dismissed," he said, smiling, and nodded to the knight who stood and walked to the door. "And Kerstin…"

The knight looked back.

"Thank you."

The knight bowed and walked out.

William sat at his desk long after Kerstin left. He didn't know how to aid the two spies. He wished to speak with them face to face but, he couldn't pull them from their mission for that. He didn't know what they meant by a dark power; the letter had been so vague on the subject. But it had sounded almost fearful. He stood and began pacing.

"A dark power?" he asked himself aloud, raising a hand and rubbing the back of his neck. A thought hit him as he left his office. He strode down the fine stone halls of his castle in Clystera. Coming to the doors of the library, he halted, opening them slightly into the truly grand room. Three levels tall and the size of three ballrooms, it was the greatest library of the known world. So, unsurprisingly even at the late hour, there were people, mostly scholars, reading at various tables. Years ago when William had taken his crown, he had decided that knowledge such as this has a right to be shared. He had ordered the library be made open to anyone who was willing to make an appointment, free of charge. Scholars and country folk were welcome to come into the castle and use the library.

William walked down the center of the main path coming to the desk, where he found Errina the High Librarian sitting.

She looked up and smiled, "What might I help you with my King?"

"I was wondering if you could show me to the books we have on the history of the Kingdom and continent?" he replied.

"I most certainly can," the woman said, not the slightest bit affronted at the strange request.

William followed her to the back portion of the library and down a set of stairs to the sub level reserved for restricted books. Whether deemed dangerous or just delicate, they had been placed down here. Three minutes later they stood in front of a small section surrounding a desk.

"Would you like my help finding something in particular?" The librarian asked.

William hesitated. "Yes, I think so. I remember reading an old legend about magic on the continent when I was a boy. I was hoping to read it again," he explained. "It was about a boy and a solider who fought, one had light powers the other dark powers."

Errina tapped her lip in concentration, looking around the space. Her eyes locked on a book she opened it skimming through the table of context. "No," she murmured placing it back on the shelf. She continued for a few minutes until she seemed to find something. "Ah!" she exhaled and pointed to the table of contents in a dusty, old volume and flipped to the page. "It's a short story, but I think this is the one you were thinking of." She handed the book to William who thanked her. Erinna nodded and walked away, her gate calm and professional.

William sat at the desk and began to read:

When the continent was still young, before the time of Kings and Kingdoms, there were many regions, peoples and leaders of those peoples. Each leader had their own powers, the gifts of the gods. The people prospered, conflict was rare, and food was plentiful. But, the dark god tired of the peace. He blessed a champion of his own, one of dark malice corrupting the bearers heart. The champion laid waste to the world, killing indiscriminately. When all was thought lost, a bright light appeared from a dying star. It came from the heart of a benevolent god and was given to a child whose soul was of light. When the child finally faced the dark god's champion, they fought through magic. The child released the power of the star, the dark champion harnessed the power of cold and forgotten places, and the world was made anew.

William didn't know what to make of it. Figuring it was as fittingly vague as the letter, he bookmarked the page and took the book, bidding Errina goodnight as he left the library down the red carpeted path.

# CHAPTER 27

"Well, I'll be sad to see you go," Arlin said as he and his crew faced them, their horses loaded and ready to go.

"Especially you, fine lady," he said, giving a mock bow to Ava, who smiled.

"As will I," she responded." Who else will beat your men when they get out of hand?"

Arlin and a few of the men laughed. Arlin stepped forward, looking at Ava and then Aiden. His face was a little more serious, and sad. "Good luck with whatever you're doing, stay safe, and I hope we meet again." He embraced Aiden, then Ava, and turned back to his men. "Well what the hell do you think you're all doing standing there?" he yelled waving his arms. "We have a narrow sea to cross."

Aiden and Ava turned away and mounted Raith and Spark. They began at a trot through the city backing the port. In spite of himself, Aiden couldn't help the twinge of homesickness that spread through him at the thought of all they had to do and just how far they were from home.

"What's wrong?" Ava asked gently.

Aiden realized he'd spaced out and shook his head. "It's just... I've never been this far from home. And..." he trailed off.

"We'll be back soon," Ava said comfortingly. "We can't send William letters from here. We'll have to go back to Anglen to tell him what we find."

Aiden nodded, giving her a closed lip smile.

Ava asked in a lighter tone, "So, where do you think we should go for tonight?"

Aiden contemplated for a moment. "Well, we want to go to the Tarian Mountains, so let's try to get part way to Vitre for tonight. We'll camp somewhere along the road."

"Let's hope you don't wake to a knife at your throat this time," Ava quipped. Aiden frowned and she laughed. "What? Still upset that they caught you snoozing?"

"No! I'm not," he said, even as a smile tugged at the corners of his mouth. "But let's try not to shoot any arrows at our friends in the future."

Ava stuck out her tongue. "They weren't friends at the time," she shot back.

As they rode through Avalon, Aiden noticed that the town was as lively as Gloran had been. They traveled on back roads, not alleys, but the sort of roads only a local would bother to go on. The roadsides were crowded with vendors of normal things from modest clothing to clay cups. Twice, Ava insisted they stop and try some weird food she didn't recognize, the second of which turned out to be pickled and spiced fish eyes. It made both of them cough and gag.

"I blame you for this," Aiden rasped, still coughing.

"OK, I'll take that one," she coughed back.

As much as they tried to get through the city quickly, it was nearing dusk by the time they reached the outskirts.

"Well, I think we'd better just get a little outside the town before dark," Ava said, looking annoyed at how little ground they'd covered.

Aiden agreed, and they headed out along the main road. The farther they rode from the town, the less worn the path became. It was nothing more than two wagon wheel paths by the time they ducked off into the mossy woods. They continued deeper into the trees, finding a small opening in the forest already supplied with a campfire ring and stumps to sit on.

"Well, this is my kind of camp spot," Ava said, hopping down from Raith and looking around. "I assume you want to stay here?" she asked Aiden

"As long as no one tries to kill me in my sleep."

"Then let's stay here," she said, unfastening her bed roll from Raith and rolling it out across the cushy moss next to the fire ring.

"I'm gonna go get some wood for a fire," Aiden said, walking deeper into the woods. The forest was green and vibrant, with loosely spaced but large trees, their canopy so vast it blocked the sky entirely. But, as darkness fell, the forest still seemed to have a light to it, a light and something old that Aiden couldn't quite put his finger on.

Aiden came back into the camp with a bundle of dry sticks in hand. Ava had placed their bed rolls beside each other next to the fire ring. Aiden set the twigs in the ring and walked over to the nearest tree, he began pulling lichen from its bark.

"What do you want for dinner?" Ava asked, seeming to realize that they hadn't restocked the food in their packs since Gloran. "We don't have any food."

Aiden stiffened. "Shit, we don't, do we!" He paused trying to think if they had anything

"Shit!" Ava laughed. "It'll be fine. I can go hunt something or I'm sure there's something else edible in this forest." She walked over to Raith, grabbing her bow and quiver. "I'll go look for something. You get the fire started."

"Ok, stay safe," Aiden called to her.

She waved a hand, giggling, and walked into the deep woods on silent feet. Ava assumed there must be something in such a forest, it seemed almost sentient. Even in the darkness overhead there was faint light seeming to come from every plant, from the very bark of the trees. She darted around and between trees, not needing to tiptoe on the soft, silent moss.

Then she saw a stag standing framed between two mighty trees. It ate from a patch of mushrooms at the base of one of the trees. She notched an arrow, drawing it, and aimed for the heart of the beast not twenty feet away.

The animal looked up, turning its head to the side and peering at her. She breathed, looking into the animals eyes. Black as they were, they emanated a warmth that ripped the breath from Ava's chest. She lowered her bow and the deer just looked at her, not a glimmer of fear in its face. It looked down to the mushrooms it had been eating, then back to her, seemingly trying to tell her something. It did so again, first to the mushrooms then her.

Ava didn't know what to do, she took a step towards it, and the deer did it again. She stopped. "Do you want me to take the mushrooms?" she asked inside her head. The animal stood looking at her for a long moment then walked away calmly, seeming to disappear into the trees faster than natural.

Ava walked over to where the deer had stood and crouched looking at the mushrooms. Brown white spots, she picked one turning it over and looked at the lamella. They had a faint red tinge to them. She peeled one open finding white meat that slowly turned a faint shade of pink. She knew she shouldn't trust the deer, that this mushroom was likely poisonous, but the way the deer had looked at her and the way the forest felt around her, gave her comfort.

"Find anything?" A voice said from behind her. She sprang up and wheeled around to find Aiden walking toward her.

"Is everything OK?" he asked at the sight of her face.

"I just…" she trailed off.

"What is it?" he asked, reaching her and grasping her hand.

"I think I may have just gotten a sign," she whispered.

He paused, looking at her face. She looked away, not meeting his eyes. He set his thumb and forefinger against his chin and pointed her face to his.

"What's wrong?" he asked in barely more than a whisper.

She at last met his eyes. They were soft and caring. She whispered back, "There was a stag but not a normal one. It... it wasn't scared of me and... it seemed to want me to eat these mushrooms." She breathed out, not knowing how he would react.

He paused, looking into her face, his expression still soft. "Do you trust the stag?" There was no cynicism, only a simple question, as if he were asking if he thought it was going to rain.

She paused, biting her lip and thinking about the way the deer had felt, the way this forest felt. "I do," she said, the words soft and deliberate.

Aiden smiled. "Through thick and thin and whatever else." He bent down, grabbed a mushroom from the ground, took one last look at her eyes before tipping his head back, and tossed a whole mushroom in his mouth.

"Aiden!!" she shouted, alarmed. "You can't!"

But he just smiled. "I trust you and your stag." He said it simply, like it was the easiest thing in the world.

Hearing all he said and feeling all he meant, she smiled and repeated, "Thick and thin and whatever else." Then she tipped her head back and tossed the mushroom into her mouth.

Aiden and Ava walked back to the camp where there was now a small fire smoldering, casting a warm flickering light across the camp. They lay down on their bed rolls, Ava propping her head against Aidens chest.

"I have something for you," he breathed into her ear.

She rolled over onto her stomach and rested her chin on his chest as she looked at him. "What?" she purred, starting to feel a sense of euphoria. His face became more colorful and surrounded by a white light.

Aiden reached for his bag, sat down, and opened the top. He pulled the Bow of Starin from his bag as his vision also became starlit.

Ava's eyes began to water as he held the bow out to her. She grasped it. "How... when?" she gasped.

"I bought it from a shop in Gloran the night we went to that restaurant," he explained sheepishly.

She ran a hand down the bow, feeling every scratch inlay and every ornamental leather wrapping. Tears streamed down her face as she caught sight of the words carved in the shaft. The silver letters popped with the light of the flame, seeming to bend and change shape as she looked at them.

"Thank you," she said, her voice breaking. Ava looked to his face again and set the bow beside the bed roll. "I love you," she blurted out, climbing atop him, the world spinning and colors popping in her vision. "Do you love me?"

"With everything I have," Aiden said back.

Ava dipped down, kissing him slowly. He leaned up as she pulled away and kissed her back just as slowly, his hand on her hips. Aiden decided in that moment that whatever else may happen along the road, he would be hers... and if she would have him, she would be his, thick and thin and whatever else.

# CHAPTER 28

Ava could feel the sun warming her face, light shining through her eyelids, as she lay curled against Aiden, who still had his arms wrapped around her from last night and was breathing slow and deep into her hair. She shifted, shimming herself further into his warmth.

He opened his mouth and murmured, "How you doing?" And he nuzzled her neck with his nose.

"Great after…" she began.

She turned toward him, her tropical eyes warm, but as her gaze neared his face, they snagged on something. Her eyes hardened on something over his shoulder. In blur of movement and a flash of steel, Ava was on her feet, Starlight gripped in both hands, her legs spread in a battle stance. In a wicked feline snarl she spat, "Who are you?" She said each word deliberately, her voice descending into more of a growl with each word. m

Mastering himself from the shock of what had just happened, Aiden rolled over and grabbed Starin along with an arrow. He darted to his feet, standing beside Ava and finally seeing to whom she'd been talking to. Aiden nearly fell on his ass at what he saw.

On one of the stumps surrounding the still smoldering fire sat a girl. Or not a girl. She was shaped like a young female figure, but here eyes were bright, vibrant green as if the were the crown jewel of the mossy forest surrounding them. She was clothed sparingly in leaves and moss. Her eyes were fixed on her outstretched finger watching a small red worm inch along.

Aiden bow was still drawn and aimed between her eyes. "Answer her," he snarled.

The girl finally glanced up from the worm, seemingly to have forgotten they were there by the look of slight shock on her face. Then, a warm, somewhat mischievous smile replaced her surprised expression. She seemed not at all worried about the arrow fixed on her face and the tip of the sword pointed at her.

"That's no way to treat the one who led you to your dinner last night, now is it?" The girl's voice sounded young and not entirely human, but it was the casualness with which she spoke that told Aiden to stand down. She spoke without fear of them... spoke like no threat in these woods could do her harm. Ava seemed to have felt the same because she too lowered her sword, placing it back in its scabbard and dropping it to the ground.

"Who are you... please?" Aiden asked, adding the last word as an afterthought.

The girl smiled. "My name, is Alva," she said simply.

"And why are you in our camp, may I ask?" Ava pressed.

Avla's head snapped up. She looked not angry but a bit annoyed if not offended. "Your camp? You're in my home." They all paused.

"Your home?" Aiden asked. "You live here?"

"Yes," she answered a little sharply. "Me and all others of Sylvanwood."

Aiden straightened. "Did you say we're in Sylvanwood? But that's at least thirty miles from where we set camp, at least according to the map I have." He looked around at their bags as though the map might already be spread before them ready to read.

Avla smiled at him, then looked back at the worm. "I'll talk to you later Henry," she whispered to it. The worm bent its head up to her and she set it down on the mossy ground were it burrowed back down into the soil. "The wood has a way of bringing people to it," she said as her gaze returned to them.

"And, why would it have brought us here?" Ava asked, her voice finally returned to normal.

"Many reasons, perhaps to meet me, maybe to find each other…"

Ava's chest tightened and she cut the girl off. "Were you watching us last night?"

The girl let out a bemused laugh. "No," she said now smirking at Ava. "But the forest, the forest was."

Aiden's gut twinged in discomfort as he looked around the camp.

But Ava continued. "And who are you to the forest, may I ask?"

Avla raised her arms gesturing around. "To this forest, to this forest, I'm the queen, the guardian, a friend. I am the patron of the forest and creatures in it."

Aiden had no idea what to say in response and so he just stood there, Ava at his side.

"Well, I assume you would like to know why the forest has brought you here?" the queen asked, brows raised in an amused expression.

"Yes, we made that clear," Ava said, starting to get annoyed.

"We brought you here because I want to ask you what you intend to do about the Dark King," Alva explained.

"What Dark King?" Aiden asked, gut twinging in an entirely different way.

"The one assembling forces in the mountains east of here," Alva replied. "My friends told me you've been looking for information on them."

Ava stepped forward "How do you know that?"

"Oh, don't worry," the queen teased. "I'm not telling anyone your secrets. I just want to know what you intend to do about him."

"And why is that any of your business?" asked Ava.

"Well, depending on what your plans are, I might be agreeable to help."

It was Aiden who said, "We were sent by the King of Anglen to find all we can about the King of Orenth."

"Oh, William sent you," she said, raising her arms and standing. "Then you are friends of mine."

"How do you know William?" Aiden asked.

"I'll admit I haven't seen him in years.." she began.

"Years?" Ava questioned. "How old are you? You don't look any older than us."

Alva smiled more mischievously and answered, "I'm as old as the forest. Not aging is just a perk."

"Well, then, will you help us?" Aiden asked.

Avla stared at him, shocked that he was ready to partner with a seemingly magical being they knew so little about.

"Like go with you? No, but I'll tell you what I can do to help." She walked over to stand in front of them and studied them a moment, preparing to explain further.

It occurred to Ava that she could try to read the mysterious creature's thoughts. She closed her eyes and focusing, she tried to get to the thought plane. She could feel Aiden's slight disappointment. Directing her attention to the girl, she sensed nothing but a monumental wall of greenish white light.

"Nice try," Alva crooned. "But I learned how to block magical invasion long before you or your land came to be. I'm not lying. I too want the Dark King to fall, and I will help you." She gestured for them to sit, just as new stumps sprouted from the ground beside them, the old stumps melting back into the forest floor. Aiden and Ava sat.

"The one you seek is with his forces in the Tarin Mountains, west of here. I expect you will go there now, and I bid you pass through Sylvanwood." She paused, picking at her moss green nails, and then continued, "I shall also bestow you one great gift."

Aiden tensed further in anticipation. Alva's eyes flicked to a nearby tree. Following her gaze, Aiden found a large hollowed out knot. Alva stood and walked to the tree, reaching inside and pulling out a small pink flower bud. She waved a hand and vines wrapped around it, holding it fast. The vines continued wrapping themselves into a necklace with no fastening.

Alva smiled at it. "It's quite pretty isn't it?" Aiden and Ava remained silent. Holding the necklace out, she walked to Ava. "Stand," she said softly. Ava stood facing the queen who laid the necklace around Ava's neck. "When the time comes you'll know what to do."

"Wha…" Ava began, but Alva set a finger against Ava's lips and she fell silent. With another wave of the girl's hand the vines encircled Ava's neck, not tight but well fit.

Alva turned slowly, favoring the woods again. "Goodbye, oh brave ones. I do hope we meet again." She laughed softly as she walked in between the trees, stepping behind one and not appearing on the other side.

# CHAPTER 29

Aiden and Ava spent the rest of the day walking west through Sylvanwood. No matter where they went in the forest there always seemed to be a wide path beckoning them on through the trees, their way seeming to glow with color and life. With the guidance of the forest they were out of the woods by late afternoon, emerging onto a grass covered hill. They mounted Raith and Spark and began to descend toward the plains. They spent the next three days traveling north along a wagon road. It had begun fine and wide but the farther they traveled north, the drearier it seemed to grow. At the edge of Sylvanwood, it had been nearly crowded with families and merchants all heading for villages east, west and south but the nearer they came to the Tarin Mountains, the colder the air felt and the darker the sun dimmed.

"I don't like this place," Ava said on their second day after Sylvanwood. "It's cold and the light isn't shining."

"I know, but we'll be there soon," comforted Aiden.

"Yeah, but what's our plan when we do get there?" Ava replied with some exasperation.

"You know, that's a great question," Aiden said looking at her with a goofy smile that made her laugh. She sky seemed to lighten slightly, before… plop… plop, plop, plop and it started to pour.

Ava looked up at the gray sky and her face fell. "What the hell did I do, world?" she grumbled, distasteful eyes watching the gray mass wiring above them. Aiden started laughing. Ava only flipped him off.

"Want to find a spot to wait it out?" he asked.

"Yes, Aiden," she said, seeming to blame him for the rain. "No shit, I would like to find a spot to wait it out."

Ava steered Raith toward a lone oak tree. Aiden and Spark followed, and they tied the horses to the tree. Ava sat on a rock beside one of the larger roots.

Sitting beside her Aiden wrapped his cloak around the both of them. "What's wrong?" he asked.

She sighed and set her head on his shoulder. "I just want... I wish we could be at our apartment back home. I want to talk to Phil and go to the market."

Aiden wrapped his arm around her. "I know. We just have to find out what's happening in these mountains, and tell William in Clystera. Then we go home for a while. OK?"

"Yeah." She turned her head to his and brushed him a kiss. Ava pointed. "Hey, the rain stopped." She stood and walked to the horses and untied their reins. "For you my good sir," she said handing him Spark's lead.

"Why, thank you, dear lady. And look, the gods even saw fit to give us a little sun." Sure enough there were thin rays of sun breaking through the dreary clouds.

"Let's walk the horses for a bit. They've been carrying us for a while," Ava said, reaching into her bag and pulling out an apple. Placing her palms at the top and her fingers at the bottom of the fruit she rested the apple against her thigh and with a rocking motion pulled her palms apart along with either side of the apple breaking it in half.

"Here you are," she said, handing a half to Aiden. "And for you," she added, giving the other piece to Raith. Aiden fed his to Spark.

The rest of the day was spent in conversation as they approached the mountains.

"Gods damn!" Ava spat as they came atop a hill, for the first time catching a full view of the Tarin Mountains. They were tall, sharp, bald, and wreathed in fast moving fog, making it impossible to peer into the range.

"Gods Damn!" Aiden agreed, standing beside her on the hill. Ava gulped. "Well, so much for this feeling like a vacation," Aiden chuckled. "Well, let's get on with it."

An hour later they were at the mouth of a canyon, the large rolling green hills replaced with towering cliffs to either side. "Do you think it's safe to travel this road?" Aiden wondered.

Ava looked at him and rolled her eyes. "Obviously not."

"But you wanna take it anyway?" He flashed a grin. "Let's take it 'til we see something, deal?"

Ava nodded and they headed into the canyon.

"What a shit place this would be to get trained here," Ava said, sneering at the fog above them.

"Is that what you think the Dark King is doing here?" Aiden asked.

"I mean, Alva said compiling forces," Ava replied.

"Fair enough, so what do you think? We just try to get a feel for Orenth's numbers and strength and report back to William?" he suggested.

"I think so, but we should try to find out his plans if we can," she added.

"Agreed."

"People…" Ava said, pointing up the road.

Following her gaze, Aiden spotted them as well. Two men rode on horseback down the road. Aiden could hear them talking, but couldn't make out the words from the distance.

"Hide, you think?" Ava whispered beside him. He pointed to a gap in the narrow canyon side about thirty feet up. They made for it, leading Spark and Raith by the reins. They pulled into the small crack and lead the horses to the back, now hidden by the curve of the opening. Aiden came to the edge of the opening and poked his head around.

"I'm glad to be out of that place for a bit. The commanders are driving me mad," the first man said bashfully.

"Careful, if they hear you saying stuff like that you might get something even worse," the second man replied in a nervous grumble

The first man scoffed loudly. "Who's gonna hear us out here? We are at least twenty miles from the fort, and the country folk won't come within thirty miles of the mountains."

"Whatever, just don't get me in trouble." The two men passed the opening of the alcove.

"You think we'll have time to stop at a tavern on the way?" the second man asked.

"I'm certainly gonna make some time."

"Did you bring money for ale?"

"No, I'm a member of the King's army. I don't need money for ale. They'll just give it to me."

"And if they don't…"

But the men were too far away for Aiden to make out the man's answer.

Ava walked up beside him. "Sounds like we have twenty miles before we get to have any fun."

Aiden turned to the horses. "Who feels like a run?"

Raith huffed in agreement pushing her head into Ava as Spark stomped the ground. They left the alcove, mounted the horses and began to ride.

"So, they said fortress," Ava said loudly over the noise of the wind and clip clop of hooves.

"Yeah, I think we leave the horses a mile or so out," Aiden added. "Somewhere safe while we find a way in."

"It should be night by then. You think we'll be able to sneak in?"

"I certainly hope so. Either way, we should be able to get a sense of their numbers."

Ava gave a firm nod.

They rode for a little longer and then dismounted. Aiden turned to the horses, "You have to stay here for a bit. We have to go do something, but we'll be back for you as soon as we're done." Aiden stroked Spark's head and scratched him above the nose.

"Same to you, Raith," Ava said, again splitting an apple, this time into quarters, and gave one piece to each horse and the last to Aiden.

Scrambling up the hillside, they did their best not to drop rocks down as they made for the top of the small, loose peak. They could hear the dull noise of the camp not far off. Looking back, they could see the road curve around, leading further through the canyon toward the far side of the small peak.

Poking her head out from around one of the larger boulders on the hillside, Ava spotted two short towers suspended between the greater peaks to either side. "There are guard towers at the top of this hill,' she reported.

Aiden came over, resting a hand on her shoulder as he looked with her. "Wait till dark?" he whispered.

"Sounds good," she whispered back. Ava walked back behind the rock. She found a spot where, sitting at least, they would be fully out of view of the path below if any unsuspecting soldier were to pass by. She sat down leaning against the rock. Aiden sat next to her.

"When we get back to Anglen, do you think William would be OK with us asking for some time off?" she asked.

"I think so. We should definitely ask though. I would like to sleep in our bed again," Aiden admitted.

"I know, and Phil's cooking... we'll be able to have Phil's cooking and your friends."

"Yeah, you'll get to know my friends," Aiden said, leaning his own head back against the rock.

"And didn't Ganic say we get some kind of free happy hour or something?" Ava asked.

"Drunk," Aiden muttered.

"Well, fuck you, and don't you dare act like you enjoy booze any less than I do."

Aiden cracked a smile, eyes closed. "I'm more of a sweet tooth kind of guy."

"You do know they make sweet drinks with alcohol?"

"Maybe for fancy princesses."

"Well, boyfriend of said fancy princess, when we get back, I'll be introducing you to the wonderful experience that is cocktails," Ava replied mockingly.

"You might find it hard to find a bar back home that sells *cocktails,*" he said, pronouncing the last word strangely.

"Wanna bet?" she asked.

Aiden opened one eye to look sideways at her. He raised the brow in question.

"If I can find a bar that sells cocktails, you have to do one thing I ask you," she demanded.

"I already do that," he said and closed his eyes again.

"Whatever." A moment passed before Ava spoke again. "Do you think you'll want to live back home forever?" she asked as casually as she could, though she couldn't entirely pass off the weight the words held.

"Do you?" Aiden asked just as casually.

"No," she answered, holding her breath for a long moment afterwards, waiting for an answer.

"Then we won't."

She leaned forward twisting slightly in her spot against the rock to look at him fully. He opened that one eye at the sound of her moving. "Just like that…?" she asked.

He opened the other eye."Yeah."

"You'd leave your home just because I want to?"

"Uh, I mean I might want to visit back sometime," Aiden considered. "I have friends there, but, yeah."

Ava had been thinking of this since they began this mission. It had been keeping her up some nights. And there he goes and answers it just like that.

"I… I…" Ava stammered.

"What is it?" he asked, propping himself up on his elbows, a crease forming between his brows.

"It's just… I wasn't… I've always wanted to see more of the world, more than I got the chance to as a princess and more than I thought I'd be able to after, and… I was worried that you wouldn't."

He gave her an easy smile. "It's my home yeah, but I don't have anything keeping me there now except the people. But I love you." He said it so easily, like it was just a fact of his life. "If you want to live somewhere else, then we'll live somewhere else, everywhere else if you like."

"I love you too." She'd said it when they were in Sylvanwood, but that had been in the midst of a mushroom induced haze. But not this time, her head was clear, there was nothing making her say it. Nothing making her stay with him. She could easily get up and leave forever, ride Raith off into the sunset and… But she halted that line of reasoning. It felt alien in her mind. None of those things are real possibilities. None of that is anything she wants. All she wants is…

Aiden was smiling vaguely.

"What?" she asked, and gave him an unsure smile in return.

"Nothing," he said.

"Your face isn't saying it's nothing," she protested.

"I just like looking at you."

Ava can't help the laugh that breaks from her lips.

"Where would you want to live?" Aiden asked after a beat.

Ava's laughing slowly came to a stop as she considered. "I want you to see Attica at some point. I know it's not much now, but I'd like to show you whatever's left of where I grew up."

"I'd love to," Aiden encouraged. "And where after that?"

"Everywhere," she said with a giggly smile.

Aiden laughed. "Everywhere it is."

They fell back into silence for a few minutes.

Aiden was the first to break it this time. "I'm glad I met you."

"I'd hope so considering you just said you love me," Ava replied with her eyebrow raised.

"Obviously because of that, but also... the world just feels like it's gotten so much bigger since I met you... in a good way," he added, not wanting his words to come off the wrong way. "Before I met you, it felt like the whole world was inside that town. Now... now it feels more like a point, like that place, everyone and everything I'd known is nothing more than one part of an adventure."

He paused and Ava asked, "Had you ever been outside of the town?"

He shook his head. "Other than the woods and fields just around the town... no. Gloran was the first time I'd seen the ocean, the first time I'd seen more than the fifty whatever buildings back home."

"I was with you the first time I ate a wild mushroom," she said.

Aiden smiled. "And did you enjoy your mushrooming?"

Ava blushed. "I wouldn't say I didn't enjoy it."

Aiden would take it a step further, he'd like to. Ava certainly looked like she wanted to. But this wasn't the time or the place. She seemed to see the thought process on his face or maybe she was just reading his thoughts. She nodded, still smiling, confirming that she was reading his thoughts.

"What are we going to try to do once it's dark?" Aiden asked. It was a hell of a way to kill the mood, but it wasn't like he was doing it because he wanted to. Ava knew that. She knew it exactly. She knew exactly what he'd rather be doing.

"Well, we travelled across a continent to get here, so I think we should try and get inside and find out whatever we can," Ava said, saying what they both knew they had to do.

Aiden sucked in a deep breath holding it for a few seconds before bellowing it out again slowly. "Yep." He turned his head to her slightly hesitating for the span of a breath before asking, "Are you...?"

"Yes," Ava said, slumping down slightly and leaning against him.

He'd been about to ask whether or not she was as nervous as he was to be spying on the military base of a foreign king that they knew basically nothing about, but it was a dumb question in the first place. No shit she was nervous. She closed her eyes and stopped moving. Within a minute her breathing had deepened into sleep.

"Ava," Aiden shook her gently. Darkness had fallen in earnest a few hours ago, but Aiden thought it would be better to give any guards a little while without light to get sleepier, and he hadn't wanted to wake Ava any sooner than he needed to.

"It's time to go?" she stirred, leaning up and looking at him. "Go time?"

"I think so," he answered and she nodded, standing and pulling her hood over her head. Aiden matched her and poked his head out around the rock. "The guards are still there."

"Then let's help them take a nap," Ava suggested.

He chuckled and they stepped out from behind the rock. Covered in their black cloaks, they were barely visible even to each other. Aiden headed toward one of the towers. It stood about three times his height above the ground. Walking to the far corner, Aiden began to climb the protruding bricks.

"I'll climb the other tower," Ava said and she disappeared into the darkness.

Aiden ascended the bricks, getting to the edge, and peering through the gap in the battlements. The lone guard was leaning against the battlements to the left of him. Not giving himself time to doubt, Aiden hauled himself over the edge. The guard's head snapped to him at the sudden movement, but not before Aiden buried his fist in the man's throat. The man fell to his knees, clutching at his neck. Aiden pulled the man's hand away and wrapped his own arm around his throat, squeezing 'til the man went still. Aiden dragged him to the corner where he wouldn't be visible to anyone looking toward the tower.

He looked to Ava's tower, catching sight of her standing there in the light of the torch, but she wasn't looking at him. She was still as death, facing... Aiden turned to look at the back side of the mountain and nearly fell to his knees. There was a fort, as the two men had said, with three main towers on the outer wall and what looked like a great hall. The structure of the fort was big but, it was nothing compared to the camp filling the valley. Thousands of tents stretched to the mountains, thousands of fires illuminated them, and the soldiers looked like ants from the height of the tower.

"Gods help us," Aiden sighed. There was no way of counting the exact numbers, but he knew there were more soldiers here than in the entirety of Anglen's Army.

"Hey," someone said softly behind him and before he could think, he drew Starlight. "It's me dumbass," Ava said at the end of his sword.

He dropped the blade to his side then put it back in its sheath, over his shoulder. "Sorry," he breathed. "I didn't see you come over."

She nodded also looking shocked and scared. "What do you think we do now?" she asked.

"I don't know... Do you think we should try to get into the fortress and get an idea of what they intend to do with all these men?"

"If you think so," Ava sighed.

"Fuck us!" he laughed hollowly.

"Let's go," she said. "Fast, light, hurt if you have to?"

"Agreed," Aiden replied.

Ava dropped down onto the base of the tower and they started along the wall making their way down to the main fortress.

"Guard," Ava whispered. She inched ahead and drew up her blade, sneaking up behind the man, and slammed the pommel into his head. He dropped to the ground, and they continued toward the next tower. Aiden climbed a ladder to the top and knocked out the guard with his own blade. There was a ring of keys on the man's belt. Aiden grabbed them and dropped back down to Ava. She started running down the walkway without another word. Right as Ava neared the next tower, a soldier stepped out.

Catching sight of Ava, he took a step for her. "You're dead..." He was cut off as Ava drew her dagger from her belt and threw it into the man's exposed throat. Ava knelt to grab the knife. Aiden ran past, climbing the ladder to the top where the guard was looking at Ava over the edge of the tower. Aiden knocked him out, watching a trickle of blood run down his temple. Aiden dropped back down to Ava.

"Too close," he breathed.

"Yeah," she muttered back, showing her first sign of nerves.

Aiden led the way out of the last tower and ran half bent over down the stairs to the ground level of the fort. Spotting a small wood door in the side of the main building, its top curved to match the stone work, he tried to open it, but the door only clanked against the bolt of the lock. He drew the ring of keys from his pocket and fit the dirty tarnished one most matching the lock into it. It slotted in and he turned the key. The lock gave a grinding sliding click as the bolt pulled back. Aiden pulled the door open and Ava followed him into the small hallway.

"There are voices ahead," Ava whispered behind him.

He stalked down the hall, looking through the gap in the boards of the door on his left. The room on the other side was large. A round table sat in the middle surrounded by a group of men, all talking and gesturing to the table. Aiden couldn't make out what was on the table. Focusing, he tried to hear what they were saying.

"The troops need more training," said a voice.

"No, they don't they need..." countered another that was cut off.

"But how will we get the troops east?" a third voice interrupted.

Aiden pulled back from the door to face Ava. "Did you hear that?"

She dipped her chin in agreement. "Let me look," she said and he stepped aside. Leaning up to the door, she looked through the gap.

A voice rung through the space. "Silence!" A man wearing a crown and fine black clothing with gold thread stepped into view.

"The Dark King is here," she whispered over her shoulder to Aiden.

The King continued. "I don't care to hear all your petty problems. When the time comes, you will be ready to move the men and take action. If all goes well, the siege of the east will go even smoother than Attica."

Aiden could see Ava go a little stiff at the mention of her home. The King sniffed then took a long breath opening his mouth wide. He closed it and licked his lips. Ava went even stiffer.

"He just noticed us," she whispered, feeling the King's thoughts as he looked at the door.

"But in the meantime, I believe we have some unannounced guests," he said in a croon that devolved into a snarl.

Ava turned to Aiden, "How?"

"It doesn't matter, run!"

He turned and made to do so, only to find a wall of dark, a depthless swirling black void, as the book had said, like the gaps between the stars. Aiden froze as the door behind them opened, and the men poured in, grabbing them and hauling them into the room. They were thrown on the ground at the King's feet. Aiden's face slammed on the stone floor and he could feel blood beginning to flow in his mouth.

The King sniffed again. "Well now, who might you be? Spies, assassins, just stupid kids?"

Aiden spat out the blood pooling in his mouth.

"We aren't telling you shit!" Ava yelled with every bit of wrath and hatred she could.

"Maybe not now." He flicked his fingers and... WHAM! Everything went dark to Aiden, the edges of the world pulling in to shut him off from consciousness.

# Chapter 30

The next impulse going to Aiden's brain was the shock of cold as... splash! The icy water hit Aiden like molten steel. He opened his eyes and thrashed, but his hands were bound to a thick wooden post with metal manacles riveted to either side of it. Aiden was kneeling, and it was with no small amount of fear that he realized he wasn't wearing a shirt.

"Well then, boy," one of the King's men sneered. He squatted down at eye level with Aiden. "Are you going to talk now?" he asked, scraping his thumb nail across Aiden's cheek.

Aiden cursed at the man, foul enough that the din of the men around them went silent, and the man's expression went rageful.

"Well then, boy, we'll have to do this my way. I'm only sad the King couldn't be here to see it. He had to go do important things, you see, and your death just doesn't qualify."

Aiden flipped him off through the manacles.

"Begin!" the man shouted. Out of the surrounding crowd of soldiers in the courtyard walked a tall man, broad shouldered and muscularly built. Aiden knew something was coming, but it still wrenched his gut to see the long iron tipped whip the man carried.

"Do your worst," the first man said.

The tall man walked around slowly, making sure Aiden could see as he dropped the tip to the ground and let the whip drag across the dirt. The man left Aiden's field of vision and Aiden brought his head back straight. He rested his brow against the post and took a deep breath, right before... CRACK!! With the sound of a cannon blast behind him, Aiden felt the raging, throbbing pain and the cold trickle of blood as it ran down his back.

The man walked back in front of Aiden, squatting again. "Feel like talking now?" he asked.

Aiden vision was too blurry with pain to make him out clearly, but he still spat in what he hoped was the man's face.

The man thrashed away, stood abruptly, and yelled, "Again, again, ten more!"

Aiden rested his brow on the post again and... CRACK! He couldn't help it as a shutter went through his body and his back arched away from the pain. He rested his brow again, and again... CRACK! He rested it again CRACK! and again... CRACK! CRACK! CRACK! At the ninth, Aiden couldn't stop it as his back arched. The whip had landed on a previous blow, cutting even deeper. He screamed, ripping his throat apart as he roared, and before he could rest his brow again... CRACK! The man walked back over. Aiden's vision was nothing but popping lights and flashing colors.

He heard the man say, "It'll stop if you'll just tell us what we want to know."

Aiden shook his head, his brow scraping against the metal bracing of the post.

"Again!" the man shouted and CRACK! "Get some water and salt!" he then commanded.

Aiden could see someone run ahead of him and hear the sound of something being poured into water and splash. They threw the salt water on his back. He arched again, everything burning and... CRACK! Again in the same spot and he felt the iron tip of the whip fracture bone in his back as it dug deeper.

Aiden caught a glimpse of someone walk to the first man, whisper something, and then run into the closest building. The crowd grew quiet again. Terror, not the fear of pain, but gut wrenching, soul melting terror ripped through him as he saw them drag Ava into the opening before him. His vision sharpened to perfect sight, all his own pain forgotten as they threw her to her knees before him. She was crying, tears streaming down her face. There was a line of dried blood on her throat coming from her hair and a bruise on her cheek.

"Aiden, Aiden, No!" she whimpered.

He shook his head trying to clear it. "It's OK. It'll be OK," he said, but he knew the words were hollow even as he said them. There was no one, and nothing to save them. Aiden thought his heart might have stopped. He wished it had as they hauled a stump with a curved notch between them. Aiden could feel something deep in himself twinge, something that he had both never felt before and that scared him, as something leaked out. The area around them seemed to grow a little brighter. Ava's eyes caught on him, wide and more shocked than fearful. He slumped in his chains, the post holding him up. His body had failed him, his mind had failed him, his will had failed him, and he had failed her.

A grizzled, giant of a man walked out from the crowd, and everything went silent. Tears began pouring down his eyes at the massive axe the man carried. He walked to Ava's side. Another, smaller man forced her head down as the giant raised the ax.

Aiden felt something break in him. The twinge in his soul cracked, a sliver of what lay beneath his skin exposed. Light erupted, and with the wrath of a dying star, that light engulfed the world.

# III

*Fate Is A Good*
*Friend To Have*

# CHAPTER 31

Ava stood from the round table. "We can continue this discussion later," she said a little sharply, scanning the faces of the men surrounding it carefully. A serious expression was still locked on her face, as it had been last week, and the week before, and before. Most of the men looked to her and nodded. Some were still looking at the maps and papers on the table. She nodded back to them and left the room.

She swung the walnut doors wide as she exited and left them that way. She walked at a clipped pace down the magnificent white stone passages, her hands held stiffly at her sides, ready to draw weapons at any surprise these days. The passage was dim in the fading light coming through the windows, the sun setting over the far reaching forests and plains, green with the recent rain. She turned, making down another hall. Passing a few rows of flamboyant armor, she turned right and began up a large spiraling staircase. Looking up the open center of the stairwell, she could see to the top of the western tower.

Five minutes later she was at the top level and opened yet another walnut door. She entered the great room of the living space at the top of the tower. She closed the door behind her, clicked the lock into place, and looked back to the room. At the end, there was a curved wall conforming to the side of the tower, a large window covered most of it. Through it she could see the entirety of the city stretching far into the distance down below. The river ran down along its edge with yet more fields and forests beyond it. But she didn't care. She walked across the room, flipping off her shoes as she went, along with her sword and cloak which she let clatter to the floor.

The great room was flanked by two doors, both of matching walnut. She bit her lip, and her chest went a little tight. She walked over to the door on the right, the one that would have the fairer view of green forests and white mountains in the distance. She sucked in a breath. Bowing her head, she took another breath and looked down at the handle. It was shining silver. Everything in this place was shining: the silver, the wood, the stones, even the masterfully made food seemed to shine. It only made her angry, made her want to scream and rage. Had she been here in another time, in another life, maybe another world, she would have loved it. The finery, the people, the city and all its life. But now, now, it just felt like a slap to her face.

She continued staring at the door handle for uncounted minutes. A tear dripped down her nose. It missed the door handle and landed on the stone floor. She turned the handle and looked up. Walking into the room, she looked around. There were two beds in the room. The one on the right was made neatly with the edges tucked in the walnut frame, certainly not how she had left it. Mary must have come in while she was in the meeting. She didn't care. She flicked her eyes to the one on the left, and it made her chest clench to the point of pain. She looked over it just long enough to see that nothing was wrong and ripped her eyes back away. The steps of her bare feet were muffled as she walked over to her bed and took off everything save her undergarments. She did it slowly, not even caring if she was cold. She couldn't be bothered to put on night clothes.

She climbed into the bed and lay on her back. The ceiling of the room sloped up towards the great room, following the curve of the roof just on the other side. She turned her head to the side and looked back to the other bed. Another tear left her eye and ran onto the bed sheet. Another followed it as she pulled the blanket free of where it had been tucked in. She climbed beneath it and curled up on her side. It was now truly dark outside and the window between the bed offered nothing but pale moonlight. She shut her eyes. Another tear dripped down her cheek, and another, but she could feel her body relaxing. As she lay there her mind kept going, thinking but wanting to forget. But, eventually, even it succumbed to sleep.

# CHAPTER 32

She was screaming, sobbing. She could barely see his face through the tears in her eyes, could barely see him. But she could see the red, so much red, splattered across him, and across the stones around him. She screamed again, her throat shredding.

""No! No! No!!"" She bellowed the word, bellowed it again and again. Something moved to her left, and Aiden lightened, the world lightened. She kept screaming at him. Someone said something, and the person to her left moved closer. Aiden was wrestling against the chains, red spraying as he fought, the person moved again, swinging something upwards, and the world went blank.

No, not blank. It wasn't a lack of something, it was something added to the scene, like... light. It was light, flooding all around her. It was engulfing the world, the people, the fortress. But the light didn't touch her; it flowed around her like water, like swirling fog, an ever fluid writhing mass of photons, blocking out all the horrors surrounding them, wiping the world blank and blank again. It kept going and going. She didn't know for how long but eventually it stopped. It disappeared, whisped away into the crevasses of the world, and slowly, so slowly, as though rebuilding itself in the wake of what had just happened, the world came back into focus.

She blinked, shaking her head trying to clear it. She lifted her head, memory coming back. Then she remembered what had happened before the light and jumped up, trying to find Aiden. There he was, slumped down with only the chains on the post holding him off the ground. She wrenched her head around looking for the men, the fortress, the entire army that had filled the valley. Though she couldn't see the valley from the slightly raised courtyard, she could see the fortress, or at least what had been the fortress. There had been a fortress, or she thought there had been. She shook her head again trying to clear it. Where the structures had been, only rubble and burning wood remained. The towers were reduced to piles of the same. But the people. She looked down scanning the courtyard again. The people, the soldiers, they were nothing but charred skeletons littering the ground. She looked down at her own hands; they were still bound but her legs weren't.

She stood staring at Aiden. She could see his chest rising and falling, but he didn't move otherwise. She stumbled the fifteen feet to him, fear tightening like a snake around her with every staggering step. She reached him, dropping to her knees. "Aaa..." she rasped, her throat not able to form the words. "Aa... Aiden?" She rested her hands on his shoulder and shook him gently. "Aiden?!"

He didn't react, just sat there slumped.

She looked up, there were sounds in the distance. "The army." She said the words aloud as though reminding herself and began scrambling around looking for the man, the one who had spoken. He had the keys. She spotted a charred skeleton. It lay not five feet from the whipping post. She scrambled over to it, digging through the ash and bones until she saw them. She grabbed the keys bound on a ring and fitted keys into her manacles until one slid in. It clicked and her shackles fell away. She got to her feet and ran over to Aiden.

The distant noise was growing louder as though the entire army was stirring from a great collective blow. She jammed the first key into his lock; it didn't fit. She jammed the second, then third, then fourth and... finally, click. He was let free as she wrapped her arms around him and pulled him up. The noise was growing and the fear slithered further wrapping around her throat. With a growling grunt, Ava hauled him over her shoulder. The weight of him felt crushing as she made for the hillside from which they'd entered the fortress. She staggered forward, grunting on every step. She was at the edge of the courtyard when a glint of silver and white caught her eyes. One of the soldiers must have discarded their weapons at the edge of the wall. She dipped slightly, Aiden still slung over her other shoulder, as she snatched the weapons. They were tied up in a piece of leather, now on the brink of snapping at the most charred point.

It was slow going. Ava lost track of time as she pulled him up boulder after boulder, step after step. Only once she'd reached the top of the ridge did she dare to look back. Where the fortress had sat there was nothing but rubble and the charred specks that were once the bodies of the soldiers. She squinted trying to look beyond into the valley. A third of the valley had been wiped clean. Only black ash was left in the wake of the blast. But beyond it people were running, and even from the distance she could hear the din of an army in utter chaos. She turned, looking down the other side of the hill, and began walking down as fast as she could. In the gravel that covered this side of the hill, she slid farther than natural on every step and was soon at the bottom of the hill.

Ava looked around. "Spark, Raith!!" she called and waited, surveying the landscape. She was beginning to sag under the weight of Aiden. She knew that if she wasn't able to find the horses, she couldn't get the two of them out of the mountains. Gods! She couldn't even get herself out of the mountains.

She opened her mouth again, sucking in a breath and preparing to bellow even as her own throat screamed in protest. But the yell was not necessary. Just then, the horses rounded the corner, both moving at a gallop as though they knew what was happening. They ran to her. Spark came up beside Ava, the horses brown eyes wide, and lowered her back for Ava to set Aiden across. She grunted as she flopped him from her shoulder to Spark's back. She rolled him over so he was lying on his stomach and threw one of his legs to the other side of the horse. She grabbed his hands, pulling them in front of Spark's neck, then unclipped the reins and used a piece of leather to tie his hands together around the horse. Ava then placed his feet in the stirrups. When she had finished she ran to Raith. Standing beside him, she freed her weapons from the bundle. The noise of the army was still growing, less chaotic, more organized. The fear, ever slithering, wrapped around her neck and chest. She fastened the remaining weapons to Raith and mounted.

"Spark! Come," Ava commanded. She flicked the reins on Raith who began to run down the canyon. Spark galloped beside her, Aiden strapped on her back. Ava tucked low, heart thundering, even as the beating of hooves seemed to soothe her. Thirty minutes later, the two horses thundered down the road beyond the army. Ava looked back. Nothing, they must not have seen her.

"You can rest," she whispered to Raith's ear, tugging on the reins slightly. The horse slowed, Spark matching pace. They now moved at a trot. Ava at last took a deep breath, sitting up in the saddle. She reached into her pack still fastened to the horse right where she had left it the previous evening. She pulled out the water skin and drank, all the while trying to keep her eyes away from Aiden where he lay face down on Spark's back. Aiden was still rising and falling with breath when she finally forced herself to look at him.

Her gut convulsed. She keeled over the side of Raith and vomited, leaving a puddle of sick on the road. When she had finished, she pulled on Raith's reins bringing him to a stop. She hopped down and again looked at Aiden. Reaching into her bag, she again pulled out the water skin and a large piece of white cloth. She walked over to Aiden. Again, her gut wrenched, trying to rip her to the ground as her heart throbbed. Aiden's back was bathed in red. She had a feeling that whatever power he had just used was all that kept him from the gates of the dark god. It had to be. That, or a god of his own was looking over him. The wounds on his back were not the sort one endures but rather the kind people die from. There were deep, brutal cuts all down his back. Ash stained blood leaked from each gash, now making its way down Spark's gleaming white sides in streaks of washed out red. One of the cuts was deeper, stretching from his shoulder to lower back. It leaked blood, oozing in time with his heartbeat. Where it crossed his spine, she could see a glint of white poking out in shattered shards.

She uncorked the water skin, pouring it on the white cloth. Numbly, she began to wipe away the blood and ash.

But before she could finish the first stroke of the cloth, the flower blossom hanging at her neck began to glow. It gave off pink and green light, and the vine holding it around her neck loosened. She halted, dropping the cloth to the ground. She scrambled, pulling the necklace over her head. She held it before her, tears streaming in her eyes clouding her vision. But, 'Yes!' was her only thought, yes there was something looking over them. Alva was still looking over them. Whoever or whatever Alva was, god, deity, a being just looking to put good into the world, Ava didn't care.

"How?" she whispered to the flower bud. It glowed brighter as its petals leaned towards Aiden's back. Ava plucked the flower from the vine necklace. It now sat in her palm. She stared at it, then stretched her arm over his back and turned over her hand. The flower fell, but before it touched his back green tendrils emerged. They covered his back, sparsely at first, before more grew out of the flower, which sat squarely in the center of his form with its petals upright. The green and pink glow brightened as more tendrils shot out, finally covering his back. The glow grew still brighter, and brighter. Ava closed her eyes as the light became too bright to look at.

When the light stopped, it flickered out as though it had never been there in the first place. She opened her eyes to find the flower and all the green tendrils withering. First they turned dark gray and finally black as they blew away in the wind, leaving no trace that they'd ever been there in the first place. Once the tendrils had all disappeared, Ava could again see his back. She let loose a sob, relief flooding through her, wiping away some of the slimy fear that had gripped her. His back was tan again, marred only by white scars where the cuts had been and a small gash crossing his spine where it had been ripped apart. She sobbed again, dropping to her knees.

# CHAPTER 33

Ava opened her eyes. They burned slightly as she stared at the curved ceiling. She could feel cold sweat coating her body. It was sticky as she tore the blanket off herself and swung her feet onto the white stone floor. Her head hung between her shoulders as she sat there, perched on the side of the bed, arms braced on the mattress. She flicked her eyes to the other bed, staring at it for a long moment. She stood and walked to the walnut door.

Entering the great room she strode straight across, opening the door on the opposite wall and entering into the short hallway. Beyond it there were two doors on either side. She entered the one on the right and strode into the bathing chamber where Mary must have already filled the tub. It sat in the middle of the room, its polished silver dimmed with the steam coming from the bath. She pulled off her remaining clothes and climbed into the tub. The water was a little too hot for her to sit, but she did anyway. She once again lost track of time, sitting in the bath. It seemed to happen a lot these days. When things got quiet and she had time to think, she would lose track of time. She knew not whether she was there for seconds or hours.

Eventually, she dunked her head, cleaning herself quickly before climbing out of the tub and grabbing a towel. She wrapped it around herself and walked back to the bedroom where she dropped the towel to the ground before striding into her closet to get dressed. When she emerged she was clothed in a fine white tunic and dark red pants. She walked back to the door, sparing another look to Aiden who was still lying in his bed. She then entered the great room where she grabbed her boots off the floor and pulled them onto her feet. Lastly, she grabbed her sword, which she fastened to her back.

When she exited the living space at the top of the tower she let loose a breath, looked down the stairs, and whispered to herself, "Thick and thin, and whatever else." She began down the stairs for yet another day of meetings and preparation. When she arrived at the council chamber of the monolithic Castle of Clystera, she found a few of the men already sitting around the table, William among them. He sat at the far side of the table from the entrance in a slightly larger and more ornate chair than the rest of the court. He gestured for Ava to come sit beside him.

It was really only because he liked her and Aiden so much that she was invited to these meetings. She supposed she should be honored that he did so. William was wearing his crown today, a slight surprise given how he typically liked to run the meeting. Ava strode around the table coming to sit at William's right side.

"How are you today?" he asked, speaking too softly for the others in the room to hear.

"I'm... I'm ok," she replied softly. The hesitance was genuine, she noticed with a little shock. Last night had been the first time that her dreams had allowed her to envision escaping the fortress, without waking to her own screams and rushing to the bathing chamber to hurl her guts up.

William seemed to be able to tell looking at her. "I'm glad," he whispered back, resting a hand on her shoulder. "It will get better," he whispered to her.

"And Aiden?" she asked before she could stop herself.

William smiled. "I have a feeling his story has not finished being sung. I think this is merely... a pause for the music."

A tear dripped down her cheek and William wiped it away.

"Are we ready to begin?" one of the men around the table asked gruffly.

"Yes, I think we are," William said calmly looking back to the men surrounding the table.

"Kerstin," William said to one of the men around the table. "How has the recruitment and training for our military been going?"

Kerstin smiled. "It's going well. Based on what we know of the Orienthian army, I believe that we will be able to amass a big enough force to at least defend by mid winter."

William sighed. "Well then, winter will be here soon and the Orenth host will have to withhold any attack until spring, if they don't want to be caught with an army to feed in the snow." He finished, looking around the table where others voiced their agreement on the assumption.

Ava was barely listening as the men spoke. It was white noise. Everything felt like white noise but she came to attention as another man cut in.

"I'm sorry," he said it a little more loudly, gaining everyone's attention. Ava looked up, meeting his stare. He didn't look sorry at all, and anger flared in her at the sight of his slightly sneering face.

The man continued. "But we're basing all our estimates of their power off the panicked glances of a scared girl."

Ava's eyes were now fixed on the man.

William, seeing Ava's attention, began, "Lord Calam, we have been given valuable information about our enemies strength and..."

But the man cut William off, disgruntling a few of the council members. "We have been given information that could not only be false, but has come from some girl of a foreign court."

Ava stood, pushing her chair back hard enough to knock it over; it hit the ground with a clatter that boomed in the large chamber. She braced her hands on the table glaring at the man. She continued to stare at him, the silence of the room pressing in.

"I am no *girl*. My name," she growled, "Is Ava Corinth. I am heir to a forgotten Kingdom and have sworn my allegiance to William." She paused again and the man bristled under her gaze. "The information I have given you was not without price, and if you think you could do better, then you can go to the Tarin Mountains and try your luck."

Calam just bowed his head and shook it slowly. He looked back up still sneering at her, "Any price you were asked to pay..."

"Calam!" William breathed, looking between them nervously. Williams expression grew worse at the deathly stillness that had swept over Ava.

"Whether it be you..."

"Calam!" William said in nearly a shout, standing up in protest.

Calam paused, now leering at her. "Or the life of a no name street kid from the south."

Ava went entirely still now as the slight noises of the council room disappeared. She stared at the man. She knew who he was. She had looked into all these men when she arrived at the castle. This man's name was Calam Claris, Lord of Ertic. He ruled the second biggest port city in Anglen.

But that didn't matter to her as she loosed the dagger from where it lay hidden on her forearm and hurled it at him. It soared across the table, the silver glinting in the light from the window as it graced the man's cheek and red flashed. Everyone stared at Ava as she spat, "Aiden Windren is twice the man you are, and he's already saved your life once so speak about him like that again and the next one goes in your throat." Ava turned on her heel and stormed out the chamber.

Calam was already shouting protests in what sounded alarmingly near a sob. "Guards! After…" He was trailing off into some pathetic quarrel that William was already quashing.

Her pace was even more clipped than usual as she strode down the hallway. She didn't know where she was going. Not to her room. The sight of Aiden only made her want to scream, but where else was there in this damn castle for her to go. So she just kept walking. Eventually coming to a balcony overlooking the city, she spotted a bench and sat, bracing her elbows on her knees and resting her face in her palms. She sat like that for long minutes doing all she could not to cry. She heard soft footsteps as someone walked onto the balcony and sat beside her.

It was William who spoke. "Ava?" he paused waiting for a response.

"What?" she said back, her voice breaking.

"Ava," William said more softly, resting a hand again on her shoulder. "I'm sorry about the council room. Calam was out of line." She didn't respond and William waited before asking, "What's wrong?" He spoke softly and she could tell he knew.

"He's gone," she whispered and paused again "We… We were going to ask you if we could have a little time before our next mission. We bought an apartment and…"

William rubbed her back in slow soothing circles. "It's ok to cry," he said.

She looked up at him. She knew her eyes were red but there were no tears. "I do cry," she breathed. "But… it feels like every time I start crying I might… might not stop. I lose control and the world feels too small and too big all at the same time and…"

William smiled and looked at her right in the eyes. "But you will. Maybe not for a long time, but you will."

And at his words, the tears began flowing. They burned as they streamed down her face and William wrapped his arms around her. He held her, and she cried and cried and cried.

William also hurt. He too was on the brink of tears, but he also thought he'd gained something with the years of his age: faith, faith that things would again come to be how they should be. He was not yet to the point of believing that Aiden's story was, in any world, over.

When she finally finished, she pulled away and William let go. He looked into her eyes again and a slight bit of silver glinted in his own as he said, "I know it's hard now, but I would bet my life that the story of Aiden Windren has not yet finished being told."

"Thank you, William, for everything."

The old man nodded. "Don't give up hope. Aiden has been invited to death, but fate is still reading the invitation."

# CHAPTER 34

Ava shivered slightly as she sat in the tiny cave. She had set Aiden down beside her and laid both their cloaks over him. A day after the explosion, she was near the mouth of the canyon. Spark and Raith stood at the entrance of the cave, blocking most of the wind, but even still it was cold. It had rained last night and the water had come rushing into the cave.

Deciding the damp fire wasn't worth keeping, she stood and walked over to Aiden. Ava hauled him over her shoulder and mounted him on Spark. She had tried and tried to wake him, but even as she had, she'd known that he wouldn't wake. He continued to breathe, but she could tell it would take more than a little time to wake him. And so she packed up the miserable camp and began to make her way down the canyon. She winced against the cold, biting wind as it raced up the road. She knew she wasn't far from the end of the valley now. Fifteen minutes later, she let loose a sigh as she caught sight of the distant rolling hills and forests of the plain below the mountains. The horses also caught sight of it and hurried into a trot. Before long, they were far off into the plain.

"Now… what?" she said aloud, looking to Aiden's limp body. "I suppose we should go back to Clystera but…" she trailed off thinking. She then wondered out loud if they should try to get a ride on the Mezerek, the great river that nearly split their continent across the middle, stretching from southern Anglen to northern Orenth. "Well, are you going to answer?" she said, feeling like the whole world was pulling away. "I guess I really am crazy talking to an unconscious body." She groaned, a broken sad noise, and looked down the long, stretching road. "We can get to the Mezerek by tomorrow if we keep this pace. Then I'll use the money to charter a boat to Anglen."

They did keep the pace through that day and far into the night, only stopping for the horses to eat and drink. She split the last apple between the horses. Raith nuzzled her with his muzzle, giving her some small comfort. They reached the small town along the river by early morning. With a few hours until dark, she decided to wait. She doubted many of the captains would be willing to take her if she woke them and demanded they do so. So she sat there, Aiden lying beside her. Ava felt blank, numb. She couldn't feel the tears that fell from her face every once in a while as she sat standing guard over him, the tears thudding duly against the fabric of her pants. She could only see them fall and hit the damp dirty fabric.

The sun rose, the town waking along with it. She waited until the people at the boats were awake and moving before approaching a group of the men sitting there.

"Are any of you headed to Anglen?" she asked more confidently than she felt.

Some of the men look surprised, some sneered, but one of them, a woman who looked no older than twenty, cut in. "I'm headed to Anglen midday today."

And even with everything happening, Ava didn't find it that hard to give the woman a fake smile before she asked, "How much to bring two people and two horses?"

The woman frowned slightly in consideration. She gestured for Ava to follow her down the dock a few boats to hers. Ava made sure she could still see Aiden and the horses before she followed.

"How does 15 silver pieces sound to you?" the captain asked.

Without a word Ava reached into her money bag and pulled out five gold coins. "I'll pay five more if we can leave now and for your silence."

"We have a deal then," the woman said, taking the gold coins from Ava with a smile. "May I ask your name?"

Ava flicked her eyes to the woman. "No, you may not."

The woman's smile flickered. "Very well then, mine's Zoey. If you bring the horses over here, we can load up and head out."

Ava nodded and ten minutes later they were in their cabin with Aiden on the bed. The horses were loaded below. Ava came back above deck to see how the departure was going.

Zoey smiled and called over, "We'll be off in five minutes."

Ava nodded back and looked to the town, but her stomach fell, not in pain or sorrow but a fresh wave of fear as she caught sight of the two soldiers, the same ones that had passed her and Aiden on the way to the fortress. They were riding along the edge of the river.

Ava turned and walked at a forced gate to Zoey where she whispered, "We need to go now before those soldiers see me."

To Ava's surprise, the woman nodded, face cold and calculating as the soldiers began at either end of the dock and stopped to speak with each captain. Without another word, she walked to each member of her crew whispering something and the men all headed to their oars, not rushing, not gathering attention but casually. The nearer soldier was only one ship away.

Zoey walked back to the helm and to Ava's side before she whispered, "If this goes south be ready."

Ava had both her sword and bow strapped across her back; she took a deep breath collecting herself. The soldier left the ship next to them, moving to check their ship next. He turned to walk toward them at the same the time that Zoey yelled, no louder than a normal command of a captain, seemingly trying not to alert the soldier more than was necessary.

The man quickened, face hardening with displeasure at the sudden departure whilst he was still trying to check the ships. He broke into a jog, yelling for them to stop. Zoey did no such thing. His pace quickened, eyes now scanning the deck, the helm. He looked past Ava seeming to have missed her, but it was nothing more than a moment before the man's eyes snapped back and locked on Ava's own. He didn't know her, nor did any of the people in the courtyard but the King had and he'd left before...

"Go!!" Ava yelled, right as the soldier broke into an all out sprint for the ship, roaring both threats and profanities as he did so. The ship's crew heaved harder against the oars, pulling through the murky water at increasing speed. The soldier was nearing the side of the ship now at the edge of the docks, a slightly rusted sword already drawn from its scabbard at his side. The tip of the sword raced with each swing of his arms. He leapt, catching the rail of the ship in his chest he grunted, pulling himself over and onto the deck of the ship.

"You, bitch!" he spat, storming for the helm. Ava met his pace walking down the steps to the deck. "You're coming with me!"

Ava's expression didn't shift from the mask of cool ice that had glazed her eyes for days. The man lunged for her, slashing down in a sloppy diagonal motion. Ava parried with ease, causing the man to stumble to the side. She danced around him, back now exposed to her. His armor was constructed of poorly fitted plates that left gaps at his ribs. She flicked the small dagger out from the sheath at her wrist, blade soft silver in the overcast light. Ava didn't miss a beat, burying the tip of the dagger in between the plates at his ribs. She pulled on the dagger and brought the blade of her sword to the man's throat as she pulled him to the rail of the ship. He was letting out gasping wheezing breaths now, a guttural noise following as blood filled his lungs. He uttered something inaudible over the noise of his breathing.

"Burn in hell," Ava growled back. In one shoving motion, she bit the steel of the blade into the man's throat and left him to crumple to the ground already choking on his own blood. Ava turned, giving her blades a sharp flick, small flecks of blood spraying off them before she shoved each back into their sheathes.

She strode with brisk determination back to the helm and to the back railing where she drew her bow, spotting the remaining soldier sprinting up the bank of the river keeping pace with them. Rage consumed every line of the man's face as he stared at her. His blade too was in hand, waving wildly as he tried to run. She had an arrow knocked and drawn back to her cheek before the soldier looked up again. And in the moment that spanned a heartbeat in which the soldier saw the arrow and Ava let it go, she could see the change. His expression shifted from the kind of fear that people who are in danger feel to the kind which only those looking death in the face truly know.

With cold brutal talons, death claimed the man, iron arrow tip ripping through the soft, unprotected flesh of his neck. Shaft and fletching followed suit until the arrow passed through his body, and with a sharp thud, sank in the tree beyond him. She closed her eyes and took a breath.

When she opened them again, Zoey was standing beside her looking a little scared. Ava didn't care. "Tell no one I'm on board," she whispered and walked back to the deck.

The crew all knew to stay away. They were looking at her with wide eyes. She just walked back to the body of the dead soldier, pulled her dagger from his side, and placed it back in its sheath on her forearm. She grabbed the money bag from his hip, then pushed him to the side of the boat and hauled him over the railing. He splashed as he hit the murky water as a few scared members of the crew murmured with poorly hidden distaste.

Ava walked back to Zoey. "For your cooperation," Ava said and handed her the bag. With that Ava walked back down from the helm and below deck to her cabin.

# CHAPTER 35

"Ava," William said as the council all sat around the table, many of whom were still eyeing Ava wearily after the last meeting she'd attended. She'd skipped yesterday's meeting. But William had asked her to come to this one in particular. He'd sent Mary early this morning with a letter requesting her presence. Ava had read the wax sealed letter and strongly debated ignoring it. After the last meeting she had no interest in coming to listen to fools shame Aiden. But she decided it was important to attend even though it meant sitting there and enduring the glare of Lord Calam.

"Ava, I know you missed the last meeting, but I wanted you here today because we've had some rather large developments in our situation," William explained.

That sparked her interest and her eyes snapped away from Calam. "What?" she asked, interested.

"Yesterday, one of Lord Eren's soldiers came across an Orienthian spy attempting to get past the walls of Clystera." William paused, looking tired and old as he continued. "It is the goal of today's council to decide what to do with the man."

A murmur went around the room. It was Calam who cleared his throat speaking to William as he asked, "Isn't that clear, My Lord? We should question the man, see what he knows of the Orenths' plans." Another murmur followed, this time of agreement.

William looked each of the lords in the eye before continuing, "And if the man isn't inclined to talk, what then?"

"Then we convince him, as any other nation would do," Calam answered thought Ava couldn't help the feeling that even Calam didn't like the idea of that.

"And does that make us any better than those who seek to harm us?" The lords looked to each other skeptically and William continued, "I know there are things done in war, bad things. I have beared witness to some already." William half glanced at Ava. "But Anglen has not yet condemned its soul in this fight, not under my rule, and it is my hope that when the dust clears and the blood stops flowing, that the people of Anglen, you and I included, will still be able to sleep at night, free of the torment of vexing thoughts."

The room went silent for a moment, none of the lords looked. After a minute it was Calam to Ava surprise who said, "I agree." He raised his hand, then Lord Iris and so on until every lord at the table was raising a hand. William looked to Ava.

She cleared her throat surprised that he was waiting for her answer and said, "If I am truthful, I would have done whatever it took to obtain the information and for what those soldiers did to Aiden, but that is not to say that I am not proud to live in a Kingdom with such kind and just rulers." She also knew that Aiden likely would have voted in favor of keeping morals, so she raised her hand.

William nodded to her. "Then we will keep the man in the dungeons and in humane conditions until we feel it's safe to release him."

The rest of the meeting was devoted to the same talk of resources, men and tactics that they all were. Ava returned to glaring at Calam, though with a little more respect than before. William talked throughout the meeting always with the slow calm compassion of a man of peace and diplomacy.

The meeting ended and William stood to declare, "We will continue at tomorrow's meeting."

The lords all bowed to William and left the room. Only after they had all left did Ava realize she was still sitting at the table. Coming to, she stood and began to walk toward the door when a warm hand touched her shoulder. She turned to find William standing before her. She stood waiting for whatever comment he was going to make on her admitting that she would have tortured the man.

But when he opened his mouth he only said, "I understand."

She blinked. "What?"

William gave her that warm smile. "I understand your anger, and I don't blame you for it. I only hope that when the time comes you'll be able to let it go." She blinked again and they stood there for a moment before William asked more gently, "How are you doing?"

She thought for a moment, and she surprised even herself when she said, "Better, not good... but better." And meant it.

He rested a hand on her shoulder and whispered, "Don't give up on him."

Ten minutes later Ava was walking down a long staircase and then entered the kitchen where she found Mary. "Can I help with anything?" Ava asked.

Mary looked surprised but answered, "If you'd like you're welcome to help us make dinner for the great hall."

Ava did help Mary and the other servants, or at least try to. Mary had to step in every time she began to curdle the cheese sauce she was supposed to be making. Even as she had to call Mary for the fifth time, she was glad she hadn't just gone to her room. When she finished helping, or more accurately hindering, the making of dinner, Mary smiled at her even with Ava having made her job so much harder.

"I'm glad you decided to come down here," Mary said, giving her a smile and hoisting a platter on her shoulder to carry upstairs. "You're welcome to come again whenever you like. Help a few more times and you might be able to cook something."

Ava laughed softly. "Cooking was always more Aiden's thing."

"Nevertheless, if you ever want to come help me and the other servants, we're happy to have you," Mary said, patting Ava on the shoulder as she passed off into the hall beyond.

Ava figured if she were going to make an effort to get out of the tower she might as well go to dinner in the hall. Letting out a sigh in preparation for the noise she was sure would be claiming the hall, she began up the stairs. The temperature increased slightly as she walked up each of the three floors between the kitchen and the hall.

When she entered the great hall the noise hit her but not as firmly as she had thought it would. She scanned the hall, finding William sitting at the largest table at the head of the room. He sat squarely in the center atop a large, ornately carved walnut chair. Catching sight of her, he waved and gestured to the chair at his side. She gave a small smile and walked over while some of the people at various other tables gave her surprised looks. But she just ignored them and walked to William's side.

"Please, sit," William said, smiling up at her warmly. She did and he continued, "I'm glad to see you down here. It might just be me." He said the last bit a little more softly, then added, "But I think the food tastes better in the hall."

Ava laughed softly as she began to pile food onto her plate. She had a pleasant time at the table talking with William and the others, even finding it in herself to talk with Calam, briefly. After excusing herself from the table, she walked back down the length of the hall with a faint smile brightening her face. She continued making her way towards the staircase and had made it halfway up the tower before stopping. She turned on her heel and began swiftly back down the long staircase. Reaching the hall, she walked back up to the table but William had gone.

She looked to Calam. "Do you know where William went?"

Calam's brows rose but he answere, "I think he was headed to his study."

She nodded at him and exited the hall. She knew his study was somewhere in the south of the castle but she had never actually been to it.

"Ava? You're getting out a lot today," someone said in a questioning voice at her left. Turning, she found Mary standing there with a stack of folded clothes in her arms.

This was perfect. She turned to Mary. "Where is William's study?" Ava asked, forcing her voice to normality.

Mary smiled, and holding the clothes in one hand, pointed down the hall she'd just come. "Down this hall, take the first right, and it's the last door," she said gesturing the directions with her free hand. "I'm glad to see you so excited," the woman commented.

It shocked Ava enough that she opened her mouth. She hadn't even realized. This was the first time that she had been excited in weeks. But somehow it gave her a sort of shame to know that she could be excited about anything while Aiden was still lying unconscious.

"Ava?" Mary questioned.

Ava realized she'd been staring down the hall. "Sorry," she said and hurried away. She walked quickly, turning right down the first hall. Reaching the end, she found a tall walnut door. She took a breath and knocked.

"Enter," William said from inside.

Turning the door knob, Ava found William at the other side of the grand desk.

"Ava?" he said, surprised, and asked, "What is it?", looking a little worried.

She paused in front of the desk and took a breath. William just looked at her waiting for an answer. "I… I have a solution to our problem."

Williams' posture stiffened, barely.

"With the prisoner I mean," she explained.

He didn't say anything for a long moment before saying firmly, some small note of disappointment decidable in his tone, "I've already made my decision, as has the council. We will not harm the prisoner." His eyes were harsher than usual as he stared at her.

"I know," she said quickly. "I think I can get the information without harming him."

William's eyes narrowed. "How?" he asked slowly.

"You won't believe me," she said, looking straight into his eyes. She paused before continuing. "If you take me to him, I can show you."

William paused. "And if I do… then do you swear not to harm him?"

Ava nodded firmly.

"Regardless of what he says or tries to do?"

"I promise," she replied.

William seemed to contemplate this for another long moment before standing. He walked around the desk coming to her side and facing the door. Ava didn't move.

"Then follow me," he said softly and walked out the door. Ava turned to follow him. They began walking towards the great hall. Ava half thought that they might actually go in as they drew nearer to the door. But William turned, opening a small side door, and began descending the flowing spiral staircase. They continued down for a long way before entering into a huge chamber. Ava scanned the room and gagged at the machines littering the room. All were covered in dark red stains and a thick layer of dust where they sat pushed against the stone walls.

"Wha.." But she couldn't get the words out.

William turned to her looking strained. "Anglen's rulers haven't always been as benevolent as they are now. Before your time, before mine when my great, great, grandmother first took the crown she put an end to... the methods and tyranny used by our kings of old. Most don't remember those times but this chamber has stood as a reminder.

"Why not get rid of it?" Ava asked, cringing as she looked at the stains leading to a grate at the center of the floor.

William looked around the room sadly. "This chamber was built long before the castle, long before Anglen. Back when magic blessed and cursed this world." He paused again looking around the room. "I have tried to get rid of it more than once, but the people who built it put safeguards on this room and the rooms around it. That's the only reason we still use it as the dungeon." He sighed. "Any hope of escape is impossible with the spells left on the place. That's why we can' get the torture devices out and why prisoners can't get out."

"No one can escape?" Ava asked.

"From some of the cells, maybe yes, others no, there are some old rumors of people escaping but nothing more than that."

"Where is the prisoner?" Ava asked, trying to break William's dazed, sad look at the room.

"This way," he said, shifting his eyes away from the room and to an iron door on the left. Getting to the door William knocked. "It is William," he said clearly and the door opened.

Walking through, Ava could see the two guards flanking the door. Both looked alert. They nodded to William. William nodded back and continued down the hall to the door at the other end, also flanked by two guards. Passing that door, they came to a large room. Iron barred doors flanked it on one side. More guards were posted at the corners of the room.

"The prisoner," William said and one of the guards walked over to them and led them to one of those iron barred doors. Through the door Ava could hear someone growl.

"I'll tell you nothing," the voice on the other side of the door spat.

"Open it," William commanded to the guard.

"My Lord?" the guard stammered. "He… he's already tried to attack three guards." The guard paused for a moment. "Let us chain him and bring him out of the cell."

William frowned but nodded. Two of the other guards at the corners of the room came over to the cell. The fourth moved to guard William. The first guard opened the door and rushed in, followed by the second and third. A minute later, after much shouting, they pulled out the man. He was dirty, grime smudged across his face and darkening his clothes. His hands were chained behind his back and his ankles were bound. There was a thick iron chain connecting the manacles at his wrists and ankles. The man thrashed as they hauled him to the center of the room before Ava and William.

"He'll kill you! I'll kill you!" the man spat and thrashed still harder as they forced him to his knees and locked the connecting chain to an iron loop in the floor. Two of the guards went back to their posts. The other joined the one at William's side. Only once the man had ceased his unintelligible spitting did William slide his eyes to Ava. clearly prompting for her to show him.

"Leave us," she said to the room at large. The guards began to protest.

William gave her a slightly confused look but said to the guards, "Do as she asks."

Three of the men moved to the door, but the last looked at Ava a little suspiciously.

She gestured over her shoulder to her sword with a finger. "If he tries anything," she assured him, and the guard's face slackened a little as he walked through the door. When it had closed, Ava and William turned back to the prisoner.

"Now what?!" the man hissed. "Are you going to torture me 'til I tell you what you want to know, 'cause I'll die before I do."

William remained silent so Ava said, "You would." She cocked her head and continued, "But no, we're not here to torture you. But you will give us the information we want."

William again looked at her oddly, and she closed her eyes trying to tear back into that other plane. He flinched as the wall between the planes snapped, and she opened her eyes. The prisoner was trying to hide it, but she could feel that he was scared.

Eyes full of hate, he glared at her. "What the fuck was that?!" he demanded.

Ava concentrated on the man. "You're from Coloot," she said smiling.

The man stopped pulling at the chains.

Ava focused. "Your name is Galan and you report to…" She focused more. "You report to the Dark King himself."

The prisoner's face leached of all color. "How?" he breathed.

William was still facing the man, his expression unreadable.

"What did your King send you here for?" she asked, trying to bring the answer to the forefront of his thoughts.

The man snarled. "Like hell am I…"

But there it was. Ava flinched as she felt it. And she turned to William, "He was sent here to kill Aiden, and me."

William looked at her his expression, taking on a harsher look even as he attempted to mask it. "Only you two?" he asked.

"Mhm," Ava answered.

"What does his king want?" William asked.

"He doesn't know. His king never told him."

"Is he free, or does he serve the King of Orenth unwillingly?" William asked, his eyes returning to the man.

Ava again forced the other plane's power at him. "Unwilling," she replied.

William spoke to the man this time as he asked, "And if I were to free you, what would you do?"

Ava's gut squirmed at the thought. "He... he..." She stared at the man, not knowing what to say to the thought she'd just felt. "Why?" she asked the man.

His eyes were now dark as he looked back at her. "B... because," the man stammered, "I've done too much, seen too much. I... I just want it to end."

There was silence for a moment before Ava told William, "He would kill himself."

They all went silent for a moment and the prisoner finally bowed his head.

Now frowning sadly, Ava concentrated again. "And your children?"

The man let out a small sob. "They don't want me... they know what I am, and... " He sobbed again. "If I die in service of the King, then our debt is paid and they're safe."

William let out a sigh. "Has he been truthful?" he whispered to Ava.

She nodded. Without another word, William walked over to the door. He opened it, murmuring something to the guards.

When he came back it was with a key in hand. Ava held out a hand for the key. William nodded, handing it to her. She bent to a knee behind the man, first undoing the lock binding him to the floor, then the ones at his wrists and ankles, checking all the while that his thoughts never strayed near anything dangerous. Only once she had finished and returned to William's side did the man stand.

It was William who said in a strong voice, "You are free to do as you wish."

Tears glinted at the man's eyes, and without a word he started for the door.

Only as his hand reached for the handle did William continue, "Though if you wish it, Anglen would be honored to have you at its side."

Galan paused, half turned to William.

"It doesn't seem to me that you were ever proud to do the bidding of such a master. If you'd rather redeem yourself, I give you a way to do so."

Galan stood still for a minute. "May I have time to decide?" he asked softly, recognizing how the words put his position in jeopardy.

William nodded, however, and pulled one of the rings off his finger. He tossed it to Galan who caught it.

"When you come back to the castle, show the guards this ring and they will take you to me," William instructed.

Galan nodded, turned and left the room.

"That was a risk," Ava said briskly when she was quite sure Galan was out of ear shot.

"As was revealing your powers," he said, not looking at her. "I take it that's how you and Aiden escaped the fortress in Orenth.

She remained silent. She wouldn't tell him, let him think it was her. If he was to know the truth, it would be Aiden who told him. So she kept her mouth closed as she walked past him and out the door. The guards stepped aside and offered shallow bows as she passed.

# CHAPTER 36

She opened her eyes to the dark ceiling of the dingy cabin. It was the third week of floating along the Mezerek. With the ever changing width and depth of the river, it was impossible for boats to move quickly along it. Unlike Arlin's ship designed to smash through waves at top speed, Zoey had to carefully make her way along the river. It ended up being an ordeal every time they passed another decently sized ship. Still, she supposed this was shorter, and in another few days she'd be across the border of Anglen. It would only be a day and a half ride to Clystera, to William, and she prayed to silent gods there would be help there for Aiden.

She watched Aiden in the bed beside her for a while, watching his chest rise and fall with every deep, slow breath. Sighing, she flipped her legs off the bed and sat on the edge, head bowed and looking at nothing at all. She only snapped out of the trance when someone knocked on the door. She had the knife strapped to her arm out before the person had the chance to call through the door that breakfast was ready. She just shook her head and sheathed the knife as she walked to her bag hanging on the small dresser where she had not bothered to put away her clothes. She put on a fresh shirt and carefully strapped on her sword, bow and quiver. Taking one last glance at Aiden, she opened the door and walked out.

When she reached the deck, she found most of the crew sat around eating small bowls of porridge. Walking up to the helm, she found Zoey who handed her a bowl of the stuff as she approached.

Zoey returned to looking out over the deck and the river beyond and let out an annoyed huff. "Normally, we would be well into Anglen by now but the currents are weak and the melt from the mountains has been slim. With the water this low, we can't risk it."

Ava nodded and took a bite of the porridge. It tasted bad, but still, it was warm and with the frigid air she was happy for it. She looked around again. There was new frost covering the river banks, and the crew members were wearing more layers against the cold.

The sight of the lush green banks coated in morning frost reminded her of a milder version of what the coastal storms would do in Attica in winter. It'd get so cold out that the spray from the sea would drift up into the air and fall back against anything unlucky enough to face south and coat it in inches of ice. That was only on the coast, of course, but the thought of home sent a sort of disconnected emotion through her.

It had been years now. That thought too struck her like some invisible blow. It'd been years since she'd been ripped from her bed in the night and placed on a ship to watch and hear as the war drums of the coming ships sounded. She shook her head clearing the thoughts. They'd do nothing for her now.

"Where's the cook?" Ava asked.

Zoey gave her an apologetic, uneasy look.

Ava's thoughts must have been showing on her face. Zoey thought she was mad and offered, "I know the food's not good but he's trying his best."

Ava frowned. "I'm not going to complain."

Zoey looked at her for a moment. Ava didn't bother to put on a happy mask, let Zoey mistake her expression for distaste in the cooking.

"He's down in the kitchen, third door past your's on the left."

"Thanks," Ava replied.

Getting down to the cramped hallway, she strode to her room. She stepped in and grabbed the last few pieces of meat and potato from her bag. She left the room again, not letting herself look at Aiden. Reaching the third door down, she gave a half knock before striding in.

The cook turned out to be a thin boy who seemed to be about thirteen. "If you're here to complain!" he said as gruffly as he could with his high voice. "Then you're outta luck, that's all we've got!"

"I'm not here to complain," Ava said flatly.

The boy turned around. Seeing his face, he looked even younger, ten at most. He looked nervous, almost scared as he took in her appearance and weapons.

"I'm sorry," he said quickly. The boy did appear to be trying his hardest. His sleeves were rolled up, revealing a blistered burn on his arm, and his apron looked like the last ten feasts at the Attican Palace had been eaten off of it.

Looking behind him, Ava saw the full sink of dishes. The boy had clearly been trying to clean them, suds leaked down the side of one of the pots as she watched.

"Can... I help you?" the boy asked Ava more lightly, standing up from the bent over position at the sink where he'd been standing on a stool.

Ava looked at the boy, her face blank. She held out a hand with the meat and potatoes. "Can you make some broth from this?"

The boy's eyes widened slightly at the sight of the food. "Yes," he said slowly, "But don't you think it would taste better another..."

But Ava cut him off. "Just broth," she repeated.

He looked a little sad but took the food. "Should I bring it to your cabin when I'm done?" he asked.

"That would do well," Ava said in answer and walked out.

An hour later there was a light knock on the cabin door. Ava set *From Blood to Water* on the table. She had picked up reading where Aiden had left off. When she opened the door, she found the boy holding a small bowl of rich broth and a plate of seared meat and mashed potatoes.

He smiled. "I didn't see any point in wasting the meat and potatoes once the broth was done."

Ava looked down at both and nodded. She took the plate and bowl from him and lightly shut the door in his face.

She walked over and knelt at Aiden's side of the bed. "Dinner time," she whispered softly, setting the food on the side table. She pulled him up into a slight sitting position against the headboard. Grabbing the bowl, she slowly brought it to his lips and poured some of the foggy looking solution in his mouth. She tipped the bowl back up and grabbed the rag on the side table to wipe away the slight bit of broth from his chin.

"We'll be back home soon," she whispered. "Or at least I hope we'll be." Sighing, she picked up the bowl and again poured the broth into his mouth.

When the bowel was eventually drained she set it down and gathered the bandages and salve from his bag. Ava walked back over and carefully turned him onto his side, then pulled up the cloth of his white shirt. She pulled off the bandage to reveal the still gaping wound the whip had left in his back. It had been made smaller by the flower but was not healed. She felt numb as she spread salve across his wound and attached a new bandage.

When she'd finished she took a bite of the food the young boy had made of the leftovers. Apart from a slight bit of salt, it was unseasoned. She wasn't sure what compelled her to do it, but she stood, grabbed some of the bandages and salve and got up. Getting to the kitchen door she knocked.

"Come in," the high voice of the boy called back.

Ava opened the door and walked in. The boy half turned to see her. He began to say something nervously, but she cut him off.

"Are you busy?" Ava asked.

He glanced at the now small pile of dishes in the sink and shook his head. Ava walked over to the tiny table and sat. He just watched her, confused.

"Come on," she said, not looking at him as she laid the salve and few different bandages on the table.

He walked over. "What are those for?" he asked, looking at the salve and bandages.

She looked up at him frowning slightly. "Sit down, they're for your arm."

"What?" He looked down at the burn as though he'd forgotten it. "That's ok," he said, his face heating. "It was my mistake anyway…"

But she just glanced at the chair, indicating for him to sit, which he did, looking a little uncomfortable. "Give me your arm," Ava ordered.

The boy stretched his arm across the table. Grabbing it gently, she examined the jagged, slender burn that stretched half the length of his forearm. She stood and walked over to the sink where she found a bar of soap.

"How did you get this?" she asked.

"Making the seared chicken last night."

She reached for one of the bowls he'd cleaned and filled it with water from the jug to the right. She walked back over to the table and, after sitting, began using one of the clean cloth bandages as a rag to clean the blistered bloody burn. He winced when the rag touched, it but quickly relaxed.

"What's your name?" he asked.

"Ava," she said plainly, not bothering to look up from his arm.

"My name's Eli," he said.

Ava grunted. She wasn't the sort to try to make conversation with people she barely knew on the best of days, let alone these days, but Eli seemed to have no qualms about making it for the both of them.

"What are you doing here?" the boy asked, looking politely curious. "Zoey told us not to bother you when you came aboard."

Ava wiped the cloth along the length of the burn, and he winced again.

Ava stayed silent for a long moment before she replied, "I'm trying to get home, to a friend."

Eli continued looking at her, then at the bandage she was now wrapping around his arm. "Who... who is the person you brought on the ship?" he asked tentatively.

Ava stopped wrapping the bandage. Eli flinched, certain he'd said the wrong thing, but she just began wrapping the bandage again. Ava replied, "He's a close friend."

Feeling he'd pushed his luck enough, Eli fell silent and looked down at his arm. They sat in silence for a minute while Ava put salve and bandages on the next part of the burn.

"How old are you?" Ava asked quietly.

Eli straightened slightly. "Ten and a half," he said a little proudly.

Ava again remained silent for a moment, then asked, "And how did a ten year old become the head cook on a ship?"

"When I was little, I was living on the streets of a small river town in Laconia." He hesitated but then went on. "One night I was on the docks looking for food, and a dog attacked me. It had me by the arm when Zoey got there and beat it off.

After it ran away Zoey told me I could either keep living on the streets or join her crew and help in whatever way I could."

Ava tied up the last bit of the bandage and leaned back in her seat looking at Eli. "So you came aboard and Zoey just made you head cook?"

"Well... not exactly. At first she had me try to work as a member of the crew. But I was more of a burden so rather than have me get in the way of the crew she made me cook."

"And was there a cook before you?" Ava asked.

Eli shook his head. "Nope, the crew used to take turns making each meal." He laughed softly. "If you think the food's bad now you should have seen it then."

"Yeah..." Ava said, looking at him intently, too intently for the meek answer she'd given. "Who does Zoey work for? And why is she going to Anglen?"

Eli squirmed in his seat. "Why do..." But he trailed off at Ava's sharp look. "I don't know who she works for. But she's going to Anglen for trade."

Ava smirked. He was telling the truth on the first count, but the second... "I haven't seen any trade goods."

Eli was shaking slightly.

"I'll ask you one more question. Does she mean to harm me, my friend or Anglen?" Ava watched him force the shaking away.

"No," he said blatantly.

Still facing him, Ava closed her eyes and flinched as she opened the door to the other plane a little wider. She opened her eyes and something flashed behind her. The light was gone as soon as she turned. Looking back at Eli, she re-focused. She felt fear... and truth. He was telling the truth. Ava closed the plane, trying to shake away the feeling the flash had left behind. Another part of her wanted desperately to know what it was, though yet another thought was telling her she already knew, like a book she'd read a long time ago and couldn't remember the whole plot.

"Very well." She stood without another word and left the room.

# CHAPTER 37

Ava awoke, still covered in cold sweat, and ripped off the thin blanket covering her.

"Ava!" someone yelled to her right.

She turned to find Mary.

"Are you ok?" the woman asked, looking startled.

"Yeah, yeah, can you leave for a little bit?" Ava asked, still out of breath from the dream.

"But I'm tending to Aiden," Mary protested.

Ava was now walking to Aiden's bed where Mary sat with a bowl of steaming water beside her.

"What is it? What's wrong?" Mary asked.

Ava shook her head, hoping beyond hope she was right about the light in the dream. "I just need you to leave for a little bit," Ava said a note of hysteria in her voice.

"But!" Mary began.

"Please," Ava said.

Mary opened her mouth looking at Ava then closed it. She began again, "I'll be right on the other side of the door if you need me." Turning on her heel, Mary grabbed the bowl of water and walked out the door shutting it behind her.

Ava turned looking to Aiden. His face was impassive as he lay there, his chest still rising and falling slowly. Ava took a deep breath. She closed her eyes and took another before ripping through to the other plane. When she reached it she could see red through her eyelids. Opening them, she found him. It was Aiden, but he was shining bright as a star under his skin. And under his skin on the left side of his chest where his heart should have been, there was a pulsing, almost beating light. It was beating with the rhythm of a heart. Thump thump,

thump thump. Ava found herself transfixed, not able to look away from the beating light.

"Aiden?" she heard herself breathe in that other plane. She reached out a hand, her fingers inches from the thin skin covering that starlight heart.

"Aiden." She leaned a little closer looking at his blank face. Her fingers skimmed the thin skin, and the world flashed, flashed so bright she couldn't see anything, so bright her eyes snapped shut and the orange light burned her through her eyelids. Then the light dimmed somewhat, but still brighter than the room had been.

When she opened her eyes, she was indeed not in the room at all. The best word she could use to describe it was blank. The place went on and on and on. With no sense of scale, she couldn't tell. It might have stretched ten feet. It might have stretched beyond the sun. She spun on her feet, looking around her. Nothing there was nothing. She looked down. The bottom of this place was covered in water, totally opaque, white water. She kicked her foot and the fluid splashed, sending ripples that ceased not a foot from where they began. Somehow, this sent a shiver down her spine. The water wasn't viscus. The ripples should have gone further, and the fact that they didn't made her uneasy.

She stomped and the same happened. "Hello?" she bellowed.

No echo, no lingering bit of noise, the place was completely silent, more silent than life could be. She supposed that sound was swallowed the same way the ripples were, in the abyss of a place.

"Hello?!" she bellowed again louder.

Nothing, nothing at all in this white space. She looked down at herself. She was wearing, not the night clothes she'd been in, but... Her breath caught at seeing her blood drenched leather breastplate, then the blood drenched dull green pants and gray shirt. They were the same clothes she'd been wearing in the Tarin Mountains when they'd infiltrated the fort, when they'd been caught, when they'd whipped Aiden, whipped him until he bled and bled. This was his blood; she was covered in his blood. She gulped and gulped again.

When she looked up, the place was still blank, still silent. She looked down again as the blood, Aiden's blood dripped into the white water and disappeared under the still surface. She watched as a tear of shock or fear or grief dripped into the water and did the same, not diffusing in the water, just disappearing like it never existed.

Seeing nothing else to do she began to walk. She walked and walked, not knowing how far. She might have thought she was walking in place if it weren't for the too short ripples her feet left in the white water. So she continued and walked and walked, shouting to the empty void occasionally, always to the same silent response. Ava continued to ponder what this place might be, where it might be. Seeing no end to the void, she sat. The water felt like air. She saw it displace, but it had no temperature. Touching it with her hand, she could feel nothing at all, nothing but the firm textureless ground a few inches beneath. She lay down. Maybe if she fell asleep, she could escape this blank prison.

She did fall asleep, lying on her back in the water. But when she awoke, it wasn't to the cool tower bedroom. No, she was still in the white place, except, not white, not silent any longer. Sitting up, she twirled to see the faint red glow in the blank distance. Whether near or far, she couldn't tell, but the noise sounded near. And there was hissing, splashing and... Ava felt her heart stop.

There was screaming, Aiden's screaming. She nearly fell back to the ground as she tried to sprint. The faint red grew brighter, deeper red. She kept sprinting, and a yell broke from her lips. Her voice cracked, weeks of fighting, of waiting for her to come back to herself, came pouring out at once.

As though the pressing blankness of the place finally cracked, she broke through. It was all she could do not to fall to her knees. Aiden was there, sagging on his feet. His left arm and leg dripped, blood vanishing into the water. But he had his sword held high, and his eyes fixed on something. Ava followed his line of sight to… to… to the most grotesque thing Ava could imagine. No, she couldn't imagine this.

This was a thing from a nightmare one had to force from their minds or else live in eternal fear. Prowling on all fours, it circled Aiden. The thing had no skin, like its skin had been flayed from its body. Ava could see the bloody red fibers of its muscles extend and contract on its lanky frame. Its tendons were taut as bowstrings. White blood dripped off them. Ava could even see milky bone glinting in places.

She tried to scream but only a broken noise escaped her lips. But it was enough, the creature's bloody ears twitched. It turned to Ava. Two sets of blank eyes, four total, fixed on her for a second before the creature opened its maw in… in… Ava stumbled back and her throat caught. It smiled. The damn thing actually smiled at her, revealing row after row of needle sharp teeth, flanked by two massive fangs. The thing began to speak, and it was the most wretched noise Ava had ever heard, would ever hear. There was not a noise worse than this, not in a world as light as theirs, dark as it may have seemed these past months. This thing, that voice, it made her think of dark places, the sort of places people bury for fear of what they might spread.

In a shrieking, hissing growl it said, "Well… who might you be…?" It took a step toward her, clicking noises sounding, revealing a slender six fingered paw tipped in long razor thin claws, which it scraped and tapped against each other.

Someone yelled, a human yell, and Ava's head snapped to Aiden. "You're fighting me!" he demanded. Though his words were fierce, Ava could see his knees shake as he took wide-eyed glances at her.

The thing turned back to Aiden, moving too lightly, too nimbly. "My fight..." the beast said slowly, "Is with all..." It smiled more broadly, revealing further rows of teeth. "All who bleed, all who scream, all who suffer and live, die and survive." It took a step towards Aiden.

Not knowing what else to do, Ava blurted, "What are you?!"

The beast stopped, claw tipped paw in mid step, as it turned its head first, then the rest of its body back to Ava. "Me?" it hissed more softly. It's voice had a sickeningly human edge, all the hate of evil men and more. "I am the one thing that all other things fear. I am everywhere and nowhere. I'm in your very bones..." The thing trailed off, now pacing back and forth before her.

"What are you?!" she repeated, voice still shaking.

The creature smiled once more, and Ava saw something pool at the tip of its fangs, deeper red than blood. Nearly black, the liquid glinted.

"Pain!!" it screamed.

Ava only had time to see the beast's exposed muscles contract before it flashed red and she felt her side rip away. The beast had torn her arm off. She dropped to her knees, feeling her throat rip itself apart as she screamed. She clutched for her missing arm and found that she grabbed it. It startled her so much that she gagged down her scream. Looking down, still feeling like her arm had been ripped off, she found herself holding it. Just above her elbow she saw a thin pink scratch. It hadn't even broken the skin. She felt Aiden's movement as he rushed to her. He stood with his back to her as he faced the beast that now paced back and forth in front of them. Ava gulped, still breathing heavily as she stood.

"Now do you understand girl?" it said. "I am the one thing you can never escape."

This time Ava was waiting as it lunged, claws swiping for her as she drew her sword. But Aiden caught the beast's blow, sparks flying as its claws scraped against his blade. It lashed its head down for her, fangs dripping black venom, but Ava was ready. She brought her blade swinging up, driving it through the thing's open maw. Her blade split through it, and she drove the blade right to its skull.

The beast shrieked in fury and leapt back. It began to circle again, its limbs seeming to grow even more lanky. Right before Ava's eyes, she watched the skinless, red flesh on the thing's snout knit back together. It growled and lunged faster than anything should be able to move. It leapt high over them, and, turning in mid air, it brought its razor claws down at their backs. They both spun and had barely enough time to raise their swords before the claws fell against them. It snapped its jaws at them and leapt back. Not pausing to circle this time, it darted to their side, and twirling on its front paws, it exposed its back to them as it slashed viciously with its rear claws. Flicking her wrist, Ava released the dagger strapped to her arm. It fell into her hand, and she flung it at the beast. It moved fast enough to avoid getting hit in the glinting tips of its vertebrae but not fast enough to avoid the edge of the blade from slicing at the tendon on the beast's rear leg.

It was an accident. She hadn't been aiming for its leg. But it was enough. As the creature landed and tried to spring toward them, she heard the SNAP! The tendon pulled apart, and the beast crumpled to the ground. Aiden grabbed her by the arm to pull her away from the tumbling mass of claws and teeth that flew past them. Ava glanced around for the knife but it had disappeared beneath the white water.

The beast crashed to a stop. Thrashing with claws, it got to its feet, limping as it walked towards them. The white severed tendon hung limp at its foot. Ava drew her bow from her shoulder and notched an arrow. Pulling it back to her cheek, she let it fly. The thing swiped the arrow aside like a tossed ball. It took one more step before, in that too fast way, it slashed its claws. Still twenty feet away, it couldn't hit them... except Ava watched as all six of the beast's razor sharp claws detached and flew from its thin paw. Ava lunged to the side, but Aiden, too slow with his injuries, was struck. Ava heard the bone crunch as the claw embedded itself in his shoulder. He screamed, louder and hoarser than in the fort.

Ava turned, a scream of her own on her lips, but something hit her and sent her weapons flying from her hands and arrows from her quiver. The beast was upon her before she could so much as blink. It knocked her back, and with a paw to either of her sides, it stood over her and smiled.

"It would appear, that the game is..." It trailed on the word for a moment. "Up," it hissed. Its ugly bloody head, blank eyes and white teeth were not two feet from hers. Venom sizzled and reeked as the beast fell against her leather breastplate. She crawled backwards, her back to the ground, not willing to turn from the thing. It walked too, keeping over her. She moved a little farther, feeling something under her hand and stopping.

"Nothing, escapes, me," the thing hissed again, teeth bared at her. "For I am pain, and I am everywhere."

In a lazy movement, it swiped across her stomach. She was on fire. She was being burnt alive, ripped apart, and set aflame. But even as she shrieked and thrashed, she kept hold of the thing beneath her palm. The thing held up a clawed finger and scratched it against her cheek. She could feel the shredding fire grow hotter. The beast finally dipped its head not two inches from the sliced cheek.

"I am everything," it purred, closing its blank eyes and sniffing her cheek.

Ava struck, clenching her hand still tighter around the hilt of the dagger as she drove it into the beast's neck, knocking it to the side. She held tight to the dagger, letting it flip her atop the monster. Holding the handle with both hands, she ripped it toward her, straight through the beast's throat. Not giving the beast time to react, she flipped the dagger in her hands and buried it in the beast's skull. Bone crunched and cracked and finally thudded as the hilt of the dagger slammed into the beast's skull. Dark red reeking blood streamed down. With a final shudder, the thing ceased moving.

# CHAPTER 38

Aiden shot up, thrashing in pain. He tore at his shoulder, eyes still shut. He screamed as he fell off something. The sudden feeling of his stomach fluttering shocked him enough that he opened his eyes just in time to see the elbow that connected squarely with his eye. It snapped him from the flaming pain of his shoulder as a feminine yell hit his ears.

"What the!" someone yelled under him.

He stilled. He knew that voice. His vision finally cleared. For a euphoric, confused moment he didn't know if he was dead and that's why he was seeing her, or if he was just knocked out and his brain was pulling fragments of memory together in a dream. Either way, he was happy for it as he looked at her. Stuck half under him, Ava was sobbing. He pushed himself to his knees. She did the same.

"A... Aiden?" she asked, barely able to get the words out through a sobbing smile.

He leaned forward, and before she had time to react, he had his arms wrapped around her, tears of his own burning down his face. "Ava!" His voice cracked on the word.

Aiden squeezed her tighter, and she gave a strangled cough. He released his grip enough to look into her face. Her smile was wobbling, and she pulled him back, holding him just as tight. They sat there for a minute. An hour? He couldn't tell. He was only grateful to be out of that hell, out of that prison and back with her, wherever... wherever. He pulled back to look about the semicircular room, the ceiling had a curve. Pulling back further he reached over his shoulder only to find air.

"Where?" he began but stopped at Ava's chuckle.

She smiled at him, still sitting on the ground, hands now set limply in her lap. She laughed again, and he stared at her dumbfounded, then to the rest of the room again.

"Where are we?" he asked slowly.

She giggled one last time, tears still staining her face as she stood and reached an open hand down to him. He took it and she gently pulled him up.

"Aiden, welcome to Clystera."

His mouth sagged open as he looked at her and question after question filled his head. "But!" he began and stopped. Orenth, the post, and the white place?" The words spilled out one on top of the next.

She smiled again, grabbing his other hand.

"How?" he asked.

She stood on her toes and kissed him. "I have no idea about the blank place, but the rest, the rest I can tell you." And so she did. For hours, they sat on the bed. When she told him about the flower, he stopped her.

"It did… what?" he asked and reached around to his back where, sure enough, something twinged and burned. "Ow!" he grumbled, and she laughed. "That's not funny," he said in mild outrage, even as he could help laughing himself.

When Ava had finished telling him what had happened, there was already golden light peeking through the window. When it was clear she was done, he stood and held out a hand to her.

"Wanna go to a cafe?" he asked.

She burst out hard, laughing half crying. "You… you've been in a coma for months and the first thing you want to do is go to a cafe?!"

He gave her a pretentious look. "No, the first thing I wanted to do was hug you."

Ava stared at him for a long moment, then hopped up. "Well, when you put it that way."

She walked over to her dresser and grabbed a clean set of clothes. She pulled off her nightshirt as she walked across the room, left in nothing but her underclothes.

Aiden stifled a yell.

"What?" she asked, eyes widening.

He pointed at her. "Your, stomach."

She looked down and stumbled slightly as Aiden walked over to her side. From the top right to the bottom left of her stomach they could see six slender scars. Aiden watched as Ava slowly ran a hand across the scars.

"Do you think?" she began.

But knowing what she was going to ask, he shook his head. No, he didn't know about the blank place or realize that the monster had been real. He too had thought it was some kind of fucked up nightmare.

Ava looked back up to Aiden. "Take off your shirt."

He did so, ripping off the baggy white shirt. Sure enough, Ava pointed to his shoulder where a triangular mark showed in the shape of a claw.

"I guess the white place was realer than we thought," he breathed, looking back up to her.

Ava walked over to him and ran a finger along the scar . Her eyes slid to the second one at his hip. "And this one?" she asked, looking to where the scar slid behind him.

He frowned. "Right before you got there, it found me."

At that, Ava looked up to him, frowning herself. "Found you?"

"Yeah, I'd been running from it 'til you got there." He paused, eyes seeming to grow haunted. "But I... I think it was more letting me get away, letting me run. Not long before you got there, the water rippled and it came out, like it'd known where I was the whole time." His voice broke on the last word.

Ava wrapped her arms around him. "It's gone now."

When Ava finally pulled away, it was to put on the fresh set of clothes she'd dropped. A blue shirt, black pants and the leather breastplate. She pulled open the lid of the chest at the foot of his bed and handed him a matching set.

"Shall we?" she asked, smiling again and holding out a hand for him to follow.

"We shall," he answered, his face brightening.

Reaching the door, Ava grabbed their swords. She. handed Aiden his and strapped her own to her back.

Aiden reached out and opened the door for her. "Lead on," he said in a kingly voice.

At the bottom of the staircase, they began down the hall to the right. Halfway down, they turned again, this time into the main entrance hall of the castle.

"Aiden!" someone yelled and stumbled.

Aiden turned around to find William flanked by a nervous and shocked looking Mary.

"Aiden?" William said again, more quietly this time.

Aiden broke into a smile, showing all the warmth he could, as he strode over to William and slung his arms around the man. "William!" he said, releasing him.

"Ha!" William began. His eyes snapped to Ava, joy glinting in them. "How?"

Ava gave him an elated smile. "That's a long story."

Aiden looked over his shoulder, smirking at her as she continued.

"And one that we will tell you later," she offered.

"Later?" William asked, raising his brows at her. "Do you have somewhere better to be?" It was a rhetorical question. He was the King. What better place was there to be than with him?

But Ava just slung her arm through Aiden's. "As a matter of fact we do," she said.

Aiden, feeling this wasn't going at all well, opened his mouth to intervene, but William just shook his head chuckling, too happy with the moment it seemed to let anything taint it.

"Well, then you two better get going," he said. "Though I do expect a grand story when you get back."

Ava smiled and pulled Aiden by the arm, headed for the end of the hall. "Thanks Will!" Ava called over her shoulder.

Aiden smirked at her as Mary snapped some remark, but they were already approaching the grand walnut doors. As they stepped outside, the warm sun kissed Aiden's cheeks and truly warmed them for the first time since the edge of Sylvanwood. He arched his neck back, wanting to feel the warmth and to hear the sounds of life all around him.

He'd never actually been to Clystera. His parents had taken him on a few trips before he could remember, he'd been told, but never anywhere as grand as the city spiraling out before him. White stone and colored roofs gleamed in the sunlight. It took him a long moment of looking down at the city, the bright building and bustling streets and rolling hills beyond, before he finally looked back to Ava. She was smiling faintly looking up at him. He smiled back.

"Where to?" she asked softly.

Without answering, he tugged her by the hand and they began into the city. They stopped at street vendors. Ava bought him all sorts of foreign goods she recognized from Attica, the last of which was a pickled and fried sheep eye that she admitted she just wanted to see him try. Only after they had sat at a trash can for a minute while Aiden vomited it back up did they continue.

Ava led them down the street. "When I was little," she began, "My parents and I visited Clystera, and there was this fancy glass cafe where we ate breakfast." She continued tugging him down the sidewalk, eventually reaching the corner.

"There!" Ava shouted, pointing down the adjacent street. Aiden followed the line of Ava's arm, and the building sitting on the far corner shocked him. Rising four stories tall, it was built of barely white tinted glass and fixed together with mat black metal fastenings. Aiden began walking down the sidewalk. Ava followed at his side.

He turned his head to her, "Why were you and your parents in Anglen? It's on the far end of the content from Attica."

Ava huffed. "For years my mom and dad were on this hunt to help foreign nations in exchange for oaths to help should Attica call. They managed to help a bunch of smaller ones. They wanted to make a deal with Anglen, but William needed nothing at the time. So, he only invited us to visit and wished us well."

They reached the corner where the carriage director stood in the middle of the street, signaling for them to stop.

"And when Orenth attacked?" Aiden asked tentatively.

Ava shook her head vaguely. "They were efficient if not merciful. Attica fell before anyone got there. Orenth slaughtered the incoming armies. A few turned back, but there was nothing to be done."

Aiden wrapped an arm around her.

"All ways cross!" the director called.

Ava's face split back into a smile as she tugged him across the road. The front doors of the cafe were also made of glass. Grasping the black metal door handle, Aiden opened the door, giving a mock bow and gesturing for Ava to enter.

She smirked at him and did a mocking courtesy to match. "And they say chivalry is dead," she giggled, again grabbing his hand as they walked into the cafe.

At the matching reception desk stood a young man dressed in a maroon button up shirt and khaki pants. "Welcome to Palais de Verre!" he announced.

Aiden was able to detect the light and quick accent as the man dipped into a shallow but polite bow. "How might we serve you today?" he asked, grinning with stark white teeth.

Ava stepped forward. "We would like to get coffee and breakfast."

The man nodded. "Right this way." He led them up the first two flights of stairs leading to the top angular floor, then to the far side of the room jutting out, overhanging the street below. He led them right over to the overhung section of the floor. Aiden couldn't help it as his stomach squirmed at the sight of the carriages racing below.

The receptionist laid two menus on the table before them. "Your server will be with you shortly."

Aiden nodded as the man left, then scooted his chair closer to the table. He was looking over the side of the chair when he heard Ava giggle. "What?" he asked, looking up at her.

"Scared of heights are you?"

"No!" he said, looking her in the eyes even as he felt color rise in his cheeks.

"Liar," she said, holding his stare.

Aiden looked away, shaking his head. Aiden saw the movement as someone walked up to the table beside them.

"Eli!" Ava exclaimed, looking to the young boy. "What are you doing here?" she asked, beginning to smile.

"Hi!" the boy said, smiling back at Ava.

"How are you here?" Ava asked, as the boy straightened his shirt and pulled out a pencil and notepad.

"After you were dropped off past the border of Anglen, the rest of the crew and I made our way up the river to Clystera. When we got here, Zoey decide we would stay for a while. Then, she got an application for another cook. The guy was definitely better than me, so Zoey accepted…" He paused for a moment looking curiously at Aiden.

Following his line of sight, Ava coughed. "And let me introduce Aiden, Eli Aiden, Aiden Eli."

"I take it this is the friend you were talking about from the boat?" Aiden asked.

Ava nodded, then turned back to Eli. "But anyway, what'd you do after Zoey found the other cook?" she prompted.

Eli shrugged. "She told me I was welcome to try working as a member of the crew again, but that wasn't really my thing, so I told her I'd rather try my luck in the city. That's how I ended up here." Ava roughly patted the kid on the shoulder. "Nice going," she chuckled.

"Anyway," he began looking between Aiden and Ava. "What would you like to order?"

After ordering, Ava began to fill Aiden in on all the goings-ons of the court, and all they knew of Orenth's movements since the fort.

Only when she'd finished did Aiden ask, "And Orenth really hasn't made any move to weaken Anglen since?"

Ava shook her head. "Other than blocking a few trade ships here and there, nothing."

Looking at her intently he asked, "And what do you think?"

She rubbed her face with a hand. "Militarily, I think we have a good shot. For months Kerstin's been building up an army. William had him start right after we left home. But as to the Dark King, I have no idea."

Aiden nodded.

"And here you go," someone said to their side as Eli appeared, bearing two plates and two cups of coffee.

"Thanks," Ava said, turning to him and taking the plates.

Eli nodded and returned to the stairs leading to the floor below.

"Does William know what really happened at the Tarin Fort?" Aiden asked more softly.

Ava shook her head slightly. "I was waiting to tell him."

Aiden nodded. "Well, I guess we can tell him today." Aiden began eating his food, surprised at the quality of the eclair and sandwich. They continued to eat, taking their time as they talked over what they wanted to do once all this was over.

When they'd finally finished, Ava gestured for Eli to come over. She pulled out a silver coin from her bag and paid for the meal.

"See you soon," he said, taking the coin.

Ava and Aiden stood and turned toward the staircase. Aiden reached into his money pouch and flipped a single gold coin onto the table.

Ava nudged him with an elbow as they strode down the stars. "What was that?" she asked, smiling.

"What was what?" he answered, not quite meeting her eyes.

"The gold coin you left."

"A tip."

Ava smirked at him. "A tip worth way more than the meal."

"He'll make use of it. And if he helped you at some point, then he earned it."

They reached the front desk, and the man who had seated them held open the door. "Do come back," he called after them as they crossed the street, making their way back to the castle.

# CHAPTER 39

When Aiden finally caught sight of the front gates of the castle, he knew something was wrong. The guards stood too stiff and the gate was barred.

"What happened?" he demanded of the nearest guard.

The guard scoffed. "And who are you?" he asked sternly, if not a little rudely.

Ava walked up beside Aiden and pulled out the necklace from within her shirt. She showed it to the guard.

He nodded. "Someone came, he said he'd made a deal with the King and needed to speak with him. The man went in and a little bit later Kirsten called for the gates to be barred and the watch to be doubled."

"Do you know why?" Ava pressed the guard who shook his head, moving to open the gates.

"Thank you," Aiden said curtly as he and Ava broke into a brisk walk up the steps to the castle doors.

"I think I know what's happening," Ava whispered as they made their way up the steps. "A few days ago one of the lords caught a spy from Orenth trying to sneak into Clystera. I integrated him, with magic," Ava said at his questioning stare. "We deemed that he wasn't a threat, so William offered him a deal and gave him time to think about it."

Ava stopped when they reached the walnut doors of the entrance hall. Grabbing one of the handles, Aiden pulled a door open and strode into the entrance hall, Ava on his heels.

"Mary?" Ava said looking to the side of the hall.

Mary was standing near the wall, a small pile of letters in her hands. Mary turned to face them as Ava walked over, her steps clipped as she did so.

"Where's William?" Aiden asked.

Nervous as she looked, Mary answered quite calmly. "He and the other lords are in the main council chamber in the west wing."

Ava thanked the woman. Breaking back into their brisk walk, she and Aiden made it to the council chamber in a few minutes. Opening the door, they entered into the fray of shouting lords and dukes, all arguing. Aiden and Ava strode to Williams side. He nodded, catching sight of them and gestured to a pair of seats at his side. They sat and William stood.

"Quiet!" he roared to the room at large.

Slowly the room fell into silence, some of the assembled lords still muttering with those beside them. But William just stood and waited until every member of the assembled group had ceased talking.

"A few hours ago, we received information from an Orienthian ally," William began in an authoritative voice. "You've all been summoned here so that we might hear their full testimony and decide our next moves from there."

William surveyed the room, the men and women surrounding the table. Aiden did the same, his eyes snagging on a young man sneering slightly at Ava. But his eyes snapped back to William.

"Bring him in," the King commanded.

It was only then that Aiden noticed William wearing his crown. Crafted from both gold and silver, it was an elegant band wrapping around his head. The crown peaked up at the front, displaying the shining clear stone carved with the crest of Anglen. The doors on the far end of the chamber opened and a slender middle aged man strode in, flanked by a guard on both sides. They did not restrain him but stood too close to be entirely comfortable with his presence.

"To those who have not met him, this is Galan, former spy and informant of the King of Orenth. He has decided to aid us in whatever battle may come between Orenth and ourselves."

The room was unnaturally silent, the quiet only broken by the soft footsteps of Galin and the guards. Someone coughed. Aiden turned to find the same man that had been sneering at Ava looking at William. Aiden could have sworn that William sighed slightly as he looked.

"Yes Calam?" William answered, looking to the man.

"How is it we know this man speaks the truth? You just said he hails from Orenth."

William turned from Calam and spoke to the room as he answered, "Although I cannot go into the exact means through which we have ensured this informant's validity, we have determined without a doubt that what he speaks is true."

Calam stared at William for a long moment. William held his stare.

When Calam opened his mouth to speak, Aiden leaned forward in his seat and asked loudly to Galan, "Is it true that you hail from Orenth?" Aiden asked the question firmly but with none of the animosity that Calam and some of the others seemed to show towards him.

"Yes, Lord, I come from a small town in the south of Orenth."

Aiden nodded. "And if this is the case, then why is it that you have chosen to help those who seek to rival the ruler of your homeland?"

Galin looked to his feet for a moment before answering. "I only ever helped the King of Orenth to protect my family. The Orienthian King may be powerful and influential, but he is not loved," Galin said quietly. "He's forged himself an empire, but at the cost of his people."

Aiden heard another cough. He raised his head to find not Calam but a young woman looking at them. She was dressed in a black dress embroidered with golden leaves. Her golden hair was bound in a loose braid.

"Sir... Galin," she said, addressing the man. "I hate to interrupt the story of your people, and I do hope we have time to return to the subject, but if you don't mind informing us of the crucial information for which this meeting was called, I think we would all be very appreciative."

Galin nodded again. "Of course, My Lady. I have urged this meeting be called so that I might inform you of Orenth's latest movements."

The room went perfectly silent in the pause between his words. Aiden could see the tenacity of the men and women around the table as Galin continued, "The Dark King intends to have his army attack in three and a half months' time."

The statement was plain, flat, and the silence was allowed to persist for only a moment longer before the room exploded into shouts and arguments. People shot to their feet, called him a liar and an anarchist. William stood, attempting to shout for silence, but he coughed, doubling over slightly, reaching for a handkerchief. Aiden stood, grasped William's arm and helped him back into his seat.

But it was Ava who stood in his place. Standing, she shouted for silence over the din. Nothing happened, and so releasing the dagger strapped at her forearm, she spun it in her hand and slammed it point first into the walnut table. The thudding crack rang through the room. The tip of the dagger was buried inches deep in the wood. As the crack of the impact met their ears, the Lords and Ladies of the court fell silent as one. All eyes were fixed on Ava. They sat down one by one, Calam waiting until Ava fixed her eyes specifically on him.

Her voice bordering on a growl, she said, "Regardless of what you think on this matter, when your King…" she said, emphasizing the word and gesturing a hand toward William… "Calls for silence, you shut the fuck up!"

The people stared at her as she returned to her seat and directed her attention to William.

Having recovered, William directed his attention back to Galan. "Are you sure that he intends to attack in three months?"

Galan nodded. "He wants to attack once the snow has a chance to stick. He hopes that it will slow anyone that might come to your aid."

William surveyed the room. "Anderis?" he said looking at an older man. "Do you think you will be able to fortify the western edge of the northern territory by such a time?"

"I believe I can," the man responded, with the slightest hint of uncertainty.

"And you, Josephine, will you be able to fortify the southeastern territory?"

"I believe I will," she responded in kind.

"And Kerstin, how is the formation of our army going?"

The knight's face fell slightly. "It has been moving faster than expected, but we… we will not be ready to meet a host in three months. The men are still green and the rate of recruitment is bound to drop when the snows fall."

The atmosphere of the room went cold and stagnant at his words. William stretched up an arm and rubbed at the back of his neck, a look of contemplation painted across his face.

"Annalise?" William called.

Aiden peered around the table looking for whom William was speaking to.

It was the woman dressed in the black and gold dress that answered. "Yes, William?"

"Who could we call upon that would be able to get here in time?"

She grimaced. "None with a standing army near large enough. We might get some Aid from Drenai, but our only allies with strong standing armies are too far away."

"What of Nicora?" another Lord cut in.

Annalise looked to him. "They have a small standing army, but I doubt they would be able to ready it and make it here by the time Orenth does."

William shifted in his chair, and Aiden ran a hand through his hair looking to William.

"Send emissaries to both as well as to Uqbar," William ordered. "Ask them to block all trade with Orenth and to send us soldiers if they can."

The words fell and after a brief moment of silence, the deafening squalor of the Lords, Ladies, Dukes and others grew again. Aiden leaned forward resting his elbow on the table and his head in his hands. He thought of their apartment back home with the soft bed and small kitchenette. It had none of the grandeur of the castle but it also had none of the politics.

Ava nudged him with an elbow. He looked up, she leaned closer. "I might have an idea," she whispered.

"For what?"

"For an army," she answered.

His brows rose. "Where are you gonna get an army from?"

"I'm not sure I can, but I might be able to."

Aiden frowned. "Is it safe?"

She just looked at him like he was an idiot. "Of course not, but where's the fun in that?"

He stared at her for a long moment. Then he dipped his chin in agreement. They both pushed their chairs back and stood.

Ava cleared her throat loudly and the squalor died. Everyone once again turned to Ava, William along with everyone else.

"I have an idea," Ava said. Her nervousness forced her voice to be a little louder than usual, but it remained firm and steady.

"And?" Calam said half sneering at her.

"Barataria," she said.

Calam burst out laughing, some of the others joining him. "Drake Jagger…?" Calam laughed out. "Lord of the pirates, why would he help us?" Calam choked slightly as his laughing subsided. He patted the table. "Drake Jagger is the most ruthless man on the high seas. Not even armies dare cross him. He helps no one without a price… a price never worth paying. And somehow you think he'll just help us?"

There were nods of agreement at Calam's words and he continued, "He's killed men for asking for his help in the past. And so I ask again, why would he help us?"

All eyes were on Ava now, but her face was a mask of stoney ice as she stared Calam down.

"He wouldn't!" another Lord called out and the words where echoed. William just sat in his chair, eyes intently but warmly directed towards Ava.

"He wouldn't help us," Ava conceded and her words were cold. "He would help me."

Calam's smug smile died. "And why would he help some nobody from Attica?"

The room stayed quiet as Ava paused and took a breath, "Because I am Ava Corinth."

Someone murmured something at the end of the table.

Ava continued, "Crown princess, high heir to the Attican throne… and he owes me a favor."

# Chapter 40

Aiden walked back into the tower room of the castle, a step behind Ava as the door thudded shut.

"Well," he said, walking to the couch by the fireplace and plopping down.

"That was interesting," Ava smirked as she sat beside him. "More so than usual." She stretched long ways along the couch and rested her head against Aiden's leg. "That was the most the council has done since I've been here. It's usually just meaningless arguing and a status update from Kerstin." Ava looked at him. "Wasn't Kerstin the knight you were talking about back home?"

"Yeah, I haven't had a chance to talk with him yet." Aiden nudged Ava, "So what's this debt the King of the Pirates owes you?"

Ava laughed softly. "He has a son about our age, bit of an asshole. But anyway, he took one of his father's ships and managed to get it all the way to Gildea before he was caught by the Guildean soldiers. The pirates have a treaty with the Republic of Gileda. Crossing into their waters violated it."

"And the punishment?" Aiden asked.

"Death, just like the pirates would have done if a Guildean soldier had shown up at Barataria."

"And how were you involved?" he asked, beginning to unbraid her hair, though Ava didn't notice.

"My parents had sent me to study there for a while. They wanted me to have some idea of what foreign courts are like. I saw them bring this pirate kid into the city. I didn't think he meant any harm by it, so I went to the regent and asked that she spare him as a favor to me."

Aiden paused his unbraiding. "And they just did it?"

"Well, not exactly. Gildea is a pretty competitive place so she made me an offer. If me and Archer... the son," she added, realizing she hadn't told Aiden his name. "Were able to fight off a beast of her choice, then his freedom was won."

Aiden laughed aloud. "Beast? She had you fight a beast to earn his freedom?"

"Yep, it's a weird place," she said, now inspecting her nails.

"And your parents were ok with this?" Aiden asked, surprised.

Ava scoffed, "They never found out."

"What'd you end up fighting?" he asked.

"She ended up picking a wolf."

"The beast you fought was a wolf?"

"Yeah," she said, looking back to him, less amused. "Archer managed to get scratched across the face in the first thirty seconds and spent the rest of the fight running around the arena while I fought the damn thing."

Aiden finished unbraiding her hair. She flinched, reaching a hand behind her head.

"Did you?" she began to ask, but instead grabbed the pillow from the other end of the couch and flung it at his face. To both of their shock, the pillow burst open as feathers went flying around the room. They fell to the ground, and Aiden spat the remaining ones out of his mouth. Ava, overcome with laughter, rolled around on the soft rug, still half laughing a minute later when Aiden came down to the rug and kissed her, a few feathers still lodged in his hair.

The next morning when Aiden walked across the great room of the living space to the adjacent bathing chamber, he found that the feathers had already been cleaned up. When he finished bathing, he came back into the bedroom where Ava still lay snoring and hanging half off the bed. He pulled on his clothes, strapping Starlight across his back, before walking over to the bed.

"I'm gonna go to breakfast," he whispered, brushing the hair out of her face.

She, not bothering to open her eyes, muttered something indescript. He left the room, making his way down the long spiral staircase and into the great hall where he found the long tables loosely scattered with people talking. He made his way towards the head table where William gestured he sit at his side.

"Well, I'm glad to see that one of you two is able to get up before noon," William said, smiling warmly.

"Well, you know it takes a lot of energy to fight monsters and politics," Aiden countered.

"I suppose it does," William said, shrugging.

"What monsters do you speak of?" William asked, a curious expression painted across his face.

Aiden frowned slightly. "That might be a discussion for later in your study. We have a lot to talk about."

William frowned, setting down his fork with a faint clatter. "Anything very important?"

Aiden dipped his chin, his face going slightly taut.

"Then we will do so as soon as Ava awakes," William decided.

Someone walked up to the table before them.

"Morning, Mary," William said in greeting as she set a plate of roasted lamb on the table.

"William, Aiden," she replied and turned reproachful eyes to Aiden. "If I may ask, what in the gods' names caused all those feathers to be scattered across the couch, floor, table and rug this morning?"

Aiden almost choked on the potato in his mouth and swallowed it before answering. "Ava... threw it at my face. And, well, you saw what happened."

Mary set down her last plate. "Do try not to feather the east tower anymore." Though she said the words curtly, Aiden could have sworn she chuckled as she walked away. William certainly made no effort to hide his amusement as he laughed.

Ten minutes later Aiden spotted a man dressed in a black tunic and light armor walking into the hall with an antler hilted sword at his side. Hopping up from his chair, Aiden made his way around the table and down the hall.

"Kerstin!" Aiden called out, raising a hand above his head. Kerstin tuned slightly, looking for the source of the call. Their eyes met and Kerstin just stared at Aiden for a long moment, an expression of confusion across his face before his eyes went wide.

"Aiden?!" He took a step and Aiden smiled. "Aiden!"

Kerstin began walking quickly toward him. The knight wrapped his arms around Aiden, squeezing him tightly. They stood there for a moment before releasing each other.

"Is that really you?" Kerstin asked.

Aiden chuckled, breaking into a bow and splaying his arms. "Aiden Windren at your service."

"Oh stand up," Kerstin said, grasping him on the shoulder. "You've gotten big. You were down here last I saw you." Kerstin waved a hand around his stomach.

"Bigger than you!" Aiden shot back and indeed Aiden now stood a few inches taller than the knight.

Kerstin let out a laugh. "Big words coming from a young guy. But let's eat." Kerstin directed them to a nearby table.

Aiden didn't bother mentioning that he'd just eaten a full breakfast. He ate another as they talked. Aiden told Kerstin about everything that had happened since he left home, meeting William, and later Ava about whom Kerstin took a bit of an interest in.

"And she really almost split you in two when you met!? I thought I taught you to tail someone."

"Yes, she almost split me in two," Aiden said sardonically. "And I bet she'd knock you on your ass too."

"It sounds like I really should meet this girl. I've seen her in the meetings, but I've never had a chance to actually talk with her." Kerstin picked up his glass of orange juice and, tipping it back, drained the remaining liquid. "I suppose I should have thought nothing less after she threw that knife at Calam."

Aiden coughed while drinking his own orange juice, causing it to splash across the table. "Ava did what?" he asked half laughing.

Kerstin grinned slightly. "Not that long before you came to, Calam pissed her off, talking shit about you in a meeting. He wouldn't shut up even when William told him to and she flung a knife at his head," Kerstin finished somewhat plainly.

"I'm going to take a wild guess and say he's the one who was glaring at her the whole meeting?"

"Yep," Kerstin said, pouring himself another glass of juice.

Someone yawned at Aiden's side and sat down beside him. "Morning," Ava half yawned again, looking between him and Kerstin who gave a polite nod.

"Did you get your beauty sleep?" Aiden asked, finishing his juice and reaching across the table to grab a plate off the stack for her.

"Can you not tell? It is called beauty sleep," Ava muttered back, now piling pastries and eggs on her plate.

Aiden smirked, then looked to Kerstin. "Kerstin, may I introduce you to Ava. Ava, this is Kerstin."

Ava lifted her head and looked around Aiden. "Aren't you the general?" she asked.

Kerstin flicked the medal on his uniform. "I am."

"Hmm," Ava said and went back to eating her eggs.

"Ava, once you're done with breakfast we have to go talk to William," Aiden told her.

She nodded and poured herself a cup of coffee. Aiden returned to conversing with Kerstin for the remainder of the meal.

After finishing her food, Ava stood tapping a finger on Aidan's shoulder and jerked her chin towards William. "We should go," she said.

Aiden rose to his feet and so did Kerstin. The knight walked to Aiden's side and faced Ava who raised her brows. He stretched out a hand. She looked at it, then at Aiden who smiled. Ava grabbed it even though Aiden could tell she was fighting the urge not to roll her eyes.

"It was a pleasure to meet you," Kerstin told her. "And regardless of what our fellow council members say, I appreciate what you have done for Anglen."

Ava looked a little surprised but thanked him.

They made their way up to the table where William still sat, now engaged in conversation with Annalise. Spotting their approach, he stood and said something to the woman before walking around the table and down the few steps to meet them.

"Good morning," he said to the still sleepy looking Ava. "Aiden seemed to think that this was a conversation best taken in my study."

Ava nodded, looking more serious and glancing at Aiden. He could tell she was a bit nervous about telling William. To be fair, there was a chance that he would be pissed that they'd been back so long and Ava hadn't told him. Either way,

William led the way out of the great hall and into the entrance hall. Five minutes later they sat in William's study.

"Well, what is it?" William asked, looking between them.

Aiden looked at his feet for a moment not wanting to meet William's eyes. "We wanted to tell you the rest of the story of what happened in Orenth."

Williams' eyes narrowed and the old lines of his face hardened. "The rest?" he asked, looking at Ava.

It was Ava who answered the unspoken question. "I didn't understand it all and didn't want to tell you 'til Aiden woke up," she said, holding Williams' stare.

"So what is the rest of the story of Orenth?" he asked, looking back at Aiden with a nervous expression painted across his face.

"Do you remember the letter we sent you from Gloren?"

"Yes… you mentioned a skirmish with the Orenthian Navy and that there were some rumors of one with dark power." He said the last few words a little unsurely. "But what does that have to do with your time in Orenth?" he asked, returning to solidness.

Aiden was about to open his mouth to answer when Ava did so. "The rumor we told you about, it was true," she said bluntly.

William looked blankly for a moment. "True how?" he asked more urgently than before.

"True, as in the King of Orenth does have dark power." Aiden answered.

Ava pulled out a satchel he hadn't noticed she'd brought with her. Aiden and William both watched as she pulled the magic book out and flipped through it, stopping on a page. Ava cleared her throat and began to read:

BY FAR THE RAREST OF THE MAGICAL GIFTS, THE FORM OF MAGIC KNOWN AS RAW POWER NEITHER TAKES A FORM NOR HAS IT EVER PROVEN TO HAVE A LIMIT. UNLIKE OTHER TYPES OF MAGIC THAT ARE DEPLETED AS THEY ARE USED, AFTER WHICH THE WIELDER MUST THEN REST TO RECOVER THEIR GIFTS, WIELDERS OF RAW POWER HAVE NO KNOWN LIMIT TO THE FORCE THEY CAN UNLEASH. THOUGH THE MOST POWERFUL OF THE BRANCHES OF MAGIC, IT IS ALSO THE MOST VOLATILE. IT CAN NEITHER BE CONTAINED NOR BLOCKED. IT IS SYNTHESIZED IN THE FORM OF LIGHT OR DARKNESS, BOTH SAID TO BE COMPLETE IN THEIR EFFECT, EITHER THE LIGHT OF THE STARS THEMSELVES OR OF THE DARKNESS BETWEEN THEM.

William's face was impassive as he asked, "What do you mean to tell me by this?"

Ava met William's stare again. "He seems to meet this definition," she answered.

William said nothing for a moment and Aiden broke the silence. "Or at least he has the power, but we don't know how powerful it is," Aiden added before William could respond.

William opened his mouth and closed it again. He did so again and finally gestured for Ava to hand him the book. He set it on the desk before him and leaned forward. He read scanning back and forth over the pages as he flipped through. A minute went by, then another, and another. They sat in silence as William read. Aiden watched the clock beyond his desk, mind drifting to a more pleasant place in the cool southern spring.

William removed his hand from the page of the book and leaned back up straight in his chair. "Are you certain?" he asked Ava and Aiden.

Both nodded.

"And there's one more thing," Aiden said.

"What?" William asked sharply, looking at Aiden.

Aiden gulped. "So do I," he said softly.

"You do… what?" William asked, voice still sharp.

"He controls light," Ava said.

Aiden thought William might yell, but he just froze.

"William?" Ava asked, uncertainty lacing her voice.

Without warning the King sprang into motion. Standing from his seat, he half ran to the book shelf. Moving faster than Aiden had ever seen, he ran a finger along the titles, row after row of books. Not finding what he was looking for, he came back to his desk, and yanked open the drawers one at a time. With a noise of satisfaction, he halted his frantic searching. Moving in near reverence, he stood, an old slightly tattered book lay in his hands. He shifted his grip, holding the book more firmly and looking between them.

"Follow me," were his only words before breaking into a swift walk out of the study.

Aiden and Ava both scrambled slightly. Ava grabbed her bag and was hot on Aidens heels as they exited the room, following William. Twice Aiden tried to ask where they were going.

"You'll see," was William's response both times.

They reached the great hall and turned right down the corridor across from the great hall. They turned again, reached the end of the hall, and entered into a monumental atrium. It was three stories tall. The walls were lined with books, thousands, hundreds of thousands of them. Aiden would have stopped to spin around and admire the sight if it weren't for William continuing right to the front desk.

A slightly older woman stood at the round desk in the center of the massive room. "William," she said in a surprised greeting as they approached. "What can I do for you and…" she peered around him to Aiden and Ava. "Your friends?" she finished.

"Hello," William said. "I need you to take us to where we found this book." He held up the old leather bound volume for her to see.

"Of course," she said.

Walking through the gap in the round desk, she began to lead the way toward the back left side of the library where they came upon a reinforced door. She pulled a key from her pocket, fit it in the lock, and turned it. The lock gave a light click and she opened the door. They began down a long staircase leading down to a sort of catacombs of bookshelves and study desks. They were led a little way farther, delving deeper into the somewhat gloomy space before halting at one of the larger study areas.

"Here we are," the librarian said, turning to look back at them. "Can I help you look for anything in particular?"

"No, we'll be fine. Thank you, Errina," William said.

The librarian inclined her head before walking away back toward the staircase.

Aiden was about to ask why they'd come down here, but William opened the book. Flipping through the pages and finding the one he wanted, he handed it to Aiden. Glancing down at the page, Aiden could tell it was a story. Ava moved closer to his side, also looking down at the page. Aiden began to read. The story was short and it took him only moments to get the main idea. Aiden looked back up to William who now held a similar book in his hands.

"William?" Ava began. "You're not suggesting that this myth is what's happening?"

William didn't answer and just handed them another book. This one just had a picture depicting two people facing off, one wreathed in darkness, another in light.

"And how do we know if this is true at all?" Aiden asked. Ava echoed the question.

"We don't," William said without turning to them. "But on the off chance it is, I would rather we be informed on the topic."

"Wait wait wait!" Ava said, walking over to William and pushing down the book in his hands "Do you honestly think there's a chance that Aiden has the heart of a star?"

Aiden laughed. "Well, can't you tell?" he said in mock pride.

Ava and William both turned unamused expressions toward him.

"William, even if there is any chance that this is happening, what can we do to prepare? Aiden has no control over the power."

Aiden shivered at the words, remembering what had been happening when it did come out.

"Perhaps you are right. Maybe there is nothing to be done, but if there is, don't you think it's worth knowing?" William asked.

"Yes, of course. But war is upon us, and we have no allies. Even if this is true, it'll mean nothing if we all die in a battle we are unprepared for!" Ava retorted, voice growing into a near shout.

William continued to read, but he did look up after Ava's harsh response. "So, then, what do you propose we do?" he asked Ava, his voice rising in turn.

"We focus on the problem at hand, getting allies in this war we are about to have to fight!"

"And if this is the case? If the Orienthian King does have this power and we are unprepared for it, then what?"

Ava bared her teeth slightly. "Then it won't matter anyway because by that time Anglen will have fallen just like Attica." Her face seemed hollow at saying these words.

William stilled his frantic reading of the book.

Aiden stepped towards them. "What if you, William, along with whomever else, continue to study these books, learn all you can about their contents. In the meantime, Ava and I will go to Barataria and try to make an ally of the pirates."

William closed his eyes and looked to the ceiling for a long moment. He let out a sigh. "If this is all just leading to the doom of my people?" he asked, sounding older and more tired than Aiden had ever heard.

Ava grabbed his hand. "Then we walk to it proudly, and the people will too, just like my parents did," she said, solemnity filling the room.

Aiden touched William's shoulder consolingly.

"Very well," the old man said. "You two go, along with Annalise as my official emissary."

Ava nodded. "Ok then, shall we go get ready?" she asked.

"You two go. I'm going to read here for a while longer."

Ava nodded again, and letting go of William's hand, made her way toward the staircase. Aiden squeezed William's shoulder before following. Aiden met Ava at the base of the stairs.

"Thick and thin, and whatever else," she whispered softly as he approached. Standing on her tippy toes, she kissed him briefly before leading the way back up the stairs.

# CHAPTER 41

Aiden walked out the front gate of the castle and down the steps to the stables. The sun was warm and the air cool when he got there. He was able to spot some dark storm clouds building in the distance as he approached the stables. Ava stood next to Raith, bags and weapons already strapped to the black haired stallion.

"Morning!" she called over, offering a tight lipped smile as he approached and untied the reins of Spark who also was laden with extra weapons and supplies. Ava pulled herself astride and dawned her slightly dirty black cloak. Aiden followed suit. They began at a trot down to the gates of the castle grounds where they were set to meet Annalise. The storm clouds to the north were now swirling, and Ava groaned at the sight of them pouring rain down upon the road they would be traveling. Reaching the gates, they found Annalise dressed in a white and gold embroidered dress and matching cloak.

"Greetings!" she called to them, riding a chestnut horse, and jerked the reins for it to join them.

"I've been informed that I am to accompany you on our journey to Barataria. You are Aiden and Ava, is that correct?" she asked, riding beside them.

"We are, and that is," Ava said, offering a small smile to the woman.

"Good," she said. "Then I officially introduce myself. I am Lady Annalise, emissary to King William." She smiled.

"Aiden and Ava, knights of Anglen," Aiden said in response.

Annalise nodded and they rode in silence for a few minutes.

As they passed the inner gates of the city, Annalise spoke again. "I've arranged passage on one of William's ships for us. We will leave from Gloran."

Aiden turned his head to the woman. "We already have a ship," he said mildly.

"Oh, William didn't mention you charting one of his ships."

"We didn't," Ava said.

Annalise blinked. "What do you mean you didn't? We must arrive flying the official colors of Anglen," she said a little too sternly.

Ava turned her head to reply. "No, we don't and we won't. I've already written to a friend, and we will be traveling with him."

Annalise looked outraged. "And did you ask William if this is ok?"

"Nope," Ava said mildly.

"Then we must take the other ship," Annalise protested.

"Nope," Ava said again.

"We are traveling on official Anglen business and must act accordingly. So we will either go back and ask William, or we will take my boat!"

This seemed to have taken it too far for Ava who pulled back on the reins of her horse and turned to face the woman. "This is not some court matter. This is a mission, one you have been invited on."

"Excuse me, but I outrank you," Annalise tried to cut in.

But she was cut off as Ava continued, "And it is to me that the King of the Pirates owes a debt, not to you or William. So you will listen to Aiden and me on this mission!"

Annalise looked near to outrage as Ava flicked the reins and continued down the road out of Anglen. Aiden flicked his own reins to follow. He heard Annalise mutter something before flicking her own reins to come up beside them. They rode on in silence for a while. The sky darkened as the first drop of rain fell.

"Shall we make camp here?" Annalise asked, squinting up at the dark sky.

"Not yet," Ava said lightly.

"But it's about to rain," Annalise said in a tone of misunderstanding.

"You have a cloak," Aiden said, looking at her.

Annalise's eyes widened as she looked down at the thin white cloak. "This?" she said, a little panicked.

Aiden frowned at her and pulled out a second dirty black cloak from one of his bags. He tossed it to her. She held it in two fingers squinting at the dirt. She only put the cloak on when the rain started, and all three of them flipped their hoods on.

"So when are we going to make camp?" The Lady asked.

Aiden saw as Ava smirked in front of Annalise.

She replied, "We'll be getting on the ship tomorrow morning."

This time it was Annalise who stopped. "It's still a full day's ride to Gloran!" Panic was now clear in her voice.

"No," Ava said. "It's a full night's ride to Gloran."

Annalise tried to argue that they should make camp for a while but upon finding out that neither Aiden nor Ava had even brought a tent, she gave up. They rode through the night. The rain finally lifted near dawn, and they were able to see the expanding ocean in the distance as light finally graced the Earth.

Aiden flicked off his hood, took a deep breath, and tipped his head to the sky. "Hey, you guys wanna go get a quick breakfast at the restaurant on the way into town?"

Ava smiled warmly, flicking her cloak off her head.

"The one with free food," Aiden said as he pointed ahead to the restaurant.

"Where are we going that has free food?" Annalise asked, politely, though Aiden had a sneaking suspicion that she was more concerned with the safety of free food.

"Just to a restaurant. We're friends with the owner," Aiden said in answer.

Reaching the restaurant, they dismounted and led the horses to the small podium where the same women still stood.

"Hello," she said a little tensely.

"Could we get seated for breakfast?" Aiden asked, smiling politely

"Of course," she said and waved a hand to someone inside. Out came a young boy. "Feed and water our guests' horses," she told him. The boy walked over, taking each of the reins and led the horses out of sight around the edge of the building.

"Right this way," the woman said and shot one last nervous glance at Ava as she led them into the building and up to the second floor. They sat at the table overlooking the harbor. The receptionist handed out menus and left them with a polite dip of her chin.

"What are you going to have?" Annalise asked, looking up at Ava from her menu.

Ava hummed for a moment in thought before answering, "I think I'm going to get… the garlic fried grouper. And you?"

Annalise also looked down at her menu. "I think, the black salt scallops."

Aiden looked down at his own menu. He scanned both pages looking for biscuits but found none. "Hey Ava, do you see any biscuits and gravy on the menu?"

She scanned her own menu. "Nope, but I bet you can ask for some."

"You would really come to a place like this to order biscuits and gravy?" Annalise asked, looking at Aiden in surprise.

"I'm not a big fan of seafood in the morning," was his only reply.

The waiter arrived in few minutes. They ordered their food, Ava and Annalise both ordering fancy and expensive dishes and Aiden getting biscuits and eggs all covered in gravy. When they all finished their meals they made their way back down stairs.

"We're meeting Arlin at 11:00." Ava said, making for the door right as someone stopped in her path. The man towered feet above her as she looked up. A frown had already crossed her face, but disappeared the moment she realized who it was.

"Haven't seen you here in a while," he said. looking down to Ava and holding out a hand. She took it. "And you, Aiden," he said. Even through the peppering of small fighting scars, the man's smile was warm.

"It's good to see you, Draxon. We would stay but we're in a bit of a time crunch," Aiden said. The clock beyond Draxon's shoulder already read 9:40.

"Oh," the man said, looking a little put off.

"But next time," Ava cut in.

"Next time we'll have a rematch," Draxon nodded in understanding and the three of them moved to walk around him. "Hey, you two," he said, remembering something. "There's been talk of Anglen recruiting soldiers. Is that true?"

Aiden turned back. "We can't tell you anything but, as friends, be safe out there."

Draxon made a gruff noise of thanks and turned away, making back for the bar.

"What did it take for Arlin to agree to take us to Barataria?" Aiden asked lightly as they remounted their horses in the small stable at the side of the restaurant.

Ava reached in her pocket and, drawing out a silver coin, she flipped it to the stable hand. They rode out and onto the main street leading down to the harbor.

"I had to promise that you and I would give Zach a rematch," Ava replied.

Aiden laughed. "Well maybe he's been practicing."

"Practicing his shit talk," Ava shot back.

"What sort of competition is it that this Zach wants a rematch in?" Annalise asked, pulling up to ride beside them.

"He and his buddies challenged us to a friendly brawl last time we rode on Arlin's ship," Aiden answered.

"A friendly fight was the cost of passage across the ocean?" she asked, sounding a little disgusted at the idea.

"Not really," Ava said laughing. "It was more of a joke."

Aiden shook his head. "I bet Zach really does want a rematch though."

Ava made a noncommittal noise and shrugged. They passed the small inn next to the harbor. Aiden straightened in his saddle and strained trying to peer over the ships and people to spot the Sea Storm. Its sea green and red paint flickered in the light. Aiden pointed to it across the bay and they turned their horses. They were able to ride nearly to the docks, but with all the people they were forced to dismount and walk. Aiden and Ava led the way through the crowd. Annalise followed behind when someone called their names and they turned to look. They saw someone waving in the crowd. Aiden was able to make out the messy, spiky brown hair as Arlin's first mate approached them. Ava called over a greeting.

Zach hurried to catch up with them. "Are you three headed to the ship?" he asked. Ava nodded. "So am I," he said. "Follow me. I can get us through this pigsty faster."

He led as they made their way away from the crowded docks and walked along the side of the stone brick road and past the theater. The theater really was a magnificent structure. Hewn from stone, it towered up into a peaked roof.

"Is this where that message was painted?" Aiden whispered to Zach.

"Yeah... It was a shame. The theater's perhaps Gloran's most wonderful experience. They hire people from all over the world to do shows."

Ava pushed by a person walking the other way in her haste to join the conversation. "Have you ever been?" she asked Zach eagerly.

He nodded smiling faintly. "A few times, as a child. I grew up on Arlin's ship. His father raised me on it along with Arlin and his sister. His father used to take the three of us to see a show every time we visited Gloran."

The Sea Storm finally broke into view as they rounded a bend in the road that encompassed the bay. Ava sped up her pace, tugging a mildly protesting Raith along in her haste to get to the ship. Aiden joined her. They tied their horses at hitching rail on the dock before walking along the reinforced plank to get aboard. The deck was neater than Aiden expected as he surveyed it. It was stocked with more than a few barrels of what smelled like rum. Aiden could see crates of more liquor piled against the far wall. Zach grasped him on the shoulder and turned him around. He was grinning toothily as he surveyed him and Ava for the first time fully, now out of the crowds

"My favorite overconfident sailor!" Ava crooned as she smiled and wrapped her arms around him briefly. Aiden did the same.

"Arlin's in his office," Zach said to Ava's unasked question.

They walked over to the head of the ship, Annalise keeping close as they opened the door and walked to the end of the short hall and into Arlin's study. He didn't look up from the papers on his desk. They only could see his messy red hair for a moment before Arlin noticed them and looked up. His eyes widened at the sight of them, and he smiled warmly as he came around the desk and hugged the two of them.

"You two are looking well," he said, stepping back and taking a better look at them.

"Only better than you," Ava said curtsying.

"Well, I certainly hope you don't look like a rag tag pirate from the edge of the world, Princess."

Ava laughed.

"So how'd things go after we dropped you two off in Avalon?" Arlin asked.

Aiden frowned briefly. "Not so well... but I think that's a story for another day," he replied.

The captain gave him a questioning look but nodded."And who's this?" he said, holding out a scar flecked hand to Annalise.

"Lady Annalise of Anglen," she said as she dipped into a small courtesy before shaking his hand.

Arlin inclined his head. "We'll leave as soon as all the cargo is loaded," he said and made for the door. The three of them followed him out onto the deck where the crew was still loading more rum and other crates onto the deck while still others brought them below. Some of the men flashed smiles at

Aiden as they walked by loading the ship and readying the sails.

Zach walked aboard. Leading Raith and Spark by the reins, he tugged them along. Spark walked calmly down below deck, but Raith pulled back. Ava swore, running over to help Zach as Raith tried his best to throw the man into the water. Aiden and Arlin both bent over laughing as Ava grabbed the reins and tried to calm Raith down. But the horse just kept bucking and neighing at the plank. Aiden reached into the bag at his waist and pulled out an apple.

"The noble knight," Arlin crooned still laughing as Ava struggled and swore violently at the horse. Aiden griped the apple in both hands as he walked over and with a sharp movement he snapped the apple in half. He held out one piece of apple to the protesting animal. Raith stopped fighting. The horse's nose fluttered and his eyes flicked to the apple. Aiden held it before the horse and smiled. The horse stretched his neck trying to get the apple but Aiden stepped back. The horse's eyes narrowed and it huffed, stepping forward and reaching for the apple again. Aiden led the horse all the way onto the deck of the ship before finally giving him the apple. The horse snatched the apple and with a last huff followed Spark down below deck.

Aide turned back to Ava smirking. She stuck out her tongue as she walked back over to Arlin. Aiden broke the remaining part of the apple in half and tossed a quarter to her.

"I'm glad to see that even the mighty Ava struggles with something now and then," Arlin said, still chuckling.

"The men are ready," Zach announced a little more seriously. They followed Arlin and the mate to the helm of the ship where the captain called for the men to begin rowing. The ship gave a slight lurch as all the men now seated heaved on their oars and they pulled into motion towards the mouth of the port.

"So what's the real favor you need for getting us to Barataria so quickly?" Aiden asked, standing at the captain's side.

"Only the fight with Zach and his buddies," Aiden scoffed slightly. "I'm just happy to have an emissary on the boat. This way I get to trade with the pirates and their law prevents them from trying to raid my ship."

"So that's the real reason," Aiden said, nudging Arlin's shoulder.

"And that I like having you guys around," he retorted, grinning. They stood in silence for a little while watching the edge of the bay loom closer.

"Drop the sail!!" Arlin shouted to the crew who ceased their rowing and moved to follow the order. The boat lurched again, harder, as the wind pressed against Aiden's cheeks and the small waves started to clap against the hull of the boat.

"So what really happened in Orenth?" Arlin asked lowly.

Aiden grimaced. "Your word that none will hear what I tell you?" Aiden whispered back.

Arlin nodded.

Aiden sighed, "We got to Orenth and made our way north to the mountains. Then we followed a road up through them for a while. Some soldiers passed by and we overheard them talking about a fortress." Aiden shifted on his feet and moved to rest his arms on the rail of the helm.

"We followed the path 'til we heard noises in the distance. We hid the horses and went to investigate. That night we snuck into the fortress and got close enough to hear what was happening in the great hall. The Orenth King was there." Aiden stopped again and Arlin waited for a moment.

"What happened?" the captain asked, more gently than usual.

"They found us. When I woke up, I was tied to a post. They whipped me bloody before hauling Ava out," Aiden explained as he watched Arlin shutter out of the corner of his eye.

"How'd you get out of there?" Arlin asked.

Aiden debated lying. "We... I... Magic," he began, not having really made up his mind.

This time Aiden sensed it as Arlin turned his head toward him, taking a small step back and causing the ship to wobble slightly as he turned the wheel.

"Magic, like the stuff that died out centuries ago, in myths?"

Aiden nodded solemnly.

"Well, Gods damn!" Arlin swore, raising a hand to his brow and wiping it.

Hours later and after a long nap in their cabin, Ava awoke to find that the storm clouds from the previous night finally broke and the warm sun shone down onto the deck. Aiden and Arlin were still perched on the helm watching as the crew sprawled across the deck playing cards and basking in the good weather. Ava walked out onto the deck, an open wine bottle in hand, as she spun on her feet and caught sight of Aiden. She gestured for him to come down. She turned again, walking over to plop down on a coil of loose rope next to Zach and the others playing cards.

"Go!" Arlin half crooned at Aiden, giving him a light nudge with his elbow. Aiden stood, walking down the steps and over to the group where he sat and slumped against the rope pile at Ava's side.

"You guys still owe us a rematch," Zach said in a somewhat mocking taunt.

Ava hummed. "I don't much feel like fighting but... I could be persuaded to play a game of cards," she said .

Aiden had to fight the urge to laugh at the confident look on Zach's face.

"You're on, what're the terms?" asked the first mate.

Ava hummed again, taking another swig of the wine. "How 'bout this?" she proposed, handing the bottle to Aiden. "The loser has to get up in the center square of Barataria and shout whatever the winner decides."

Zach's eyes narrowed for a moment, but he stuck out his hand. Ave grasped it and gave a too gentle shake. Zach gestured to the man shuffling the deck of cards, and he dealt the cards out between the two of them. Ava picked up her cards and, looking at them, she nearly coughed.

Zach smirked. "Not liking your chances now princess?"

Zach was still cursing fifteen minutes after the end of the game when Aiden and Ava walked below deck. They went to the end of the hall, reaching the oak door. Ava raised her hand and tapped lightly with the back of her knuckles.

"Who is it?" Annalise called softly from the other side of the door.

"Aiden and me," Ava called back.

They heard footsteps on the other side of the door, and with a scraping noise, the door swung open.

"What is it?" Annalise asked, stepping out now dressed in a black and gold tunic.

"You should come up to the deck. The sun's out and food'll be ready soon."

Annalise looked at Aiden, and her brows rose."You want me to go and socialize with the sailors on deck?"

Ava huffed. "We're gonna be on this ship for at least two weeks. There's nothing that can be done to shorten the trip so you might as well get used to it."

Annalise's brows remained high.

"Oh come on, Zach's going to want a rematch after the game of cards he just played with Ava," Aiden said, trying to convince her. "You can watch."

"For a short while only," she agreed, still looking skeptical.

The three of them walked back up onto the deck. Zach stood near the mast and glared at Ava as they emerged. Ava winked and Aiden led the way back over to the group playing cards. Arlin called down from the helm, telling Zach to get the food from the cook below deck. Zach flashed an unamused expression up to Arlin.

"Oh that's nothing compared to what you're going to have to do later," Ava said, grinning mischievously as Zach moved away. The sailor flashed her a rude gesture and the people around them laughed.

"Well you really got him riled up," another of the sailors said, grinning.

"I suppose so," Ava said casually.

Annalise finally sat down on the edge of one of the crates, her posture clearly more stiff and formal than any of the others.

"But just think about how he's gonna feel when he finds out about this," she said and pulled out a white card.

Aiden had to stifle a laugh. A red two gleaned in the corner of the small piece of thick paper. The group bent over as one, laughing. Aiden heard Annalise's gasp. Ava grinned wider and gave as much of a bow as she could, sitting with her legs crossed.

"You cheated?!" Annalise barked. But even she couldn't hold back a small huff as they all looked at the card.

"Well, I mean, I feel like it's more on him," Ava chided. "He did agree to play cards. But I never agreed to play fairly."

Zach walked back on deck and the group hushed. In his hands he held a pot and a stack of wooden bowls.

"Lunch!" he yelled, setting the pot on the crate beside Annalise and handing out bowls.

Coming to Ava he held out a bowl and she smoothly slipped the card into his now empty hand. He stared at it for a long moment. Ava shifted, turning slightly where she sat so the mast was no longer at her back. She rolled over backwards and stood.

"You...?" Zach began to say, confused.

"Cheated!" Ava finished for him.

Zach's eyes widened.

"Couldn't leave without that fight," Ava said, smirking as she unstrapped her weapons and tossed them at the base of the mast. She rolled her neck and took off her loose over shirt.

"You guys doing a team fight or just you two?" Aiden asked, looking over at Ava.

"Just us," Zach answered.

Though he sounded angry he was grinning as he pulled off his own shirt to reveal a large, faintly sea green dragon tattooed across his back. The tail of the beast wrapped around his middle and below his hip. Looking at him now, Aiden noticed just how much bigger Zach was than before. He'd been nearly skinny the last they saw each other. But now he stood nearly as wide as Arlin. His bare chest gleamed faintly with sweat as he shrugged his shoulders and raised his fists.

"Loser owes the winner two kegs of their favorite alcoholic beverage!" Arlin shouted.

"I wouldn't mind two kegs of Barataria's finest," Ava said.

Aiden moved out of their way and leaned against the crate at Annalise's feet. "This'll be fun," he said, wiggling into a more comfortable position and resting an arm behind his head.

A few of the others also moved to find better places to watch.

"Let's dance," Ava muttered and she lunged forward fist raised. She swung faster than Aiden had expected. Zach leapt back. Ava did the same and stood, hands half raised, waiting for him to attack. He did and she swung up an arm, deflecting the below upwards. In that moment, Zach left his lower body unprotected. Ava buried her knee in between his legs. Zach dropped to his knees and was now positioned lower than her. She slammed a fist into his face and jumped back. Zach let out a slightly choked noise and didn't rise from his knees. Ava not sparing a glance, faced the small assembled crowd on the ship and bowed, flourishing her arms flamboyantly. Aiden shook his head grinning as he chuckled under his breath.

Ava bowed again to the other side of the group. Aiden looked behind her to Zach who stood suddenly. Everyone stopped their applause and Ava's face snapped into a confused expression. She turned, looking for the source. She had turned just in time for Zach to be face to face with her as he slipped a foot behind her legs and pushed her over. Ava gasped in surprise as she fell. She hit the ground and scrambled to get up, but Zach swung an arm and his elbow connected with her unprotected face. A few people, including Annalise and Aiden, cringed at the blow. Zach slipped an arm around her throat and locked it with his other. Ava thrashed and, picking up her legs, she pushed against the mast. They both went flying backwards. Zach's back hit the deck. He groaned in pain, but his grip held strong. Aiden watched as Ava's face grew red, then purple. She looked nothing short of rageful as she patted Zach's leg and he let go.

Zach stood and grinned with all his white teeth as Ava bent over on her hands and knees coughing. Aiden couldn't help it as he bent over laughing. He thumped the deck with his hand

and the rest of the crew watching joined in. Annalise raised a hand to her mouth trying to hide her chuckling.

"I look forward to receiving my kegs," Zach crooned as he walked over to the open water barrel and began washing away the blood smeared across his face. It took Ava a minute for her coughing to subside. When it did Aiden was still bent over laughing. She stood and walked over to the pot of soup and grabbed two bowls of the sweet smelling liquid. Ava handed one to Aiden. She looked thoroughly unamused as she sat beside him and took a sip.

"I take it that is not how you intended for the fight to go?" Annalise asked, still seated on the crate beside the pot.

"No," Ava said flatly, sitting across from Aiden leaning against the mast.

Aiden craned his neck looking up at Annalise. "She was expecting to wipe the floor with him."

Aiden looked back down at his soup and lifting the bowl he went to take a sip right as someone grabbed the bowl and forced it up into his face. The hot liquid splashed and covered him. By the time he'd wiped his eyes, Ava had already sat back in her spot against the mast and was giggling. Aiden could hear Annalise and the others laughing too.

Aiden licked the hot soup from his lips. "My compliment's to the chef!"

# Chapter 42

"How long do you think it'll take to get to Barataria?" Ava asked later that night as they lay on the deck near the front of the ship.

"I don't know, maybe two weeks," Aiden said. One of the clouds above them shifted and the deck was cast into moonlight. He raised his arm, and using his finger, traced its outline. "What's the plan when we get there?" he asked, still pointing at the sky.

Ava sighed. "Well, assuming none of the pirates stop us before we can get to the bay, we'll stop there and ask to see Drake Jagger."

Aiden finished tracing the outline of the moon and turned his head to Ava. "Will he recognize you?"

Ava made an unsure noise. "Probably not... but his son will." Ava shifted to lean her head against him. "And after we get back to Anglen? Then what?" she asked in turn.

Aiden sighed long and deep. "Then... then we'll see. Maybe Orenth will back down if we're able to get enough allies to defend."

"And if they don't?" Ava said, meeting Aiden's eyes. "Do we fight?"

"Do you want to?" he asked slowly, a feeling of uneasiness seeming into his thoughts. He was most loyal to her, yes. But he was loyal to William too, and if they conflicted...

Ava looked back to the sky. "We took an oath, and all our friends live there. I say we fight."

Aiden nodded, that weight lightening. "We'll fight then," he agreed.

Ava laughed softly. "How's it that we went from strangers in a backwater town in Anglen to this?"

Aiden chuckled. "That is a good question." His stomach growled. "I miss Phil's cooking," he said.

With a tired groan, Ava stood up and said, "I'm going to bed."

Aiden glanced at her before returning to looking at the star speckled sky. "I'll be in, in a little bit," he said faintly.

Ava nodded and walked away down the deck. Aiden listened as her footsteps faded and the only noise became the slight breeze and the slapping of the waves against the hull. The stars twinkled and the clouds once again moved to cover the moon. He sat, resting his head against the bracing at the prow of the ship, and continued to watch the clouds above, mind oddly blank…

His first thought before opening his eyes was panic as something cold and wet splashed on his face. He opened his eyes, whorling. He was still sitting on the front of the deck and a small crowd of sailors were surrounding him. Arlin stood among them with an empty bucked tucked under his arm.

"What the hell!" Aiden cried out, scrambling to his feet and glaring at Arlin who seemed to be trying not to laugh.

"Last person up gets splashed," he said and the assembled crowd spread apart. Aiden shook the water off his arms, cursing under his breath, and began walking back to the door leading down to the cabins. As he neared the door, the handle turned and out walked Annalise. She yawned, stifling it with her hand before looking at Aiden. She looked him up and down before returning her gaze to his face.

"Did you fall overboard!?" she asked, sounding throughly worried.

"No," Aiden said flatly and, sidestepping her, he walked down to the cabin. Ava was sitting on the bed reading the magic book. It took her a second to look up from her book. "Oh!" she said in surprise. "Arlin really wasn't kidding! He dumped the bucket of water on you?"

Aiden gave her another unamused look. Ava smirked and reached into the backpack sitting at the side of the bed. She tossed a fresh set of clothes to him. He changed, pulling off the sodden salt smelling clothes and replacing them with the fresh ones that smelled faintly of the small jar of honey Ava had snuck from the castle kitchens.

"What do you think about us giving Annalise a little run down before we get to Barataria?" Aiden asked, fastening the belt of the fresh pants and looking up to Ava.

She set the book in her lap. "What do you mean?"

"Well, from what you've told me, it sounds like a violent place. Don't you think it would be best for her to know a little more about how to negotiate her way out of a conflict?"

"Hmm," she said and tilted her head to look at Aiden's bag sitting against the wall.

Following her gaze, he found the bag. He unfastened the top buckle and snatched out a slender dagger. "We have this and neither of us are using it," he said, showing her the dagger.

"All right then," she said and hopped up from the bed.

She grabbed the knife right out of Aiden's hand and made for the deck. Aiden followed. The deck was loosely scattered with sailors all trying to get breakfast. Some were still yawning as they stood in line before the fresh pot that had been set on the crate. Annalise stood near the front of the line. Ava leaned against the wall connected to the helm. When Annalise exited the line, she walked over to the side of the ship where she sat on another crate and prepared to eat breakfast. Aiden walked over, Ava keeping at his side.

"Good morning," Ava said tentatively as they approached.

"All dry now?" Annalise asked.

"Yeah... Arlin dumped a bucket of water on me for *sleeping in,*" Aiden admitted.

Always wanting to find a rationale, Annalise commented, "I think that was just because they found you asleep with how they were joking about it after you left."

"Anyway," Ava cut in, seeming to sense Aiden's growing annoyance. "We want to teach you some stuff before we get to Barataria."

Annalise raised her eyebrows.

"Here," Ava said and held out the dagger.

"And what am I supposed to do with that?" she asked, not taking it.

"You are supposed to learn how to use it," Ava answered, clearly a little annoyed that she hadn't taken it.

"And why would I need to learn how to fight?" she asked again, her voice still smooth and calm.

"Because..." Ava began.

But Aiden cut in, "Because we don't think that the people we're likely to meet there are as willing to talk their way out of conflict as you are. It would make both of us feel a lot better if you were more than dead weight in that case." Aiden finished.

Annalise's brows rose higher. "Are you expecting that we will be attacked?"

"No," Aiden said a little too quickly.

"But it is a possibility," Ava said, seeming to have reined in the temper that rose any time she had to speak with the emissary.

Annalise looked between them and didn't answer for a long moment. "Allow me to finish my food, then we will train in… whatever way you see fit."

Aiden and Ava both ate their own food sitting at the front of the boat and watched the waves in the distance. When they returned to the main deck of the ship, it was to find Annalise now dressed in a fine, light blue tunic that looked like it cost its weight in silver.

"I'm ready," she said as they approached. She was smiling but stopped abruptly at a look from Ava.

"Do you care about those clothes?" Ava asked.

Annalise looked a little affronted and looked down to survey herself. "Yes."

"Then you might want to change into something you care a little less about." Aiden said, moving to sit back on the crate beside the pot.

Annalise tried to reply, but Ava snapped back and five minutes later Annalise emerged wearing an old and slightly ragged tunic of Ava's. "Now am I dressed adequately?" she asked, visibly annoyed.

Aiden nodded.

"I'll start," Ava said.

Aiden took one look at the expression covering Ava's face and insisted that he be the one to teach Annalise first, t help her survive Ava's turn if nothing else.

"Can I have the knife?" Aiden asked.

Annalise handed it over. Aiden threw it, and it stuck into the mast. He walked to a small pile of scrap wood sitting on the edge of the deck and pulled out two pieces about the size of the knife. He tossed one to her and walked back to face her.

"Well, here goes," Aiden began. "You just try to defend and get away. Sound good?"

Annalise nodded and stood tall holding the stick before her.

"Bend your knees," Ava said from her perch on the crate.

Annalise did so, and without further warning, Aiden attacked. Moving slower than he usually would, he slashed with the stick. Annalise gasped and raised her own stick in a half hearted block and stumbled back. Aiden stepped back and returned to a casual standing position.

Annalise stood, an indignant rage flickered across her face as she began to yell. "I wasn't ready!! Ava had just told me to bend my knees and...!" She held her arms tensely at her sides while she yelled and gripped the stick so tightly her knuckles went white. Annalise ceased her yelling after a minute, a little out of breath and causing most of the crew to glance over to see what was happening.

"Well, do you have anything to say for yourself?" she demanded of him.

Aiden casually crossed his arms holding them in front of him. "If I were an attacker, how would you have fought?" he asked, keeping his voice steady and calm.

"And what does that have to do with you just lunging at me?" she hissed, still looking livid.

"I am an attacker," Aiden said simply and he threw the stick at her before charging.

Annalise again screamed but raised the stick in time for it to make contact with Aiden's chest before they both tumbled to the ground. This time when they both had risen Annalise walked squarely up to Aiden, looked up at him for a long moment lost for words, and punched him. He let her, and a small trickle of blood ran from his nose.

"Well, there's no need to do that," he said, pinching the bridge of his nose and tilting his head back.

"No... No need!" she shouted.

Ava chuckled from the crate.

Annalise wheeled to her. "And what's so funny?"

Ava held a hand out gesturing to Aiden. He laughed softly before tipping his head back forward. He released his nose and unbuttoned the few buttons near the neck of his shirt. Annalise watched, her mouth pressed into a thin line, as Aiden stretched the collar of his shirt to reveal a red and purple mark on the left side of his chest.

"Ava's laughing, because if I were an attacker... I'd be dead." He finished pointing to the stick now left forgotten on the ground.

The next week of the trip was filled with more training, which Annalise slowly grew more adept at. Aiden and Ava trained together every morning. Arlin or Zach occasionally joined them. They switched to training Annalise when she eventually came above deck. Once Annalise's lesson was over, they ate breakfast, sometimes eggs, sometimes porridge. Arlin steadily taught Aiden more and more of the workings of the ship as they stood together at the helm while Arlin steered. The inconsistent weather of southern fall broke into warm cloudless skies of the northern equator. Warm breezes blew and the crew started shedding layers of clothing, eventually shifting to doing their duties shirtless. Still every day, the temperature grew.

Aiden's sword whined as it scraped against the edge of Ava's, and a bead of sweat dripped from his chin. He was forced to jump back as Arlin's elbow barreled toward him. Arlin's movement distracted him and Ava's foot connected with his ribs. At the same time, Arlin knocked into Aiden, throwing him off balance. Ava was still advancing on Arlin. She lifted her leg to kick him. In the moment she stood on one leg, Aiden now on the ground, swept her other. She came crashing down, and they all groaned and writhed from the respective impacts. Aiden was the first to get up and offer a hand to the other two. Someone shouted from the head of the ship, and Arlin rubbed at his ribs as he moved to answer. Aiden and Ava followed, making their way past the crates where Aiden grabbed his discarded shirt. He pulled the loose, white fabric over his head, covering the one lasting jagged scar across his back.

"What is it?" Arlin asked, reaching the young sailor who hung out from one of the bracing ropes. The sailor stood leaning out over the turquoise sea.

"There, right over there, Arlin," he said, and Aiden could detect a northern accent. The sailor pointed a finger out toward the blue green expanse.

Arlin squinted and the sailor handed him a brass and walnut telescope. Arlin extended it and looked.

"You see the mushroom shaped rock? That's the first bit of the Balearic Archipelago."

"And?" Arlin asked, having fixed the telescope on a point on the horizon,

"Barataria is half a day's travel past it. We'll be there tomorrow morning," the sailor explained.

Arlin grinned and handed the telescope back to the man. He turned back to Aiden and Ava. "You two ready to have some fun?" They grinned back.

Arlin walked past them and shouted to the deck, "Ready the ship! We arrive at first light!" Then he walked over to the front most mast and untied a knot, dropping the sail the sail farther.

The young sailor jumped down from his perch and made for the helm.

"I'll go let Annalise know to start getting things ready," Ava said, walking away.

Aiden made his way back to the cabin and slowly began packing their bags. When all their belongings were packed, he took his weapons back to the deck and found a nice spot overlooking the sea to work. He pulled a small stone from the pouch he'd brought and, dipping it in the bucket of water beside him, he began to sharpen. Ava came by at some point and handed over her weapons too, smiling toothily as he looked at them, and with a sigh, he grabbed them too. He slowly made his way through, honing each edge and resheathing it. He even managed to sharpen the precisely shaped blade of the dagger Ava kept strapped to her forearm. He popped it back into its sheath frequently, checking not to change the resistance of the holding mechanism. It wouldn't do for the blade to fall out of the sheath randomly.

The day seemed to slip by as he sat there ensuring that each weapon was as sharp as the day it was made. The sea only seemed to grow more turquoise throughout the day and slipped into a greenish blue as the sun fell, casting the ship into orange light.

"Here," someone said to his side. He looked up to where Ava held out a bowl. He grabbed it, and she sat beside him with another bowl sitting in her lap. Aiden took a bite of the warm stew and looked over the water to the distant land mass that had appeared at the end of the archipelago.

"Are you ready?" Ava asked calmly.

Aiden took a long moment to answer. "I think so, but you'd know better," he answered.

Ava blew on her stew. "I think you are."

They both sat and ate for a moment, Aiden picking out the bits of beef to eat first.

"Do you really think it'll go smoothly?" he asked and set down his bowl to lean back on his palms.

"With the pirates? No," Ava answered. "Drake Jagger won't want to help us. He doesn't want to help anyone. It'll just be a matter of whether or not he honors the debt."

"And if he doesn't?" Aiden asked in equal calm.

"What will we do?" Ava sighed and leaned back against one of the crates. "Well, you did spend all day sharpening our weapons."

Aiden chuckled. "So... what? We fight our way through the biggest pirate stronghold in the world?"

# CHAPTER 43

Someone banged on the door. "Up, ya love birds!" Zach called through the door.

The two of them rolled out of the bed. They dressed in silence, Aiden tucking his knife into his boot and Ava pulling on a long sleeve shirt to conceal the knife strapped to her forearm. They sheathed their swords and left the room. Aiden opened the door to the deck and was met by the warm yellow glow of dawn. It leached into his face and he took a deep breath, closing his eyes. When he opened his eyes again Ava was walking to the head of the ship. The turquoise expanse of Barataria Bay lay beyond. The two great towers at the entrance of the bay gleamed. Aiden could see the glint of steel off the arrows lodged in the ballistas on each. Aiden followed to the head of the ship.

"Raise the main sail!" Arlin called from the front.

Aiden felt the ship slow in the water. They glided past the two great towers and into the bay. Aiden reached Ava at the front and poked his head over the edge of the ship.

"Well, that's inviting," he said jokingly and pointed over the edge to the sea bottom littered with broken ships.

Ava looked for a long moment and didn't answer.

Aiden stepped beside her. "You ok?" he asked gently.

"I..." She shifted on her feet. "Was this a good idea?" she asked, seeming resigned to the truth that it wasn't.

Aiden wrapped a hand around her shoulders. "If it isn't, then I'm here to help fight our way out."

Ava smiled slightly, still looking at the fast approaching dock.

"Thick and thin, and whatever else," he said even more softly.

A few minutes later they and Zach stood at the side of the ship as it slid into place along the dock. A few of the sailors hopped over to the dock and secured the ship. Zach set the plank against the dock and the three of them walked down. Arlin joined them a moment later along with the young sailor with the accent.

"So what now?" Aiden asked, looking between Arlin and Ava.

"We wait," Arlin said gruffly.

"For, what?" Aiden asked cautiously.

"Since we weren't flying a pirate flag coming in, they're gonna send someone to come check who we are."

"And how…?" Aiden began.

He stopped as a group of five men came walking down the dock. The men were all dressed in similar coats, swords hung at their sides. The one in the center wore a slightly tattered tricorn. The man grinned as he approached and a single gold tooth glinted.

Arlin stepped forward and announced, "We're here with an official emissary of Anglen."

The man's grin faltered and he stopped a few feet from Arlin. "And why has an emissary of Anglen come here?" the man asked, sneering as he looked between the five of them.

"For me," Ava said stepping forward. "I'm here for an audience with Drake Jagger."

The pirate's sneer disappeared and he grimaced. "Might I ask why it is that Mr. Jagger would have any interest in you?"

Ava stared right back at the man as she answered, "No, you may not."

The man bared his teeth, gold tooth glinting. The pirate to his right rested a hand on the hilt of the rusted sword. It curved more than an Anglish blade, broad across the belly and clipped at the tip. He rested a hand on the pommel at his side. The man took a step closer to Ava.

Aiden stepped between them, flashing his best under pressure smile. "How about..." he said, raising his hands as the men's attention shifted to him, "We all just take a breath? You guys can give Mr. Jagger a heads up that we're in the area and looking for an audience."

He paused, looking to see what the men's reaction was. They said nothing and he continued, "And in the meantime, we'll stay here, make ourselves at home on the ship, and wait to hear from you."

The man's teeth slowly disappeared behind his lips and he stepped back. The pirate at his right moved to hold his hands behind him. The gold toothed man finally nodded and without another word all five of them turned leaving the dock.

The ship was tense that night when they ate dinner. The shallow din of the bay and city beyond were audible, yet the crew ate in silence. Arlin had returned to his study right after the pirates left. Ava had gone to sleep in their cabin , as had Annalise. Aiden sat alone on one side of the deck, the remainder of the crew was scattered across the it. Aiden watched as the young sailor with the accent ate at the head of the ship. The young man just sat there overlooking the city. His shoulders were slumped, and he didn't touch the bowl of food sitting on the taffrail. Aiden didn't quite know why, but he stood and moving casually he went to sit beside the man. The man's head jerked to the side and he gasped as Aiden sat beside him.

"It's just me," Aiden said one hand raised in dismissal.

The young man sighed. "Is everything ok?" he asked softly, returning his gaze to the city.

"Is everything ok with you?" Aiden asked.

The sailor looked at him. "What do you mean?" he asked suspiciously.

Aiden glanced at the city. "You haven't looked away from that place since we got back on the ship."

The man frowned. "And what is it to you?" he asked again.

Aiden looked back at the city. "You've been lookin' at that tavern the whole time," Aiden said and pointed to a small wooden building at the corner of one of the streets. Aiden looked back to the man and noticed that his face colored as he looked back at the tavern.

The two of them sat in silence for a long moment before Aiden once again spoke. "I'm Aiden," he said plainly.

"I know," he said.

The man didn't continue, and Aiden didn't think he was going to. Figuring he'd made him uncomfortable enough, Aiden moved to stand. He was reaching down for his bowl to leave when the man spoke.

"The tavern, it's my brother's."

Aiden stilled, looking at him with curiosity.

The sailor continued. "I left Barataria as soon as my debts were paid, and… he didn't."

Aiden sat back down. "Is he still here?" Aiden asked softly.

The man sighed. "If he's alive, he's here. Nothing would have gotten him to leave. He loved it too much, didn't care to see the rest of the world like me." He looked back, seeming to have forgotten something. "I'm Jacques, by the way."

Aiden smiled faintly and held out his hand. Jacques shook it, meeting Aiden's eyes before looking back to the city.

"Are you gonna go see him?" Aiden asked.

Jacques laughed sardonically. "I can't."

"Why not?"

Jacques pointed to the biggest and grandest of the inns just beyond the center of the dock. "I was born here and left. I haven't paid tribute in years. The moment I step off the docks and onto the land, I'll be arrested."

Aiden raised his brows. "Aren't you going to come with us to go see this Jagger?"

Jacques shook his head.

"But we'll be with an official emissary. They're not allowed to arrest you."

Jacques chuckled again and reached for his bowl. "You really don't know much about Barataria do you?"

The night seemed to warm as Aiden sat there beside Jacques. "Only what I've been told by Ava and Arlin," he admitted.

"Barataria doesn't really play by everyone else's rules. It's a power and a people unto itself."

Aiden looked up to the big inn on the hill. "Is Jagger a fair ruler?" Aiden asked plainly.

Jacques cocked his head as he too looked at the inn for a long moment.

"If he considers you one of his own, if you're born here or somehow earn your place here, then he just might be the most devoted ruler I've ever known," Jacques replied. He took the last few bites from his food and stood. "I'll see you tomorrow. I doubt we'll hear anything for a day or two."

Aiden nodded distantly and kept looking over the city for a long while before he too stood to go to bed. The next morning Aiden woke to the feeling of dirty fabric hitting his face. He leaned up in bed and pulled the black traveling cloak off his face.

"Put that on," Ava said as she dressed in her usual clothes and thin leather chest plate.

Aiden blinked with drowsiness and rubbed at his eyes. "What for?" he asked, yawning. Ava didn't answer and Aiden groaned. "Are you about to get us in trouble?" he asked as Ava strapped on her weapons. She still didn't answer.

A few minutes later they were both dressed and armed. Ava opened the door to the hall more gently than he'd expected. He followed her down the hall and up the stairs to the door. She opened the door and they walked out. Aiden blinked again. The moon still hung high in the sky. Both the city and bay were cast in soft pale light.

Aiden looked to Ava then at the city. "No," he said flatly.

Ava frowned.

"Nope, I'm not gonna do it," he said and crossed his arms.

Ava crossed her arms too, looking a little amused if nothing else. She opened her mouth to speak but Aiden cut her off shaking his head.

"You didn't even let me try to convince you," she argued.

"I know," Aiden said, looking her straight in the eyes. "It was intentional. I don't want to be convinced."

"But if…" she began, but stopped as Aiden turned to go back to their room.

"I want to sleep," he said with his hand on the door when something hard hit his head and cold liquid splashed down his back.

"Ow!" he yelled, turning back to where Ava stood.

She had one hand held before her and the other covered her mouth as she tried not to laugh. "My bad.." she said as Aiden took a step towards her, an unamused expression etched across his face.

"I didn't realize the bowl had water in it." She gave up the act to try to hide laughing and grinned at him. "Come on… Don't make me go alone," she pleaded, still grinning.

Aiden groaned again. "What do you want to do?" He asked, resigned to the fact he was not going to get his full night of sleep.

She just flashed a feral smile and vaulted the side of the ship down to the dock. Aiden followed, vaulting the railing and landing on the dock. They both pulled up the hoods of their cloaks. Ava led the way at a brisk walk to the end of the dock and up a side street. Even at night the city was hot. Aiden could feel sweat running down his body under the thick fabric of the cloak, though it could have been the water Ava had thrown on him. Ava rounded the side of one of the buildings and peered up the main street.

"Anything?" Aiden whispered at her shoulder.

"Nope," she said and, at a more casual gate, she began walking up the street. They repeated this up street after street, always breaking off onto side streets before reaching people or to avoid bright lights. Ava still didn't tell him where they were going, but he had a pretty good idea when they stopped at the end of one of the small side streets and ducked behind a pile of crates someone had left at a back door. Aiden poked his head around the crates and surveyed the inn at the top of the hill. Beyond the end of the alley was the courtyard of the inn. A few people sat slumped against things, talking or half asleep, clearly drunk.

"I take it, you want to get into the inn?" he asked looking back at Ava.

She gave a curt nod and gestured for him to move so she could look. He did so.

"Unless you think we can just walk past those people I don't see how," he said plainly.

Ava didn't answer and without another word she darted back down the alley. Aiden followed and Ava turned to the left and went left again. A short minute later they were looking at the side of the inn. In the pale moonlight he saw Ava's teeth flash as she smiled up at the building. She pointed to a window high up on the side of the building.

"That's where we need to get to," she whispered looking back over her shoulder.

Aiden nodded, meeting her eyes, and looked back to the window. The top of the frame hung just five feet below the peaked roof.

"What's inside?" he asked, still looking at the window.

"Archer's room. Or at least it should be based on the view he told me he had from his room when I met him," she answered

Aiden chuckled. "Your plan to win the favor of the King of the Pirates is to break into his son's room?"

Ava shrugged. "I don't think he'll snitch, but it would be nice to have some idea about his father."

"I guess," Aiden said and turned to her. "I have an idea." He must have been grinning a little too broadly because her eyes narrowed.

"And what is it?"

"Well, wouldn't that spoil the surprise?" he said and tapped her on the shoulder before breaking into a crouched run to the side of the building. He could hear Ava moving behind him. She followed as he reached the side of the building and pressed his back to it between two of the curtained windows. Ava hit the wall beside him and pulled her cloak further over her face before reaching over to do the same to his. Aiden ducked as he passed by the next few windows and finally reached the rusted iron drain pipe leading to the gutter at the top of the building. He watched as Ava looked the pipe up and down.

"You're not serious," she said and reached out a single finger to wipe the pipe. "You want to climb the sopping wet, disgusting pipe?"

"Scared?" Aiden crooned and she frowned. "Any better ideas would be welcome," he said.

She looked at him, then the rest of the building, for a long moment before sighing and slumping her shoulders. "Get on with it."

Aiden grasped the pipe and, cocking his foot at an angle, was able to fit his toe in between the pipe. He twisted his foot to lock it in place. He could feel the vibrations in the pipe when Ava started climbing. The pipe was wet but roughly made with plenty of texture to hold onto as they climbed… twenty feet, then thirty. Aiden reached the top and grabbed the gutter, hauling himself atop it and onto the shingled roof. He shook his burning forearms before kneeling to reach a hand down to Ava. She was breathing heavily when she reached for his hand. They grabbed each other's wrists and Aiden helped pull her onto the roof.

"For the record, I hated that bit of the plan," she said, still panting.

"And I hate being woken in the middle of the night and having water thrown at me… again."

Ava choked on a laugh as she looked at his still sodden cloak.

"If you hated that, you're really going to hate this," he warned.

Ava's laughing stopped abruptly as Aiden walked up to the peak of the roof overhanging the window. Ava looked at him, then over the edge of the window. Aiden held out a hand. Ava grabbed it and, moving slowly, lowered herself over the edge of the roof. They held each other by their forearms. Ava gently released the edge of the roof as he lowered her down. Aiden was kneeling with a leg on each side of the peaked roof.

"Can we get in?" he asked softly.

Ava hummed. "I need to be a little lower," she called back up.

Aiden lowered his chest to the peak of the roof, squirming slightly as the shingles dug into his chest. "Better?"

"Yep," Ava said. She swayed slightly, hanging from his arms. She jerked and something popped before a scraping noise and a sharp click rent the night.

"It's open." Ava pulled in closer to the building and gently released Aiden's wrists.

"You can come down," she whispered.

Aiden grasped the edge of the roof and, sliding his legs off the side, lowered himself until he hung before the open window. Ava's knife was still jammed, holding the window and lock open. He swung on the edge of the roof, rocking his legs back and forth, until he caught the toe of his boot on the window frame. He careful placed his other foot on the frame, and even more carefully, grabbed the top of the window frame with his other hand. Aiden then lowered himself through the window entirely. Ava stepped up on a small table and, with a tug, pulled out the knife, resheathing it back on her forearm.

They now stood in a small room strewn with clothes.

"I thought you said this was his room?" Aiden asked, grabbing one of the silk shirts.

Ava gave him an *obviously not, what are you thinking* kind of look. "This is his closet. His room is on the other side of the door."

Aiden looked at the door. "And what's our plan when we get in there?"

"Wake him up without... alerting everyone here?" Ava said, shrugging.

"And if he tries to yell?" Aiden asked, brows furrowed

"Um... punch him?" Ava said, sounding not at all sure about it.

"I hate your plans," Aiden said flatly and opened the door.

The adjacent room was large, reaching to the top of the peaked roof. At the other end sat a large four poster bed. Ava crept by and, moving quickly, made her way to the side of the bed. Aiden joined her and looked down at the half drooling face of the red headed boy about their age. A half dressed girl was lying at his side. Aiden's mouth dropped open slightly, and he looked over to Ava, splaying his arms in a gesture of bewilderment. She merely shrugged and moved to the side with the girl. She pointed to Archer, then to him. Aiden scowled but moved to Archer's side.

Ava had a hand above the girl's shoulders and shook them in the air to signal what she was about to do. Aiden held out his own hands and watched as Ava held up three fingers. She dropped one finger, then another, and upon dropping the last one she gently shook the girl's shoulders. Aiden did the same for Archer On Ava's side, the girl gasped slightly, and Ava pressed a hand over her mouth. The girl struggled for a moment. Ava held a finger to her lips. The girl saw and stilled. On Aiden's side Archer muttered something and rolled over.

Ava looked at Aiden then back down to the girl as she slowly removed her hand and whispered, "Stay quiet. We're not here to hurt you. We just need to talk with Archer."

The girl's lips trembled. She shook slightly but nodded, trying to cover herself. Ava pointed to the cushioned arm chair against the wall and held out a hand. The girl carefully grabbed it and sat up out of the bed. Ava leaned over and took one of the blankets off the foot of the bed and handed it to her before leading her to the chair. She sat wrapped in the blanket, still shaking, and nodded to Ava.

Ava nodded back, smiling slightly, and walked over to Aiden. She frowned, gesturing to Archer. Aiden frowned back. Ava stuck out her tongue as she lifted the pitcher of water on the side table and emptied it on the boy's face. He tried to jerk up, but Aiden clamped a hand over his mouth, forcing him back down onto the bed. His eyes were nothing short of irate as he glared up at Aiden. He kept thrashing, and Aiden grabbed one of his arms before pressing his knee into the boy's chest. Archer looked around the room to where the girl sat, now crying silently, then back to Aiden, then... he stilled and blinked. He tried to say something, but the words were muffled. He was looking at Ava who flicked her wrist and the dagger popped out.

"Just calm down," she said, holding up the knife. "We're gonna let you go and you're going to stay quiet."

Archer resisted and Aiden forced him down again. Ava flipped the knife in her hand, resting her thumb on the pommel as she angled it at him.

"Right?" she continued in a hushed command.

The boy looked between the two of them, then at Ava for a long second before dipping his chin, at least as much as he could with Aiden holding him.

Aiden slowly let go and removed his knee. Archer held his hands up and kept looking between them as he slowly leaned up to a sitting position. Ava popped the knife back into its sheath and smiled at Archer.

"What the hell do you want, Ava?" Archer said, sneering at her.

Her smile vanished. "We needed to talk," she said and crossed her arms.

"In the middle of the night, after like seven years, now is the moment we *need* to talk?" he asked, gesturing to his naked torso. Aiden grabbed one of the shirts off the floor and tossed it to him.

"And who the hell are you?" Archer asked, turning his attention to Aiden. Aiden didn't answer. Archer pulled the shirt over his head and stood, taking a step towards Aiden who didn't budge.

"Where here to talk, not fight," Ava said lazily. She walked over to the chair beside the girl who now sat, still wide-eyed but mercifully not shaking. Ava plopped in the chair, crossing her legs and yawning. Aiden grinned slightly, flashing his teeth and stepped away to sit on the foot of the bed across from Ava. Archer tracked Aiden as he did so, seeming to debate what to do when Ava again spoke.

"I'm here to call in your debt."

Archer didn't do anything for a moment, then his face blanched and he sighed, bowing his head. When he looked up, Ava met his eyes. "What do you need?" he asked.

Ava smiled. "Good, I thought you'd take a little more convincing." She uncrossed her legs and leaned forward to brace her elbows on her knees.

"My partner and I are here with an envoy from Anglen. Where here to get the aid of your father and you're gonna help us."

Archer pulled a stool out from under a small table and sat on it facing the two of them. "And what makes you think I have any power to help. My dad does nothing for no one unless it helps him or Barataria," Archer finished.

"You're his son," Aiden said unamused. "I'd think you have some sway over what he does."

Archer gave a tight lipped smile shrugging unsurely.

"Cut the bullshit, Archer!" Ava whispered in a quiet but aggressive voice. "I know your father was planning to go to war to get you back when you were a kid. I saved him from having to go to war. He owes me!"

Archer scoffed. "You saved me from nothing."

To Aiden's surprise Ava smiled and leaned back in her chair. "That scar on the inside of your thigh says otherwise. As I recall, without me wrestling the wolf off you, it just might have continued higher."

Archer reddened and he glared at her. Ava held the stare still smiling faintly.

Archer gave in. "I'll see what I can do."

Ava grinned, flashing all her teeth as she did.

"I'll come down to the docks when I know something," Archer offered.

Ava again cut him off, walking back to the closet. "Don't bother. We'll come back with the others. Oh, and do tell the guards to expect us. It is such a hassle to sneak in like this."

Aiden shook his head at her gloating as he followed and gave an apologetic nod to the girl still sitting in the chair.

# CHAPTER 44

"Where in the raging sea fearing hell have you two been!?" Arlin roared as the two of them calmly walked down the dock, the morning sun now casting the bay into warm light.

Annalise stood at his shoulder, a look of worried disapproval painted across her face as she stood with her arms crossed. Aiden had the decency to look a little ashamed. Ava, on the other hand, walked right up to the two of them and bowed at the waist, splaying her arms in mock reverence. She straightened, giggling.

"This is serious," Annalise said, taking a step forward. "We told the guards we would stay on the ship. You two just trespassed on pirate land."

"Where were you?" Arlin growled, looking the most angry Aiden had ever seen him.

Ava just smiled and moved to side step the two of them but Arlin moved in her path.

"Where, were…"

"We had to have a chat with someone," she said, sighing, and again tried to step around him.

Arlin grabbed her arm and forced her in front of him. He had just opened his mouth to speak when Aiden answered the question.

"We went to talk with Archer Jagger."

Both Annalise and Arlin's faces looked surprised.

"And how did you get him a message for a meeting?" Annalise asked, looking surprised and impressed.

"We…" Aiden began but trailed off.

Arlin's eyes narrowed.

"We met him in his room... unannounced," Ava added with a hint of hesitation.

Annalise gasped and Arlin again grabbed her arm.

"You did what? Whose idea was this!?" he demanded.

Ava just took a step closer until they were nose to nose. "You're really starting to get grumpy in your old age," she whispered.

With a slight click and a slicing noise, Ava popped out the hidden knife and pulled it through Arlin's belt. His pants dropped, and he lunged to pull them back up. In that moment of confusion, Ava stepped past him and walked through the door down to the cabin.

Aiden was still half lost for words ten minutes later when he and Arlin stood at the helm of the ship overlooking the bay. Arlin was still fuming. After getting a piece of rope as a sad replacement for his belt, he'd tried to go confront her but Annalise had talked him out of it. He asked Aiden to come with him up to the helm but still hadn't spoken a word. Aiden just stood there, not wanting to break the tense silence.

Lucky for him he didn't have to as Arlin asked, "Are you sure no one saw you other than Archer?"

Aiden nodded. "None, other than a girl who was there, but I don't think she's much of a concern. She seemed to know Archer pretty well. I think he'll make sure she doesn't say anything."

Arlin dipped again into silence for a minute, looking out over the bay before sighing. "What were you two thinking? Why not just wait to have an official meeting?" He turned and looked at Aiden waiting for an answer.

"Ava doesn't think Drake Jagger will help without Archer on our side to help convince him."

Arlin made a small noise of acknowledgement, looking back over the sea and sighing. This time, Aiden saw his shoulders relax and his breathing finally steady.

"Next time you're going to do something dangerous, just... think about how it might affect people," the captain admonished.

Aiden's face heated. He suddenly felt incredibly small at Arlin's side.

"Zach, Annalise, Jacques, the rest of the crew. Just... just think about them next time."

Aiden realized that this was one of the few moments that he had ever seen Arlin show his fears, his fears as the captain, as the commander of men. Aiden was glad that he had no such responsibility to others. Everyone he worked with was his equal, free to make their own decisions. But Arlin, he seemed to be carrying the weight of every mistake on his shoulders, every loss, every bit of pain.

Aiden nodded slowly and deliberately. He and Ava against the world. He wished he could keep it that way. No other pressure, no other peoples' backs to watch.

"I will. I'm sorry to have put them in danger."

Arlin smiled vaguely and gripped Aiden on the shoulder, meeting his eyes before walking away down the deck.

When Aiden entered the cabin twenty minutes later it was to Ava sitting on the bed reading. He was about to open his mouth to speak when she did.

"I know what you're going to say."

He stilled, waiting for her to answer.

"I know it was reckless to go straight to Archer to talk. I won't do it again. When we go back to talk with him we'll bring Annalise and do it right." Her words were heavy and they shook slightly.

"What is it?" he asked, sitting on the bed beside her.

"I'm just... tired of things being out of our control. I liked it before when everything we did, we chose to do, before William sent us out." A tear dripped down her face. "I miss my home, my parents. I used to feel untouchable in the Attican Palace with all the guards and my parents around all the time. They spent so long getting allies and making sure we where safe. But as soon as we needed it, it all failed."

He wrapped an arm around her and she leaned against him. they sat like that for a moment.

"Gods help anyone who tries to touch you," Aiden offered.

She gave a shaky laugh. He held her for a moment before speaking again.

"It'll go back to how it was, someday," he whispered into her ear. "Not like it was then, but someday soon we'll be back home in the apartment, eating Phil's cooking, going to the market, and buying meat from Frank." He held her tighter.

"Someday," she repeated and slowly stopped shaking. She tilted her head to him. "Thick and thin?" she asked

"And whatever else," he answered and kissed her.

The following morning they got their answer. Archer probably had spurred the process along, a good sign for his loyalty after their first interaction. Aiden and Ava were sitting on the deck eating breakfast with the crew when three men, better dressed than the others, came walking down the dock. Two of the men wore black tricorns, a red feather poking out from the brim of one of them. Aiden bumped Ava with his elbow, and she looked up from her food. The crew quieted as the thump of the men's boots sounded on the plank leading onto the ship. Aiden watched as Arlin walked down the stairs from the helm. Aiden and Ava stood to join.

Aiden tapped Zach on the shoulder as he walked by and leaned in. "Can you go get Annalise?" he whispered.

Zach strode across the deck and disappeared through the door.

"What can I do for you fine fellows?" Arlin asked, flashing a small grin and looking at the man in the front.

The man in the red feather in his tricorn was impassive as he responded, "We've been sent to take you and your emissary up to the inn for your meeting with Mr Jagger."

The other two men were staring at Aiden and the rest of the crew.

"Of course," Arlin looked over to Aiden who nodded curtly. "Our emissary will be out shortly."

The man dipped his chin slightly and crossed his arms looking around the ship.

"We will also be bringing two others for the meeting," Arlin added.

The man looked back at him, responding, "No."

Arlin didn't look at all surprised. "You see, Mr Jagger knows one of the people I would like to bring and both were sent by King William of Anglen to attend this diplomatic meeting."

"And we were sent to take you and the emissary, and we will take only you and the emissary," the man retorted, his words growing harder as he spoke.

Arlin's pleasant smile was still plastered across his face. Aiden could tell Ava was itching to say something, but she too had a calm smile.

Aiden took a deep breath, and one more before stepping to Arlin's side and reaching for his neck. The two men flanking the first both grabbed the hilts of their swords. Aiden turned the palm of one of his hands to them, trying to make it clear that he was not reaching for the sword on his back as he pulled off the necklace that William had given him.

He held it out by the chain showing it to the men. "This is the Crest of Anglen, given only to its knights. Our King has requested that Ava," Aiden gestured to her, "and I attend this meeting. And as you said, we intend to follow our orders."

The man's face heated almost imperceptibly and he glared at the two of them for a long moment before nodding. He turned to one of the men at his flank. "Go tell Mr Jagger."

The man looked unhappy at the command. With one last leering look at the crew he turned on his heel and walked back down the dock.

He had surpassed their sight when Annalise finally walked out onto the deck. Dressed in a black and gold tunic, she had clearly been spending the time since Zach left to get ready. She smiled warmly at the two remaining men as she approached and again the one in front dipped his chin.

"All ready then?" Arlin asked and turned to Zach who had followed Annalise back on deck. "You're in charge while I'm gone."

Zach grinned a little too broadly.

Arlin shook his head slightly as he returned his gaze to the men. "Lead on."

Without another word, they turned and walked off the ship. The six of them walked in silence through the streets of the city, now loud and bustling with the life and the activity of its waking hours. Aiden was a little shocked at just how alive they were. People bumped into them as they walked down the broad road, leading everything from carts to horses and tropical birds. The sides of the street were lined with market stalls and shops. Were it a different day he would truly have loved to just roam the streets with Ava. But the men kept a brisk pace. Before long the crowds of people thinned, and they came out at the entrance to the courtyard before the inn at the top of the hill.

The front door of the inn was flanked by guards, which Aiden recognized as nothing more than a show from their absence the previous night. Nonetheless, the guards opened the doors and the group walked in. Jagger's two men led them to the end of the hall, flanked all the way down by doors and staircases, with tattered paintings in between. They reached the end and the two men opened a door and waved their arms for the four of them to walk through. On the other side lay an almost grand hall, at least in size if not in decorum. The tables on either side of the aisle leading up to the head table were still covered in dirty plates and goblets, half eaten dishes sat scattered on grimy platers throughout.

But Aiden looked back to the head table, the only one in the hall not laden with any dirty dishes. Behind it sat the biggest man Aiden had ever laid his eyes on. Even in his chair he was as tall as a normal man. His shoulders were of a matching build. His beard looked like black wiry fur flecked with gray hanging down onto his chest, iron rings holding it in braids. It was partially missing on the left side of his face where two jagged, slashing scars lay. One came from the back of his neck to the base of his hairline and the other from his temple through his eyebrow and across the bridge of his nose and down across his mouth. His face was hard, but Aiden got the impression that that was its normal state. He didn't stand as they approached. Aiden followed the lead of the others as they walked up to the other side of the table, rested their hands on their chests and inclined their heads. Aiden craned his neck to watch for when they looked back up but they didn't. He was starting to wonder what they were going to do when the King of the Pirates grunted, and they all stood straight again.

"Make plain your business," he demanded gruffly.

In the moment his mouth was open, Aiden saw the deep groove that ran through his teeth right where the scar lay. His voice matched his general presence. Aiden looked to the others. It was Annalise who stepped forward without hesitation. She smiled broadly and warmly as she looked up to the man. Aiden realized that there were no others in the room with them. The two men had closed the door behind them, and more surprisingly, no guards were placed in the room.

"Mr Jagger, we are here to request the aid of Barataria on behalf of Anglen and its citizens," Annalise began. War is looming and we were sent here to discuss terms of your help."

The man didn't react for a moment. Aiden had to give it to Annalise; she hadn't faltered when it came time to say her part.

"Why would I ever send aid to some dog shit foreign Kingdom?" he asked as though no reason of morality, of saving innocent lives, had ever even occurred to him.

Aiden couldn't help but shift a little bit at the coldness of the answer.

"Well, not only because you'd be helping the people of Anglen, the men, women and children unable to defend against an attack, but also to forge a strong relationship with Anglen," Annalise offered.

He didn't so much as blink at the statement. This man really didn't seem to care if every person on the continent died.

"The unpreparedness of you people is the fault of your government and not my problem to solve," he said blatantly. "You and you people have nothing to offer me or Barataria that we don't have or want." He leaned forward in his seat. Aiden couldn't help but want to lean away at the motion. "So I ask again why I would I help you." His words were not a question this time, but rather a means by which to frighten them. If Aiden was honest with himself, it was working. He clearly wasn't expecting an answer.

301

"You wouldn't," Ava said and stepped forward.

The Pirate King's eyes wrenched to look at her. There was an anger, a wrath in them, that Aiden had never seen. Something about it told him with infallible clarity that it could never be soothed, not by any of them, not by any person, not by the gods themselves.

"But... you will help me!" Ava said with more bravado than Aiden felt he could have in the presence of this man.

Jagger stood and his black, leather, boot-length coat swayed. He wore a sword on one hip, merely a short sword to him and what would have been a great sword to any normal sized man on his other. Two baldrics hung from either shoulder, one holding some sort of metal balls, the other holding more daggers. In his belt hung a length of red and brown stained fabric.

He braced his hands on the table as he looked down at the group of them. "And why would I help some insulting lass like yourself!" he roared across the table, his dark eyes now burning, though his face remained relatively calm.

Aiden could feel Ava fighting the urge to cower, but she replied, "Because you owe me a debt."

Jagger bared his teeth slightly as he surveyed her. "A bold claim," he said softly but didn't shift his gaze from Ava. "But I'm afraid you have no claim to my services. Every debt I've owed has been paid or the owner killed. I'm not in the habit of listening to false claims made by little girls from far off kingdoms!!" He truly roared the words this time.

Aiden tried to summon words to Ava's aid but none came out. To his sides Annalise and Arlin both opened their mouths, seeming to want to say something as well, but quickly closed them. Jagger grabbed the table before them and, with a flinging motion, slid it along the floor and out of his way with such force that it ground fresh marks into the floor. It crashed into the next table, forcing that one into the wall, causing a boom that hurt Aiden's ears and shook the rafters of the room. But the Pirate King's way was clear as he walked right up to Ava and looked down at her. Aiden watched her right hand fidget and knew she was debating popping out the small dagger.

But she just took a breath, closing her eyes, and looked down at the floor even as he stood not three feet from her. Aiden too was fidgeting, wanting to reach over his shoulder and grab Starlight before Jagger could get any closer to her.

Ava took another deep breath, and with the calm calculation of a princess said, "I am from a far off kingdom, one that no longer exists."

The Pirate King's eyes widened the slightest, nearly imperceptible bit in doubt. "And what fallen kingdom do you hail from?" he said in as much of a croon as his growling voice would allow.

Ava finally looked up, meeting his stare full in the face as she answered, "I hail from the east. I am Ava Corinth Princess of Attica and high heir to the throne. And you owe me the life of your son, Archer Jagger."

Long moments passed in which no one spoke. Aiden could see out of the corner of his eye Annalise and Arlin exchanging nervous glances. Aiden continued to hold his breath. Things were about to go either really right or really wrong. He could feel it, the charge, a precipice upon which they stood, not knowing whether the dirt beneath their feet would bear their load or not.

But apart from that, there was another charge, a real one in the air. It took Aiden a minute to remember where he'd felt this sort of oddness in the surrounding air before. He was struck with a whole new wave of fear when the realization of when he'd last felt it hit him. It was like a physical blow to his emotions, to his soul. It pinned him with the kind of fear that caught him partway between an impulse to run and a desire to kill the man before him, before that man could do them any harm.

Jagger was the first to speak again. He spoke so softly that had there been any conversation in the room he would have been inaudible. But they did hear him, not that they would have needed to hear his words to understand his meaning.

The charge in the air had become palpable now. It was the same sort of power that rent the air when they'd first met Alva, the same kind that he'd felt when the King of Orenth had sensed them. He hadn't known it then. The sensation had still been new and unfamiliar. But he recognized it now. He recognized it, and unless his eyes were deceiving him, he saw it too. Red mist was rolling off Jagger's shoulders, waves of it that pooled to the ground, forming sticky dark puddles that looked sickeningly like... Aiden didn't want to finish that thought.

"Run... before I turn you to ribbons where you stand," Jagger growled.

*Run*, Aiden thought, *run*. Perhaps it was an exaggeration. Maybe it was the sort of empty threat that leaders throw around to make better deals, maybe... It wasn't. Aiden knew it, and he had no desire to stand around and wait for Jagger to enact the threat. Maybe Aiden's own power would have saved them, but that felt like a big maybe, a maybe he had no control over and one that could just as easily kill them.

These thoughts all happened in less than a second, of course, less than a second in which he'd grabbed Ava by the wrist, pivoted on the ball of his foot, and sprinted.

# CHAPTER 45

No one said anything for a long moment as Archer walked down the dock. Annalise hadn't left her room since getting back to the ship. Ava hadn't been inclined to either until Zach had informed them all that Archer was walking up the dock, at which point she'd wrenched open the door of their cabin and ran on deck.

It had been a few hours since their interaction with Drake Jagger, a few hours in which they'd expected to receive a messenger or at least a letter telling them that they were to leave Barataria. But much to their surprise, no such command had reached them. Annalise had seemed inclined based on the brief few words she'd mumbled before entering her cabin to leave anyway, but Arlin hadn't said anything. Zach not having been there to see what had happened, served as the encouraging voice telling them that not all hope was lost...

'Bullshit,' Aiden couldn't help thinking when Zach said this. He'd been ready to have less than a warm welcome but not... not that. No part of him had been expecting Jagger to turn them to ribbons for asking. What did this leave for William? In the best case, there was always the chance that they'd overestimated Orenth's military.

"Where in the gods damn fucking hell were you!" Ava ground out.

Archer raised his brows in a gesture so nonchalant that Aiden half thought Ava might attack him for it on the spot. Archer didn't answer until he was fully on the ship, coming to stand before the four of them: Zach, Arlin, Aiden and Ava. Aiden didn't think Annalise would be coming out to join them. The rest of the crew watched but gave them a wide berth, finding places to sit on the far side of the ship where they would be able to see what happened without risking any involvement.

"You could give a fair few pirates a run for their money with that language," Archer said, sliding his hands into his pockets.

"Your balls must be made of brass coming here after that!" Ava snarled.

"Oh, how about *Thanks Archer for coming all the way down to our ship to talk though what we're going to do to convince your dad to help us, even after I so rudely woke you up in the middle of the night unannounced.* That might be a better way to greet me."

"Coming all the way down to our ship," Ava said, turning away from him slightly and seeming halfway between screaming and laughing. She chose to laugh, high and disbelieving far from her normal joyous giggle.

"It was a favor that I came down here. It isn't a good look for the son of the King to come down and socialize with the foreign trash that washed up in the bay."

"You best watch who you're calling *trash*, boy," Zach growled.

"Oh, don't go getting all offended. I know you're not trash. But that's what most of the captains in this bay are thinking right about now."

Ava let out a sigh.

Archer looked back at her. "What is it now? Is something not to the liking of the high queen, princess royalty of the Kingdom of…" He made a motion with his hands.

Aiden gave him a flat look.

"This is shit as apologies go," Arlin bit out. He was doing a better job of hiding his anger from showing on his face, his words though… He was just as mad as the rest of them.

Archer let out a bark of a laugh. "Apologize? I'm not here to apologize."

"Then why are you here?" Ava asked in a tone that bordered dangerously on a threat.

"As I told you. I'm here to help plan out how we're going to convince my dad to help you."

"I don't know if you forgot the date or if you're just dumb," Zach started. "But they've already been to talk to your dad."

"Neither…" Archer said, sounding unamused at the insult. No one spoke and Archer continued after a moment. "I'm here now because it didn't matter what you said in that meeting. He was going to turn you down either way."

"If you knew he'd never help us then why didn't you just say that when we visited you?" Ava spat. "Rather than let us go to him and threaten to *turn us to ribbons*," Ava finished, quoting Jagger.

"He didn't turn you away because he's not going to help you." Archer said like it was obvious, taking a step back to lean against the railing of the ship as he spoke.

"He did it as a test to see how you'd handle it. You did well, you know," he praised. "Most people would be half a day's sail away by now."

"He said that just to scare us?" Aiden asked flatly.

"Mhmm, just one of his things," Archer said with a faint shrug.

"So how are we going to get him to say yes?" Aiden asked. Ava still seeming stuck between anger and numb shock at his side.

"Well… I'd recommend you not just demand that he help you."

Beside them Arlin muttered something to Zach and the latter walked away, ducking through the door to head below deck.

"How else are we going to get him to help?" Ava asked.

"Well, the debt got you in the door per se. Now you have to make it worth it for him to help you."

"We don't have anything else to offer," Aiden said.

Archer raised his brows then gestured around the deck like it had all the answers. "Of course you do. Don't you have an emissary somewhere on this ship?" Archer asked, looking around as though Annalise might just pop out of the floor boards.

"We do and she'll be here in a minute," Arlin said.

"Great, does she have permission to negotiate on behalf of your King?"

"I think so," Ava said. She seemed to have forgotten her anger, realizing that there might still be some hope.

"Then you have everything you need," Archer said, clapping his hands together.

"Meaning what?" Arlin asked slowly. Aiden knew he was thinking about Archer's gesture around the ship.

"Meaning... that all you need to do is find something that Barataria needs, that you can supply, and make a trade deal. And lucky for you, I know everyone here. I also happen to know what everyone wants."

Zach came back with a hesitant Annalise not long after, meeting them all in Arlin's office. It took them a few minutes to catch her up on what Archer told them.

Aiden had never been upset to have Annalise tagging along, but this was the first time he was grateful to have her for more than company. They spent the better part of an hour having Annalise come up with a potential deal to propose to Jagger. Then Archer judged whether or not that would appeal to his dad. This plan of course hinged a great deal on whether or not Archer was an accurate judge of his father, but they didn't exactly have a better informant.

"So... the biggest import you need is... *booze?*" Annalise asked, sounding a little distasteful. "Along with," She looked back down at the list of other potential exports before her, "Steel, root and stem vegetables, and oak timber?"

"That's right," Archer confirmed.

Annalise didn't say anything back so Ava jumped into the conversation. "And when can we get another meeting with your dad to discuss this with him?"

Archer made a face, seeming to consider for a moment. "Let's give it a few days. I need to talk to him before you do. I'll get some of the officials together and have them tell him about all these things we need. That'll get the idea in his head. A day or two after that you guys can ask him again, and I'll come to try and help smooth things over."

They all said words of agreement or made similar gestures. Archer made for the door. Aiden knew Arlin wanted him off the ship but he couldn't help asking quickly before Archer had a chance to leave.

"Hey, Archer, how do you know that all the people need this stuff and your dad doesn't?" Aiden asked.

Archer half turned back looking over his shoulder at Aiden. "My dad isn't exactly the easiest person to talk to. I'm easy so people tell me and I tell him."

"So why haven't you told him about all this stuff already?"

"Because we haven't had any way of getting it even if he did know. Figured I wouldn't bring it up 'til there was a reason to." And with that Archer turned back and walked off the ship with all the nonchalance of a prince.

# Chapter 46

Archer smiled. "Morning dad."

Jagger didn't say anything or look up from the list he was reading, only nodded slightly in an acknowledging sort of way. Archer caught a glimpse of the list as he sat down on one of the two cushy brown leather chairs. It was labeled something about GDP. Of course that was less of a true gross domestic product and more of an account of all the stuff Barataria had managed to plunder within their boundaries. Still the number at the bottom of the page was considerable, more than considerable, it was a kingdom's ransom.

"What's that?" Archer asked more for the sake of getting his dad talking than really having any reason to know.

"Haul from the quarter so far," Jagger grunted.

Archer nodded vaguely. So much for getting his dad talking about something before bringing it up.

"I heard that you had some people visit you earlier." Jagger froze his sifting through papers. He didn't lift his head but his eyes locked on Archer. "Mhm."

A prompt for Archer to continue. " … Do you know,"

"Who she was?" Jagger asked.

Archer always knew or suspected rather that there was a fine line with his father that he'd best never cross. Not that he'd ever done so, but bringing up this particular bit of the past felt like it came dangerously close.

"Yeah…"

"I do, and I take it you're here because you want to help her."

Archer didn't answer.

"Part of me always hoped you'd grow out of this loyalty for people," Jagger said resoundingly.

Archer knew it, but it still stung a little bit to hear it aloud.

"Would make you a better leader if the time comes," his dad continued.

"I... I know," Archer responded slowly, head dipped to face the floor.

Jagger made another sound of resignation, nodding his own head a few times in quick dips. "You're a better person for it," Jagger said slowly.

Archer looked up a little surprised. A long moment passed.

"I know you can't just help them."

"We protect our own," Jagger began. "In a better world it might be otherwise. But we don't live in that world, and the day I lead with a heart instead of a head is the day I am no longer fit to be King." Jagger stopped looking at him for a few moments, sifting through the papers as he waited. "But you already know that... So tell me why you think I should help them?"

Archer gave him a small smile before calling, "Come in!"

His dad raised a brow but seemed unsurprised. In shuffled a few people Archer had picked out. They made a line a little to the side of Archer.

"Please tell the King what you told me," Archer said, looking at the first man.

The man looked uncomfortable. He wore a leather apron that seemed so worn it was barely thicker than a piece of cloth. He gave Archer one more nervous glance before looking back to Jagger and dipping into a deep bow.

"Mr. Jagger, it isn't that I'm trying to be a nuisance, it's only that young Archer here's asked me to come and inform you 'bout some things been making work difficult for the other smiths."

"And what might those things be?" There was no animosity in Jagger's tone, but still his voice was enough to make the man more nervous.

"It's the steel we have here. Ya know we're making a lotta things, anchors and chains and weapons, the like. And, well, I t's the steel here you see. Stuff we're able to make is shit for forging things, and the steel we manage to bring in from raiding, we can get by with it if need be, but, it just ain't ideal ya see."

Jagger briefly glanced at Archer before looking at the next man and asking him the same. The man gave a similar answer involving needing more timber. With the trees that naturally grow on the island, it's near impossible to make a very good ship. The grain isn't straight enough, making cutting straight pieces that won't warp or bow in water a nightmare.

Jagger repeated his routine of glancing at Archer before moving to the next person. He didn't have to ask the last woman standing on the far right what the issue was before she started speaking though.

Barataria didn't have a queen. Archer's mother had died before Archer was old enough to remember her. But if there were any woman on the island with enough power to rival a queen, it was this one. She wasn't tall, and was pretty in a take no shit sort of way. She wore an old set of black overalls stained in places and had her hair tied back in a bandana.

"We need more booze," was her comment. She didn't say anything for a heartbeat though Archer had the impression she did intend to continue.

"You want more booze, Yayna?"

"Laugh all you want ya old pile of shit," she said.

Archer had to give her credit. She was probably the only person in all of Barataria, and a good bit of the rest of the world, who would have said that to his face.

"But it ain't me who needs booze, gods know I can get all I want. But people are sick'a drinking that piss poor moonshine we make outta da sugar cane. They want good dark beer. Fill 'em up more before they puke, and good dark beer comes from the south, ya know the places that don't send ships up our way."

"And how do you know that this is such a priority to my people?" Jagger asked.

Archer knew his dad wasn't going to like hearing Yayna's request, but she was the person with the most sway among the people, and Archer wasn't above using that to convince his father.

"I know, because unlike you, I'm not such a sad old bastard as ta only ever drink alone. I also, in case you'd forgotten, run the tavern you sleep above, along with nearly all the others in your bloody kingdom."

Jagger waited a long moment after she finished before speaking again. "I will speak with my son now."

The two men needed no further cue to get out. They both dipped into swift bows, their eyes never meeting Jagger's as they shuffled back out the door. Yayna was trying to say something about if he had a chance to get them booze, he'd better take it, but his dad let out a growl that Archer felt in his chest. She finally blushed a little with nerves as she quickly pulled the door closed behind her.

"I could have done without having to talk to that woman."

"You could have," Archer said, "but she's right about people wanting alcohol, and the people respect her too."

Jagger glanced out the window for a moment. "Before you finish this proposal, I want to know something." He looked back tearing his eyes away from the harbor at the bottom of the city. "Why does me helping them matter to you?"

Archer hadn't thought about that question. His dad almost never asked why people did what they did. He usually relied on past actions to predict what people were going to do. Even as a kid, Archer couldn't remember a time he was asked why he did something. It always seemed like an accepted reality that they were what they were. His dad was what he was, a cold, efficient, born leader, and Archer was more empathetic, better with people, lead more greatly by his emotions.

"Sorry?" Archer's mouth was slightly open. He closed it realizing it gave away how surprised he was.

"I want to know why these people matter to you."

Why did they matter to Archer? How the hell was he supposed to answer that. There was the obvious answer of that he owed Ava his life. But that was obvious, his dad knew that. His dad wouldn't have gone back on a debt of his own either.

"Because... I don't know I... I think, I think we've been alone in the world too long, the pirates I mean. And I know we don't need anyone. I know we're just fine on our own."

"The rest of the world's a dangerous place," Jagger added.

"I know it is, but it's big, and we're alone, and... Well, I like the people who've come here. I think they're good, and with how they talk about their king it sounds like he's good too."

"Good people make weak allies."

"Maybe, but they make loyal ones too."

Jagger didn't ask any more questions for a moment as Archer sat in the chair waiting. Then he asked, "What else do we need?"

Archer sighed too softly for his dad to notice. Back to the topic. "We also can't grow any root vegetables here. They might be on the list of things you could demand."

"Would I be demanding?" Jagger asked.

Archer gave him a look. "They're desperate and your... you, every word that comes out of your mouth is a demand to them right now."

Jagger nodded and Archer stood to leave. "Smart boy," Jagger muttered as much to himself as to his son. "Tell them to come back tomorrow morn. I'll see them then." Archer closed the door behind him as he left.

His mother would have liked Archer, Jagger thought to himself, more than she did him anyway. Gods, the fights they had had about all the harsh decisions he'd made back then. Archer would have agreed with her he knew. Archer would be fighting back now if he'd ever had someone set an example of it. Archer might not make a great king, the other captains would never have him, but he made a good one, better than Jagger at least. But one step at a time on the road to change, Jagger thought as he stood from the desk and left his office.

# CHAPTER 47

Annalise flat out refused to go back to the tavern at the top of the city. "You may not have heard the threat he made if we don't leave him alone, but I am not in the business of ignoring advice from powerful, *violent* men." This was her first of a few arguments as to why they should set sail to leave rather than go back.

But all of these were trumped by points from Ava. "Annalise, we either get Jagger's help now, maybe die early, or we can go back to Anglen, and wait to be killed by Orenth. We don't have another option. All Anglen's other allies are far away and aren't powerful enough to save us even if they could get there in time."

Annalise gave a look of uneasy, but not outright, dismissal.

"We go up there. We say our part. You make a trade deal and we leave. That's it," Ava blurted out, exasperated.

A more patient person might have bothered to finish fully convincing Annalise that this was their only option, but that person was not Ava. Zach was again charged with commanding the ship in Arlin's stead. Arlin was already waiting on the dock, standing beside the tall slender boy who had been sent to summon them. Ava joined them not waiting for Annalise to mull over the point any longer.

"She's right, you know," Aiden said in a near whisper.

Annalise's eyes flicked to him, reproach already tainting them, but that quickly softened into empathy and a moment later, fear of another kind as she fully understood his meaning.

"They really have that many men?" she asked, matching Aiden's tone.

He gave an unsure half shrug. "There's no way of knowing how many soldiers Orenth has now, but if they've managed to recover to where they were... we could be outmatched even with the pirates."

She gave him a tight lipped expression before rolling her shoulders and making a noise of resignation. "Out manned you mean."

"Sorry?" Aiden looked down at her. Past them on the docks Ava was waving for them to come.

"We might be out manned, not outmatched."

Aiden couldn't help his small smile as he followed her down the plank and onto the deck. The trip through the city was starting to feel more familiar at this point, one curving poorly planned street leading into another, until they came face to face with the inn. It's sign waving slightly in the breeze, too old and tattered to be legible.

"This'll be where I leave ya," their guide said and walked off around the edge of the building.

The same guards were stationed at the doorway of the inn. They opened the doors without any reaction. Aiden and the others had just turned to face the main doors that would lead to the dining hall where they'd met Jagger before when a light casual voice sounded.

"Well... If it isn't my favorite gold diggers." Archer strode past them as Ava shot him an insult that made him chuckle. Archer made to push open the doors but the guards did it for him. Archer gave one of the men an incredulous look.

"Son," Jagger began as they entered. The hall beyond was silent for a moment. "This meeting is private." The statement did little to encourage Aiden that Archer's involvement was going to do anything for their chances of Jagger accepting their proposal.

"I know, that's why I didn't invite any drinking mates," Archer said and, walking around the table his father sat at, he took a seat in one of the smaller chairs. Jagger grunted but said nothing more. He waited for Aiden, Ava, Annalise, and Arlin to line up before him and bow before speaking.

"What will you give me and my people in exchange for our aid?" A simple enough question.

Beside him Aiden could practically hear Annalise's heart hammering. "We... um, excuse me. I speak on behalf of the government when I say that Anglen is willing to offer." She rattled off numbers and rates for commerce. "These figures would be updated every year to adjust for any inflation or change in value of products and all commerce between our two nations would be tariff free."

Jagger gave her a hard look. "Double for the price, and they will be tariff free on our side. You and yours will still pay any tariffs invoked by Barataria."

Annalise's mouth dropped open slightly. "Mr. Jagger. That, that just isn't possible. The numbers I've already stated are the best deal Anglen is able to offer that still leaves a reasonable margin of profit..."

Jagger cut her off. "I don't give a shit about Anglen's profit, and this would leave Barataria, quite well off."

"Mr. Jagger." Annalise began sounding outright desperate now.

"Don't test me, girl. You're desperate. You need something I have. I'm not in the business of fair deals. You'll pay what I demand or you and your kingdom can burn in the flame of your enemy," Jagger growled.

Annalise snapped back to her fear of half an hour ago. She stood ramrod straight and did not speak another word.

"Now Corinth," Jagger began.

Ava stepped forward.

"I am a bad man. We both know it, and I don't intend to fight it. No debt would make me willing to send my men to war and death on my behalf…"

He stood and walked around the table. The thud of his boots against the wood of the floor caused a few pieces of silverware around the tables to rattle. He stopped before Ava, his expression was still hard but not angry. His eyes held none of the wrath that made Aiden run the last time.

"Still, I thank you for the life of my son."

It was an oddly serial moment. Jagger agreed to send the required troops to Anglen. He said they'd be ready to set sail within the week, that updates would be sent, and that he himself would be coming with them. And just like that the man was gone, ducking to fit through one of the door frames leading out of the hall. He moved surprisingly quickly for a man of his size.

Aiden could only assume the others were also at a loss for words.

"We did it," he said softly.

"We did it," Ava repeated.

"We're still alive," Arlin said, touching his torso as thought to confirm that he was still in one piece.

"We'll be broke," Annalise muttered, far more subdued than the rest of them.

"Hey," Aiden started. "I went fifteen years of my life without needing a coin. It's better to be alive than rich."

"You're right," Annalise said with a slightly hysterical laugh.

"Congrats," Archer's voice reminded Aiden that it wasn't just them in the room. Archer was smiling, it seemed this really was the outcome he was looking for. He walked with them on the way back down to their ship.

"What did he mean by that thank you?" Ava asked.

"He... My dad's an unusual man," Archer started. "You heard him say that no debt would ever get him to send his people to war."

"Yeah, so my debt was worth nothing to him," Ava said, sounding a little annoyed, as thought it hadn't been worth saving Archer's life.

Archer let out a small laugh, bowing his head to the ground and shaking it, in apparent humor at some joke none of them understood. "No, not at all. I'd imagine it gained you quite a lot actually."

"He said he'd never send troops for a debt," Arlin barked. "What the hell did the debt gain us?"

"Him!" Archer laughed. "It gained you my dad coming with you. He was willing to send our army to war because it gave him a chance to twist your hand to get us the best trade deals we've had in a century. But he's going because *he*," Archer emphasized the word, "owed you a debt, as my dad. As harsh a man as he is, he's going personally to fight because of his debt to you."

Ava gave Archer a satirical look. "Great, I saved a prince's life to get one extra solider great use of my limited princessly time."

"Firstly, my dad wields two swords, and you've seen him. He's no normal soldier."

"Fine, two very big swords," Ava added. They crossed onto the wood of the dock, nearing the ship.

"Think what you like, but you'll be glad he's fighting on your side. More glad than you know."

Aiden thought he might know what Archer meant, but... that was a hope for a more certain time, not a hope to rely too much on. Feelings and fear were little to trust the lives of his fellow people to.

# CHAPTER 48

To his credit, the Pirate King kept his word. Throughout the week they watched as ships all through the harbor were gradually loaded with the supplies they would need for the few weeks journey back to the shores of Anglen. They saw little of Jagger or his men, only seeing them on the few occasions for which Ava, Annalise and Arlin were summoned back to discuss more of the logistics of the transport. Jagger informed them that he had already sent word back to Anglen of his agreeing to come.

Annalise was a little put off by this fact. "He didn't even consult us on the contents of the message," was her fuming retort when Arlin told her to stop complaining on the walk back to the ship.

It was two nights before they were secluded to depart when Aiden again spotted Jacques sitting at the head of the ship and peering into the city. Something about the thought of his just sitting there made him do it. With a quick noncommittal word to Ava sitting next to him, he stood and moved at a brisk pace as he walked right off the ship and along the dock. The streets were slowly growing less crowded as he made his way up to the inn at the top of the hill. When he reached the inn he strode right to the front doors. There were no longer any guards and it took him a minute to find a servant.

"Excuse me," he said politely to the young man, "could you get Archer Jagger for me?" The servant looked a little surprised at the request but agreed.

Five minutes later Aiden was still standing in the hallway, admiring a worn painting that someone had clearly taken a sword to at some point based on the gaping tear in the canvas. When someone stepped beside him, he turned to see Archer who stood close but not so close as to be rude.

"My father wrecked this in front of the merchant who owned it for beating a boy bloody at the docks."

Aiden raised his eyebrows and Archer went on.

"The boy had been playing with a kite that got tangled in the merchant's mast. When my dad found what had happened he marched down to the docks with the kid. As punishment, he took the most valuable thing the merchant had on his ship."

Aiden nodded his head vaguely thinking that was the end but Archer continued.

"He wrecked it in front of the man before hauling him to the tower at the entrance of the bay."

Aiden could feel a twinge of something slimy in his gut as he considered what Archer might be about to say.

"He whipped the man before hanging him from the tower... as a warning to anyone who might come here and hurt his people."

Faster than Aiden had expected, bile burned in his throat. It was an effort not to puke at the thought of someone being *whipped* and killed.

Archer seemed to notice Aiden's thoughts. "He's not a good man," Archer said plainly, not a hint of shame or apprehensiveness tinting his words. "No King of Pirates ever could be."

Aiden supposed he agreed with the statement.

"But for the things he loves, he'll do anything, be anything... and he loves his people."

But this seemed to conflict with what Jacques had said.

"If he loves his people so much then why does he have such strict tax rules?"

Archer looked a little surprised at the specificity of Aiden's question.

"What do you mean?" he asked thoughtfully.

"Only that one of the men on our crew who used to live here said that if you don't pay the taxes then you can't come on the land of Barataria?"

"Oh," Archer said, seeming to understand. "Well, not one cent of the taxes goes to anything but the welfare and protection of the people. Not paying the taxes is like not protecting your neighbor."

Aiden looked around the room, the inn.

"None of the money goes to him?" Aiden asked disbelievingly.

Archer chuckled. "He's the greatest pirate in the world. If he wants money he'll just take it. Even most of the money he takes goes to the people." Archer shook his head as though everything he'd just told Aiden was obvious. "Anyway, what is it you came here for? Should I get my dad?" he asked, still looking amused at Aiden's ignorance.

"No…" Aiden said slowly, not knowing exactly how to ask his next question. "That crew member who used to live here but can't come ashore."

Archer nodded, looking a little skeptical.

"I was wondering if he could come just for a little bit." Aiden could sense that Archer was about to say no and continued quickly. "Not anywhere, just to visit one place."

Archer didn't answer, looking unsure of what he wanted to do.

"Just as a favor to me, not any part of our agreement," Aiden finished, conceding to the realization that this was a lost cause.

But Archer still didn't answer. "Let me think about it," he said finally to Aiden's surprise.

Aiden just nodded kindly to Archer and left the inn. By the time he got back to the ship the sun was already starting to dip, casting the bay into the bleary pink orange glow of dusk.

Ava smiled warmly as he entered their cabin. "Where'd you go?" she asked lightly.

Aiden sighed. "I was trying to see about getting permission for Jacques to see his brother before we leave," he answered, plopping on the foot of the bed and falling backward to look at the ceiling.

Ava's brow scrunched. "What?" she asked, not seeming to understand.

"The sailor on Arlin's crew with the accent," he said, straining his eyes to the side to look at her. "His brother lives here, and there's some rule Jacques broke that makes it so he can't come onto the land of Barataria," Aiden explained.

Ava just shook her head chuckling. "Well, aren't you such a good knight," she said before plopping down on the bed beside him to look up at the ceiling above.

"You excited to go home?" he asked her, and he could feel her smile.

On the morning they were set to leave Archer finally came down to the ship. Aiden and Arlin gave friendly waves from the helm as Archer climbed aboard and came up to meet them. "You get your wish," he said plainly.

Arlin raised his brows at Aiden, but Aiden didn't answer. As he and Archer walked away, Arlin called, "Be back soon, we set sail in an hour!"

Aiden raised a hand in recognition but was already on the steps down from the helm and scanning the deck looking for Jacques. As he expected Aiden found him standing at the prow of the ship. Aiden made his way over, moving a little faster than usual, Archer walking at his side, until they stood in front of Jacques.

"Do you want to see your brother?" Aiden asked, maybe a little too frankly.

Jacques looked surprised and almost affronted, almost, until he caught sight of Archer and asked back, "Are you serious?" His words were a little rushed as though too caught up in the idea to keep his composure. Aiden and Archer both nodded and smiled. Jacques took a deep breath before returning a firm nod.

Aiden and Archer really didn't see much of the visit. They had walked up to the tavern and when they got there Jacques had asked them to wait outside while he went in to find his brother. They stood in silence for a few moments before Archer started pointing to different ships in the bay and recounting stories of different pirates sailing each one. Some of the stories ended in triumph, others, mostly those of the ships that had large sections that seemed to be made of new wood, had suffered defeat.

"Most of the ships here are old enough to have fought against Gileda before the treaty was brokered, at least the bits that haven't been replaced. My father signed it not a month after he announced himself High King."

"Your father was willing to sweep all the animosity under the rug?"

Archer laughed, side eyeing Aiden before returning his gaze to the bay, still chuckling as he said, "If you were a wolf and you had three cubs and a deer carcass, and then another wolf comes and kills one of your cubs in the fight over the carcass." He paused a moment. "Do you continue fighting 'til all your cubs are dead and the both of you are too bloody to eat the thing?"

Aiden thought about the metaphor, his respect for the man beside him increasing as he did. "I just didn't take you dad to be…" Aiden trailed off.

Archer finished for him, "One to forgive his anger, think things through, take the best course of action whatever it may be?" Archer laughed softly. "His anger may hide it, but he didn't become the most feared man on the high seas by always leading with his emotions."

Aiden shrugged in agreement.

Archer gave a small smile. "Except of course in the heat of battle," he said with a more wicked grin than Aiden had yet seen. "And gods help anyone unlucky enough to cross blades with him."

Thinking about it, Aiden figured he agreed. He, himself, was taller and bigger than most. That man, even sitting, that man has made him feel like a twig he might snap in his fingers.

They continued to stand in silence waiting for a few minutes longer. Aiden watched the progress on the Sea Dragon in the bay below before he finally asked in a voice slightly smaller than usual, "When will you be crowned King?"

Archer took a moment to look around the city around them before answering, "I won't."

Aiden frowned in confusion. "I'm not sure I understand?"

"The Kingdom of Pirates is not like that of other courts," Archer began to explain. "Our kings are decided by two things, neither of which is blood. It's decided by who is ruthless enough to take it, to declare themselves King of the Pirates, and whether or not the others think you're good enough to rule." Archer finished, a slightly haunted look on his face.

"And if they don't find someone worthy?" Aiden asked, feeling he might not want to know.

Archer huffed. "That one's easy, they die. If a pirate declares himself the King and the others disagree, then they set aside their differences long enough to kill that captain and his crew."

"Do you intend to be King?" Aiden asked.

The haunted look returned to Archer's face, but he was saved the discomfort of answering by the opening of the door behind them as Jacques stepped out. Upon seeing him Aiden noticed three distinct things: he was crying, his mouth wore a wide wobbling smile and there was blood leaking from his nose and brow.

Aiden didn't know where to start. "Are you ok?" he blurted out, beginning to reach over his shoulder to his sword while looking beyond him into the tavern.

"Yes, yes!" Jacques said, holding up his hands for Aiden to stop reaching for any weapons.

On the walk back down to the ship Jacques explained that when his brother had first saw him he punched him in the face, but after that he'd calmed down and talked. Jacques just kept thanking both of them for allowing him to visit. When they finally did reach the ship Aiden could see the men moving to put the oars in place. He was about to move to climb on when Archer loosely grabbed his arm and bade Jacques to go ahead, which he did after thanking both of them one last time.

Archer then said, "That was a good thing to do for someone you barely know. Not a very pirate-like thing, but a good one." He sighed briefly, "And to answer your question."

Aiden almost told him he didn't have to answer just to get rid of the haunted look in his eyes, but curiosity kept him from doing so.

"No, I don't have any ambition to be King of the Pirates, and if truth be told I hate the whole concept." That was the last thing Archer said before releasing Aiden's arm and walking away.

Aiden climbed aboard the ship and made his way up to the helm where he joined Arlin and Ava. Arlin grinned at him, "Jacques seemed quite happy when he came back aboard." Aiden grinned back.

"When do we set sail?" Ava asked, looking over to Arlin.

"Jagger's going to come over and tell us where to sail within his fleet. Then we head out."

And sure enough the Pirate King walked onto the dock not twenty minutes later flanked by two men. If Aiden had to guess that was the closest the man's face ever came to a smile. He walked aboard and straight up to them where all three of the hosts gave slight bows.

He grunted in response and then gave his orders. "Me and my ship will lead the fleet. You are welcome to sail at my side if you see fit. If you don't wanna, then sail towards the middle of the pack." He said this plainly, no animosity now, just plain orders.

Arlin nodded deeply.

"So, you are going to be coming with us to Anglen?" Ava asked, like she hadn't really believed him before when he said he would be.

The King of the Pirates paused. Aiden thought it might be in confusion at the words, but he answered nonetheless. "My army will sail nowhere without me at its helm, and I will not be coming back to this bay with a debt," he growled back. Jagger then nodded to his men before turning and walking back off the deck.

Within the next half hour the fleet had set sail, and Arlin was racing to meet Jagger's own ship at the head of the fleet. The Sea Dragon had finally caught the massive black and red pirate ship just as they crossed between the two great towers at the entrance of the bay and made their way out into the open sea.

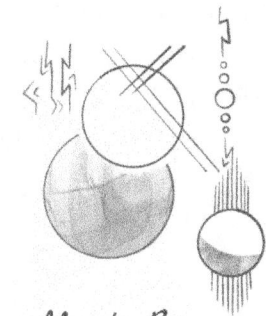

# IV

## Fierce A Leader Must Be

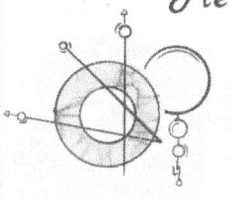

# Chapter 49

Aiden was stuck in a state of numb relief for the following weeks as they made their way south. He could tell Ava was as well, the two of them continued life on the ship as they had before, but now had a tendency to halt training in favor of just sitting on the deck and drinking with the crew.

Still, they did train. Annalise occasionally joined too. She'd improved greatly. By no means was she going to win against any trained fighter, but Aiden did feel confident that she could defend herself well enough to get away. He couldn't help but feel a small sense of relief at the thought.

The weather had grown colder as they traveled south. The scorching sun of Barataria had faded to be replaced by light clouds and chill breezes. In Anglen it would already be mid fall and the trees of the forests back home would soon be adorned in all shades of red, orange and yellow, as bright as the high masts of the Pirate King's ship to their left. Aiden had seen little of the King since leaving Barataria. He had invited them over to his ship for just a few brief meetings about what he should expect when they arrived in Anglen. He'd been less than pleased at the lack of information they had to offer on the enemy.

Jagger and his mate told them as much. 'We will need to learn our enemy's intent as well as their numbers if we are to win," he'd said gruffly, looking not at all pleased by the whole situation. He sighed at the four of them standing there, the most calm noise Aiden had heard him make.

"You came here asking for my aid to fight an enemy you barely know wants to fight you. You have no useful information that might give us an edge against them, and you have given me no time frame as to how long you intend for me and my men to stay in Anglen."

The meeting did not improve from there. Later that night Aiden couldn't help the feeling that he was indeed leading these men into a trap. He pondered the thought as he lay awake in bed, Ava snoring lightly at his side while he stared up at the ceiling. Aiden didn't know how long it had been that he had been staring up at the ceiling, but eventually he pulled off the blanket, taking care not to wake Ava, though he doubted he could if he tried. He dressed quickly, strapping on all his normal weapons and daywear. He spared one last glance back at Ava before easing the door open and making his way up onto the deck.

He looked up at the helm and the sailor steering the ship gave him a sleepy nod. Aiden walked up to the man who rubbed his eyes as he approached.

"Evening Aiden," the sailor said blearily.

"Yeah," Aiden said in a slightly hushed and hurried voice. "Could you maybe sail a little closer to the red ship to our left?" he asked quickly.

The man's sleepy brows rose slightly.

"And come back when I wave?" Aiden added.

The man's brows rose higher. He had clearly been keeping a healthy distance from the Pirate King's ship compared to the others. Four ships' widths stood between them and the other.

"Please?" Aiden pressed.

The man sighed. "Well, shit," he hissed.

Aiden watched as he turned the wheel slightly and they drifted vaguely towards the ship. Aiden flashed him a grin and ran to the mast, climbing up it and walking out along the lowest brace of the sail that hung not twenty feet above the deck. The ship with the red sail grew closer. When it was close enough Aiden looked to the man at the helm and nodded before breaking into a run and leaping.

The chilled air whipped through his hair and the sea seemed to be raging under him in contrast to the smooth expanse out beyond. He hit the deck and rolled immediately, ducking behind a stack of crates. He poked his head around the edge and watched the pirate at the helm of this ship. He too was drowsy and didn't seem to have seen anything as Aiden darted from the cover of the crates and tucked behind a barrel. He knew where the cabin he wanted was. He'd seen through the window from his own ship. He just had to get off the side of the helm without the other man seeing. He took a breath. This was fine, he could do this, he thought to himself. It wasn't a bad idea all, to sneak onto the ship of your tentative ally who was known for having a temper.

With another deep breath, he made his way to the far side of the ship from his own. The man on the helm was leaning on something and facing towards their own ship. Reaching the far side of the ship, Aiden crept up the steps to the helm, taking care to keep his black cloak covering him and his face. He was at the top few steps of the staircase when the man yawned and, letting go of the wheel with one hand, he stretched and began to turn. Aiden's chest tingled with the feeling of being caught, but he grabbed the rail and flipped himself over it, hanging off the side of the ship. Through the tiny gaps in the thick posts he watched the man finish stretching and go back to facing the other side of the ship.

Aiden huffed a slight breath before hauling himself back over the railing, silent as the swishing sea beneath him. He crept around behind the man and to the back right corner of the ship. He peered over the side of the railing and down at the window he intended to enter. The light was still glowing faintly and he smiled. With one last glance back at the man steering the ship, he again hauled himself over the railing and climbed down over the ornamental carving of Scylla to the window. He hung on one hand, bracing his feet on the carving, as he pulled the knife from his boot and slit it in the gap between the two flaps of the window. He slid it up and the latch gave the faintest of dull clicks, just nearly audible over the soft patter of waves. His breath was racing now. The bit of sea spray on his face was cold as he fitted the knife back in his boot and opened the window on silent hinges before climbing in.

Archer sat at a desk on the other side of the room, head bent over something. The same girl lay sleeping in the bed. Aiden grinned and turned, shutting the window. This time he flicked the latch with a deliberate click. Archer jumped lightly, craning his neck in his seat to look toward the noise. Aiden was prepared for him to shout, but Archer just sat there with his mouth open for a moment before closing it.

Archer stood to face him, then shook his head and chuckled slightly. "I really should start locking my windows," he whispered, clearly not wanting to wake the girl.

Aiden mock frowned. "It was locked, so you're going to have to do more than that if you don't want to have late night meetings."

Archer still just shook his head grinning. "So what is it that was so pressing you had to come and talk to me in the middle of the night?"

Aiden's smile slowly died.

"What is it?" Archer asked more quietly, glancing to the door.

Aiden sighed. "We don't know anything for sure, but we haven't been entirely honest about what we suspect."

Archer's eyes had narrowed. "And what is it that you suspect exactly?"

Aiden couldn't help fidgeting with his hands. "I just wanted to warn you to stay away from the King of Orenth. Whatever else may come, stay away from him."

Archer didn't look convinced. "Why?"

"We don't know for sure," Aiden answered quickly.

"You already said that but what do you think?"

Aiden could feel his face coloring. "I'm not supposed to have told you anything. Just promise me, if things go south you'll stay away." Aiden finished a note, a plea evident in his voice.

Archer held an inquisitive stare for a long moment and to Aiden's surprise relaxed and glanced to the bed. "Ok, I'll give you the benefit of the doubt," he said smiling. "Don't worry I'll get the word around… quietly."

Aiden smiled, saying "thank you," and turned to leave back through the window.

"Hey, don't get dead out there."

Aiden smiled more broadly. "You either," he answered and, flicking open the window latch, he climbed back up the carving at the back of the boat. Reaching the rail at the helm, he peeked through the gap. The pirate at the helm was now leaning the other way, facing slightly away from the right side. Aiden took the chance. Keeping low, he pulled himself over the rail and darted back to the deck where he made his way from pile of cargo to barrel to the second mast part way down the deck. He climbed and, even moving fast, he heard a noise of surprise from the helm. A moment later a lantern was lit, casting faint light along the deck of the ship and making the sail nearest the helm show red between Aiden and the pirate. Aiden walked bent double along the bottom edge of the sail. Grabbing one of the bracing ropes, he was able to lean out and flail his arm. It took a minute but he caught the eye of Arlin's sailor and their ship slowly began to move closer, almost casually. Thirty feet, twenty. Aiden could hear the man on the red sailed ship grumbling something about "this anglish prick." Fifteen feet, twelve. Aiden bolted down the remaining length of the sail brace and leapt.

He could hear the gasp of the pirate on the red ship. Admittedly, it did look pretty bad jumping from their ship, his black cloak swishing in the lantern light. But a moment later he hit the deck, and in a smooth roll, he stood and stepped behind the mast of Arlin's ship. Aiden could feel the faint noises of outrage coming from the pirate ship, but Arlin's sailor had already begun his lazy drift away from the red ship. Only once they were again a good distance away did Aiden step out from behind the mast. Walking casually, he made his way back to the door leading down to the cabins, not entering until he flipped a gold coin to the sailor steering.

"Keep this between us?" The sailor nodded and Aiden nodded back, an accomplished smile painting his face as he crept back down the hall and into his cabin.

The room beyond was bathed in soft candle light emanating from the bedside table next to which Ava sat, leaned up in the bed and half glaring at him as he met her eyes. Aiden gave a guilty smile.

"And where have you been?" she asked, sounding more than a little annoyed.

"Having a chat with Archer." She frowned and Aiden pulled off his cloak and weapons. "You do know that other boyfriends go to bars and flirt with girls to piss off their girlfriends, not sneak onto pirate ships and risk getting killed right?" Aiden gave a dumb shrug.

"I've never been with anyone else. How was I supposed to know that," Ava replied with a sarcastic glare.

He smiled and gestured to her in an *are you really any better?* sort of way.

"I suppose I cant judge," Ava admitted, sighing.

Aiden gave a nod of agreement.

"And what was this chat about?" she asked.

"I told him to stay away from the King of Orenth."

Ava's eyes went wide.

"I didn't tell him why," Aiden cut in before she could respond.

Ava still frowned as she sat there looking at him now just in his shirt and breeches. "And you didn't think to invite me?"

Aiden knew he shouldn't, but he couldn't help it as he smiled and said, "I didn't want to interrupt your snoring."

Ava scowled. "I don't snore."

"Yes, you do," he said and walked over to sit on the bed beside him

"No, I don't."

"Yes, you do, cutie little princess snores."

In an instant she had grabbed him by the collar of his shirt, pulled him backwards until he lay on his back across the bed.

She climbed atop him and pinning his arms. "No, I don't!" she argued, leaning down closer to him.

"You do," he whispered and, pulling his head up quickly, he kissed her. She started to move, trying to pull away, but instantly stopped and kissed him back.

The next morning Aiden walked out onto the deck with bleary eyes from the excursion last night and after. When he got on deck, Zach smiled at him in that way that Aiden knew meant he was making fun of him. Aiden just ignored him, not really caring what it was about, and yawned as he walked up the steps to the helm of the ship where Arlin stood with two bowls of stew sitting on the railing next to him.

"Mor-ning," Aiden yawned as he took a place at Arlin's side.

"Morning," Arlin said back and something in his voice to told Aiden he was on the brink of laughing.

Aiden looked up from the bowl of stew he'd grabbed. "What?" Aiden asked, meeting his stare.

"You look tired," Arlin said, not at all answering the question.

Aiden frowned. "So do you," he said dully and returned to eating his stew.

"Me and the rest of the ship."

"Whatta you mean?" Aiden said, silently cursing the hour, this was too early to play games.

Arlin smirked, "Well, after the auditory performance coming from your cabin last night, of course."

Aiden almost dropped the bowl as he half spat out the stew. He could feel his face burning. And now Arlin burst out laughing.

Aiden was fully aware of the teasing grins and laughs of the crew as he made his way about the ship that morning. He found Ava sitting, leaning against the front most mast looking over the sea, a bottle of wine in hand. She seemed totally unaware of what the ship had heard as she squinted up at him in the sunlight and gestured to a spot beside her. He sat, and could still feel his face burning as the eyes of the crew kept darting to them at the front of the ship.

"Do you know how long we have 'til we reach Anglen?" she asked mildly while handing him the bottle.

Aiden shook his head. "You'd have to ask Arlin," he said after taking a swig. Maybe wine would cure his embarrassment.

Ava just tilted her head back to the sun and smiled. The weather was still growing colder as they made their way south, but the rays of sun were warm and Aiden couldn't help smiling as they shone on his face. Ava took back the bottle and downed the last bit of wine before standing. She reached down a hand to help him up. He followed her as she made her way towards Arlin, right past Zach and a group of laughing sailors.

"*Avaaaa!*" Zach crooned mockingly at Aiden whose cheeks instantly turned back to tomatoes. He didn't meet their eyes.

But Ava glanced back at him, seeing his face, then looked at Zach and the sailors before stopping to face them. She grinned and bowed at the waist, splaying her arms in mock flamboyance. "You're welcome," she said in an audible whisper as she stood, grinning toothily. The whole group looked surprised, but Ava just turned back to Aiden. She looped her arm through his, and they walked back up to the helm. Aiden's cheeks returned to normal.

"Morning captain," she said and, walking behind Arlin, she flicked his captain's hat off, catching it and fitting it on her own head. Arlin chuckled, not looking away from the sea ahead of him.

"How long 'til we reach Gloran?" Aiden asked, bracing his forearms on the rail between Ava and Arlin.

"Four days, if the wind holds," Arlins said back.

Ava plopped the hat on Aidens head. "You could be a captain," she said, looking at him in the hat.

Arlin smirked down at him and snatched the hat, placing it back on his own head. "You two really are a pair!" Arlin chuckled.

"A pair that just got Anglen a fleet," Aiden said, smiling out at the wide open sea.

# CHAPTER 50

The morning was cool as Kerstin road alongside a small envoy of guards, emissaries and generals. They had left Clystera yesterday and would be meeting Aiden and his fleet in Gloran. Kerstin couldn't help reciting the word in his head. Fleet, army. The two joking, rascal kids had actually done it. Anglen had an army. If the scouts he'd been sending to their borders and to neighboring kingdoms were to be believed, then they would need it soon. Just yesterday William had received a letter from the King of Laconia saying that Orenth had requested to pass men through the Via the Mezerek. Though the King wished him the best of luck, he would not risk refusing. The council had expected that they would be receiving the same from Avalon. So he and the generals had been sent to meet the fleet. The sun had broken over the mountains to the east and looking far ahead it was glinting on the rippling surface of the sea. On the horizon, Kerstin smiled as the small shapes wobbled in the distance.

It took them the better part of a day to get to the gates of Gloran. They were greeted by the city's Lord. He was a plump man named Harald, but Kerstin had only ever heard him referred to as the Captain. It was an odd title considering, at least as far as Kerstin knew, the man had never owned a ship. He was called this by everyone except William who just seemed to refuse to call him by anything other than his name, often to the slight annoyance of the Captain. Lord Harold smiled tightly at them as he sat perched on his similarly fat horse.

"Morning!" Kerstin called as they approached. He knew William had sent word ahead that this is where the pirate fleet would be landing. Though William had assured them that the pirates were coming on his invitation, the Captain still seemed nervous at the idea of pirates staying in his port. He was a businessman and the idea of pirates staying in his home seemed like a fair reason to be worried. Still, the Captain had seen the ruin just a few soldiers had wrought all those months ago and had pledged to do all he could to stop it from happening again.

Lord Harald kept his tight lipped smile as he waved his welcome to the envoy. Reaching him, the generals and emissaries all gave their greetings to the Lord. Most still attempted to maintain the pompous greetings Kerstin usually only tolerated at the castle and for formal parties. The Captain too seemed to find the formal introductions tedious.

He gently cut in as the third general introduced himself with a full formal title. "I suggest we meet the harbor master now," the Captain interrupted, clearing his throat. "The preparations are nearly done for our guests, and Drake Jagger's letter said he would be meeting us there."

The general looked slightly affronted at the interruption, and Kerstin silently scorned the man for being so caught up in his own pompousness.

"Yes, let's!" Kerstin answered before the generals could protest. The Captain gave him a grateful smile before flicking the reins and directing his horse along the main road leading down the hill and to the docks.

The city seemed aware of their visitors based on the panicked hush of the city. Every other time Kerstin had visited Gloran the streets had been bustling with vendors and revelers the docks covered in people and cargo. Now the streets were sparse and the docks empty of any cargo, all the docked ships having pulled their boarding planks.

"When was the city informed that this is where the pirates would be making their landing?" Kerstin asked, shifting slightly in his seat to look at the Captain.

"I announced it to the city the day after I received the letter from William."

Kerstin nodded, turning back to the road ahead of them. Reaching the end, the Captain led the group along the edge of the bay for a little ways until they reached the large double towered building of the harbor master. Ancient ballistas sat perched on the high towers, the night time oil lamps perched just behind them.

The Captain stopped at the small stable at the side of the building and tied the fat horse to the post. Kerstin tied his own mare to the adjacent hitch and turned back to view the sea. From the incoming fleet he could make out two ships at the front of the armada. One was slightly larger and beared vibrant red flags. The other had turquoise sails matching the color of warm waters, much unlike the freezing bite of the water lying in the harbor beside them. Kerstin looked back to the company. The rest of the emissaries and generals had now hitched their horses and were following the Captain through the worn oak doors of the building. Kerstin followed and they entered into a large reception room at the far end of which sat a desk. The woman sitting behind it gave a curt nod as Lord Harald walked to the door behind. The rest of the group followed, Kerstin taking up the rear. They all entered into a cavernous office. Small desks flanked the sides of the room, people sitting at each and speaking with others of all sorts. At the other end of the room sat at a grander desk. Behind it was a ruddy man who looked to be in his mid forties. Kerstin had heard of the Harbor Master of Gloran. None of the rumors had been good. Looking at him now, Kerstin had the distinct impression that the rumors were both true and would become a prevalent issue in the weeks to come.

"Good morning Icarus," the Captain said from the front of the group. The man didn't even dane to respond as he looked up at the Lord of the city and the company of high ranking officials standing before his desk. Kerstin made his way around the others to the desk.

"Are all the preparations ready for our guests?" the Captain pressed toward the stone faced harbor master.

"No," he responded flatly, leering at the Captain and then the rest of them. "And they will not be."

The Captain looked genuinely surprised. "But all the messages you had sent me…?"

The rest of the company was muttering between themselves and looked to both the Captain and Kerstin.

The harbor master continued to leer. "Idle chatter to keep a mulling Lord in line."

The Captain now looked wholly affronted. "Do you mean to tell me," he bit out, "that you have not only disobeyed my commands but also those of our King."

He shot a nervous red faced glance to the company. Kerstin, seemed to be the only one not entirely surprised.

The Captain continued, "You would send away the only ally we have and not even tell anyone!" The Captain's voice rose now under the pressure of his anger and the clear pointed attention of the others.

One of the generals stepped forward slightly. "This will mean treason," he said in a gruff voice that Kerstin knew lacked the conviction to do what he was saying.

"I am your Lord," Harald said, taking a step closer to the desk.

"You are Lord of the city!" the harbor master shrieked. "I am law unto myself in this harbor. You boast of your imagined power here, but I am the ruler! I have the power, and you have lost sense and your influence, *Great Captain!*" The harbor master clapped his hands.

Out of the shadows and doors in the dark places of the room leaked soldiers clad in black armor that clung tightly to their torsos. The company gave out yells of shock, but Kerstin was already looking for exits. Not yet drawing it, he tested the weight of his sword at his side. He was the only one off the company armed with anything more than a small dagger or ornamental swords as he again scanned the room and the soldiers. The harbor master was now grinning in a way that told Kerstin, told him in his bones, that something was wrong, wrong beyond the soldiers, beyond the ineptitude of the harbor master.

"Well, I am a businessman after all," he sneered and moved around the desk with the confidence of total control. "And the Orenthian King had a better offer…!"

Kerstin took a breath then another, closing his eyes.

When he opened them, the harbor master hissed in an air of vile nonchalance, "Kill them."

Kerstin drew the sword from his side and in the first move cleaved it upwards and through the jaw bone of the nearest soldier, splitting his face in a grotesque mess. He then grabbed the dagger from his waist belt and flung it at the soldier before the door. It hit the metal breastplate of the soldier's armor and deflected to the side. It was enough though and the force of it knocked the soldier back. Kerstin could feel the impending horror of what had been done but he didn't let himself think about it, not now, as he rammed his shoulder into the iron braced door. He felt the bones in his shoulder groan as the nails of the bracing popped out and the half splintered door burst open on the second slam.

He bolted for the stables, only steps ahead of the soldiers. Sliding on the slick boards, his hands raking against the ruff wood, he scrambled back to his feet and bolted for the horses still hitched at the small stable on the side of the building. Kerstin ripped free the reins of his horse, flinging himself atop it. He could hear the soldiers raging through the front exit and glanced back at them then to the other horses. With a flash of steel he slashed the reins of the other horses and, swinging the flat side of the blade, he slapped the rump of the nearest one. It reared on its hind legs before bolting into the shocked soldiers. The horse trampled one as the other horses, frightened by all the commotion, also bolted. Some joined the other in trampling the soldiers, others ran in all directions. Kerstin didn't know what was made of the soldiers. He'd already slapped the reins, dug in his heels, and sent the horse down the curve of the harbor at a gallop. The few sparsely spaced people shrieked and jumped out of the way as he roared for them to do so.

Kerstin's heart twisted at what he'd just done. He may not have liked or even respected the people in the company, but he never would have chosen for them to die, certainly not like they were destined to now. There was nothing to be done of that now. They were likely already dead and Kerstin alone couldn't have done anything for them anyway.

He turned his head forward and, had he not already been in the heat of battle, he may very well have collapsed at the sight of the small host of ships flanking either side of the narrow entrance to the bay, their presence unknown to the oncoming fleet of pirates. Something swooshed by and with a crack of fragmenting wood a ballista bolt stuck into the ground at his side. He tucked lower over the back of the horse, scanning the bay, city, mountains and hills around it for any method of alerting the pirates, alerting Aiden.

The mouth of the bay! Far from the docks at the mouth of the bay lay the twin set of towers in between. Kerstin knew that there lay the thick, spiked chain that had once been raised at all times before a king of old had commanded it stay lowered for trade.

He yanked the reins and the horse plowed down the street, keeping to the contour of the bay. He glanced back under his arm. He could hear the distant shouts of the soldiers and huffed in cold smugness at the sight of the riderless horse kicking its way along the road far behind him. The buildings on his right began to decrease in size and were replaced by dense oak forest flanking Gloran. The noises of the city and shouting guards faded into the thundering clatter of the horse's hooves on the dirt and gravel street. The eastern tower loomed higher and higher. Kerstin could now make out the small fortifications at its base.

The guards yelled as he approached. Guards not soldiers, the men at the base of the tower wore normal leather and metal armor bearing a stag on the chest piece. Kerstin shoved a hand down the collar of his shirt, catching the small chain of his necklace with a finger and ripping it above the collar of the shirt. He heaved on the reins and the horse slowed. Kerstin jumped off it, still moving, and stumbled before the still shocked guards, some of whom now had weapons drawn ready.

He held the necklace away from his neck, brandishing it at the guards. "I'm General of the King's forces!" he shouted, half out of breath from the ride over. Blank shock covered the guards' faces. Kerstin moved for the door to the tower as a few of the guards seemed to snap out of the shock enough to come forward. One of them beat Kerstin to the door and fitted a key.

"How can we help?" the guard asked.

"Whats wrong?!" demanded another.

"We need to raise the chain!" Kerstin bellowed.

The guard did not seem to understand. "The chain?"

Kerstin glanced again to the bay, to the armed ships sitting at the mouth of it, just out of view. No alarm looked to have been raised yet, but that would change the moment the chain came above the water.

"The old chain blocking the mouth of the bay, the ship breaker?" Kerstin pressed. The guard's eyebrows went up, still not understanding.

One of the older men stepped forward. Gray tinged this man's beard, "This way," he said and stepped past both of them, leading deeper into the base of the tower.

Kerstin turned back to the rest of the men, still looking too surprised to know what to do. "Five of you meet me at the top of the tower as soon as the chain is up," he ordered. Without waiting for an answer, he followed the older guard who led them down a flight of stairs and through a heavy iron braced door. In the room beyond sat a horizontal wooden crank and beside it a gear linked to a spool, stretching twenty feet high to the top of the ceiling. A massive barbed iron chain was held, filling only a small portion of the spool. Kerstin pointed to one of the levers on the crank while he ran to the lever on the other side. The old guard reached for the handle and, before starting to push, yelled for more guards to come. Not waiting for an answer, the two of them began to push. The wood groaned with age as the crank began to spin, slowly. One clink of the iron chain reached the spindle, then another. Kerstin shouted for more men, and he could have hugged them as three of the youngest and fittest guards burst through the door. Their faces were now set in determination as they filled the two remaining spaces on the crank. Kerstin stepped aside for the third to take his place.

He was already moving for the door as he yelled to them, "Whatever else, get the chain up!" The oldest nodded and Kerstin sprinted up the staircase.

The towers narrowed in diameter as he raced up the higher levels of it and finally onto the top where three men stood beside the already loaded ballista. This one made the two of the harbor master's hall look like crossbows by comparison. The bows of the machine stretched twenty-five feet from one side of the tower to the other. Kerstin pulled himself into the mounted seat and, using the levers attached to counterweights, pointed the great spear-sized bolt toward the nearest of the ships flanking this side of the bay entrance. Some of the guards' mouths were open in shock while others muttered words of question at the action. But Kerstin didn't bother to answer as he watched the ships crawling with black armored guards. He slammed a hand into the large lever sitting before him. With a whoosh and the twang of the anchor rope thick bow string, the bolt flew. Right to the center of the deck. It plunged through the meager boards with a crash. Kerstin heard the splash as the bolt flew all the way through the ship and into the water of the bay below. The soldiers of the ship shouted, but Kerstin didn't bother watching them as he yelled for the men, still wide eyed on the top of the tower, to load another bolt. It took them a second but they responded, heaving the crank of the ballista and pulling the rope back before two of them grabbed another bolt and fitted it in the massive grove of the machine. Kerstin aimed it at the second ship now clearly in disarray at the sight of their fellows sinking into the bay. He again slammed the lever, this time sending the bolt through the deck of the second ship. Three more ships sat at this side of the bay mouth. Kerstin had managed to blast a hole through the deck of one more before the remaining two began to shoot flaming arrows at the tower.

"Duck!!" Kerstin roared as the arrows flew, some skimming against the stone of the tower. The remainder flew over the men perched below the ballista. A few stuck in the broad bow arm, blocking Kerstin. With the bolt already loaded, the impact of the massive arrows caused the ballista to fire again. This time it struck one of the men sprinting across the deck. From the tower Kerstin saw a small mist of red as both the soldier and bolt disappeared into the bay below. Another volley of arrows flew. The guards bent over double as they still moved to load another bolt. Two arrows struck the bow arm that Kerstin was crouched behind. The third slipped below the arm. Kerstin gasped in pain as it plunged in the wood of the seat, grazing the edge of his calf and ripping through the flesh and muscle of his leg. The guards slowed, not knowing whether to help him or load the bold. Kerstin answered for them as he roared to get the bolt loaded. The moment the guards cleared the front of the huge bolt, he fired. This time it speared right through the mast and into the deck. Kerstin groaned as he reached down and surveyed the shredded side of his leg. One of the guards ran forward already holding bright white bandages the gods knew where from. Another was ripping out the burning arrows from the bow arms before they could set it aflame.

Kerstin pushed away the hands of the man trying to bandage his leg. As he met his eyes, Kerstin's own shined with tears he couldn't suppress. "The other ships," he pointed to the remaining five or so stationed at the other side of the bay, "If they come in range, sink them too."

The guard nodded again, still trying to wrap Kerstin's leg.

"You must!" Kerstin yelled, and the man cringed back slightly before nodding more vigorously. Kerstin returned a curt nod before snatching the cloth from the guard's hands and limping across the top of the tower and back down the spiraling staircase. His horse was still standing near the entrance to the tower, its head darting to and fro in the chaos.

"Where's the nearest place outside of Gloran I can get a boat?" Kerstin demanded of the guards.

One of them ran forward and kneeled next to Kerstin. The guard grabbed the roll of bandages beginning to wrap them around his leg.

The guards looked between each other. "Sometimes my cousin leaves a small one on the coast about a mile up," one of them said pointing further east beyond the tower.

Kerstin gave a short lived smile replaced by a grunt and wince as he again stood. The guard who told him of the boat stepped forward leading the horse and mounted it.

"The hell are you doing?" Kerstin demanded, stumbling toward the horse.

"You won't be able to sail it like that," the guard said genuinely. "I'll come with you."

Kerstin didn't like the idea but had no time to argue the point. "Fine," he said and turned back to the remaining guards. "Soldiers will be arriving here shortly. Do not let them lower the chain!"

The guards had gone pale faced and some began to tremble. Kerstin's heart fell as the weight of what he was asking them to do landed on him. He knew his next words might doom them but he added, "Hold it 'til nightfall at least. Then if you can, run."

"How many are coming?" one of the older ones asked. Kerstin could feel the adrenaline beginning to fade.

"I don't know," he said. It was all he could do to stop his voice breaking. "It could be just a few. It could be a legion." He paused for a moment. There was no reason to lie to them now. "We've been betrayed. The Harbor Master let Orenthian soldiers into Gloran. I don't know how many. I don't know how. But I do know that if they get a chance to ambush the incoming fleet… then we won't have a chance in the war to come." It was shit as pep talks go, but he wouldn't lie to them, not to the truly loyal guards of the kingdom.

He watched as the men looked out to the road before them. Perhaps the youngest of the guards there, not a wisp of hair covered his chin was the first to speak. He spoke not in a prayer, or plea, or any other kind of fear, as he hooked his arms around the necks of two of the other guards at his sides, both of similar ages, one boy and one girl. All three had burning red hair and looked as green as any guards or soldiers Kerstin had ever known, but he also didn't think he ever had as much respect for any, as he did for this one, barely fourteen, as he said loudly, to everyone in the vicinity. "Well, if I had to die today, I'm glad it's with you fuckers!" He finished grinning. "Do what you have to," he said to Kerstin, with the kind of honest innocence of youth that he'd seen in Aiden when they'd first met. The kind that had made Kerstin, even then, know that Aiden would never wave in conviction, and nor would this boy.

Kerstin hauled himself onto the back of the horse, the other guard helping to pull him up and they shot off. They followed the road back down toward Gloran for a few hundred yards before they slowed. Kerstin had to admit he never would have known the way on his own. The guard led them through a patch of trees along what looked to be nothing more than a game trail. It remained this way for a while before it opened back onto the cold sand of the coast. Kerstin looked left to the fleet and sighed at the sight of the lowered sails. The horses' hooves sprayed cold wet sand on their feet and Kerstin reached down to check the bandages on his leg. It stung when he touched it, and his hand was covered in dirty diluted blood and sand when he lifted it.

The guard glanced back over his shoulder, "How are you doing?"

"Fine," Kerstin grunted back. "How much farther?"

The guard pointed ahead to a small shape on the beach ahead of them. The boat turned out to be a small daysailer, barely five feet wide and fifteen long. Still Kerstin was grateful to see it. The guard pulled on the reins and the horse slowed to a stop. The guard slung a leg over and held up a hand to help Kerstin down. Kerstin took it begrudgingly and was glad he did as he nearly collapsed upon hitting the sand. The moment he seemed sure Kerstin wasn't going to fall over the guard ran to the boat, throwing his weight against the prow as he shoved it off the shore and onto the water. Kerstin tugged the horse's reins pointing it back towards Gloran before slapping its rump and sending it galloping back down the cold beach. The guard pointed at the rear of the two places to sit in the boat. The moment Kerstin was in, the guard finished pushing the boat out into the water and with a smooth step climbed onto the prow. He walked around Kerstin on the side of the boat, holding the small mast and causing the whole boat to lean as he did. The man grabbed the rope tied to the corner of the small sail and with a flicking motion wrapped it around a small wooden tie point before pulling the sail out and into the wind. The boat's boards groaned and they were off for the looming fleet.

# CHAPTER 51

Aiden was sleeping peacefully, the cold light of the morning shining through the window in the wall of their cabin. He was awake, but by no means ready to climb out of bed. Right as he pulled the blanket high over his chest he heard the whoosh of wind as the cabin door opened and Ava walked in. He listened to her feet on the boards as she attempted to not wake him. He maintained his silence as she climbed into the bed on the other side. She blocked the light coming in from the window as she leaned over him. The mattress sagged under the weight of her palms and she leaned her face closer to his. His mask broke and though he didn't open his eyes, he smiled. She giggled.

"Guess wha-a-t?" she taunted, plopping down on the bed beside him and resting her chin on his chest.

He just lay there smiling vaguely.

"Guess?" she continued to taunt.

"And why would I do that when you are about to tell me?"

She nudged him with an elbow.

Aiden opened one eye. "Jagger, smiled?" he asked skeptically.

She propped herself up slightly with an arm on his chest. "No, but Zach just spotted Anglen," she breathed, grinning.

"We're almost home!" he sang out.

Moving faster than she could react, Aiden swept her up in his arms and stood up. She yelled sharply in surprise and batted away his laughing as he carried her through the door and up onto the sun kissed deck. If he was honest, it was freezing without a shirt. He held Ava a little tighter as he carried her straight to the prow of the ship before setting her down. He wrapped his hands around her waist where she stood in front of him, facing the other away. Hid teeth glinted toward the green and gray mass tinged blue in the distance sitting before them.

"Almost home," Ava whispered and, craning her neck back, looked up at him behind her.

"Almost," he whispered back.

The peaceful moment was cut short as Zach called over. "Well aren't you a disgustingly cute sight for the morning?"

A rough and calloused hand clapped Aiden on the back. He cringed at the cold touch, arching away from it. Zach stepped beside them, bracing his forearms on the railing and looking out over the sea to the land beyond.

"Don't act like you're not homesick too, Zach the heartless sailor," Ava shot back.

He chuckled. "I would never! I'll finally have a chance to drink all that ale you owe me," he sniped.

Ava hissed back jokingly.

They all stood there for a long moment looking out toward Anglen before Zach said more flatly, "Jagger called a meeting for later this morning before we get there to discuss our arrival."

Aiden and Ava both nodded vaguely as Zach walked away, back to the helm of the ship where Arlin stood at the wheel.

The morning went by too slowly. The distant land seemed not to grow any closer as they sat in their normal morning group eating breakfast. Annalise joined them a little late as usual, again wearing the fine white clothes for their arrival back to Anglen. She smiled down at the group, grabbing a bowl of food, and to Aiden's surprise sat on the deck of the ship, completing the small circle.

Arlin came down not long after, informing all of them that they would be going over the Pirate King's ship in twenty minutes for the meeting and that they should be ready to cross over. Annalise looked a little nervous at the idea, and after the last meeting, he couldn't really blame her. If it hadn't been for Arlin, she would have teetered off the board between the two ships and plunged into the steel water. She had thanked him the moment she was back on the ship and hadn't seemed keen on the idea of crossing again since.

"We'll rig up a rope," Ava whispered, giving a knowing glance to Annalise who sighed softly, before standing.

"Well, I must go get ready for the meeting," she looked down at Aiden, still shirtless. "I… suggest you do the same."

"You don't think he'd appreciate my beautiful bare chest?" Aiden crooned back in mock hurt.

"I'm afraid not," she said laughingly and walked back to the door that led below deck.

Aiden did indeed go down to the cabin and change into a fresh pair of breeches and a new white shirt, this time bothering to strap on his dagger and sword. He brought Ava's weapons when he came back up. The crew was already moving the broad plank they had used to walk between the ships before. Rather safer, he thought, than the method he'd used to go talk to Archer. Annalise was waiting for them on the deck dressed back in the black tunic with gold thread. Her hair was tied into a perfect braid. Ava thanked him as he handed over her weapons.

The three of them walked over to the edge of the ship, where both Arlin's and Jaggers's helmsmen were steering towards each other. Only once they were within eight feet or so did the sailors drop the plank between the ships with a thwack. Ava stepped forward first, having produced a rope from somewhere. She tied one end to the rail of the Sea

Dragon and, walking as though it was just another day back home, strolled across the plank not even bothering to look down at the raging cold water below. When she reached the other side where Archer and three of the other pirates were waiting, she tied the remaining rope to the rail and waved for Annalise to come across. Annalise gulped and Aiden heard one of the pirates chuckle over the roaring of the water. Aiden followed the nervous emissary as they crossed to the other side of the ship where Archer was standing, grinning at them.

Only once all of them were over did Archer speak. "My dad wants to go over the final planning for our arrival in Gloran and maybe get some idea of where we might be heading after that."

They did indeed talk about the arrival and what might come, with Annalise proving most of the answers all in well articulated points and gentle rebuttals. The Pirate King seemed happy with the plan, or at least Aiden thought so based on the lack of wrath emanating from him. They were eventually instructed to go back to their ship, where they would sail just a little ahead of the fleet into the bay. From there, their two ships would land and meet with William's company in Gloran.

The rest of the day was spent in revelry that a few weeks ago Annalise might have run from screaming. She certainly had loosened up on her standards of how to behave. Between the three of them, they drank a bottle and a half of Arlin's wine before he told them to stop drinking him dry and go do something else.

"You two should spar with Zach," Annalise said, clearly a little drunk. "We could use some entertainment," she gestured to the rest of the sailors sitting around the deck.

Ava shook her head. "I'm too happy to fight," she said far less drunk than Annalise who, unsurprisingly to everyone on deck, turned out to be a light weight when it came to drinking.

Annalise scoffed. "Well, if you two babies won't, then I... will," she said and stood.

Aiden was taken aback. So were the others. Zach grinned from the other side of the group. Aiden began to raise his hand to shut down the idea on the grounds that Zach was twice her size and actually knew how to fight.

But Ava grabbed his arm grinning, "Let her have a go."

"Really?" Aiden asked incredulously.

"Yeah," Ava said a little too casually for Aiden to ignore. He raised a brow and she just shrugged.

"So what about you Zachery? Are you a sissy too or will you fight?" Annalise crooned.

To his credit Zach didn't seem to want to but stood at the first sound of teasing from the others. "I'll go easy on you," Zach sighed. He couldn't help sneering at her as the two of them began to circle, he still holding a bottle in one hand. The sailors behind him laughed. Zach looked back at them to grin. Annalise struck, not precisely or well, but the punch to his face was enough to knock him down. Her fist connected right on his jaw bone as he looked back. Zach hit tripped over a jagged deck plank and hit the ground with a heavy thud. He propped himself back up on his arms after a moment, looking slightly surprised at her. Annalise cursed, holding the hand in her other, she shook it. Zach and the others including Aiden broke out laughing.

"Still wanna fight?" Zach asked not bothering to get up.

"Yes," Annalise said but everyone watched as she still cradled her hand. she then amended the statement. "Well, maybe later."

Zach grinned, his chin begging to turn red. He snatched one of the small tankards of ale from the crate beside him and handed it to her. Zach grabbed another, done with his bottle. "To the lady who knocked me on my ass before I saw it coming!" he toasted and everyone cheered.

But the cheer was cut short at the yell from one of the nearby ships. Everyone quieted, listening for the noise. There was some commotion on the ship to their right and a moment later someone roared, "Drop all sails!! Full stop!!"

Again there was a moment of calm, then the ship was in chaos as the message was repeated to other ships and eventually the rest of the fleet. Within five minutes every ship in the fleet had lowered their sails and were slowing to a halt. Arlin was striding along the deck giving orders when the ship veered closer to them and dropped a plank to board.

Arlin, Zach, Aiden and Ava all walked over to the side of the ship. The captain of the ship strode across. He was another young captain, maybe even younger than Arlin. The man looked split between panic and anger at the group of them.

"What is it?" Arlin demanded, stepping forward.

"The harbor chain is up in the bay."

"What?" Ava blurted.

"Your port..." the man sneered, "has raised a ship breaker blocking the entrance to the bay. So either they want us to stay out in the open water or they don't want us at all."

"That chain has not been raised for nearly a century," Annalise responded in surprise. "It was commanded that it stay lowered long before King William took the throne, and they know we are soon to arrive."

The young captain sneered at her too. To her credit she'd sobered up more than Aiden would have thought she could on such short notice.

"Well their intention is clearly not to let us in, now isn't it? To port!!" the man roared to Arlin's man at the wheel.

The man looked frantically between the new captain and Arlin, who nodded.

"We'll meet with Mr. Jagger and see what he wants us to do?"

The man huffed off and strode across the deck, two of his own men coming across the plank to flank him. One was young, no more than twelve and barely came to Ava's shoulder. The other looked similar to Zach in every regard but demeanor. The three of them strode to the other side of the deck to their own ship, pulled up the plank and veered away. The bigger of the two men flanking him, grabbed the plank they'd been using to get from ship to ship. The moment they were close enough, he dropped it to the deck of Jagger's red sailed ship. The three of them walked across, signaling for the rest to do the same. The five of them, including Zach, came to the plank this time. Zach walked immediately behind Annalise, a hand on her elbow, as they made the crossing, Annalise blushing the slightest bit.

They were led by Archer into the Pirate King's study where they waited for a long minute in silence before he finally entered. All of the calm that had covered his features before was gone. He again had the sense of red, misty rage pouring off him as he surveyed the lot of them.

"I will ask this once and only once." The words were a growl, that resinated in the floor boards. "Why is it that the kingdom I have come to aid has just blocked entrance to their shores from me?" The Pirate King's hands were tense. The white yellow calluses of his knuckles, formed Aiden guessed by years of beating the shit out people, stretched under the strain.

An hour later Aiden was thanking the gods for Annalise, who even drunk, seemed able to calm Jagger, to at least some degree. She explained that they had no more idea as to why the chain was down than he did.

His red fuming anger finally slowed and he invited them to sit. "Then we wait here until we can get a person onto land to see what's going on."

"When will this person be sent to see what's happening?" Aiden asked, already planning how he and Ava would get on the team.

But just then more commotion roared from the deck. The Pirate King stood sharply.

Archer groaned. "And what in the sea fearing hell's wrong now?" he muttered and followed his father out onto the deck with the rest of them.

"What is it?" Jagger roared to the ship.

All eyes flicked to him and one of them answered, "A daysailer's approaching. There are two people on it from what we can tell."

"Show me!" Jagger roared.

The pirate led them to the starboard prow of the ship. There it was a small boat bobbed along no more than five hundred feet from the Sea Storm. The Pirate King's face was an unreadable mask of calm as he looked out at the boat.

"Orders sir?" the pirate asked.

"Take them aboard. If they make a move, dye out sails fresh red."

The pirates on ship insisted they all stay back when the boat arrived. Well, insisted might be a kind word for the string of curses they shot at Annalise when she walked back to see how close it had gotten. The uproar sounded again when the boat reached them. The group of them from Arlin's ship were shoved to the back when the two men were hauled aboard.

"He's wounded!" one of the pirates called out. Jagger was already at the head of the group. Aiden could hear the pleading of one of the men at the head of the crowd. It sounded like the Pirate King talked with the two men for a while before one of the pirates shoved to the back of the crowd where Aiden and the others still stood.

"Which one of ya's Aiden?" the man growled.

Aiden stepped forward. Without a word, the man grabbed him by the upper arm and began wrenching him to the front. Ava yelled, but Aiden looked over his shoulder, giving her a reassuring glance. The man pulling him pushed his way through the others to the small circle formed at the center. The man only let go when Aiden was standing right beside the Pirate King. And only then did he look down at the two men.

One of the men Aiden didn't know, dressed in Anglish armor he looked to be about thirty. Aiden glanced at the other and had a double take. The man's skin was pale and he looked more tired than usual but he knew him.

"Kerstin?!" Aiden asked breathlessly.

The man tilted his head up to Aiden and grinned for a moment before nodding. Aiden looked him up and down and gasped at the bloody mess of bandages wrapped around his lower leg.

"Someone get a doctor!" he shouted and tried to kneel down to Kerstin, tried because a hot, giant vice-like hand grabbed him by the upper arm and nearly picked him up off the ground as it hauled him back.

"Not yet," the Pirate King didn't remove his hand from Aidens arm.

"But!" Aiden began.

But Jagger cut him off. "Not until you explain to me who these men are and why I shouldn't paint my sails with them.

Aiden was out of breath as he answered, "Because this man is in charge of William's forces in Anglen." Aiden panted, not technically correct but correct in practice. He winced under the Pirate King's grip.

"And the other?" Jagger pressed, staring wrathfully at the other frightened looking man.

"I... I" Aiden stammered.

"He's," Kerstin winced, "one of the guards at the tower that raised the chain. He helped me get to you."

"And why is the chain raised?" Jagger bit out.

Kerstin tried to sit up but failed.

"Please," Aiden pressed, "let someone fix his leg, then he can answer all our questions."

There was already a small pool of blood seeping from the bandages around Kerstin's leg.

The Pirate King stared daggers at the knight for a long moment then glanced at Aiden. "Rammrook!" he yelled.

There was some scuffling from behind them, and a moment later, an old man slightly bent with age shuffled into the circle, kneeling at Kerstin's side.

"Fix him good enough to talk. I want him in my office in five minutes."

The doctor gave a curt nod, not bothering to look back, and seeming used to this kind of *do the best you can in not enough time* kind of order. Aiden sighed and before he could brace for it was again yanked through the crowd by the hand that had still not let go of him. Aiden and the Pirate King both passed the edge of the crowd where the rest of Aiden's group still stood. Ava's eyes flared at the sight of Aiden being guided half off the ground, but he gave her a severe look and she remained silent.

"Office, now," he growled and, reaching the door, shoved Aiden in before holding the door for the rest of them to enter.

They all did, everyone but Ava bowing their heads slightly away from the man. She looked him straight in the eyes, but he didn't seem to care as he followed them into the room. He stood there blocking the door, the rest of them pushed back against the desk.

"I will say this once... if this is some elaborate plan to stab me in the back... it will fail. I am King of the most brutal kingdom on water or land and whatever you think you might be able to do to overthrow me will fail. So if you are planning to stab me in the back say so now, because if you don't... I will take pleasure in every moment I spend pulling you apart bone by bone and string you up as a warning!" His voice rose on every word of the last sentence. The red mist again seemed to swirl around him. Aiden shook his head trying to clear it of the mist and the feeling that came along with it. None of them so much as parted their lips. They stood like that for a minute before the King's face slackened just the slightest bit.

"In that case, your friend," he looked at Aiden, "will be in here any minute." He walked around to the back of the desk, towering over all of them. Even Arlin looked to be brushed aside as Jagger walked by and sat in the huge polished wood chair.

Sure enough, a minute later the door opened and the old doctor carried Kerstin in with the help of another pirate. Aiden immediately pulled one of the chairs forward for them to set him in. Kerstin's leg was now bound in fresh bandages, tainted red where the wound lay, but no longer leaking the copious amounts of blood as before. The other two men hurried out of the office. Then Jagger slid a slightly disdainful look between them.

The Pirate King gave Kerstin a moment to get comfortable in the chair before he began. "So, captain of King William's forces, why is the chain up?"

Kerstin's face blanched, and he hung his head between his shoulders. "We've been betrayed," he said softly.

Aiden went tense, and he felt Ava do the same at his side. The others didn't seem to be breathing either. Only Jagger seemed unsurprised by the words. Aiden's eyes flashed to the Pirate King, he... he was smiling, smiling in a way that made every instinct in Aiden's bones tell him to get out of the room before it turned.

But he just asked in the calmest tone Aiden had ever heard from the man, "By whom?"

Kerstin looked up at the man flinching at the look. "The harbor master," Kerstin wheezed. "He smuggled Orienthian troops into Gloran. I raised the chain so you wouldn't enter their trap."

Jagger made no effort to thank the knight. "How many?"

Kerstin shook his head. "I don't know. They will have killed the whole company I came with by now."

Aiden's chest tightened and he felt his feet begin to wobble as he watched Kerstin who saw the change.

"William was not with us."

The room went silent for a moment as Archer walked in the room, halting against the wall just beyond the doorway. Jagger surveyed his son for a long moment then the rest of them. He pointed to Ava and Aiden. "I'm told you two are skilled in matters of stealth?" He paused waiting for an answer.

"We are," Ava said.

The massive pirate grunted his acknowledgment. "Then here is what you will do."

Both Annalise and Kerstin made noises of objection at the command in the words. But Jagger let out a low vicious growl, and they fell silent immediately. Aiden could have sworn he saw that red mist dancing around Jagger's shoulders.

He pointed to Aiden and Ava. "You two along with my son will lower the chain." He pointed to the others. "And when it's down we will enter the bay."

Kerstin blinked. "Did you not hear me tell you it was a trap. They are waiting for you in the bay! There are ships flanking either side of the entrance!"

But the King's smile only grew more blood thirsty. Archer was looking surprised as though he didn't think his father would have given him a mission. The look danced in his eyes for a moment longer before it was replaced by a look Aiden'd never seen on Archer's face before, calm and understanding.

"You three leave at nightfall," Jagger ordered the three of them. "Be ready, the moment the chain is down we'll be there."

The plan was simple enough, Aiden thought half an hour later as he and Ava prepared in their cabin. If not a little cocky and brazen. He wondered how many of the Pirate King's men would die in the battle.

He and Ava had been silent since the meeting, and it was she who finally broke the silence. "I hope Archer doesn't fuck this up," she spat, shoving yet another dagger into her boot.

Aiden smirked, "Are you really still mad at him about the wolf thing?"

She flicked her eyes at him, daring him to make fun.

He just raised his palms. "Have you ever been in a battle?" he asked her. She'd been in Attica but...

"No," she said softly. "The mercenaries had taken me before the fight started."

Aiden nodded vaguely. "What do you think of Jagger's plan?"

Ava smiled. "I think he has a better chance than you think."

Aiden frowned, but Ava's smile grew feline and he realized why she'd been so quiet in the meeting.

"You!" He said and laughed.

She smiled back. "The Pirate King will win this fight. He doesn't even think he'll lose a man," she said, still smiling.

Aiden tucked another dagger in his belt and pulled on his black cloak. "Anything else that you read?" he asked.

She placed a finger on her lips in consideration. "The temper wasn't faked. I don't think that man's ever had a calm thought in his life."

They stepping out into the hall and walked up on deck where they found Archer waiting. Aiden had to blink a few times before he realized who it was. Archer normally dressed in dirty pants and a colorful shirt, but he now was wearing black from head to toe. He donned light leather armor, a full-sized sword strapped over his shoulder, a short sword strapped to his side and, Aiden blinked, the same small, slender dagger strapped to his forearm that Ava did. Archer grinned between them, looking them up and down.

It was a little too frankly for Ava's liking and she snapped at him. "What are you doing here?"

He pointed to the side of the boat. "We're taking the little boat to land," he answered.

Aiden nodded and the three of them walked to the side of the ship where the boat was strapped. Someone had replaced the sail with a black one, not the easily visible white of before.

Aiden gestured to the empty prow of the ship. "You two want to go over the plan before it's time to go?"

They both shrugged, walking to the place he had indicated. The sun was already shining cold pink in the dying day.

"So, has anyone ever been to this tower we're supposed to break into?" Aiden asked, leaning against the rail of the deck.

Ava shook her head.

"Nope, but my dad questioned your friend."

Aidens eyes flashed. "Questioned?"

"They just talked," Archer said, raising his hands. He continued, "Your buddy said that the mechanism for the spool is in the sub-level of the tower. The left tower with the spool also has a ballista on the roof. We'll have to take it over and use it to destroy the other ballista before they can get in."

They went over how they would take over the tower until darkness fell. They ended on the idea that they would all enter the tower at the same time, sneaking up to the base through the trees as far as they could. Fingers crossed they would be able to incapacitate some of the soldiers before they alerted the others. Or at least that was the plan as they lowered themselves into the daysailer. Arlin bid them well and left before the pirates came over. Unsurprisingly, Jagger came over a moment later. The surprising part was that he wished them all the best of luck, not just his son. The girl who had been in Archer's room came over too, sticking close to the Pirate King. She wished them safe passage, seeming a little timid in front of them. Archer pecked her on the cheek, smiling as he whispered something to her. She smiled back. Jagger nodded and, with a sharp yank of the rope holding the boat, it was free and they drifted ahead.

They hadn't even brought a lantern and relied on the almost nonexistent light of the thin crescent moon to guide them. Not that there was much need of guiding with the giant brazier that had been lit atop the tower. They rowed in silence, Aiden slowly gaining that quiet calm that came before violence. The land loomed closer and with two fully fit rowers on either side of the boat it was moving a lot faster than it had been with Kerstin and the guard. Meanwhile, Ava sat at the front of the boat looking out toward the tower.

"Why is there always wind when we don't want it and never when we do?" she demanded of the world.

Archer laughed. "The way I see it, you're not the one rowing the boat."

Ava's head turned back to him and, though Aiden couldn't make out her face, he could tell her eyes were flaring at him. Aiden sat in the tight silence for a moment longer before choosing to do something about it.

"My god you two," he scoffed. "You had to fight some wolf together forever ago and it didn't go so well. Does it really matter now?"

Archer's head snapped to Aiden, then to Ava. "Well, that's not why she's mad at me," he told Aiden.

Ava grumbled from the prow of the boat.

Aiden raised his brows knowing no one could see. "Oh yeah?" he asked and hoped Ava could hear the smile in his voice.

"She doesn't like me because before any of the stuff happened in Gileda…"

"Archer!" Ava growled again.

He snickered. "She asked me to Taramin, when her family stopped in Barataria on the way to Gileda."

"Taramin?" Aiden asked, confused.

"It's a dance in Barataria. We have it once a year and dear Ava asked me to it… but I was already going with someone, so I said no. And since you're only allowed to go with an invitation from someone living in Barataria, she wasn't able to go at all."

Aiden looked between them twice then burst out laughing.

"Shut up," Ava whispered.

He didn't.

"Aiden be quiet," she said more urgently.

He ceased his laughing to look over his shoulder at Ava and the beach beyond. Archer did the same.

"Stop rowing," she whispered.

They both obeyed, turning in their seats to look at the beach where they could just make out the forms of two people. They scanned the beach for others. There were none.

"Water?" Archer breathed barely audible over the noise of the rippling water against the shore.

They'd drifted closer now. He pointed to himself and then to the water. Aiden frowned and watched Ava dip a finger into the steely mass and shutter. Aiden sighed, then nodded. They all slipped into the water, their cloaks fluctuating near the surface as they swam. Their heads barely penetrated the surface and it was a struggle for Aiden to keep his breath steady in the frigid water. But they swam. It took them no longer than five minutes to be at the edge of the shore. Together, they crept up, lying on their stomachs in the shallow water and shimmying as close as they could to the un-suspecting soldiers. They again looked between each other only barely able to see the outlines of each others' heads. Aiden in the middle held up three fingers. He took a breath and dropped one, then another. He took a final deep breath before dropping the last finger.

The three of them shot to their feet. Water sprayed as Aiden grabbed the dagger from his boot and began to sprint at the soldiers. They were dressed the same as those in the courtyard of the mountain fortress: black armor with the Orienthian crest upon the chest. He took another step and flung the dagger. It soared and the first of the soldiers shouted right as the pommel of the poorly thrown dagger thudded into his face. His fellow looked down with a cry on his own lips, right as Archer barreled into him with a knife as his body slammed into that of the other soldier. A crunch sounded as the knife cracked through bone. He pulled away a moment later. Ava had already reached the other soldier who writhed on the ground as she held him against the small log they'd been sitting on.

"How many soldiers are in the city?!" she snarled. The soldier just smiled and blood gleaned on his teeth.

"You're dead," he whispered.

Aiden picked the knife up off the ground and held the point to his chin. The man spat in Ava's face. Blood and spit speckled her skin in the faint moon light. Barely contained anger painted across her face when she closed her eyes. When she again opened them, they were sharper as she fixed her stare on him. She started to breathe more heavily as the man shuddered. Archer looked between the two of them confused. But Ava held that stare a moment longer before picking the soldier up by the collar of his breastplate and slamming his head back down into the log. He went limp, a trickle of blood running from his head.

Archer's mouth opened. "He might have told you!" he protested.

"No, he wouldn't, not with the Orenthian King to scare him into silence," Aiden said softly. He looked to Ava inquiringly

Her face was grim. "Half a legion," she answered to his unasked question.

Archer was now looking between the two of them. "What the hell was..." he began to ask.

Aiden didn't let him finish and pointed in the direction of the tower looming above. The forest before them was thick and almost pitch black with the canopy above. Aiden and Archer started for the forest. They were forced to move slowly through the woods, not wanting to lose their footing in the blackness. But soon enough they saw the light of the lanterns at the base of the tower begin to peek through the trunks of the trees. They slowed further, crouching as they made their way under a fallen tree. They remained bent double as they came up to the edge of the forest and halted.

No more than twenty feet beyond the tree line lay the fence surrounding the base of the tower. Aiden's breath caught in his lungs and his mind went cold and blank at the sight of what the soldiers had done to the tower guards. They had been carved beyond recognition, their bodies hanging broken and contorted on the spikes atop the fence. In the light of the lanterns inside the small courtyard he could see the puddles of dark blood pooling on the grass. Aiden felt the others stiffen and heard their breath catch beside him. Three of the bodies looked to be no older than Aiden himself, maybe younger. Siblings or relatives of some kind, each had burning red hair, now matted and sticky with blood.

They all looked over the fence then beyond it. There were no more than ten soldiers seated and standing. Aiden could make out three that sat around a small fire, two more at the entrance to the courtyard, two at the entrance of the tower, and the rippling shapes of the final three moving through the posts of the fence.

The moment of silence ended. Ava snarled and Archer winced at the noise. "They're dead," she growled, with all the viciousness of her emotions, shifting to pull her mother's bow over her head. She notched an arrow.

"Which ones?" Archer asked in a whisper. Ava didn't respond, but the answer was plain enough. All of them. She wanted all of them dead. Aiden rested a hand on the arrow Ava had notched. Her eyes flashed and she looked at him, tear streaks already shining under her eyes.

"Let the two of us get in position first."

She nodded after a moment, her lips pursed. "Do it quick."

Aiden and Archer didn't disappoint. Within moments they had pulled back just behind the tree line splitting in different directions. A moment later they were creeping along just on the outside of the fence bent double. Aiden halted mere feet beyond the edge of the gap in the fence forming the entrance to the courtyard. A heartbeat later Archer crept up on the other side. Silently, Aiden reached over his shoulder and grabbed the bone white hilt of Starlight. He had a dagger in his other hand. Archer did the same and they shared a glance before Aiden turned his head. Finding Ava tucked behind a tree, he took a deep silencing breath, rage already boiling under his skin, and nodded.

No sooner had he done so than the arrow flew. Its small shining head soared and, with a guttural noise, found its mark in the throat of one of the soldiers. The other solider let out a scream. Aiden and Archer were already moving and he was dead a moment later, Aiden flicking his blade as he ran by into the courtyard. The soldiers at the base of the tower yelled and the others plunged into momentary chaos. They didn't waste the opportunity. Archer had ended two more of them, blood spraying the air before they'd drawn their weapons. Another arrow flew over Aiden's shoulder, sinking into the throat of an approaching soldier. Aiden ran for the next one, spinning on his feet, as the man launched a sloppy slice at his torso. Aiden finished the spin by sinking the knife into the man's side. He heard soft, fast footsteps behind him and another arrow flew, plunging into the leg of a soldier a few feet beyond. The man fell to his knees and the soft footsteps passed him. Ava had already pulled the bow back over her head and held her sword in one hand as she cleaved it right through the neck of the knelt soldier. Aiden heard the roar of another soldier behind him. He spun but the roar was cut short with a clanking thud. The blade of a dagger plunged into the side of the man's armor, right up to the hilt. Aiden looked around, Archer grinned at him even as the Pirate King's son spun on a graceful pirouette, the length of his blade sticking through the gap between the soldier's armor just below his armpit.

The shouting stopped. Aiden was panting slightly. The three of them looked at each other, sparsely coated in sprays of blood. Aiden looked to the tower, listening, and he sighed at the calm silence. Archer pointed to the door but Ava was already storming for it. She reached it first and, with more force than was necessary, stuck a dagger in the gap between the door and the wall. She yanked on it, but the door didn't so much as wobble. She tried twice more before Archer stepped beside her, a small wavy piece of metal held in his hand. Ava glared at him but stepped aside as he fitted it in the lock. It took a moment of wiggling the metal and the lock clicked open.

"I'll get the ballista," Archer whispered and, pushing the door open, started at a feline, quiet sprint up the steps.

Aiden and Ava didn't consult each other before racing down the steps. They found the room Kerstin had spoken of filled with only a few men. They made quick work of it. The element of surprise was on their side and all but one of the soldiers was denied the time to raise his weapon.

Aiden surveyed the spool and crank Kerstin had told Jagger about. Sure enough, the spool reached to the ceiling of the room and a crank lay in the center of the space. A gear system connected the crank to the spool and on the side of the spool a huge toothed ratchet held it from unraveling. Aiden walked over to it trying to find how one would unlock the pin when...

"Out of the way!" Ava shouted from behind.

Lucky for him, Aiden obeyed as she brought down the soldier's massive dane axe on the pin. It cracked and the two of them jumped back toward the door. This was again lucky, as the pivot holding the spool groaned and, with the sound of a cannon blast, snapped off. Aiden took one look at what it began to do and grabbed Ava's wrist. He was sure it hurt as he picked her up off the ground, pulling her up the stairs by the arm. But he didn't care as the sound of the spool crashing around the room boomed. He could hear the spiked chain gouging into the stone. The tower shuttered and shook as it finally pulled the spool tight against the wall of the room. Aiden looked to Ava, both of their eyes wide with fear, face stark white and drained of color. It took him a moment to snap out of the sudden shock.

"Archer!" he said.

Ava understood as the two of them ran up the steps, not bothering to quiet their feet after the booming of the spool. Aiden was wheezing by the time they reached the top of the tower. The soldiers were dead, blood strewn across the large flat top of the tower. The very first rays of light were starting to paint the sky and lighten the earth as Archer struggled to pull back the rope to load a bolt.

"Get in!!" Aiden shouted to him.

Aiden and Ava each went to a side of the massive ballista, grabbing the rope crank and turning it. Aiden let out a groan of effort as the rope clicked. They grabbed one of the huge bolts, longer and thicker than a spear. It slotted in. Archer began using the levers of the machine to point it, not at the harbor, but at the other ballista mounted tower flanking the entrance to the bay. The glowing sky now shown bright enough to make out the shape of the structure. Archer pulled another lever, aiming the bow just a little higher than the top of the tower. Whoosh, the bolt flew, flexing slightly through the air. It hit with a crash that rang through the bay, through the city, and plunged through the stones of the tower.

"Again!" Archer said and they repeated the process loading the ballista and firing.

The first rays of the day were piercing the sky by the time the fifth bolt split the air, crashing into the tower and it crumpled. The remaining stones collapsing, the top half of the tower fell, covering the side of the bay in a plume of gray dust. Aiden took his first deep breath since the previous night and turned, smiling to the incoming pirate fleet.

# CHAPTER 52

At the other side of the tower, Ava didn't move and she didn't smile. Her gaze was fixed on the city at the other end of the bay. Archer too had walked over to the side of the tower and was looking grave. 'Half a legion' but what was half a legion to someone who'd never seen an army before, at least never an army with a number associated.

Aiden's smile was short lived as he joined her to look out at the half a legion. He felt something oily in his gut. Half a legion, it turned out, was more soldiers than Aiden had seen since the mountains. He balked. They were lining the coast with more black sailed ships along it. The pirates, they were about to sail through the open mouth of the bay right into... a trap. That's what this had been, from the start. They had thought that they had seen past the trap but this, the soldiers had known it didn't matter that Kerstin got away. It didn't matter to them if the whole fleet came into the bay, they were ready and...

Aiden turned back to the incoming fleet and was utterly lost for words as five... five of the Pirate fleet continued their sail to the bay. The Sea Dragon at the front was flanked by Jagger's own ship and three more of the pirate fleet. Five ships against the rows of soldiers on the shore and the remaining Orienthian ships near them.

"What the hell are they doing?" Aiden voiced aloud looking back and forth between the five ships and the coast of the bay. Smoke was starting to bloom from some of the buildings.

Archer and Ava both turned to watch the pirates. Ava too wore an expression of blank shock. Archer paled, his eyes narrowed on the red sailed ship now pulling slightly ahead of the Sea Dragon. He smiled and gave a small laugh.

Ava heard the noise and her eyes snapped to him. "What the hell's funny!" she demanded of him.

His smile just grew, not truly happy but cruel, cold even, as the first warm streaks of light began the day. Ava took a step toward him, a hand pointing behind her to the ships about to sail right into this trap. She opened her mouth to speak but Aiden did so first.

"What don't we know?" he asked quietly.

Ava halted, half turning to Archer, and he watched as she closed her eyes still facing him. He shuttered. She'd had it with not knowing. She'd had it with Archer's vagueness. His mouth was half open before her eyes.

She just stood there gaping at him. "What in the gods' names is he?"

"What?" Aiden blurted before he could stop himself.

Ava didn't answer, she just kept staring at Archer.

"What is who?" Aiden asked again.

Archer looked at them. "You'll see," were his only words before he looked back to Ava. "That's a neat trick," he said, then turned on his heel and, at a jog, began back down the stairs to the base of the tower.

*Fine fuck both of them,* Aiden thought as Ava followed Archer and not answering Aiden's question.

A minute later they were all at the base of the tower, Aiden and Ava having raced down to join Archer. Aiden was still confused and looked between the two of them as Archer untied the two remaining horses from the stable. Aiden again looked between the two of them as Ava mounted one of the horses and reached down a hand to help him on. She was now grinning too.

"Where are we going?" he asked.

"To the battle," Archer answered curtly.

Ava, tired of waiting, grabbed his arm. He mounted the horse and a moment later the three of them were thundering along the dirt road to the city.

Aiden kept glancing to his right as they rode. The small portion of the pirate fleet was about to collide with the first of the Orienthian ships. A minute later they did. Arrows arched in the sky as the ships came into range of each other. The approaching ships slowed and engaged in combat. All except the red sailed ship, it plowed right ahead toward the coast. It came into range of the soldiers on the coast and, even from the distance, Aiden heard the whoosh as the soldiers loosed their arrows. Aiden's gut clenched and he watched the deck of the ship. But it was empty. The sailors must have been below, ready for the arrows to pepper the deck of the ship. The next of the five ships broke through toward the coast. The Sea Dragon this time was just a little behind as the red sailed ship reached the coast line of the bay. Its sails had somehow been lifted. The prow of the boat crashed through the outer wooden branches of the dock. It turned as it did so, exposing the flank of the ship to the awaiting soldiers who loosed another volley of arrows. /They again thudded into the empty deck of the ship.

Aiden and the others crossed the edge of the city, the horses now galloping on wood and stone as they made their way to the center of the bay. The side of the ship made contact with the stone wall of the upper dock, bumping into it with a splash and hollow thud. Not a moment later did the crew burst from the deck. Aiden's mouth was dry as he watched the pirates stream from every door onto the deck. Before the soldiers could ready another volley, the pirates were upon them clashing.

Aiden's heart was starting to really race now.

"Switch me!" Ava shouted over the clatter of the hooves below them and the din of the battle ahead.

Her words snapped him out of it. He stopped focusing on his breathing as they switched hands on the reins. In the blink of an eye, Ava had dipped down to one side of the horse. She kept a hold on the horn of the saddle and, as her feet contacted the stones of the cobbled street, she was bucked back up into the saddle now perched behind Aiden.

"Cool move!" Aiden shouted over the rushing wind.

"Thanks!" Ava shouted back.

Aiden again looked up to the ongoing battle right as a figure jumped the gap between the red sailed ship and the edge of the stone harbor. The Sea Dragon made the same maneuver, its own men begging to pour onto land. Something smacked Aiden in the back of the head while Ava shouted some apology. A moment later Aiden knew what the thing had been as a twang sounded and an arrow whizzed by his head. It soared toward the oncoming battle, hitting one of the black armored soldiers in the small of the back. He crumpled and some of the nearby soldiers turned just in time for her second arrow. This one landed just below the collar bone, sinking right through the black metal as the man fell. The soldiers in the rear lines were now turning, looking to them. Aiden reached over his shoulder and again something smacked him in the back of the head.

"Really?" he shouted.

But he still grabbed his sword, pulling it from its sheath as they neared the soldiers. He saw the glint of Ava's sword in the corner of his vision and Archer's at his side where he rode bent low over the back of his horse. Up ahead Aiden saw something red burst into the air, but he was denied the chance to see what it was as they finally made contact with the soldiers.

Aiden didn't have his familiar sense of violent silence this time as they plowed through the first few of the men, all of whom died either from the horse plowing through them or the already fast moving slashes of Aiden and Ava's swords. Aiden continued to slash at the men standing below them, praying against the occasional blade that made it close enough. Yet still the silence didn't come. He heard every clash of blades, every clank of armor on armor, every shout and shriek of the dying men. Still he fought, Ava doing the same behind him, as they both slashed and stabbed down at the men. Blood sprayed, coating his legs, his chest, his face, his mouth, misting the very air in the rage of moving bodies. He heard a shout beside him and watched as the formerly white, now red speckled horse Archer had been riding buckled, an arrow sticking strangely out of the side of its head. But Aiden's moment of lost attention cost him, Ava too. As one of the numerous soldiers made it through and, with a flash of steel, hacked through the front leg of his own horse. Ava yelled behind him as they both pitched forward. Aiden's face contacted with wet stone, the impact ringing through his bones, his teeth. Something heavy landed atop him and was quickly off again. He could taste coppery blood in his mouth and stars popped in his vision as big as the soldiers around him, blocking them from view as ringing began in his ears, instantly blocking out the din of battle.

Through the gaps in the stars he saw the oncoming black armored soldiers pause, a few of their heads turning over their shoulders. Aiden saw the face of the nearest, originally pink and ruddy in the cold, blanch of color. Aiden's vision was going red and frilly around the edges. But the stars and red frills were denied the ability to block his remaining sight as something else did. It too was red, but not the same. He could see the line between the red frills and this other red, so saturating it overwhelmed his vision. But again he was cut off as something contacted the side of his head and the world went dark before the impact had registered.

The next thing Aiden knew he was being hauled along bent over the shoulder of someone in a fireman's carry. The ringing was still there, deafening, yet he could make out faint sounds beyond it. He opened his eyes, red still coated the right side of his vision as he stared down at the cobbles moving fast below him. Legs flashed in and out of view. A moment later steely water flashed by, swirling red leaking into it from the stone, then wood planks. The legs slowed. he felt the person carrying him lean forward and set him against something. A man, it was a man who had carried him. The man set another person down at his side, a girl. He knew the girl, knew her well, he cared about her but, or... maybe that was a dream, maybe he'd never even spoken with the girl. Everything was so fuzzy, sight, thoughts, sound, touch, taste... it was all like he was really far away from his senses.

The man grabbed both of their shoulders forcing him back to lean against something. Then he quickly stood and shouted something Aiden couldn't make out. The man leaned over him, his face no more than a foot from Aiden's. Aiden blinked, trying to bring the man's face into focus. He said something too. He couldn't make it out over the ringing, something about 'Ok'. Then the man was gone, racing away. Aiden's gaze followed him and, with a dull shock, Aiden realized he was on a ship. There was something red out beyond. He turned his head to the side. Ava... Ava was sitting beside him. That was her name, and he did know her. He loved her, though think and... and something. She was sitting there. She was moving, grabbing his face, forcing it toward her. She shouted something and he blinked, blinked again. The ringing began to quiet and he blinked again. This time some of the stars finally winked out and he could make out what she was saying.

"Aiden!!" she brought her face closer. "Aiden!!" she shouted again blood and tears were mixing on her face.

"Ava?" he said, the words seeming to come from somewhere very far off.

She sighed, wrapping her arms around him. He blinked again and his attention was pulled back to center, ahead of which was a cloud of red swelling and blooming in places as it ripped into the black armored soldiers. Where the red mass met with the soldiers, more red sprayed. Aiden continued to blink, squinting, trying to see through the red mass to the figure within. His words were slurred as he tried to ask what was happening.

"It's Jagger," Ava said.

It took Aiden a moment, or maybe a minute to register the words. "Jagger?"

But indeed the figure in the middle of the cloud was the Pirate King, standing feet taller than the other men. Other pirates fought near but not beside him. None of them seemed dumb enough to come within the circle of death that Jagger was now forcing through the soldiers. Aiden just watched, still unable to do so much as lift his arms.

The battle was quick from there on. Jagger kept coming in and out of view as they fought. The Pirate King did indeed fight with that great sword held in a single hand, a full sized sword in his other. It didn't seem to matter that the Orienthian soldiers were clad in thick metal armor, for where the blade hit it went through, cleaving the panicked forces apart. The blood they sprayed just floated out to join that of the cloud which spun and swirled, suddenly materializing to block or attack the soldiers. Arrows flew into the shield only to drop and disappear in the gore coated ground.

The Orenthian forces began to splinter as the last of the lines were pierced. No sooner did they break than the remaining soldiers gave in, turning and stumbling on the uneven body covered ground, and bolted, half staggering, as they tried to run towards the city. Those few buildings that had been smoking now illuminated the streets with fire light. The glow made visible his targets as the red cloud, at last writhing and with a shutter that lasted a heartbeat, exploded toward the retreating soldiers. They fell or at least most did. All those within sight of the Jagger fell as the cloud hit them. The rest were taken care of by the pirates and Arlin's crew who swept from the edge of the docks and into the streets, bows twanging as they were fired.

But the blackness again covered Aiden's vision as the world went silent.

The next thing he knew he was in his cabin. The ringing had ceased almost entirely, though some of the red on the right edge of his vision remained as he peered up at the raftered ceiling of the ship. He heard something to his side and couldn't help groaning as everything from his face to the base of his spine screamed at the movement. He did manage to turn his head enough to see who was sitting beside his bed. With a slight shock, he realized it was the doctor Jagger had summoned before.

The old man looked at Aiden with a wry smile as he said softly, "Well, you gave death a damned good shot, boy." He chuckled.

Aiden tried to sit up but gasped in pain as he did so and the man rested a hand on Aiden's chest.

"Don't move…" He paused, waiting for Aiden to meet his eyes. "I'll go get ya friends. They've been wanting to see you." The man pressed a little harder with his hand and Aiden winced. "Now don't try ta move."

A moment later the man was out the door and Aiden was left alone in the room. The small pieces of furniture had been moved to accommodate a stool and small table of medical supplies at the bedside. Aiden lifted a hand reaching for his booming head. He could feel bandages but dropped his hand as the door again slid open. Ava, quickly followed by Arlin and Kerstin, walked in. Through it felt like tearing his face in half, he tried for a grin. Arlin was the only one who really smiled back. Ava tried for one but it didn't meet her eyes. And Kerstin, Kerstin was just standing there like the world had just gone to shit.

"What's..." Aiden tried to ask but with a shock his face felt like it was on fire. He tried to cough but his chest burned with the attempt and his whole body clenched. They moved to his side, and by the time he had calmed enough to look at them again, any pretense of normal-ness had gone from Ava. Aiden just looked around, down at himself trying to see what had happened but Arlin held up a mirror and Aiden looked.

It took him a moment to register what he looked back at; the right side of his face was peppered with purple and blue, the edges of the bruise twinged with yellow. The other had a strange half moon shaped, near black bruise. Arlin angled the mirror down to his bare chest where purple and blue again speckled his left ribs three more than the rest, probably broken.

The doctor walked back in and came to sit on the stool beside the small table. He began without warning as he explained each of Aidens injuries. "Ya have three broken ribs and a bunch more bruised ones on your left side, a bad concussion, subconjunctival hemorrhage... you're bleeding in your eye." He answered to their confused looks. "And ya sprained da hell outa your back." He finished with a commiserating smile "But...!" He began, finally smiling. "You will make a full recovery, and will be back on your feet in two weeks."

Arlin let out a laugh and everybody looked at him. "Bullshit!" he said, looking at the other two. "Five gold pieces says he's on his feet in five days."

The doctor gave a half disapproving, half impressed smile. "I must say, I gotta give it ta ya boy. I ain't never seen someone take a horse kick to the head quite so well. Though with how ya friend's talking, sounds like that toughness might just be part a ya."

# CHAPTER 53

Five days later Aiden indeed thought Arlin would have been right about him walking, that is if Ava hadn't flat out refused to help him until at least a week had passed. So he was forced to wait in bed while she kept him company. Kerstin had informed the both of them that he was working with Jagger about where to send forces. William had contacted them not long after the battle. Kerstin had sent the messenger right back with news of what had happened and asking for any instructions on what to do. Kerstin left the ship right after telling them all this. He apologized but claimed that there was too much planning to do for him to stay. A few of the others had come by to see him, but most of the time had just been spent in the room where Ava continued to read her way through the magic book.

She had been sitting in the small cushioned seat built into the cabin for most of the day when she finally asked, looking up from the book, "You mind if I try something?"

He glanced down at the book. "Something magic?"

"Yeah, I'm not sure if I can do it. This says there's a chance I can but..." She shrugged. "I might as well try."

He nodded and she closed her eyes, bowing her head slightly. Nothing happened.

Aiden stayed silent for a long moment. "Is it working?" He eventually asked quietly.

Ava opened her eyes and frowned. "It would appear not." She paused. "You can keep reading your book. I'm going to keep trying. you'll know if it works."

He shrugged again and picked up his book.

Ava too had been hurt in the battle, fourteen stitches stretching over her shoulder and across her back. But compared to Aiden, the doctor had said she barely had a scratch and he wasn't to worry. '

"You can't be the only one with cool scars", she'd said when he voiced concerns about her not being on bed rest.

It wasn't until the last day of his Ava-imposed imprisonment that her attempt finally worked. It almost made him jump out of the bed when he first heard her voice say something, not across the room, but into his head. He groaned, rubbing his ribs where the sudden jolt had strained them before staring across the room at her.

"The fuck was that?" he demanded, staring at her across the small space.

She blinked for a moment. "Did you hear it?" she asked a little breathlessly, as though she'd been straining to do it.

"Yeah, the creepy whispering in my head. I heard it." His voice was split between commending her on the new ability and telling her to stay out of his head.

Ava smiled wryly. "I've been trying to do that for the past day.

"That was what you wanted to try?"

She nodded.

"What did you say?" he asked.

Ava frowned, annoyed, then closed her eyes. Her expression shifted to one of concentration and the voice sounded again, echoing like a thought in his mind.

"Wanna leave the cabin?" it asked, and when she again opened her eyes, she smiled right as she reached for the crutches the doctor had provided.

A few minutes later they both stood on the deck of the ship looking out across the harbor to the still red flecked coast.

"Oy, you two!" someone called.

They turned, Aiden taking a moment longer to do so with the crutches.

"You lost me a bet," Arlin said down from the helm of the ship, but he smiled and a moment later had signaled for one of his men to take his place fixing the lines. He walked down to meet them. "It's good to see you back on your feet," he said and gripped Aiden on the shoulder.

Arlin had a fine cut raking across the seam of his eyebrow but seemed otherwise unharmed by the battle.

Aiden smiled back before giving a pointed glance back to the coast and city beyond. "What happened?"

Arlin too looked to the edge of the city where the majority of the battle was fought, his eyes seeming to go far off. "We won," he said a moment later and looked back to Aiden, then over to the red sailed ship near the coast.

"Jagger turned the tide. He fought off most of the men on his own and gave cover for the rest of us…" Arlin paused for a moment. "That's how we managed to get to you two and Archer. He saw you went down and fought off the soldiers long enough for Zach and me to get to you."

Aiden let out a long sigh looking to the battlefield. "Thank you," he said, looking the captain straight in the eyes. He nodded, "Really."

"You should thank Zach too. He helped get the three of you out."

"I will," Aiden said in answer.

Arlin again nodded and turned from him. But Aiden saw through the slight red on the edge of his vision as the captain hesitated, looking Aiden up and down on his crutches before he spoke again. "Kerstin, Jagger, and some of the others are setting out to meet King William and the other Lords in Clystera tomorrow… if you feel up to going."

Aiden did indeed want to go. Ava initially shot down the idea on the basis that he just got back on his feet and they know that there are soldiers in Anglen looking for them. But she'd been convinced by the time they reached the coast. They took one of Arlin's small boats to meet with Kerstin and the others planning on going to Clystera the following day. The first pirate they saw on the dock was able to inform them that the people they were looking for were in the old city hall that the Lord of Gloran had occupied prior to the battle.

"Top of da hill, big building with windows," were the actual directions he gave, but they remembered the building from their previous visits.

It took them a little while to get to the top of the hill with Aiden how he was. The others were in a meeting when Ava knocked on the door. Archer answered, his arm hanging in a sling. He smiled at the two of them, his eyes lingered on Aiden's face for a moment. He stepped aside and gestured for them to enter the great room of the large house where Kerstin, Jagger, and a few men that Aiden didn't know sat in circle around the table. They all looked up as the three of them walked back over. Kerstin smiled. Jagger gave a calmer look than usual.

"It's good to see you on your feet," Kerstin said and gestured to the table. "We're planning what to do with the fleet..." He trailed off looking between the others.

Jagger met the silent prompt. "I'm going to have a portion of my force remain here to protect Gloran and the northern coast against ships. A small force is going to be sent on land to support the standing army that William already has in place at Clystera. The remainder are going to sail to the southern edge of the continent to serve as a protective barrier as we've still got no idea where the Orenths are coming from.

Aiden nodded vaguely.

"Will you be riding to Clystera with us...?" Kerstin asked tentatively, glancing at Ava.

"We will," Aiden answered.

Kerstin nodded, still smiling and turned back to the others. "Are we decided on where the fleet will be going for the time being at least?"

The others surrounding the table made noises of agreement. They gathered their things and made their way out of the room, no doubt going to make the arrangements they'd just discussed.

"When will we be going?" Ava asked after they'd all left.

"Tomorrow morning," Jagger answered. "The funeral for the dead will be tonight at the bay. After that we're free to go."

Aiden nodded slowly.

"Are we to attend?" Ava asked respectfully.

Jagger turned to face them for a long moment before speaking again. "You fought in the battle. You should honor those who died in it."

That was answer enough. Minutes later they were again walking down the main street with Kerstin striding at Aiden's other side.

"What happened to the people you came to Gloran with?" Ava asked to Kerstin.

"The harbor master had them killed."

"And the harbormaster?" Aiden asked, still trying not to squirm.

Kerstin let out a cold laugh that made Aiden start. "It turned out that siding with the murdering invaders didn't go so well for the prick."

"Yes, but what happened to him? Do we have him?" Ava pressed.

Kerstin shook his head. The three of them reached the end of the street, coming out to the edge of the docks. Kerstin pointed down the street to the left away from Arlin's ship, which Aiden now saw docked at the somewhat repaired remains of the wooden docks below.

"He was dead before the battle started."

Aiden's head snapped to where Kerstin was pointing. Far down the street, dangling from the jutting center beam of the roof, hung a figure.

"I can't say I feel all that bad for the man," Kerstin said coldly.

Aiden stared at the dangling corpse for a long moment, then turned. "I can't either."

Kerstin understood and accompanied them all the way down the docks to Arlin's ship before excusing himself, saying that he really must get back and put together the company that would be going to Clystera with them tomorrow. Aiden and Ava both said goodbye and promised to meet him at the town hall at first light. Arlin again met them on the deck of the ship. He was giving orders to his crew but paused to speak with them.

"I heard you two are heading out with the others for Clystera tomorrow."

"We are," Ava supplied.

Arlin sighed. "Ah well, I knew you two brats wouldn't bless us with your presence forever."

Ava laughed.

"I had your horses brought to the stables just beyond the dock." Arlin pointed over Aiden's shoulder to where a small, four penned stable sat nearly hidden behind the adjacent building.

Ava chuckled again, walked up to Arlin, and wrapped her arms around him. "Don't let Zach cry too long after we leave."

Arlin laughed.

"We'll see each other soon," Aiden said.

Ava stepped away and he too hugged Arlin, a little gently with the remaining injuries. The two of them walked across the deck of the ship and back down to the cabin.

"Should we pack?" Ava asked when they eventually closed the door.

Aiden looked around the mess of a room. Old clothes littered the floor and the side table was still covered with various bottles of medicine and bandages from the doctor.

"That… would probably be a good start," he said.

She smiled vaguely and, without another word, handed him his bag, pressing it into his free hand. "Well, if you're good enough to ride to Clystera, then you're good enough to help pack."

"Oh but my face, it just hurts so much and…"

She looked up from where she'd knelt to pick up the scattered clothes. Brows raised, she stood, walked right up to him and kissed him on the cheek. "All better? Now pack."

He gave a wry smile and obeyed, stuffing all the clothes, then more carefully the books and other things he had scattered around the cabin into the bag. Ava took the medicine from the small table and before long the space was again how it had been when Arlin first showed them to it.

"Ready?" Aiden asked, opening the door to the hall and looking over his shoulder.

"Yea…" Ava turned back quickly and crossed to the other side of the room, opened the cabinet and pulled out one last bottle of wine.

"Drunk," Aiden muttered and left the doorway.

The sun was beginning to fall when Zach found him on the edge of the docks looking out at the fleet now begging preparations to set sail again.

"The funerals are about to start," Zach said softly.

"Where?"

"A little way around the bay to the east."

Indeed, when Aiden turned to look off in the distance there were torches lit. A minute later Ava had joined them and they started walking along the edge of the bay. Soon the stone turned to wood, then sand. The assembled group was standing together on the sandy shore. Small boats lined it. Each tied by short ropes, they floated just a few feet into the bay.

"Glad you came," someone said beside him. Aiden started slightly on his crutches. Archer gripped his shoulder, steadying him. "My dad wants you and Ava to help."

"Help?" Aiden asked.

Archer glanced at the boats. "You'll see."

Archer led them to the center of the group of pirates. A few members of Arlin's crew stood among them. The three of them broke through the crowd to a small clearing. A large fire filled the center and on the other side of it stood Jagger. Archer stepped away into the crowd and the Pirate King gestured for the two of them to join him by the shore. They did, the crowd parting to allow them forward. When they reached the edge of the water, two men set a large clay pot before them. Another set a large coil of rope. Three more came forward and, without a word, they dipped the rope in the clay pot. It came out dripping with something smelling faintly of olives. The three men went about tying the rope to the prow of every boat. Pushing the center ones out first, they tied the two ends of the line of boats together, forming a large flowing circle.

Aiden tried to count the boats, but before he could finish something was shoved in his hand. He let go of his crutch to see who it was. Archer stood solemn faced as he forced a bow into Aiden's hands.

"Just do what we do," Archer whispered and pushed another into Ava's hands. He handed each of them an arrow, a piece of cloth was wrapped around the shaft near the head.

Aiden looked around the crowd, all of whom now held bows and arrows knocked. He did the same with his own arrow. Ava and Archer stepped beside him as the group began to light the arrows. Some lit them with torches, others with small fires. The three of them followed Jagger to the main fire at the center of the clearing and lit their own. Then they retreated back to the shoreline. The pink light of the dying sun was still casting light over the circle of boats floating out toward the mouth of the bay.

"Draw!" Archer commanded.

As one the bows of each pirate in the group groaned. Aiden held his hand at his cheek, the screaming pain of his muscles muted in the moment.

Archer spoke:

As you came from nothing,
you return to nothing,
to the salt of the sea you beg haven,
to a realm beyond this world,
where the pains of the wrath may never touch
you, may gods abandon you, and death welcome
you, to warm lands of jade water and golden
ale, on the beaches of everlasting peace!

The stillness held for a moment longer before Archer loosed his arrow. Another heartbeat and the rest of the arrows flew. Orange dots peppered the pink sky. The first of the arrows landed on the boat. In a whoosh Aiden felt the warmth as the fire raced along the rope between the boats. One last heartbeat and the ring of boats was alight in the darkening water.

The next morning Aiden rolled over in the bed, pressing his face into the pillows, but winced as the pillow pressed against the bruises there. Ava's feet thudded against the boards of the floor and a moment later she had thrown his cloak on him.

"Come on, we have to get up to the town hall."

Aiden mumbled something.

"If you keep Jagger waiting, I'm not defending you when he beats you."

He flopped onto his back and she muttered something he chose not to hear. Thud! Aiden grunted and opened his eyes. Ava had thrown his weapons on him.

"It's cruel to throw things at a crippled man," he muttered but stood from the bed. Strapping the sword to his back, he shoved the knife in his boot and another in the sheath at the back of his waistband.

"Oh well, I'm cruel, but I still saved your life more times than anyone else," she snapped back and tossed him a bow.

"What am I supposed to do with this?"

"Shoot bad people."

He frowned. "I'm shit with a bow."

"Then to shoot me dinner tonight," she said and handed him a slim quiver. He opened his mouth to reply but she cut him off.

"It doesn't weigh much, just bring it."

Aiden grabbed the two loaded packs leaning against the wall near the door. "Ready?" he asked.

"Thick and thin," she said, grabbing the pack and walking out the door.

The light of the sun was just barely visible as a glow on the eastern side of the horizon. Aiden had chosen to forsake the crutches today and had to fight not to limp while getting to the horses in the stable. Spark neighed and bumped her chest against the edge of the pen when they approached. Raith stomped his feet. Aiden reached a hand out, pressing it against

Spark's muzzle for a moment before opening the pen. The horse walked out, stopping just past the entrance of the pen, and stood still as Aiden strapped the pack to the back of the horse's saddle. Ava did the same and, in the light of the moon, he saw as she flashed a smile.

"To war then?" she asked.

"To a new adventure," Aiden said back and pulled up onto Spark's saddle with a wince, flicking the reins.

The others were waiting in front of the town hall, already mounted, similarly covered in dark cloaks.

"Morning," Ava said and they nodded,

"We should get going. We're expected in Clystera by tonight," Kerstin said.

The group slipped into motion. Kerstin rode at the front, Jagger at his side for most of the morning. Aiden and Ava chose to ride at the back. Aiden still felt half asleep long into the morning but was finally prompted to move in front of the group by the growl of his stomach. The other horses neighed as he squeezed his way by. Jagger's black shire stallion sounded more like growl, Aiden thought, which seemed fitting for the man. Still, the two men at the front of the group directed their horses to the side for Aiden to join them.

"Morning," Kerstin said, looking at him then squinting at the bright road ahead of them.

"Morning," Aiden said lightly to both of them. "I was wondering. Are we going to stop at one of the taverns on the way for food, or will we just eat while we ride?"

"I'm not sure." Kerstin looked to the Pirate King at his side. "Any preference?"

Jagger frowned. "You know anywhere good on the way?" he asked gruffly.

"Assuming they don't throw Ava out, I do," Aiden admitted.

The Pirate King raised his eyebrows, a shockingly normal expression for him. Aiden smiled back, tugged on the reins and turned around to join Ava at the back of the group.

It turned out that the tavern keeper did try to kick them out when he saw Ava. His effort, however, was halted the moment Jagger ducked through the doorway. They ate quickly. Aiden and Ava likely would have eaten with their hoods on and their heads down. Kerstin, however, was having none of it. He promptly took off his cloak showing the silver Clysteran armor, after which most of the tavern goers left. Still, they ate fast and were back at the horses before anyone had the nerve to talk to them.

Out of the blue, Aide heard the words, "Can you hear me?" He almost jumped. He certainly shuttered at the sound of Ava's voice in his head. He turned to face her, nodded, then tilted his head this time trying to send words back.

"And you?"

Ava flinched but nodded. She was used to feeling other people's thoughts by now, but they had a weird feeling when directed at her. Her face went a little colder.

"There was a boy in there with a necklace... an Orienthian crest."

Aiden went still for a few moments considering what to do next."Should we tell the others?" he thought back.

She didn't answer for a moment. "Let's tell Kerstin and Jagger to stay on guard, nothing more for now. They might want to fight or find him."

Aiden nodded and, moving casually, walked over to Kerstin who smiled and said, "I'm glad we stopped for food.'

Aiden walked right up to him, willing his own eyes to chill. "Stay on guard," he whispered so the others would't hear.

"What?" Kerstin began.

Aiden shook his head, barely. "Tell Jagger."

Aiden didn't wait for an answer before turning and walking back to Spark and Ava. He dipped his chin.

They continued to ride long into the afternoon. Aiden couldn't help continuously checking his sword over his shoulder. At his side, he saw Ava doing the same, checking her arrows and the leather breastplate. By nightfall they were able to see the outline of the castle atop the hill. Aiden shifted in his seat and watched the others shift nervously as well. The caution turned out to be unnecessary and eventually they passed through the city gates. Aiden recognized a few of the guards who stood watch. They nodded as Kerstin showed his crest.

"We've been told you're wanted at the castle," one of these men said from where he stood under the arch.

And so they did. They rode straight for the castle gates. Aiden sighed when he finally stepped out of the saddle. He rubbed Spark's muzzle and handed the reins to the stable boy. The others left their horses as well. Had he not been in a rush, Aiden would have helped the stable boy with the massive stallion Jagger had been riding. But he only turned, striding up the steps to the lit doors of the castle. The doors opened as he approached.

On the other side of the huge entrance hall stood a young boy. "Good evening m'Lords," he gestured behind Aiden. "Might I escort you to your chambers?"

None of the group answered. "Call the Lords to a meeting." Aiden said

The boy blinked. "I was instructed to bring you to ya rooms?"

"Get your Lords!" Jagger growled and the boy almost stumbled.

He took a step back. "Yes, Lord." He said, bowing quickly, and then ran uncertainly it of the room.

"Tell them to meet us in the council chamber!" Ava called after the boy. "Kerstin, will you take the others to the council chamber? Aiden and I will go get William and fill him in before the Lords have a chance to twist what we say."

The knight hesitated but nodded.

Ava led the way to William's room, she'd spent more time around the castle after all. They were at his door in a few minutes. Aiden knocked.

Someone grunted on the other side and they heard, "Come in." Ava pushed the door open and the two of them walked in.

"Hi William," Ava said. The old man was sitting at the desk across the room from the door. William stilled for a moment, then stood from the desk, turning on his heel as he walked over to meet them. He didn't say a word as he walked between them and rested his hands on their shoulders. He gave Aiden's face, still clearly marked by a horseshoe, a quick worried assessment before it seemed he deemed it not urgent.

"I'm glad you're back…" His words held more than they really said. "And with an army I hear?"

Ava nodded noncommittally.

"We do…" Aiden said slowly.

"We're calling a meeting with the other Lords."

William raised his brows at Ava. "Now?" he asked, looking between them, then out the dark window.

"Yes, we need to talk about the forces in Anglen."

William's eyes narrowed. "Forces in Anglen?"

It was Aiden's turn to blink. "We fought them in the Bay of Gloran?"

"Fought who in the Bay of Gloran?!" William asked, his tone growing more urgent, still looking between them.

"An Orienthian Legion," Ava provided. "We sent word of the battle four days ago." William didn't answer for a long moment. Then, moving faster than before, he went to his dressing room. Seconds later he came out dressed in a black jacket and pants.

"We received no letters. You said you already called the council?"

Ava nodded, pushing the door open for William to walk through. William walked faster than Aiden thought possible for the man. Aiden glanced quickly at Ava. She met his look, now grim faced.

The silence of the castle was abandoned as people began to move throughout. The halls were still left dark, save for the moonlight through the windows. The council chamber, however, was light by the time they got there. Aiden could make out the muttering of the Lords on the other side of the shut walnut door.

William shoved open the doors and the three of them walked in. The muttering ceased the moment King William walked in. The Lords and Ladies of Anglen sat around the table, some still in their night clothes, almost all of them frowning. Calam opened his mouth but shut it again as Jagger ducked into the room behind William. It was true that with his height the Pirate King needed to duck to enter nearly any doorway, but Aiden had a feeling he made a show of it on this occasion for the exact effect it had had. None of the others seemed to have anything to say. William sat down, the two chairs at his left still empty. Aiden and Ava both pulled off their cloaks and set them over the backs of their seats before sitting.

William turned looking first at Jagger, "I thank you for agreeing to aid us."

The Pirate King didn't answer.

William then turned to Aiden and Ava at his left and then Kerstin at his right. "I've just been informed that there was a battle in Gloran," he said to the assembled group.

The muttering returned.

"Battle?" one of them called over the noise.

"Yes," the King responded.

"Might we be graced with a first hand account?" Calam drawled, sneering at Ava.

William gestured to the three of them at his sides.

Kerstin cleared his throat. "The harbor master of Anglen betrayed us. By the time Mr. Jagger's fleet got to the continent there was already a small enemy fleet and host in the city. I managed to get to their ships and warn them. Aiden, Ava and one other were sent to destroy the Orenthian defenses quietly so that our fleet might be able to enter the bay. They did and the battle was fought, after which we sent a messenger to the capital to inform all of you… but it seems the messenger never made it." He finished.

"What do you mean the messenger never made it?" one of the ladies asked, then looked at Kerstin.

"The messenger never made it to the capital."

"What do you suppose happened to the messenger?" another asked. Some of the lords again began to mutter.

"We believe that the messenger was stopped."

"Someone here is lying." Aiden heard the words in his head. To his side Ava didn't so much as glance at him.

"Who?" he thought and a moment later the answer came.

"I can't tell with all the noise in the room, but I can hear their thoughts. They're racing, nervous, they… have to *do* something."

Aiden looked into the face of every Lord in the room. Some sneered. Others looked scared or nervous.

The meeting continued. They were further questioned about what happened. Calam never abandoned the sneering look he threw at both of them. It took awhile for the council to accept and agree on the account of the battle that Aiden, Ava and Kerstin told them. Jagger, to Aiden's surprise, only ever spoke to the three of them. Unsurprisingly, however, he was the first to get tired of the pointless bickering of the council disagreeing on what to do.

"It is not a great wonder that your lot needs my help if this is the best your royalty can do when it comes to matters of war." None of the group spoke as he continued, "So based on what you know, as of this moment, how many men do you think the King of Orenth has managed to get across your borders?

None of the group answered, they had the feel of a group of children who hadn't been doing their chores.

"What of Galin?" Ava asked, sitting up a little straighter.

Her next words weren't to the group. "Ready?" she sent the thought to Aiden.

He crossed an ankle over a knee. "Yep," he thought back.

"He was sent on a mission back to Orenth about a month ago. We haven't heard from him since."

"Honor-less coward," one of the ladies spat. "Probably ran back to his King."

"The way I see it…," Jagger growled, "it was your responsibility to keep this land safe. So tell me lady, have you ever seen battle? Have you ever spared so much as a drop of blood for this kingdom you claim to protect!"

"Well…" the lady began barely trembling as Aiden saw the red mist began to pour from the Pirate King's shoulders.

"Well! Until any of you have, why don't you focus on doing your jobs better and not on shaming all those whose hardships you do not know!"

The room went silent for a long moment before William spoke. "Mr. Jagger, I..."

"Guard!!" Ava screamed, but Aiden was ready and, in the moment it took him to register the words, the dagger his hand had been covering was pulled from his boot. Metal clanked behind him. A heart beat later his chair had been kicked across the room and he was standing between one of the silver armored royal guards and William. The man was only feet away, his sword already out of its sheath. Aiden didn't have time to decide exactly what to do as the sword went spearing past him for William. He lunged at the sword, his hand wrapping around one side of it. The cold edge of the blade bit into the side of his hand. He forced the blade up, missing William's head by less than a foot. Using the knife in his free hand, he jammed it upwards in the gap of the knight's armor, right under his arm. There was a shriek. Pulling on both the sword and the knife hilt, Aiden threw the soldier back first onto the round table.

A moment later the other guards were there pinning the man to the table as he writhed. All the Lords had jumped to their feet, flocking to the far wall of the council chamber. The only people left seated were William and Jagger. William continued to look startled although he stayed in his seat. The King of the Pirates looked entirely unperturbed by the incident. Ava stepped to his side and reached forward and pulled off the helmet of the... woman. A small trickle of blood ran from the corner of her mouth where one of the guards had punched her.

William finally stood and walked to their sides. "Who are you?" he asked calmly.

She spat in his face. Some of the group at the far side of the room gasped.

William only frowned. "Take her to the dungeons."

The other guards obeyed immediately, pulling her off the table and forcing her hands behind her back.

"And see to it that she is seen by a healer," Kerstin Added. We will want to question her later."

One of the guards nodded to Kerstin. She was out of the room a moment later.

"The rest of you," Kerstin began, "if you are agreeable William, I think you should return to your rooms. I'll have a guard posted outside each of your doors while we search the castle for any others."

The other Lords seemed more than happy to do so and were led off to their rooms, each with a guard, who Kerstin ordered to have their visors up at all times.

"And me?" Jagger asked after all the other Lords and Ladies had left.

William did not immediately offer so Aiden did. "You can stay in the other room across the hall from ours if you like?"

"Or we can find a larger..." Kerstin began.

But the pirate cut him off. "That'll do."

Jagger followed a little ways behind as the two of them led him up the spiraling staircase to the top living space of the tower.

"It would have been nice to have the tower empty tonight," Ava whispered to Aiden before splitting off to show Jagger his room."

# CHAPTER 54

They were woken a little after dawn at the sound of someone knocking on their door.

It was Kerstin. "You two are late," he said.

Ava hopped up out of the bed still wearing a night dress and walked to the door to open it.

The knight balked slightly.

"We'll be down in a bit," Ava huffed. "Now get out of our tower."

When they did finally make their way out of the room and down the tower to the entrance hall, they were met by Mary. She smiled at them and led them to the council chamber. The other Lords were already there, William among them.

Some of the Lords frowned. "How kind of you to grace us with your presence," Calam said across the table.

William only smirked.

"Well, then," Ava said plopping down into her chair. "Shall Aiden and I go find out what the prisoner knows?"

Aiden could have sworn the corners of Jagger's mouth tugged up. The rest of the council looked confused.

"Didn't William deem that we shouldn't..." the lady paused.

"Force answers from prisoners?" Ava smiled. "I imagine we'll be able to get answers without hurting her. Fear is a powerful tool, and she dose't know we can't hurt her."

Ava turned to William. "Yes, you two may go," he agreed. "Kerstin will lead you to the cell. Join us when you have what we need. The rest of us will continue the previous discussions."

Ava smiled at the old man and hopped back to her feet. She wrapped an arm around Kerstin's shoulders as they left the room. He shrugged her off.

Aiden stopped them on the way to the dungeons, turning and walking off down a side passage. "What the... where are you going?" Kerstin demanded, turning to follow him.

Aiden got to the kitchen a moment later. He grabbed a few apples and a bottle of wine, then turned around, "Lead on," he said.

Kerstin just shook his head.

The prisoner had been put in the same cell where Galin had been held with the same layout of guards at each corner of the room and more in the hall beyond. She thrashed against the chain holding her to the floor as they approached, spitting at them.

"You can leave us," Aiden said to the guards in the corners of the room. The men shifted on their feet for a moment, then moved to obey, keeping their eyes on the woman as they did.

When the door was shut, Ava turned to Kerstin, "Are... you staying?"

Kerstin's brows rose. "I am."

Ava looked over his shoulder to Aiden. He shrugged.

"Ok." Ava turned back to the woman.

Aiden walked to the corner of the room, grabbed the small stool. He brought it to Ava's side and sat. "What's your name?" he asked the woman, shining one of the apples on his jacket. Aiden waited until it was clear she wasn't going to answer. He looked up and frowned. Then snapped the apple in half and held out one of the halves to her. She made no move to take it. He shrugged and took a bite out of the half.

"Her name's Talia," Ava said bluntly. "She was sent by the high general of the Orienthian army to kill William."

Aiden smiled up at Ava. The woman's eyes had widened.

Aiden squinted in mock inquiry. "You know guys, I don't think Talia likes us," he said.

Kerstin chuckled, walking up beside them. "So how many soldiers has your dear king managed to get into Anglen?"

This time the woman just smiled. "You don't need your little tricks," she said sneering at Ava. "I'll tell you... he has them all."

Aiden halted his eating of the apple, "He has his whole army in Anglen?"

Talia smiled.

"Where?" Kerstin growled and she just continued to smile.

"Ava?" Aiden prompted.

She closed her eyes and the woman shuttered this time. "The south, they sailed south through the Laconian Isles. The army's making its way up the southern mouth of the Mezerek as we speak. A second force is sailing down from the northern inlet of the Mezerek. They are part way through Laconia right now and plan to meet on the eastern border."

Aiden stood. "We have to tell the others and get the army in place." He turned for the door.

But Kerstin grabbed his arm. "There's more we need to know."

"But they'll..." Aiden was saying.

Kerstin cut him off. "We don't even know how many soldiers they have."

Aiden panicked for a moment longer before settling again. He turned back to the woman. "How many men does he have?" He growled out all pretense of kindness lost.

Ava shut her eyes again and the woman shuttered. "I can't tell," Ava said breathing harder than usual.

"Tell me!" he roared at the woman.

But Talia just kept smiling. She just kept smiling.

He ripped the dagger from the back of his belt.

This startled her and she tumbled onto her back. "You're not allowed to hurt me! Your council decided against torturing prisoners!" she shrieked trying to scramble away against the chains.

"I don't care!!..." Aiden stopped abruptly and asked, "How do you know that?"

Ava shifted at his side and something silver glinted.

"How do you know that?" Aiden repeated.

The woman was truly panicked now, her eyes flicking between the two of them both holding daggers now. Aiden spun the dagger in his hand and she broke. "I don't know who, one of the council members sends letters to Orenth! He told us that you wouldn't torture your prisoners!"

"And how many men does your king have?" Ava asked smoothly.

"I... I don't know!"

"She's lying," Ava hissed,

"Can you tell how many?" Aiden asked again. Kerstin was still standing behind them.

"Her thoughts are too scattered," Ava muttered back.

"Then she'll just have to tell us." Aiden leaned forward faster than Talia could react and held the blade horizontally, the edge just pressed against her throat.

"Aiden!" Kerstin shouted, his eyes flashing. "The council decided!"

Aiden didn't relent, only said, "That was before we found out how dirty they fight..." He pressed the blade harder and a trickle of blood ran from her face.

"Fighting? You know we're going to get our answers, you fighting me is only going to make it more painful." Ava stood walking around the woman, spinning the dagger in her hands as she did.

"Fuck you!!…" Talia began to scream at him but her words finished in a cry as Ava threw the dagger down and stuck it right through the woman's hand.

Kerstin yelled.

"Get out then," Ava said coldly to the captain of the guard.

"How many men?" Aiden growled more viciously. But something changed about the woman.

"Do your worst. I won't betray my King, nor will I risk his wrath." And she spat in his face. The motion forced the blade further into her neck and more blood ran.

"Aiden! You know the punishment for breaking a council decree," Kerstin pleaded. "They'll kill you!"

The woman spoke again, "This doesn't matter. You and I don't matter. The South will be burning in cold blackness before the first soldier can get there…" She paused a psychotic smile painting her face.

"Aiden, we won't get anything more out of her," Kerstin pleaded. "Stop and we can go ready the men to march south."

Aiden took a long breath and looked up at Ava. She nodded and with a sharp movement he stood, turned and started walking back to the door.

"Your home, Aiden Windren, will burn!" Talia roared, laughing now. "In the black flames of my King. God blessed and wrath given, his might will make your people beg for death."

Aiden paused, half turning back, a buzzing beginning to fill his head. Kerstin sucked in a breath.

She continued, "He will kill each and every person in that piece of filth town you call a home. He will leave you with nothing and…"

But her words were cut short. Before Kerstin could stop him, before he could think, Aiden hurled the knife. It was over in the blink of an eye as the dagger cracked bone, sinking deep into the woman's sternum and she went limp.

"The council will…"

The council didn't kill him. Some of them thought they should but William wouldn't have it. He and Ava tried to tell them about what they had found out, but they were told that the decision on what to do now was one that the council would have to make. As murders, they would wait in the dungeons until a decision was made about what to do with them.

"Ava did nothing!" Aiden shouted at the council.

"She…" Calam shouted back, "tortured a prisoner of war!"

"Take them away," one of the ladies said.

"I will not leave my home defenseless!" Aiden roared. "I will ride for my home and I will defend it!"

"The only thing you'll be doing outside the dungeons is hanging," Calam said and nodded.

It took Aiden a second to register the gesture, but a moment later a rope was around his neck so tight he couldn't breath, the edges of his vision started to go frilly. He watched as William, the old man, made no effort to stop it. The king's only sign of distress was a tear flowing down his cheek.

When Aiden woke, he was in an unmarked cell, one that shared little familiarity to the one the assassin had been put in. This one was small, dingy, dark and wet. He sat there in silence for a long minute.

"Hello?" he called through the small iron bars in the cell door. "Is anyone there?" Someone grunted. Aiden growled through his teeth but choked, rubbing at his throat. "Please, I have to talk with William. They're going to burn the South."

The guard only shifted on his feet causing his armor to clank slightly.

"Has the council made any decision about what they're going to do about the incoming army?" Aiden pleaded with the man.

He continued trying to get the man to speak to no avail. The guard only shifted occasionally, clanking his armor. Aiden gave up his pleading when his throat started to burn and his words became muffled. He walked back to the far wall of the cell, sitting to lean against it and rub at the sharp line of bruising that ran just under his chin. This new injury was just in time to replace the burning soreness still left in his face from the battle. he sat there waiting for long hours still trying intermittently to get the guard to tell him anything. The hours blended together and soon the small bit of light coming through the bars of the door ceased. His eyelids drooped and he drifted into sleep.

# CHAPTER 55

Something clanked and thudded outside the cell in the hall. A moment later, shouting and footsteps boomed. Aiden jumped to his feet, knocking against the door in his haste to try to see what was making the commotion. The footsteps halted and a heartbeat later a second thud and clatter rang through the dungeons. Aiden could hear someone breathing heavily in the hall, but the person's breath then became steady. Light, casual footsteps sounded, moving closer to the door. Aiden backed away a step, flexing his fingers in preparation. Something small and metal clanked against the other side of the door. Click! The lock slid back and the reinforced iron and wood door swung back. Aiden raised his hands higher, blinking furiously against the light that flooded the small space.

"Don't bother," the person said.

Aiden's eyes adjusted. Archer?" It was more of a question than a statement.

The young man smiled.

"What are you doing here?"

"My dad told me I was to follow the night after you guys went to the castle. I left that afternoon and got here a little before morning. He didn't want anyone to know I was here."

Aiden blinked. "But why?"

"My dad thought there might be some kind of trouble getting your Lords to cooperate, which he needed them to do if we want to win this war," Archer explained and then paused, looking up and down the hall behind him. "But I can tell you on the way." Archer pulled off one of three bundles he had strapped over his shoulder. "Quickly," he said, handing a bundle to Aiden, who just stood there looking at it, lost. "Well, put them on," Archer said, gesturing to do so.

Aiden pulled off the covering. Inside, Starlight and all his other weapons were tightly tied into a bunch. Aiden quickly went about strapping them to himself.

Archer continued, "We have to find Ava. Then the three of us will need to get to the stables at the back of the castle. I have the horses ready there with everything we'll need to go south."

Aiden didn't pause as he looked up. You're coming with us?" he asked.

Archer nodded.

"Will your dad want you to go right to where the whole of the Orienthian Army plans on landing?"

Archer laughed softly. "You've seen how my dad fights. If I'm going to be his heir, he isn't going to be able to coddle me forever." Archer's eyes went a little colder at the words. "Hurry up, I don't know how long we have 'til more guards come. We have to be out of here by then.

"Done," Aiden said, jamming the small dagger into the gap of his boot.

Archer jerked his head further down the passage from where he'd come. "I think Ava's this way."

The two of them started a quiet sprint down the passage. It intersected with another at the end and they split to either side of the wall. Archer gestured for the two of them to check their sides. Aiden did. His side ended a short ways down with a circular room made up of cells. Two men sat at a table in the center, one large candle the only light in the space. Aiden pulled back. Archer did the same.

"Two at a small table," Aiden whispered.

"One sleeping so hard he might be dead," Archer said smiling. He stepped back to the end of the passage and poked his head around looking to Aiden' side. "Listen," he whispered.

Aiden did. The two men were talking. He strained to make out their words.

"She's a pretty little bitch of a princess," one of them sneered.

"Oh, don't let her hear that," the other one said in mock fear. "They say she's a great warrior. She might just scratch you." They both laughed. "Isn't that right little princess?"

Aiden stopped straining to hear. He had the confirmation he needed. "She's down there," he whispered to Archer.

He nodded and poked his head around the edge of the corridor one more time. "Dumb bastards," Archer muttered under his breath. "Let me see that bow?" he asked quietly to Aiden.

Aiden hesitated. "What are you going to do with it?" he asked, half thinking that if the answer was shoot them, he'd still give him it to Archer for what the men had just said.

"I won't kill them," Archer drawled.

Aiden handed him the bow and smiled.

"Watch this," Archer said and, knocking an arrow, he leaned around the side of the passage and, with a twang, loosed the arrow. It swished for a moment then something clattered. The men shouted as the light at the end of the passage went out.

"Now," Archer said a little more softly and the two of them broke back into a sprint. Aiden could just make out the forms of the two men in the light leaking from the far end of the passage. Aiden branched for the one on the left. Archer went for the one on the right. Both men were unconscious before they hit the ground.

"Ava?" Aiden said softly.

Someone to his left gasped. "I'm here!"

He ran to the iron and wood door. Archer was fiddling with one of the guards behind him. Aiden stood against the door trying to look in through the small bars. There she was, just a little too short to look through the bars of the door. Archer finished with the guard and came up beside him holding a ring of keys. A moment later the door was unlocked.

"How'd you?" she began.

Archer cut her off. "We'll explain everything later, but the next guard rotation will be coming soon and we have to go." Archer handed her one of the bundles along with the leather breastplate she usually wore.

She was faster about dressing in her weapons and armor and didn't bother to ask questions. "Ready?" she breathed, slinging Starin over her shoulders.

The three of them ran quietly through the passages, Archer leading the way. Soon they were to the large chamber with the spiral staircase leading up to the castle. They slowed a little as they reached the top of the stairs, walking more quietly, mostly through smaller side passages until they reached the back side of the castle. They stood on a balcony overlooking the forest beyond.

"How the hell are we getting out of here?" Ava gasped.

"On horseback," was Archer's answer.

From the remaining bundle, he pulled a length of rope and three leather belts with piece of metal shaped like a number eight attached to each of them.

"Put these on," he said, handing a belt to each of them. They did so. Meanwhile, he tied the rope to two of the pillars making up the rail of the balcony. He strapped his own belt on and slung both his legs over the side of the rail so he was sitting on it.

"Once I'm down, do it like this," he said and pointed to the piece of metal. He pinched a section of the rope and fed it through the upper loop of the eight. Then, he quickly undid the pieces of rope and leather holding the metal on and looped it around the bottom half of the eight then reattached it to the belt.

"Don't let go of the rope below the device," he said urgently. With a quick movement, he hopped off the edge of the balcony. They watched him as he lowered down the rope to the bottom.

"And you wonder why I don't get along with Archer," Ava said.

Aiden held out a hand as he helped her climb over the edge of the rail. He kept a hand on her waist as she fixed the metal device.

"Wish me luck," she said and hopped off the balcony. She free fell for the span of a heart beat before the rope went tight and she began the controlled descent down the rope. She reached the bottom in moments.

Aiden began the process of attaching the rope to his belt. He was about to hop when someone gasped behind him. He stilled entirely, then slowly, a weight already forming in the pit of his stomach, and looked over his shoulder to where William stood, still in his day clothes. Something in Aiden's chest tightened at the look on William's face. But the old man said nothing. He just looked at Aiden for a long moment, that strained look still covering his face until it slackened and, with what Aiden could have sworn was a faint smile, he turned back to the hall behind him. Aiden remained still for a moment, then hurried to continue hopping off the edge of the banister.

"Take the eastern gate," William demanded.

Aiden started.

William glanced back over his shoulder. "The guards at the southern gate are ready for you."

Aiden nodded tentatively.

William turned back the other way, like his walk hadn't just been interrupted by an escaping prisoner.

Aiden began the descent. He was down the rope in a matter of moments.

"What took so long?" Ava whispered, her own belt was already off. Archer was shoving it back into the bundle.

"Nothing," Aiden took off his own, handing it to Archer. They ran through the small expanse of grass to the stable where there were indeed three horses tied, Spark and Raith among them. They each mounted.

"This way," Archer said, pointing his horse toward the southern gate of the city.

Aiden hesitated for a heartbeat. "No, the eastern gate," he said. The two of them looked at him.

"Why?" Ava asked, looking at him suspiciously. Archer was matching her look.

"Just trust me," Aiden said.

They did and broke to the left. Archer threw each of them a cloak from the bundle and they rode out through the outer castle wall. The two guards stationed there looked the three of them up and down, hoods on and covering their faces. One of them grunted and the other signaled for them to go. They maintained the slow pace until they were out of sight of the guards, then urged their horses into a gallop down the empty street. They continued east to the outer gate of the city. The guards there didn't even look at them as they passed and turned right down the small road parallel to the wall. So began a long night of riding.

Aiden went through waves of panic throughout the night, thoughts of what might be happening racing through his head as they rode. They only stopped when the horses needed it, but the animals didn't protest as they climbed back on. Even Raith seemed to understand that they had to get there. They had to get the towns to evacuate. They were half way home before they came across the first town on the main road to their home. They agreed that they would make the visit fast. Ava was nominated to watch the horses when they went in. They needed to avoid the chance that they might just get kicked out on sight by the barkeep for the brawl she started on their very first mission.

It was only after walking through the door into the tavern that Aiden realized he had no idea what he was going to say to the people there.

"Aiden?" he heard someone say.

He started looking around, to where a young man had a hand raised above his head. "Ryder?" Aiden said in response.

"Yeah, what are you up to?" he asked, smiling and obviously a little drunk.

Aiden's mind was still whirling looking for a way to get these people to flee without panicking them. Ryder stood up and walked over to them. Archer remained silent while watching the man.

"Could I have a word outside?" Aiden asked the young man.

His brows rose and he shrugged. "As long as your friend promises not to put an arrow in me," he laughed and walked out the door, holding it for the two of them.

"Over here," Aiden said and led him a little way from the building.

"How can I help?" Ryder asked with a hiccup.

"Listen," Aiden began more seriously. "Orenth is here…"

All euphoria of drink left Ryder's face.

"They'll be here soon. I need..." Aiden paused, debating. "I need you to get the people of the town ready. Ideally, you would get them to flee. I don't have time to do it without panicking everyone. Can you?"

Ryder gulped loudly. "You want me to get these people to run?"

Aiden nodded, then added, "And send riders to all the other villages you can get to."

Ryder's face blanched, his eyes going slightly glazed.

"Hey!" Archer said sharply. "Can you do it?"

Ryder snapped out of it and nodded with a final look between them.

They were back on the road riding at a gallop in another minute and returned to the cold silence of pattering hooves and blowing wind. Winter was indeed coming. The cold bit into Aiden's hands and his cloak flew too much in the wind to be of any use. He knew the others must have been feeling the chill too. Neither of them were any better dressed. But still none of them spoke, only ducked down closer to the backs of the horses. The temperature dropped through the night, reaching its coldest in the early hours of the morning.

"We need to stop for the night!" Archer shouted.

Aiden shuttered, Archer's voice was the first he'd heard in hours.

"The horses won't be able to continue tomorrow if we don't."

Aiden didn't answer for a long enough moment that Ava spoke. "He's right," she said. We're going to have to stop."

Aiden gave an anguished sigh and agreed. He knew they wanted to get south as bad as he did, but they were right. Stopping was for the best, at least if they wanted to be in any kind of fit shape when they got there.

"We've been following a stream off that way for a little bit." Archer pointed left across the meadow. "Wanna stop there? We can water the horses and eat something."

Aiden nodded, tugging on the reins until Spark slowed. Then he directed the horse across the meadow. They made camp quickly, tying up the horses close enough to the edge of the small stream for them to water themselves. They made camp, not bothering to make a fire. Archer gave them each a piece of dried meat, which they all chose to eat in their bed rolls. Aiden flinched every time he forced his teeth through the tough meat, still feeling the soreness along the side of his face.

The next day was more of the same. Aiden woke at dawn to the chilled wet of the morning frost. He decided to wait a little before waking the others, at least until the frost covering his bed roll had the chance to melt. If they did indeed find an army in the South, they'd need their strength. But they were soon off, again making their way down the road. The horses were slower, but Aiden could feel Spark working to maintain the pace. His horse didn't fail him. They rode into the night, still with hardly a word to each other as the cold wet started again. It happened the same as the night before, getting colder and colder as the night progressed.

Aiden was able to make out the moon though. A thin crescent at this time of the month, it was eventually obscured. Aiden watched as the dark cloud covered it. When he looked back up moments later to see if it had yet returned, he was given a shock. Light was already poking through the clouds above them, dull and orange. But something was off as he looked up. For one, it was still the middle of the night. His quandary was solved a moment later when they rounded a corner in the road. Ava screamed first. Archer gasped. When

Aiden rounded the corner of the road, seeing beyond the trees, he too let out a strangled cry.

The glowing light was not the first hint of dawn. It was the reflection of the burning forest ahead of them. The clouds weren't clouds at all. They were plumes of ash and smoke that blocked out the moon. Looking around now, he could see the ash falling, small gray and black specks that settled on Spark's white coat. He looked back to the burning forest. The flames stretched a hundred feet above the burning trees, a morphing slithering mass of orange and white. At the base of the trees, just visible through the tree line, sat the town. It was Aiden's home, the first and only place he'd ever grown up, the place that had raised him in lieu of parents, the place that held everything he knew and loved. He could see the market where he first bumped into the mercenaries, where he'd played with Sara, Dante, Roy. Where he'd met Ava.

And now… now it and his friends supplied the fuel for the fire tearing through the south of Anglen. Aiden slung a leg over Spark, dropping down off the horse. He managed to take a few steps toward the grassland between them and the fire before he dropped to his knees and wept. Aiden continued his weeping. Ava knelt beside him at some point, Archer joined a little after. Aiden held his face in his hands and cried, then roared, and cried. And shrieked. Every pained and terrible sound he never knew he could make seemed to come out of him in those hours. He remained that way for a long while, until Archer spoke.

Aiden did not make out his words at first but Archer repeated them. "Look!"

Aiden did, and when he dropped his hands, Archer was pointing ahead to the sky. Snow had begun falling thick and fast, the big, wet flakes of the first snowfall of the winter. The snowflakes fell, breaching through the clouds of ash hanging in the sky. They fell into the heat of the flames and melted to water. The three of them continued to watch through the night. The snow accumulated inch by inch around them, and the flames of the fire diminished to wet smolders by the first light of day.

Archer and Ava had built a camp along the road at some point in the night. She tried to get Aiden to rest. With a tear streaked face, she'd given up on the effort and walked away. She came back. Aiden couldn't tell how much later, probably not long though. She carried both of their bed rolls and set one on the snow beside Aiden. He looked up. She nodded to the bed roll, and he moved to sit on it. Ava sat beside him and wrapped the other roll around the two of them. She sat there next to him for long minutes, Ava muttered something about Archer going to look for... Aiden wasn't paying enough attention to know what. He just sat there, watching steam roll off the smolders of his home.

Tears fell from his face, falling and landing on the bed roll, beginning to form a small sheet of ice where they pooled. His mind was too all over the place to make any real connections about this. There were important questions to be asked, but he couldn't... not now. He could tell when he truly began to fall into his own thoughts. He could tell and didn't care to stop it.

It hadn't made sense to him at first when he'd met Jagger, how any man could feel the wrath that Aiden saw in that man's eyes. He understood now. Jagger was no monster. He didn't wield wrath like a weapon because that's what he was destined to do. No, he held the disillusioned wrath of a man who'd lost. Aiden didn't know what, but it was clear now that he had lost something. The world had taken something precious from Drake Jagger, and the King of the Pirates would be damned if he didn't take something just as valuable back, with teeth and nails and unfettered rage if he had to. That was the reason for the wrath.

Ava spoke and it snapped Aiden to awareness. "What now?"

# CHAPTER 56

Aiden didn't answer. He only sat in the snow watching the smoldering ruin. Ava did eventually get him to come over to the small camp they had made.

"Could you help me?"

Aiden flinched at the words but looked up.

"If we're going to stay here for a bit, we need to find some shelter.

He watched as she glanced toward the ruin of the town then back to the shabby camp. "We..." Aiden coughed. "We could go over to the town and see if there's anything left to stay in."

Ava's face lightened. They were all cold, more than cold. They needed a place to sleep. She looked back at him. Her voice strained with lack of use. "Are you sure?" she asked and looked at him.

Aiden glanced back at the town through the trees. "There's no point freezing out here," he mumbled. "We can't do anything for them now." He shook his head sadly and stood up. Minutes later they had packed the pathetic camp onto the horses, just enough to walk over to the town. Aiden started leading the horses through the snow. Ava remained a minute longer to carve an arrow in one of the nearby aspens, pointing to the remains of the town. Archer would put the pieces together quickly enough when he got back. It was slow going to wade through the shin high snow while leading the tired horses. Ava caught up with them a few minutes later.

The town was cold when they got there. Less snow covered the ground, only coming up to the ankles of Aiden's leather boots. He barely recognized the streets as they walked down to the far side of the town. They turned right onto the small bridge with the letters KW engraved on the side. They made it to William's mansion, quickly finding its upper wooden levels to be gone. The lower stone ones still stood, charred black and dark inside but still standing. The massive front doors had burnt away, leaving an opening wide enough to lead the horses through. Aiden tied the horses to one of the remaining stone beams in the outer room before making his way farther into the adjacent room. He was still too numb to feel all the thoughts that came to mind being back in William's home. Still, the place felt eerie in the dark cold, like something slithered through the air. Even in Aiden's state, the feeling set him on edge. The presence didn't feel dangerous, but angry, wrathful. Ava walked in behind him.

"Do you feel that?" he asked.

She blinked at him, holding a small lit torch in one hand. "What?"

Aiden looked around again. "Something's mad."

She stared at him blankly. "What's mad?"

"Something…" he said again. "Use your power to see if you can sense it?"

She opened her mouth.

"Just try," he urged.

Ava closed her eyes. "Nothing," she said blandly. "I can't hear or feel anyone's thoughts but yours." She seemed to think that ended the discussion and went to find some good spots with the least amount of snow and ash to lay out the bed rolls.

They made a small fire later and went back to sleep, Aiden still squirmed at the feeling around them as he fought to stay away from the sinking hole of burning thoughts that at all times tried to consume him.

"Oy, you two!"

426

Aiden awoke with a start, and Ava muttered something ending in, "Prick."

"What a welcome," Archer said, smirking down at her for a moment. But the smirk died a moment later on his face. "I know where the army is."

Aiden leaned up right as the slithering anger writhed and he flinched.

"Where?!" Ava asked.

"North. They're camped about half way back to Clystera."

"How do you know this?" Aiden asked wide eyed. "You didn't ride all the way to them, did you."

"Gods no! My horse is cooked. My dad sent a raven with the news, and there's more."

Aiden and Ava both waited.

"Our armies are moving south to meet them," he sighed. "My dad says we might just have the numbers, assuming Kerstin's men can fight."

The anger around them continued to build. Aiden could have sworn it was accompanied by hissing noise, but the others didn't seem to notice.

"Can we get there in time?" Ava asked coldly.

Aiden already knew the answer.

"No, not with the horses," Archer answered. "Not in the snow. My dad's letter said they'll meet in the next few days, assuming Orenth doesn't go any further north."

"That's a fool's hope," Ava muttered, standing to pace around the room.

The wrathful hissing thing roared again closer this time.

"Well, if you have a better idea for how we might get there, I would be happy to hear it," Archer shot back, earning a glare from Ava.

"Humans did this…" the thing said, still closer.

Aiden faced the back of the mansion where the sound had come from.

"She will want to know what we have found," it hissed, "and who."

There were two of the things, the hissing spitting things. Aiden shot to his feet, whirling, looking about for anything in the dark place, in the shadows. The other two had halted their argument to watch him, both wide eyed and confused.

"Aiden?" Archer asked softly.

"What?" Ava had begun.

But he answered, "We're not alone." He whispered, trying not to sound too worried and failing as he listened for the hissing voices.

"Who's here?" Archer asked looking around the empty dark room.

Aiden dipped down, grabbing the hilt of his sword from where it lay beside his bed roll. The cold steel of the guard bit into his hand as he choked up on the blade, still checking between all the entrances to the room.

"Aiden what's going on? Who's here?" Ava demanded.

"I don't know. It's mad. It said we're humans, that humans did something."

Ava grabbed her own sword from her bed roll. Archer drew his from his side, still looking unsure at whether this was some kind of joke or not.

"Aiden," Ava said far more softly. "I know this is all a lot… but you haven't slept in days. You might just need…"

Then they heard the first growl. It was more of a rumble that sounded through the snowy night far off. All three of them turned in the direction of the noise toward the back of the mansion. It came closer but still far off, a soft almost inaudible patter accompanying it. The patter continued until the sound came from the side of the town, rattling the ruined house and causing black, charred soot to fall from the ceiling. The soft growling and patter paused for the space of a few heartbeats. The three of them spun in place trying to see where it was. The thing contacted the earth at the front of the mansion with barely a sound. Still the ground quaked, causing more soot and ash to fall along with bits of stone and rubble.

The hissing voices returned. "They're in there," it hissed, sounding savagely happily.

There was a soft sliding noise and another voice sounded from the front of the mansion. "Show yourselves."

Aiden recognized the voice from somewhere, colder and harsher than he'd last heard it.

"Is that?" Ava asked, sounding hesitant.

"I think so," he whispered. "Should we go?"

Ava hesitated for a moment, then nodded.

"Who are you two talking about?" Archer begged, sounding scared if not annoyed.

"You'll see," Ava said. "And be respectful," she added as an after thought as she walked out the door into the front room.

The horses were as calm as ever, standing with their reins still slack against where they'd been tied. Aiden followed her through the doorway and out into the front yard of the mansion. On the black and gray ash tainted snow stood Alva. She was no longer dressed sparsely in vibrant green leaves but in a suit of darker, thicker greenery, a moss cloak covering her shoulders. Her expression had changed to match. Her green eyes were blazing, not just sparkling, but giving off their own light. Her arms were held tensely at her sides and her teeth were bared at them.

Although it was true that her look alone may have made Aiden balk, it was nothing compared to the beasts standing behind her on either side. The two massive snakes were each at least thirty feet in length, heads held at the height of a man, and bodies the thickness of a person. Their triangular heads were directed at the three of them. The gray and black speckled tails writhed, leaving marks in the snow.

Directly behind Ava stood an animal that Aiden didn't have the words to describe. Standing on all fours, its head reached as high as the second floor of the mansion behind them. It had the head and body of a white wolf. Its growling mouth showed gleaming white teeth set in a black mouth. It had interconnected plates of thick green, almost black, metallic looking leaves that linked together covering its shoulders, back and chest. The eyes were the only true color on the whole beast. Red and speckled with orange, they were enough to freeze Aiden where he stood. Ava and Archer did the same beside him, all three of them staring at the beasts.

"What happened here?" Alva hissed, no warmth or joy in the words, only cold fury, colder than the icy snow around them. They all looked back to the short woman standing in front of the beasts.

"A… Alva?" Aiden asked slowly.

She bared her teeth further, the green light from her eyes illuminating the yard and shining off the snow.

"Yes Aiden, it is me…"

She paused, glancing at Ava, her eyes then snagging on Archer for a long moment. He shifted on his feet. She looked back to Aiden.

"You and your friend were good once. You fought for good. I saved your life."

Aiden felt the scar that crossed over his back twinge.

"For that I will give you the chance to explain, before I allow my friends to taste their dinner," she growled as the small points of her canines grew slightly in the silence.

"Explain what?" he asked, forcing his voice into calmness.

It was the wrong thing to say apparently. Both the snakes hissed and the wolf let out a growl that Aiden felt rumble in his chest.

"Explain the unnatural fire that has burnt my home and my friends!" She waved to the forest around them. "Explain why it took my magic to stop the fire from burning! Explain why the humans did such a thing!"

The snake on the right moved forward slightly. "Because, humans are hateful, ungrateful, and nothing more than food," it hissed, slithering toward Ava. It

"Drackon!" Alva hissed and the snake looked back. It stared at them for a moment but returned to its place beside Alva.

Aiden cleared his throat. "You already know who did this," he said softly. "The King of Orenth has invaded Anglen."

Alva surveyed him for a long moment. "The King of Orenth, a human. So tell me, did you help him? All three of you have magic in your veins. Magic burnt my friends. Perhaps I should kill the three of you."

"You really think I did this?" Aiden spat back, his anger flaring as he took a step toward her. Ava grabbed his hand but he pulled it away. "This was my home too!" he screamed. "I grew up in that town!" He pointed. "My friends lived in this town, the only friends I had for most of my life. And they just died in it!"

Alva didn't back down an inch. "Humans kill their friends all the time," she said coldly. "You, unlike those of the wood, kill for no reaso…"

She was cut off mid word as Aiden stepped forward."Be smart," Archer muttered from behind.

Alva closed her mouth looking him up and down. "What will you do now then?" she asked a little more calmly.

Aiden's mind whirled. In truth he had no idea. Make the King of Orenth pay was the only thing that came to mind. "We'll go north," he said.

She looked him up and down again. "You'll never make it in time," she responded.

Aiden bared his teeth.

"If your friend's information is true, then the battle will be done by the time you get there, and you'll be facing all of the remaining Orienthian host," she said just as coldly.

"Then I kill the remaining host."

She scoffed. "Knight of the ashes, that's your plan. You want to die fighting a lost war at your enemies feet."

Aiden's chest was getting tighter and tighter by the word. "What will you do then?" he asked. "They burned your home and friends too. Will you stand by and watch while they go on to burn and pillage?"

Alva snarled a noise echoed by beasts behind her. Then she smiled, "No. I will be going north as well. Me and mine are going to fight, and we are going to kill their army, their soldiers, their commanders, their King, and anyone else who had any hand in the burning of the forest's life."

A chill went down Aiden's spine at the tone. The other two shifted behind him.

But she was still smiling. "It would seem that we share the same enemy at the moment... Would you like to ride with us?"

Aiden didn't move, didn't look away from Alva.

But Alva looked away to the others standing behind him. "Get your weapons. We leave now."

It didn't take them long to do what she said. To be fair, she hadn't made it sound like a question. She only stood there watching them stand still. "Well?" She waved for them to hasten. The three of them strapped on their weapons and fastened their cloaks.

"What about the horses?" Ava asked, a little out of breath as she pulled on her bag.

"I don't know," Aiden said, pulling on his own bag.

The three of them left the room. Spark huffed at him as he walked by. Aiden patted the horse's muzzle before walking out into the front yard, still illuminated by Alva.

"What about the horses?" Ava asked Alva.

Alva smirked at them. "Your horses will be taken care of."

That seemed to be enough for Ava. "How are we getting there?" she asked.

Alva smirked again and the white wolf stepped forward. "Zalve will be taking us. But first..." Alva waved a hand and growing out of the ground there were three plants, each growing into a small tree about the height of a person. Branches grew out on either side.

Aiden was forced to blink. Out of the branches of the trees sprouted thick green, almost black, leaves that thickened and formed into plates that linked together growing out, the fibers of the leaves weaving together layer by layer. White veins began to spread throughout. The plant finished growing right before his eyes, producing a suit of thin, leathery looking armor, greenish black with white veins. Two more sets had grown to the sides. The sets had no helmets. Only a light chest plate, guards for their shoulders, bracers and light guards for their legs.

"You're no good to any of us dead, Aiden Windren." She gestured to the armor.

The plates of thick leaves slipped on like a second skin. They stuck close to his body, flexing with every movement.

"On!" Alva ordered and with a graceful jump and swing of her leg she mounted the massive wolf. None of them moved.

The wolf slowly turned its head to the three of them and flicked its chin backwards. Aiden took a deep breath, pushing down the anger, rage and sorrow as he walked to the side of the great beast. Wrapping a hand around one of the massive plates of its armor, he pulled himself onto its back. The others did the same, the two snakes hissing softly when they passed. Aiden could see the first rays of dawn coloring the sky to the east when Alva whistled softly. Zalve, with one last growl, turned on huge paws, making less sound than was natural, leaving paw prints in the snow. Alva let out another whistle. The wolf squatted slightly. Aiden tightened his grip on the seam between the plates in preparation, and the wolf launched into a run.

Within the span of a heartbeat they were moving faster than any horse alive. Aiden could feel the wolf's claws biting into the snow-covered dirt on every step. Feel but not hear. Its paws were no louder than that of a small dog running through snow. They cleared the town and were across the small field from which they'd watched the burning of the forest within a minute. In front of him Alva tucked down closer to the wolf's back, small flecks of snow flew into the air from its front paws, tickling Aiden's face.

Something flashed to the right. Aiden glanced to the side trying to catch what it was. But the thing was already far ahead of them. Both of them. The snakes were slithering through the snow so fast they were out of sight beyond a far off tree line in seconds.

"Where are they going?" Aiden half shouted over the noise of the rushing wind and snow.

"To find the enemy!" Alva shouted back.

They climbed over the horizon in the next hour. In all that time the wolf didn't so much as pant. It only kept the same efficient strides over the snowy ground. They hadn't taken the road, cutting straight north through the trees and fields of the countryside. The morning was still cold. The sharp flakes of snow bit into Aiden's face as they went, but the thick leaves kept his core warm enough against the bright cold of morning.

The sun was shining bright white light when the two lightning quick gray forms appeared back at the sides of the wolf.

"They are on the move," one of them hissed to Alva and she nodded.

Alva bent down close to the wolf's bobbing head. "Faster, Zalve," she whispered in its ear and the wolf's strides lengthened. The terrain shifted. The forest ended, and they began to climb a steep hill blanketed in snow. Aiden could feel the wolf's claws biting in harder against the incline of the hill as they crested it.

# CHAPTER 57

Someone knocked on the door outside.

"May I enter, my Lord?"

"You may."

Mary opened the door quietly, setting a tray down with a clank, and closed the door behind her. William didn't cease writing at his desk. She again picked up the tray, walking over the stones of the floor.

She reached his desk. "Breakfast, my Lord?"

William dotted his last line. Grabbing the piece of paper, he folded it in thirds. He poured a small bead of wax on the seam of the pages and pressed his ring into it. Then he wrote a last line on the front of the folded piece of paper.

He turned. "Thank you, Mary," he said a little plainly, reaching for the tray.

"Yes, my Lord, and… and one other thing…" She paused and he looked up. She was holding a small letter with a blue wax seal. "Sir Kerstin asked that I give this to you."

William hesitated for a heartbeat before reaching for the letter. "Thank you, Mary."

She smiled before walking away. The door thudded shut, and William sighed, looking down at the shield shaped crest. He leaned back in his chair before cracking the wax and beginning to read.

Dear William, King of Anglen

We have received reports of a fire in the South, as well as rumors about the Orienthian host's movements north. I already have men riding south to validate these rumors. The integration of the Pirate forces into our terrestrial army has gone well. The morale of the men in the camps, however, has not improved. A portion of the men still doubt the threat. Those who do believe have expressed disheartenment. Mr. Jagger has been very helpful, if not a little harsh for his part. Lastly, I have no update on the recapture of Aiden Windren or Ava Corinth.

End Report


Your loyal servant,
Kerstin Trike


William stood. "Mary!" he shouted.

The door opened again a moment later. "Yes, my Lord?" she answered.

William walked to his bed where she'd already set out his day clothes. "I'd like you to call today's council meeting early."

Mary nodded. "For what time?"

"Tell the Lords they are expected in the council room in fifteen minutes.

"Yes, my Lord," Mary said, turning on her heel this time.

William put on his clothes and began his walk down to the council room. The two guards Kerstin had insisted on stationing at his door followed alongside him, neither with helmets this time. There were two more guards stationed at the large walnut doors of the council chamber. He nodded to the men. They opened the doors, both walking in first to light the torches around the room and open the blinds of the windows.

"Leave me for a while," William said softly to the group of guards.

One stepped forward. "My Lord... we were instructed to stay at your side."

"So stand on the other side of the door."

William didn't wait to see if they had obeyed before walking over to the window and looking out over the great plain stretching out to the south of Clystera. Yesterday's snow still lay thick over the grass of the plain. The roofs of the buildings in the city and the trees beyond the plain were also painted white. William looked down at the smoke billowing from the chimneys of the buildings in the city. This was his city, his land, his Kingdom and he had let war walk right into it. He gulped, taking one more look out over the stretching land before he turned back to the great round table. Maps were still were sprawled across from their last meeting. A large map of Anglen lay at his end of the table. Little figurines crowded Clystera, marking the camps of soldiers Kerstin had been organizing throughout the city. More lay north in Gloran and a few just off the eastern coast though they had not been moved in a week or more, not since Jagger had received the last update on their position. Kerstin had only attended a few of the meetings since the arrival of the pirates. He mostly sent letters with updates.

There was one curt knock on the door and the huge slabs of walnut swung open. Lord Iris walked in, followed by the four guards.

"Good day, my Lord."

"To you as well," William said back.

"May I ask why the meeting was called early?"

"We've received reports of a fire in the South, and possible enemy movements north."

Iris sighed gravely, walking over to William's side to look over the map. "Did this report have any information about where these enemy troops are?" he queried.

William shook his head. "Only that there were rumors of the Orienthian host marching north."

They heard footsteps approaching.

"My Lord."

"My Lord."

Two more people entered the room. William sat and waited as the remainder of the Lords and Ladies of the court filled the room. The clock struck seven with only one of the chairs still empty.

William looked pointedly at the empty chair. "Does anyone know where Calam is?" he asked irritably.

A few of the group shook their heads.

"Would someone please go find him then?"

One of the guards nodded and was about to walk out the door when Lord Calam stormed in a little frantically.

"My Lords!" he huffed, out of breath, and held up a piece of paper. "My scouts just sent this."

All eyes in the room flicked to the small scroll of parchment.

"And what does the letter say?" Iris asked urgently.

Calam smiled. "It says that there's a small expeditionary force riding north ahead of the brunt of their army. My men counted no more than five hundred on horseback, preceding what they believe to be a larger force."

The room went silent for a moment.

"And what does it say of the rest of their army?" Iris pressed.

"That they are still more than a week out," Calam responded more calmly, having caught his breath.

"And when will the smaller force get here?" William asked.

"Less than a day if they ride hard."

William looked up to the official general of his armies, a fat older man that, apart from his education and a name passed down to him by better generals, was useless. As far as William knew, he'd never even held a sword or anything more than a steak knife for that matter.

"And what are your thoughts, General?" William inquired.

The man blinked and looked up, surprised he'd been addressed. "My thoughts on what?" he asked.

William made an annoyed noise. "On what we should do about the five hundred men riding north."

The General looked down at the map laid out before them, at the mass of soldiers in Clystera. "If only five hundred are coming north then it would be best to move our encampment to the southern border outside the walls. When the enemy gets here, we crush them in battle and take the rest as prisoners."

The man's words graded against William's ears. The 'we' this man spoke bothered him, like the General himself was one of the men in the army below the castle. He'd even refused to go down to the army camp with Kerstin. The Knight was who he really needed advising him right now, but Kerstin was gods knew where scouting with his men. William was left with inept war advisors like this one. He'd been a great king once, when trade and diplomacy were enough to lubricate the gears of a happy and peaceful kingdom. But now, what could he do now against an enemy that had built an army to invade before ever meeting him, who had tried to torture and kill the only people William had sent to them?

"What do the rest of you think?" William said, looking around the table.

"I think we should crush them and take them as prisoners while we have the chance!" Calam said loudly, sounding a little shocked that it wasn't the only option being considered.

Lord Iris cleared his throat. "I think we should strengthen the southern fortifications of the city, bring in all the people outside the wall, and fight them from the battlements."

"Why would we do that when we can crush them on the field of battle and be done with it? Take their soldiers captive and find out where the rest of their army is" Calam demanded.

Iris frowned. "Because that all hinges on that message being true."

"True!" Calam spat. "You doubt my loyalty?"

"I don't think that is what Lord Iris meant," Annalise said calmly. "Only that the loyalty of your scouts or the validity of their message may be false."

Calam frowned. "These men are some of the most honorable men I have ever known and sworn to serve my house. Their message is true."

Annalise didn't answer.

Calam turned to William. "Do you too doubt the trustworthiness of my men?"

William didn't answer for a long moment. "Does anyone know where Drake Jagger is?" he asked the group.

Calam looked a little affronted but one of the guards at the door answered. "He rode north to organize the forces still in Gloran, My Lord."

"And when will he be returning?"

"He did not say, My Lord."

William nodded solemnly. "And you Annalise... What do you think we should do about the coming force?"

Annalise raised her eyebrows. "I don't presume to understand military movements, My Lord. I'm a diplomatic emissary."

"Yes, you are, and I would like to know what you would have our forces do?"

Annalise looked around the table. "I would have you do as the others have recommended," she said looking back at William.

He nodded, not entirely happy with the answer. "Then, we shall put it to a vote. All in favor of sending the army to meet this smaller force and bring them back as prisoners."

Calam was one of the first to raise his hand, then the general and a few others. Iris did not, nor did Annalise.

William counted then asked, "And all those in favor of fortifying the southern walls from within the city."

Iris, Annalise and some others raised their hands.

William counted. "It would appear we have a tie at present. Would anyone like to change their vote?"

No one raised their hand, but Calam stepped forward sounding a little desperate now. "If we do not meet our enemy when we can, they will just continue to burn the country until Clystera is the only place left and made vulnerable when they do decide to attack."

William watched as cold sweat beaded on the man's brow and his fingers tensed.

"We cannot shy away from our enemies forever," Calam continued in a voice growing more aggressive. "We must stop them before they burn the rest of the Kingdom to cinders."

The council was again plunged into a tense silence as people looked at each other. Lord Iris did not remove his eyes from Calam, not until the woman beside him, one of the older Ladies of Anglen raised her hand.

"We have shied away from conflict for too long," she said in a shrill voice. "It's been left to fester. I vote that we burn it out of our kingdom now."

Iris looked at William for a long moment, then at Calam who was nearly jumping out of his seat at her words.

"Is this everyone's final vote?" William said sharply to the group. No one moved and he nodded.

"Then it is decided. We will send out the majority of our army to meet this force of five hundred, stop them and take them prisoners before the rest of their army has a chance to get north." William pointed to one of the guards at the door. "Go inform our generals in the camps to ready the men and do as this council has decided."

William was sent almost continuous updates by the various commanders in the camps. Some seemed happy with the decision. Others were decidedly against the hassle of moving the entire army to fight five hundred men already coming to them. Others pointed out that if the enemy was already coming, then it would be better to defeat them at the walls of the city.

"Dinner, My Lord?" Mary asked, gently pushing open the door and walking in with yet another tray. She set it on the corner of the desk next to where the letter that William had written that morning still sat, its wax seal unbroken, the ink of the address dry.

"Good evening, My Lord." she offered.

"Mary?" William said softly.

The servant stopped, turning back to look at him. "Yes?"

He glanced back down at the letter and grabbed it. "Can I trust that you will get this where it belongs when the time is right?" He handed her the letter.

She quickly read the note inscribed on the front. "Yes, Lord."

That was enough. He turned back to the desk and began responding to the commanders' letters piled on his desk. A few more days, a few more days and this long painful guessing game would be over one way or another. The next few days William knew would be the ones that decided whether or not he'd be remembered as a good king.

# CHAPTER 58

They crested the top of the hill and the wolf stopped. Before them lay a long expanse of snow covered field. Far off on the left the clearing continued to the edge of a small river, a tributary of the Mezerek. On the right, the tree line wavered, bending and bowing. Beyond Aiden could just make out the vague shape of the Castle of Clystera up on its hill. Before its gate lay a mass of silver. The whole of the Anglish and a large portion of the pirate army stood in lines, thousands of men ready for battle.

Yet they still were dwarfed by the mass of black that stood in lines before them, facing Clystera. It was all Aiden could do not to shout out at the size of the host that the King of Orenth had snuck through their borders. Their army had rebuilt since the explosion in the mountains, rebuilt and expanded. Tens of thousands of Orenth soldiers clad in black shining armor blotted out the white of the snow. He could hear the distant shouts from the nearer side of this massive army, generals getting their men in line to attack.

"Why the hell would Kerstin have ordered the men to face them outside the wall?!" Ava demanded of the air around them.

"They'll be crushed before they can get back inside the walls," Archer said flatly from behind.

The black host writhed and larger shapes moved among the blackness. The men shifted away from the shapes. The three of them watched as the black host was quickly filled with thousands of small orange dots. It took Aiden a moment to realize what they were, and he did just in time for the thousands of dots to fly. They soared in front of the army for a few heartbeats. Dots flew from the silver army too. The arrows contacted and the battle began. Men on horseback on both sides broke ahead of their fellows racing for each other.

"We need to go!" Aiden roared. The wolf didn't move, only turned its head over a shoulder to peer up at Alva.

She didn't speak for a second, growled, "When the time comes, I hope you are all that was promised, light-bringer."

In another heartbeat, the wolf's claws dug in. Roots and rock cracked under the force of the wolf's paws as they shot out over the plain.

"Check the perimeter of the city, Make sure no solider trying to sneak in is left breathing!!" Alva hissed her orders against the cold, sharp wind.

The massive snakes shot out, letting out hisses, cold and hungry enough to give Aiden a non-temperature-related chill, and crossing the plain in less than a minute. Aiden watched as soldiers of both sides bolted from the beasts. They rounded the flanks of both armies and were barely visible by the time they met the castle walls and climbed over them masonry crumbling in their wake.

Soon, the wolf neared the sea of black. The left side of the battle loomed closer, the frayed line of black and silver swimming in red. Aiden scanned the black unending side of the forces. His heart nearly stopped. The shapes that had been weaving among the men, they were… were… like the creature in the blank place, skinless and raw, but worse, so much worse in the cold light of reality. Their bones and teeth shined, raw flesh with white tendon keeping it together. But the beast held back from the center of the fighting, killing only the few Anglish men that managed to get through the lines.

The sea of fighting was now just in front of them. Aiden drew his sword and heard the others do the same behind him. The din of the fight grew louder, three-hundred feet, two-hundred. Aiden took a deep breath at one-hundred feet and one more breath. The wolf crashed through the Orienthian flank and the noise grew so loud he could no longer hear the growls of the wolf over the din. Aiden leaned off to the left, scanning down at the lines of the Orenthian soldiers. With one swing of his sword he had red spraying. He couldn't even tell who he'd hit with how fast the wolf was still moving. It just kept charging through the lines.

Alva turned a head over her shoulder. "I'll drop you two, Archer and Ava. Get the men back inside the walls!"

Aiden couldn't tell what Ava and Archer yelled back, but it seemed they agreed as the wolf broke through the other side of the line. It bolted just around the flank of the wall, spinning on its paws to face back at the other direction.

Ava grabbed his shoulder, pulling him around before kissing him quickly. "Tell me what's happening," she whispered in his ear and tapped her own head.

He nodded, and in a smooth movement, she slid off the wolf. Archer was already on the ground.

"Get the men inside the walls!" Avla repeated.

Ava turned to respond, but the wolf was away sprinting back into the battle before Aiden could hear what she said.

The lines were messier this time. The wolf's passes had left the Orienthian line uneven. It bounded toward them, ready to rip back into the enemy. But the enemy was ready this time as one of the skinless beasts burst from the lines, its claws already outstretched for the wolf. Zalve's claws bit into the snow more rapidly than Aiden knew was possible, pulling them to the side. The beast flew past them, trying to stretch its claws at Aiden. He raised his sword. He didn't have time to even swing, but it didn't matter with how fast they were moving. The blade contacted the outstretched leg of the beast and sang as it cleaved through bone. Blood sprayed and the beast rent the air with a shriek audible over the battle. By the time the thing hit the ground the wolf had already turned. The beast tried to right itself but stumbled on the missing leg, and the wolf had its throat in its maw in another heartbeat.

They plunged back into the battle. Something flashed and Aiden looked up. Alva was now clad in the same armor as him. In one of her hands, she grasped a long, straight stick ending in a black rock point. Alva swung the black rock, ripping through the metal armor of the soldiers. Shouts of terror and awe rang out around them.

The shouts changed and Aiden turned in his seat. "Look behind!" he screamed.

Another of the beasts raced from the back of the Orienthian host. Not bothering to doge the black armored men, its claws dug into them in its haste to reach Zalve. Aiden raised his sword, readying for the beast to crash into them. He blinked and the next moment Alva's spear was soaring through the air. It struck into the beast's chest with a crunch of bone.

Ava and Archer were through the castle walls within a few minutes, only to find the city in a state of bedlam. Children in the streets were screaming. Horses and other livestock were running like mad through the city. Peoples' belongings had been thrown out onto the street as still others ran for the far wall of the city.

"We need to get to the wall!" Archer shouted over the noise.

Ava nodded and pointed for the main street of the city. They did their best to run through the chaos. Something silver flashed in the crowd.

Archer was the first to say anything. "Guard!"

Sure enough, the man was wearing the silver armor of a Clysteran guard.

Ava reached the man first, stepping into his path. "Where are the generals?" she demanded, shouting over the noise.

The man only stared at them, then looked down at their mostly black armor. He let out a small cry and tried to draw his sword. Archer had a hand holding it in its sheath, another grasping his other wrist before the blade was out.

Ava pulled out the small gold necklace from inside her shirt. "I fight for Anglen!"

The man blinked again, looking down at the necklace for a moment, then up at her. Ava could practically see the gears turning in the guard's head.

"The generals are in the castle!" he shouted back.

It was Archer's turn to blink. "Kerstin and Jagger are watching from the castle?"

"No, we don't know where they are. General Beaumont and the others are in the castle," he amended.

Ava cursed. "Come on!"

The two of them were running again, now toward the looming, white castle above the city.

The wolf was still ripping through men minutes later. Aiden and Alva leaned off the sides of its massive back to swing down at them. They fought just at the line between the two armies. The Anglish side had since realized who the wolf was fighting for and had been giving it a wide berth, waiting behind to cut down any straggling black armored soldiers that made it through their section of the line. But the *line* was becoming more and more generous. Bodies and gore were starting to pile where the two masses met. The fur of the white wolf was coated in mud and blood, its head nearly dyed red. Still the men of Anglen held throughout the cold bright day, as Aiden and Alva cut through soldier after soldier after soldier. Something whizzed by Aiden's head. The noise sounded again, this time finished by a soft thud and slight jolt in Aidens chest. He looked down to where the shaft of an arrow protruded from his chest plate. But the greenish black material of his armor only swelled at the base of the arrow. Aiden slid his sword along the front of the plate cutting off the shaft. The green material covered the hole, leaving only a small bump, and he kept fighting.

In the city, the mayhem was thickest on the main streets where twice more Ava and Archer were attacked by Clysteran guards who mistook them for Orienthian soldiers. The crowds continued up the hill to the castle. People were trying to hide in the keep.

"We'll never get through all these people!" Archer yelled over the uproar, grabbing Ava's wrist and pointing to the side of the stables. "That way! There's a passage into the lower dungeons."

"And how the hell do you know that?" she asked, not particularly caring what the answer was.

He grinned. "You don't think I saved you guys without a plan."

It was decided then. The two of them started at a sprint along the road to the stables. Ava glanced over her shoulder to the high towers of the castle above. They reached the stables, Archer leading the way into the small storage shed on the far side.

"It smells like shit in here," Ava hissed as they climbed over crates to get to the back of the room.

"Here!" Archer pointed down at the floor.

"What?" she responded seeing nothing where he pointed.

He bent down, sweeping away some of the dust and hay with his hand to reveal a door. Ava frowned. He grinned back and pulled the small piece of rope attached to the trapdoor.

"Ladies first," Archer offered.

Ava took a breath and hopped into the gloom of the dungeon. She hit the ground hard, ankles groaning, and bits of dirt crunching under her boots. She stumbled. Archer jumped down a second later.

"This way," Archer directed.

Ava had never been in this part of the dungeon before. It was darker and wetter than the upper levels. No torches were lit except at the intersections of the passages. They did not take any of the turns though. Archer led the way further into the hill under the castle. Another torch loomed off in the distance, merely a speck of orange in the loneliness of the black tunnel.

"That's the staircase," Archer said.

Indeed it was, a steep, tight spiraling one. The steps were each more than a foot high and tapered in like pie slices to the center column.

"Hurry!" Archer urged.

Out in the battle, two more of the skinless beasts came charging for the wolf next. Aiden saw them far off, coming from the enemies side. They ran through the men side by side, splitting apart a few hundred yards from the edge of the lines. One went left and the other right. They circled around coming at the wolf from either side.

"Alva!" he shouted in warning.

"I see them!" She raised her spear and the wolf turned, standing centered and trying to keep both monsters in view. Alva hurled the spear. It sank through the shoulder of the first one, knocking it backwards. Aiden could hear the hissing spit of the other one coming closer. Another spear flew, but not from Alva. Aiden looked around to see who had thrown it. Aiden grinned a little savagely as he saw Kerstin draw his sword from atop a massive stallion, surrounded by a group of men also on horseback.

Ava's chest was burning minutes later when they finally entered a room she recognized. It was the large room at the entrance to the dungeons, the machines of pain still pushed uselessly against the far wall. They cleared the room and started up a much more forgiving spiral staircase to the main section of the castle. Archer opened the door with a soft twist of the handle. Ava peeked under his arm. The entrance hall was crowded with people. Some of them were commoners, others wore armor, and still others looked to be high born.

"We'll never get through there without one of those soldiers spotting us," Archer said.

"No, we won't, Ava agreed. "The castle guards know we have a warrant out for us," She nudged Archer aside so she could look out the door better. "But the kitchen staff probably don't know there's a bounty."

Not waiting for a response, Ava gently pushed the door open and darted to the next closest doorway. She carefully pulled it open and slipped through. Archer was through the door a heartbeat later. Ava led the way through the tight servants passages. She could hear the noise of the kitchens up ahead and slowed slightly as she walked into the room. The noise died almost immediately. Everyone looked up at the them.

Ava looked down at herself still wearing nearly black armor. "Shit!"

She was about to start yelling at the people not to scream when a woman stepped into her path. Ava had never taken Mary to be intimidating, not until that moment.

Mary was stone faced as she looked Ava up and down then Archer. "You two should not be here," she said.

The tone surprised Ava. It was not angry or scared but hushed, secretive, conspiratorial."

"We need to get to William," Ava explained as she shifted on her feet

Mary looked her up and down one last time and nodded. She turned to the rest of the kitchen. "None of you are to speak a word of this!"

Without hesitation, the kitchen crew nodded.

"This way," Mary directed them.

A horn blew and Aiden looked up from the immediate battle around him. From the back of the wolf he could see the whole of the Orienthian army. The rear lines were advancing, wheeling great wooden contraptions with them.

"The fuck?" Aiden muttered under his breath. He could have sworn Alva chuckled in front of him while he closed his eyes. Aiden tuned out the noise around him as he sent a thought out along the thin tether Ava had left in his mind.

Ava winced as Mary led them through tight passage after tight passage. Stop!" she ordered to the others and shut her eyes.

"Aiden?" she said to him without speaking the words.

"Ava!" Aiden was shouting it.

"Yes?"

"We need to retreat!" He was still shouting the thought.

"Almost there!" Ava sent back. She was panting with the effort of the conversation now.

"Hurry!" was Aiden's last word before she felt his attention pull away.

Aiden opened his eyes at hearing the yelp beside him. He looked down. Just beside his right leg he could see a shaft of a spear protruding from the wolf's side. Blood was already leaking from the wolf's wound. It wobbled for a moment, still trying to rip its front paws through soldiers. But her rear leg collapsed. Aiden was thrown backwards, tumbling off the wolf and landing with a dull thud on the gore soaked, frozen mud.

He gasped or tried to. The impact had crushed the breath out of him. His sword was still clinched in his hand, but little lights popped in his vision.

Someone grabbed him under the arms, hauling him up with a grunt. "Aiden! Aiden!" Kerstin was standing half in front of him, sword raised,

Aiden blinked, wobbling on his feet.

"You need to fight!" Kerstin shouted, then turned to parry a charging soldier, ramming him with his shoulder. "You need to fight!"

Aiden shook his head dully and raised the sword in his hand.

In the castle Mary pushed open a door and the three of them walked out into the main hall. The door to the council room stood at the far end. Two guards waited at the door, both edging in front of it and drawing their swords. Mary, however, walked right out to the guards unperturbed.

"Put away your weapons," she ordered.

The guards hesitated. "We have orders not to let anyone in, and…" The guard speaking stopped short, looking at Ava. He pulled his sword the rest of the way out. "Lay down your arms!" he growled.

Ava made no move to touch her weapons.

"We have orders to arrest you if you ever show your face inside these walls again!"

"We don't have time for this," Ava huffed.

The guards did not flinch "Lay down your arms!" they repeated.

"Gerald!"

The guard did not look at Mary. A moment later Ava was blinking at the two of them, Mary having just slapped the guard in the face.

"Let these two in, warrant or no. She is still an official Knight of the Kingdom."

The guards looked at each other, Gerald still rubbing his cheek where he'd been hit.

"Fucks sake!" Mary hissed.

Ava couldn't ever remember having heard the woman curse. She pushed the man aside. He didn't look happy but made no move to stop Ava as she pulled open the door and waved for the two of them to enter. Archer didn't miss a beat and stepped forward, walking through the door right past the frowning guards. Ava followed. It took the people in the council room a moment to register that anyone had entered with all the shouting and arguing. But when they did, the noise in the room died. All eyes were directed at Ava.

The first person to speak was one of the older ladies of the court who looked around at the silent faces of the group. "Guards!" she cried.

The two men stepped in the still open door, moving to grab the two of them.

"Leave them!" The words were authoritative although not loud. The guards stepped back out the door.

"But William…" the woman began. "There's an official order for their arrest."

Some of the other Lords and Ladies around the table seemed to agree. Ava glanced over her shoulder, trying to judge how long it would take for her and Archer to get back to the staircase and away from the guards.

"I'd like to hear what they have to say," William told the council and then turned to Ava and Archer. "I assume you have something to say?"

Ava looked back to William who, under the mask of discomfort he always wore at giving an unpopular order, rather looked relieved.

"We have," Ava replied, stepping forward.

Amidst the raging battle, Aiden was fighting in front of the wolf. Kerstin had ordered the other men to push back the bloody mess of a line enough to encompass the wolf. Alva knelt at the wolf's side. She had pulled out the spear and was shoving handfuls of green, mossy stuff that grew out of her hands into the wound, muttering something as she did. Aiden had picked up a shield off of one of the dead bodies lying in the field. He was doing all he could to slash and bash the enemy away from the wolf long enough for Alva to do whatever it was she was doing.

"We have to call the men back inside the walls," Ava demanded to the council.

Some of the Lords around the table shook their heads. A fat, pot bellied man Ava couldn't remember cleared his throat. "If we bring the soldiers in now, we will lose the offensive. We must…"

He was cut off at a shrill humorless laugh from Ava. "Offensive! Your men are getting slaughtered like pigs out there, and you talk about being on the offensive!" she shouted.

The people around the table scowled and grunted.

"You need to call them back inside the walls," She repeated firmly.

William considered as the others shot remarks back at her.

"Even if we did call the men back, they would be killed in the retreat," the pot bellied man shot back. "We could be leaving the walls open for the enemy to invade the city."

"If you don't call the men back in, you will lose this battle and your kingdom today!" Ava demanded, her voice rising on each word.

The fat man cleared his throat again. "If the men fight well, fight for their home, I have little doubt they will prevail against such a vain army."

Ava's head snapped to the man. "Tell me, I don't know your name?"

"I'm Sir General Beaumont," he declared proudly.

"Beaumont, have you ever been in a battle?"

The man's face colored almost immediately. "Well..."

"No, you haven't!" Ava spat back. "If you had, not only would you have the balls to claim that you had, but you would also have some modicum of respect for your soldiers." She took a fuming breath. "My home fell to this army in a matter of weeks. We had competent military generals... morals don't win wars, strategy and men do!" Ava took a deep, slow breath. The people around the table had gone silent. "If you do not call the men back within the walls now, they will all die, including Kerstin and Aiden. Your soldiers will die. The Orenthian Army will breach the wall, and they will burn this city to the ground starting with this castle and all of you inside it."

"How will we hold the gate while the men enter back into the city?" William asked.

"Aiden, Alva and I should be able to hold the gate long enough to get the men in."

"Excuse me, My Lady."

Ava looked. Iris was talking.

"Who is this Alva?"

"The Queen of Sylvanwood."

William straightened in his seat. Iris looked as though he has some understanding of what she'd just said. The rest looked as bewildered as ever.

"Shall we vote?" Iris asked the group.

"No." William stood. "Guards!"

Ava's heart began to race. The two men stepped back into the room.

"Signal for the men to retreat. Open the gates," William ordered.

Aiden wrenched his shield up just in time to block the downswing blow of a soldier. He plunged his sword beneath. It sung with the vibration of piercing metal. He nearly stumbled as the channel in his mind sounded again.

He could make out Ava's voice but it was strained, far off. "Retreat called! We need to hold the gate. I'll be there soon."

Right as the last word finished, he could feel the string that she'd left for them to communicate along die away, like spider silk in the wind. He ducked as a man came charging at him. Aiden spun, slashing high from his crouched position and hitting the man in the ribs. Another silver armored man raced from behind the wolf to fill his place. Aiden didn't waste the opportunity.

He ran, turning to face the other way, toward the enemy as he spoke down to Alva at the wolf's side. "Ava and Archer did it!!" He could barely hear his own words in the noise. "We need to hold the gate long enough for the men to get inside!"

A horn sounded deep and bellowing through the chaos. It sounded again, and the Anglish forces shifted. Alva tilted her head up to Aiden and nodded. She placed both hands on the wolf's side. Green light started pouring out. She grunted softly and the light grew bright enough that Aiden was forced to look away. When he opened his eyes again, Alva was sagging a little on her feet. The wolf was pushing itself back up on all fours, nothing but bloody fur remained where the wound had been. Alva teetered. Aiden grabbed her by the wrist, slinging it over his neck.

"Zalve!!" he cried.

The wolf turned. Aiden could have sworn the red orange eyes were scared at the sight of Alva hanging so limply. It stepped to Aiden's side.

"Up you get!" Aiden heaved Alva's small frame onto the back of the wolf. It didn't stand. "Me too?" he asked.

The wolf dipped a little lower in answer. Aiden pulled himself up, hooking his fingers into the gaps in the plates. Then the wolf jerked its body, throwing him the rest of the way on. The army was truly moving backwards now. The back of the lines collapsed in as they funneled toward the open gate at the far side of the field.

Avla muttered something in front of him and he bent forward trying to make out what she was saying.

"We need the snakes," Alva told him. "Call the snakes."

"How?"

"Yell for Drackon. He'll hear."

Aiden peered around the battlefield, finding no sign of the massive snakes. He raised his hands to his mouth and roared the snake's name. He called again. A moment later he heard people screams coming from the gates of the city. The two massive forms of the snakes came barreling through the crowd who tried their best to get out of the way in time. It felt like mere seconds for the serpents to clear the retreating army. The snakes came to an abrupt stop at either side of the wolf.

"What's wrong with her?" one of them hissed at Aiden.

"I think she's used to much power!" Aiden shouted back at the serpent, unsure of the right words.

The snake seemed to consider him for a moment. "What must we do?"

The wolf had been efficient at tearing through the soldiers. The snakes were better. The retreating army pulled back as quickly as they could without turning their backs. The snakes managed to hold the lines where the men failed. Wherever the snakes made contact with the enemy, thrashing, screaming and a cloud of red gore followed.

Three hundred yards from the gates, the Orenthians shifted in the back of their lines. Aiden only had time to yell for shields before the arrows were in the air and arcing over the enemy soldiers. The King of Orenth was willing to kill his own men if it meant stopping them from retreating back inside the walls. Some of the men managed to raise their shields in time. Others didn't. Aiden held his own over his head, pulling Alva against him and ducking low to cover them both. Two arrows thudded into the shield, one going through far enough for the tip to bite into the skin of his arm. He lowered the shield, breaking off the arrow shafts with the edge of his blade. Behind him, gaps lay in the retreating lines where the other men had not raised their shields in time. The arrows had also hit the front lines of the Orenthians. The Anglen soldiers made good use of the momentary weakness. Those still standing broke into a sprint for the gate.

The snakes stood their ground as the enemy charged, trying to clear the gate too. The first soldier to reach the wolf, he was ripped in half with one swipe of its paw. The last few silver armored soldiers trickled past them. The wolf started walking backwards, shredding through enemy soldiers as they came. The snakes were no longer visible in the mess of mud and blood, nothing more than stones in a violent river, churning the water around it into blood and gore. A horn blasted again and Aiden looked back. Only a small crowd stood at the gates trying to scramble in.

"We have to get inside!!" Aiden roared.

An instant later the turbulent waters of red ceased. The snakes fell back and were at the wolf's side in a matter of seconds. Aiden looked back over his shoulder. Only a few people stood outside the gates. Now far from the lines facing them, the wolf was still walking back, swiping away the arrow-thinned enemy as they came. But not for long. The gaps were being filled by new Orenthian soldiers.

Aiden looked back over his shoulder. The gate was clear. "Run!!" he cried.

The beasts didn't need to be told twice. The moment the words left Aiden's mouth, the wolf turned, digging its claws into the muddy, body laden, gore soaked earth and sprinted for the gate. The snakes followed suit. Aiden could hear the clatter as the enemy broke into a sprint trying to catch them. A hundred yards to the gate, something flashed orange just inside. Fifty yards. Arrows started flying past the wolf, past Aiden. They reached the gate. Just beyond, less than thirty feet inside the gate, he saw Ava and Archer. Each stood at the side of a catapult loaded with a huge flaming ball. Aiden reached around Alva and grabbed Zalve by the fur of her neck, pulling her to the side. The wolf moved just in time for the flaming spheres to fly. Aiden twisted in his seat to see what happened. The projectiles hit in front of the enemy and shattered. For one terrible moment, Aiden thought the Orenthian soldiers were about to breach the gates, one terrible moment before the ground the soldiers were now running on took flame.

# Chapter 59

The wolf reared, turning its head over a shoulder to growl at Aiden who didn't even bother looking back at it. He was too busy fighting back tears of relief as more catapults shot flaming ball after flaming ball over the walls. At the head of the catapults Jagger stood, red mist steaming at his shoulders.

"Aiden!" called a familiar voice.

He did indeed fail to hold back his tears as Ava ran up to him. She was crying too, smiling at Aiden like the end of the world.

"Oh shit!" she cried in a worried voice, stopping dead a few feet from the wolf. Ava was looking up in front of Aiden. He looked up too, just in time to stop Alva from falling off the wolf.

"Get her to the castle!" Ava yelled at Aiden and Zalve, pointing up the road.

The wolf turned, ready to rush her queen to the castle. Aiden climbed back up on the wolf's back to hold Alva steady.

"Let's go!" shouted Aiden.

They were about to take off when the snakes arrived, barring their way. "We can hold the gate!" one of them hissed, showing its gleaming fangs.

"Boy!" the other snake hissed in Aiden's face. "If you hurt her, you will spend the next year of your life slowly dying from our venom!"

Aiden didn't doubt it the threat, but the wolf was already shifting past the snakes and headed toward the mostly clear street. They soon reached the stairs to the castle. People yelled in fear as the wolf bounded off to the side of the stairs, running up the hill beside them. They reached the gate where a small battalion of guards were stationed, trying to keep the crowd at bay. The guards balked at the sight of the blood soaked wolf. Guards and civilians alike scrambled to get out of its way. Zalve growled and stepped up onto the stone platform in front of the door. She bent down as Aiden slid off, pulling Alva down with him.

"Open the door!" Aiden shouted to the nearest guard.

The man only stepped back farther. The wolf growled and, with a swipe of its paw, bashed the door clean off its hinges. Aiden carried Alva through the door and into the entrance hall.

"Aiden!" Mary called from the archway to the great hall.

"She needs help," he responded.

Mary glanced down at Alva. "This way," she directed.

Aiden had to jog while carrying Alva to keep up with Mary as she hurried them along. A minute later they were in a hall that Aiden had never seen before or at least didn't remember. On both sides it was lined with white linen beds. A small table sat at each one.

"Set her here," Mary commanded and pointed to one of the beds.

Aiden obeyed, lowering Alva's small form down gently.

"Will she…" Aiden started to ask, but footsteps began behind him and he turned.

Two castle guards stood in the doorway. "Your presence has been requested by the council," one announced.

Aiden ignored them, turning back to Mary. "Will she be ok?" he asked.

"I'm not sure, but I'll…"

"Now!" a guard yelled and advanced toward Aiden.

"I'll do everything I can," Mary promised.

One of the guards grabbed Aiden's arm and pushed him along down the hall. The council room was just as uptight feeling as Aiden remembered it when the guards forced him inside. William sat at the far side of the round table. The other Lords and Ladies all turned to face him. Aiden looked quite a sight, still soaked in blood, mud and bits of gore. The mess dripping onto the white stones of the floor.

"What happened?" the King demanded.

William seemed determined to keep the group silent long enough for Aiden to explain what had happened in the battle, and so he did, every part of the battle from cresting the ridge to carrying Alva into the medical ward of the castle. Some of the group squirmed and looked away upon hearing about the fighting. Aiden thought it was more than fair to make them uncomfortable after they just sent so many men to their deaths.

"What happened in between you leaving the castle and joining the battle?" William pressed, giving no hint that he'd ever seen Aiden on the balcony.

Aiden hesitated before giving the group a very shallow overview of what had happened.

"I see, and how is the battle going now?"

Aiden almost answered but impulsiveness got the better of him. "You all know that arrows can't reach this castle, do you? You're too far away."

Some of the people around the table looked confused. "What does that have to do with anything?" one man asked.

Aiden frowned. Without asking permission to do so, he walked to the far wall behind William. He pulled out the small knife tied to the back of his waistband. One of the Lords said something, but Aiden ignored him. He fitted the tip into the lock of the window latch. With a sharp twist he broke the small lock and pulled open the window.

"If you would have liked to have known how the battle was going at any point, you could have looked."

"Insolent boy!" one of the Ladies spat.

"Cowardly old lady, you all have the gall to give orders and complain about peoples' attitudes while they fight your war!" Aiden huffed, trying not to completely lose control of his emotions.

None of the group was speaking now.

"Those people just gave their lives for you," he expelled in a controlled loud whisper, pointing down at the body laden field just past the wall. The dead soldiers looked like broken ants now in the distance. He could see the Orienthian mass moving back toward the far hill.

"Do any of you know what it was like for them in that battle?"

No one answered.

"Then I'll tell you…" His words reeked of venom. "Their lungs were trying to tear out of their chests. Their hearts were beating too fast to feel. There was so much noise all they could hear was ringing. They were drenched in frozen mud and blood trying their gods damn best not to die while men and beasts tore them to ribbons. That's how your soldiers, the cobblers, masons, smiths, farmers and bread-makers you sent to war, felt!!"

It took the room a few minutes to recover from what Aiden had said.

"So until any of you are willing to go down and get on the field alongside them, don't delude yourself into thinking you have any right to belittle the dead… or those that survived who will now forever be tormented by memories of your follies."

Aiden took a deep breath, moving to stand back at the head of the table, before continuing. "Why was the army outside the walls?" he asked. "It clearly wasn't Kerstin's call. He was out on the battlefield."

"It was my mistake," William said firmly.

All the Lords turned to him, the fat man sitting up a little straighter in his chair.

"That's not entirely true," Iris said looking at William.

"It is though. I am King. It was my job to protect this realm, and I failed."

"It is true that we as a council made a bad call sending the men beyond the wall," Iris said.

Aiden's temper heated.

"Though we were also betrayed," Lord Iris continued.

That statement, however, was enough to cool it. "By whom?" Aiden asked, alarmed.

"By Lord Calam," William said, pointedly looking at the empty chair. "He gave us false information on the number of soldiers coming to our gates."

The council went on explaining their decisions, but Aiden didn't really care. At the first opportunity, he excused himself, not at all politely, to the further dismay of some of the group.

He stopped at the medical ward on the way back down. Alva was awake again at least. Zalve, it seemed, had found her. The huge wolf was curled at the side of her bed. White fur was stuck in the top of the door frame when Aiden walked in. He only had time to check that she was ok. He still had to find Ava.

Alva, it seemed, already knew that. "I'm fine. Go to her," she said softly, rubbing the wolf's head where it lay on the ground.

Aiden didn't bother to answer as he turned on his heel and made for the entrance hall. The city was still in chaos, the steps of the castle too, though it seemed the huge blood covered wolf had deterred most people from there. It took

Aiden awhile to make his way through the crowds, but soon he was back to the wall. The catapults were reloaded and restrung. He spotted Kerstin and Jagger on the ramparts. He hurried to join them.

"You saved us!" Kerstin said, looking at Jagger, and stretched out a hand. "Thank you."

Jagger didn't take the hand.

"There's still an army at your gates," the Pirate King ground out.

Kerstin lowered his hand. "How many men were lost?"

Aiden didn't want to hear the answer, but he walked up to them anyway.

"You're alive!" Kerstin said.

Aiden could have sworn something like a smile crossed the Pirate King's mouth. Aiden half grinned back.

"Do either of you know where Ava is?"

"She and my son are relaying what they know to the camp generals," Jagger answered. "We'll be going over to join them and decide what to do next."

"William just sent word down," Kiersten explained. "He's putting Mr Jagger and me in command of all military movements."

Aiden nodded. "Where are they briefing these generals?" he asked.

Jagger pointed to a short tower a little ways down the wall. Aiden nodded and started at a jog to the tower. Entering the room at the base of the tower, Aiden had the distinct impression that this is what a war council should look like. Half the people in the room were still bloody from the battle. None were sitting. Ava and Archer stood at the far side of the table bent over a map, pointing things out to the rest of the group. No one even noticed as Aiden walked in the room and back around behind Ava. He leaned against the wall and waited, listening to what they said.

"We think they came east along the Mezerek, stopped at the southern fork," Ava was saying but was interrupted by one of the generals.

"If they had landed, we would have known from our scouts in the south. They couldn't have."

"No, you wouldn't have known," Aiden said from behind. The group looked around for a moment before noticing him leaning against the back wall. Ava smiled, taking a step toward him. But he held up a hand and she stopped, looking worried.

"What do you mean our scouts wouldn't have seen them?" a battle-beaten commander asked.

"Who supplied the men for our southern battalion?" Aiden questioned.

The man blinked. The others seemed similarly confused. "I'm... not sure," the commander said slowly. "Does anyone else know?"

"Lord Calam sent a thousand men to the south as soon as King William called for the army to be assembled," and other commander responded. "It shocked everyone that the little prick would do anything without being forced, especially from so far north".

"Except Lord Calam is in Orenth's pocket," Aiden informed them. "His men would not have warned you of Orenth's landing."

The room went silent for a moment. "That's why we never got any definitive report of the fire?" someone asked.

Aiden nodded to the man.

"But there was a fire?" another asked.

"There was," Arched answered. The attention shifted to him. Aiden could have kissed Archer for that as Ava came to his side.

"Archer can finish filling you in," Ava suggested.

The Pirate King's son seemed to agree because he nodded to them and continued explaining to the generals and commanders.

Aiden and Ava were back at the castle not long after. They stopped briefly to talk with Jagger and Kerstin who promised to send word about whatever decision they made. No one in the castle seemed to care about their presence when they entered. The city's populace had already been called on to fortify the walls. Anyone who wasn't injured was working to make that happen. The tower, however, was unchanged as they made their way up the great spiraling staircase.

"You look like shit," Ava muttered.

He grimaced. "And you look like a blood soaked ray of sunshine."

"Ha, Ha," she said pinching her nose. "You stink. Go take a bath."

Aiden had no desire to disagree. He unfastened his armor in the bathing room. The leathery feeling plates thudded on the ground, and he climbed into the water. He dunked his head, shaking it softly. When he came back up the water was a muddy red. The door creaked and Ava slipped through. Her armor and clothes were already off, and she slipped into the large tub beside him.

"Well, that was a day," she said, dipping her head back to wash the blood and mud out of her own hair while pulling out her braid.

Aiden didn't speak for a minute. Then he muttered, "It's not over yet."

She leaned back up. "What do you mean?"

But Aiden knew she understood. "Even if we manage to defeat their army, the King of Orenth will crush the city."

Ava was sitting up in the tub now looking at him. "And what do you want to do about it?"

"I want to end it."

She shook her head. "We don't have to."

"No, I have to."

She shook her head again more vigorously. Tears started to line her eyes. "Your power can't do anything against him."

"The book says it does," he replied slowly.

"So just because some old ass book says you can kill this guy you're going to walk right up to the King of Orenth? He knew we were there without even seeing us last time."

He sighed. "I need you to promise me that you won't try to follow, you were trying to read his mind last time, I think he felt it, same as Alva could."

She didn't answer.

"Please?" Aiden begged. He'd given a reason of not wanting her there, but the real reason was plain, left red and beating upon his heart.

The tears still lined her eyes as she leaned in and kissed him.

# CHAPTER 60

Moonlight was showering the room through the window hours later as Aiden slipped out of the bed. Ava still lay sprawled in the sheets, eyes closed as she snored softly against the pillow. He leaned back over the bed, brushing his lips to her cheek, and pulled back before a tear could fall and wake her. He had his armor and weapons back on in less than a minute and slipped out of the room. Aiden closed their door and rushed down the steps as quietly as he could. The entrance hall of the castle was quiet. Only the noises of the city below echoed against the stones.

Then he heard, "Stop!"

Aiden whirled around, looking for the source of the noise. Out of the shadows at the base of the stairwell stepped William.

"What are you doing?" Aiden asked, trying to force his face into calm.

"I could ask you the same thing."

Aiden didn't answer.

"Though I already know what you're doing," William admitted. "I'm not here to stop you."

Aiden's body slackened slightly. "Then... what are you doing here?"

William smiled. "I want you to take me with you."

Aiden blinked, searching for the words. "He'll kill you as soon as he sees you."

"Perhaps he will," William answered, tilting his head down.

Aiden shook his head. "I can't bring you."

"You will."

"The Kingdom needs you."

William shook his head solemnly. "The Kingdom needed me. I've been ruling Anglen since I was fifteen. It's never before been in a war under my rule. Peace is all I know, but this peace we've been living in for my lifetime is not the nature of the world. It's nothing but luck that I was born in the era of peace…" He stepped closer to Aiden. "Give me one last chance to keep that peace, and maybe no more need die."

Aiden didn't answer.

"Your oath is to listen to me and protect the Kingdom… not me. Please, do your job," William commanded.

Aiden considered for a moment. Some of that familiar tightness slithered around his throat. "Ok," he finally agreed reluctantly.

With William alongside they were able to leave the city in minutes through the eastern gate. They followed the road around the wall to the edge of the tree-line. Keeping close to the thick brush, they rode via moonlight. The fires of the encamped army loomed closer as they did. A few hundred yards off they stopped. Aiden had to help William down off the horse before he slapped its rump, sending it galloping back toward the city.

"Stay low. Stay quiet. Do what I say."

William nodded.

Aiden led them through the brush to the back of the encampment. The hill sloped upwards and through the branches Aiden spotted what he could only assume was the King's tent.

"Is that where we're going?" William whispered at his side, still a little out of breath from climbing over logs and bushes.

Aiden nodded and cut down the hill right to the edge of the trees. Two men were walking along the perimeter of the tents, talking. Aiden squatted in a bush, watching them as they passed. Quietly as he could, he drew his sword in one hand, his dagger in the other.

"Are…?"

Aiden raised a hand for William to stop, and then he pounced. Running to the men half bent over, his sword went through the first man's back, right through his spine. He plunged his dagger into the other's neck. Lower the body quietly to the ground, Aiden waved for William to follow. They went tent by tent, evading all the men they could. The others… Aiden did his best to hide the bodies. They moved as quickly as William could manage. Aiden steered him around from the soldiers already lying asleep on the ground. They reached the back of the larger tent.

"Quietly," Aiden whispered, barely audible over the noise of the men talking further into the camp.

Aiden slipped through the rear flap and William followed. They ducked against the back of a huge four poster bed, Aiden poking his head over the edge.

"Come out!" demanded a figure in the shadows.

That voice, those words, they tore against Aiden's ears. His heart dropped as it hit him, it wasn't Ava he'd been sensing last time, it was Aiden's own power. In the same way Aiden could now feel the writing mass of blackness just beyond sight before him.

"Now!" the voice commanded.

Aiden stood, William following suit.

"This has been a long time coming," The King of Orenth said calmly, standing in the center of the tent.

"This does not need to happen," William responded, stepping in front of Aiden to speak to the man.

The King of Orenth raised his eyebrows.

"Your army can still leave in peace," William offered. "Our men don't need to die."

The Orenthian let out a high, humorless laugh, tucking his hands behind his back. "Of course it does."

William took another step forward.

"William!" Aiden warned.

But he ignored Aiden. "Why must this happen?" William asked.

His adversary smiled. "Because, the gods have deemed it so. They decided long ago that we would fight. You and I don't truly matter. We only serve as the gods' entertainment."

"You did all this because of some old prophecy?" Aiden spat.

The smile vanished from the Orenthian King's face. "Yes!" he screamed and raised his arms. "All I have done, I've done to appease the gods." He gestured upwards. "I would burn the world to the ground if it meant pleasing them."

William waved a hand, gesturing to the fields around the tent. "And the Gods really want the death of all these people?"

The King of Orenth smiled again. "Yes!"

A spear of black materialized, blacker than the farthest corner of the night sky. It moved before Aiden could form a thought of stopping it. It pierced William and he fell. There was a scream forming on Aiden's lips. It was joined by another on the other side of the room.

From the shadows behind the murderous King, Ava lunged, a dagger in her hand. The King turned, seeming to already know she was there. He grabbed the wrist of her hand holding the knife, forcing it to the side, and threw Ava across the tent. Aiden only had time to watch as the Orenthian smiled and conjured another dark spear that flew toward Ava.

Aiden felt something burn and before he could comprehend what was happening, light had engulfed the world. He was falling, plummeting through the abyss. He could see places as he fell, places he didn't know, places hewn from stone, places that looked as though they'd never seen light before, places that glowed in colors he didn't even know existed.

He hit the bottom of this space, landing on his chest. He rolled over, writhing, trying and failing to get a breath into his lungs. He pushed onto his hands and knees, his eyelids flapping furiously, trying to clear the flashing lights in his vision. Someone gasped beside him and he whirled. He felt something soft and wet squelching under his hands as he did. The lights cleared. There Ava lay sprawled on her back not thirty feet from him. Aiden lunged, trying to pull a foot under himself and failing. He stumbled, falling and slamming his face into the mud of this place.

"She's still alive… barely," the voice taunted.

Aiden spun onto his back, searching for the noise. There the King stood, still dressed in black finery, a sword now strapped over his shoulder.

"Stay away!" Aiden rasped, scrambling and pulling himself to his feet. Ava coughed behind him.

The King smiled. "I'm afraid not."

Aiden reached over his shoulder, a little surprised to find his own sword back in its scabbard. Aiden looked around. He didn't recognize the place they stood in, but the state of the place was all too familiar. A field, blood soaked and littered with bodies stretched as far as Aiden could see. Behind the King lay a stone table, a sort of alter. Papers lay on it, blood soaked and surrounded by bodies.

"Where are we?" Aiden demanded.

The King smiled again and began pacing around Aiden and Ava in a large circle. Aiden kept himself between them.

"This, boy, is the last place that man managed to entertain the gods."

Aiden took a double take of the field. Hundreds of thousands, more bodies than he had ever hoped to see, all lay motionless. Red leaked into the dirt.

"And you brought us here?"

The King nodded.

"Why?"

"What more fitting place for us to once again entertain the gods?"

"You're a psycho!" Aiden spat.

The King laughed softly, his overly white teeth glinting against the overcast sky. "No, I just understand the world…" He paced further and went on, "We are not the greatest power in this world. We are nothing but puppets for the greater powers to play with. You and I are servants. Our only job is to enact the gods' wills."

Aiden bared his teeth. "And this was the will of the gods…?" He gestured to the field with his sword. "The deaths of all these people?"

The King nodded. "If it were not their will, it would not have happened."

Aiden raised his sword. "So, what's their will now?"

The King drew his sword, smiling as he did. "That is for them to know and for us to discover. Though presumptuous of me as it may be, I believe they do not simply wish for me to kill you. Which is, perhaps, your one saving grace, given that you cannot command your own power"

Aiden didn't answer.

"If you could, you'd have done so by now. So, in the name of not… *not souring the performance,* I will fight you… *man to man,* as it were."

Aiden was watching the King's sword too closely to notice the dagger he'd slipped from his belt. He only had time to dodge it before the King was upon him. Steel sang as the King's blade met his half hearted block. It forced past steel, biting into Aiden's shoulder. The King spun, striking again for his feet. Aiden stumbled away, barely avoiding the blade. The King backed away a step, rotating the blade in his wrist as he did.

"The gods have no love for you, boy. At every turn they have left you to suffer. They will do the same now!"

The King struck again, trying to swipe Aiden's leg. This time as he struck, Aiden parried, bringing his own knee up to meet the King's gut.

The King gasped and stumbled back, coughing for a moment before looking back up and smiling. "You will lose, your people will die and she... will die," he uttered in a cold voice and pointed his blade at Ava.

Aiden charged, but the King had his blade back up in time to stop the blow. They turned. Ava moaned a few feet behind him. Aiden bared his teeth. He twisted his wrist and raked his blade against the King's sword while smashing his elbow against the King's head. A sharp pain split through Aiden's arm where it hit the knife-sharp points of the crown. Upon impact, the King's sword hit the ground with a squelch and clatter. The King stumbled back and Aiden punched him with his sword hand. Blood spurted where the guard contacted his face. The King of Orenth stumbled back again.

"You're a fool!" Aiden said, walking forward and punching him again.

The King spat out blood, dropping to his knees. "Perhaps? Or perhaps my death is more... entertaining?" the King uttered in a hoarse laugh.

Aiden punched him again, irate now, sword still in hand, the guard slicing across the man's brow. The King fell over, head slamming into the blood soaked mud of this place. His crown toppled off, rolling and coming to rest against the corpse of a fallen soldier. The King gave a deranged laugh, pushing himself on mud covered arms back into the kneeling position.

Aiden suddenly dropped his sword. His head filled with ringing and screaming. Sorrow and loss further drowned out the world until all he could hear was blank noise. The King began to speak noiseless words. Aiden hit again, this time with his bare fist. He threw his weight into the blow this time as they both tumbled to the ground. Aiden landed on top and scrambled to a stand over the man. He bent down and grabbed the King by the collar of his filthy black jacket, pulling him up off the ground by just a few inches before slamming his fist again. Aiden felt and heard the crunch as the King's nose broke. He let out a wheezing croak as Aiden hit again, and again, slamming his elbow in with the force of his body as the two of them hit the ground.

Aiden felt another crunch and then the noise and sorrow, fear and pain, and roaring anger took over entirely. People and places swam in his mind as he continued slamming his fist again and again into the King's face. Phil, Frank, his friends back home, Ava, William, every innocent person Orenth had slaughtered for its King's vain belief in gods. Incensed anger poured out of Aiden. The King's face was now little more than gore and splintered shards of shining bone that Aiden continued to pummel. Fist after fist, he threw punches, his knuckles slicing themselves on the shards of bone.

But Aiden didn't stop. It was wrong, he knew. He knew he shouldn't want this, that this was not the end that any of the people swimming in his mind would have wanted. But that didn't matter now. This moment was his and these fists were his. There were a thousand faster ways to end this. The sword sitting just a few feet away was one way. Starlight was his first true gift, but using it didn't feel right. No, that was a beautiful weapon, a weapon made to do good, to defend people, not to inflict pain. This task... he wouldn't tarnish that blade with this task. Killing this man wasn't something to be proud of. It wasn't something to be controlled. It was nothing more than the culmination of a prophecy and recompense for terrible deeds that the man before him willed into being and would now pay for.

Aiden could feel the flesh on his knuckles ripping, could feel the moment the King went utterly limp, could feel every ounce of pain in body and soul as he kept fighting, tears unleashed and streaming down his face. His fists continued their relentless pounding until the King of Orenth crumpled into black ash, leaving Aiden panting over the cold remains of a man that had ripped so many things, people, lives to shreds.

Aiden stood looking down at the ash, trance-like, until he heard Ava moan behind him. He turned, running over and dropping to his knees at her side, right as the edges of the field fell into darkness, flooding in until the peaceful depths engulfed them.

# Chapter 61

People were shouting far off when Aiden awoke. Steel was ringing, beasts were roaring, screams rent the air.

"Hey, you two!" he heard Archer yell.

Aiden jerked, sitting up again, and found that he was in the bed of the tower room. He looked around. Archer and Mary stood at the door. Ava grumbled at his side, starting to push herself up.

Aiden turned back to Archer and whispered in a pained voice, "What happened?"

Archer smiled, "You're one lucky son of a bitch is what happened."

Ava sat up, looking blearily toward Mary and Archer. Bandages covered her from just above her waist to over her right shoulder. "What happened?" she repeated, already sounding annoyed.

But they were interrupted at that moment by the opening of the door. Kerstin walked in, still dressed in dirty, battle stained armor.

"Well, I think Kerstin would be the best person to tell you what's happened," Mary said, taking a step back.

"And?" Ava demanded again.

"You two fuckers slept through the final battle!" Archer spat out, not seeming able to contain himself.

Mary, however, grabbed him by the upper arm. For as much smaller than Archer as she was, she did an impressive job of forcing him in the direction of the door.

"Go entertain the others. I knew it was a bad idea to let you in here," she reprimanded, closing the door behind him. She then returned to the bedside and stood next to Kerstin.

"A lot happened yesterday, Ava," Kerstin said before she could start shouting. "You really should lie back down. It took the magic nature lady you brought with you and a team of nurses to stitch you back together under those bandages. It'd be a shame for you to die now."

Ava seemed to be debating herself about whether to argue or not, but Aiden made the decision for her. He shoved his own pillow behind her back and pushed her gently, so as not to upset her bandages, back onto the pillows. This being done, Aiden turned back to Kerstin, flinching at the pain under his own bandages. He gave Kerstin a 'now would be the time to speak' kind of look.

"We couldn't find either of you or William in the morning when the alarm sounded so it was left to me and the other generals to decide what to do. At first I thought some of the council members might demand we follow their commands, but from what I heard you gave them an earful before you left, so they decided to leave the battle strategy to us." Kerstin took a breath to pause.

Mary, looking among all of them, quickly stepped out, shutting the door partially behind her.

"When I got to the wall that morning, the enemy lines were already there," Kerstin began again. "They'd assembled at night to start a siege on the city. We were woken before dawn by our soldiers on watch. By the time we all made it down there and sorted out what we were going to do, they'd already gotten some ladders on the wall. Honestly, if it weren't for those snakes and the wolf that the magic lady brought with her, they probably would have overrun us. But they held it long enough."

"Long enough for what?" Aiden asked. It was starting to seem like there would still be an Orenthian Army on the other side of the wall if he looked out the window.

"Long enough for Jagger to find his men and bring them back up the river and save us," Kerstin sighed. "He left right after you guys… escaped, to go find his forces that he sent south around the coast, you see."

Kerstin looked over his shoulder at the sound of Mary coming back through the door with a tray in hand. On it there were a few drinks, but most of the tray was taken up by bandages and a large bowl of hot water. She sat on Ava's side of the bed and set the tray on the side table.

Mary turned to face Kerstin, telling him, "I'll be changing the lady's bandages now if you wouldn't mind facing the wall."

Kerstin blushed slightly but turned to face away.

"I take it the lad is ok?" Mary asked, nodding in Aiden's direction.

Ava gave a weak smile in answer.

Kerstin's retelling was paused for a minute as Aiden helped Ava to lean up. Mary removed her shirt and began pulling off the bandages. Kerstin hadn't been lying about her injuries. It looked like she'd been half shredded before they'd stitched her back together.

"I haven't got the faintest idea how you managed not to bleed out lying on that dirt for so long," Mary mumbled.

Ava gave another weak smile and flinched as Mary pulled off the last of the bandages, leaving Ava bare from the waist up save for the hundreds of stitches that covered the wounds on her chest and stretched up to her shoulder.

"What happened next?" Ava asked with an air of trying to distract herself.

"They…" Kerstin started to say.

He was interrupted as Ava swore and slapped Mary's hand away before thinking. Mary had just dipped a fresh rag into the bowl of water and blotted it on Ava's wound.

"The fuck is that stuff?" Ava was staring at the bowl like it had fire in it.

"Water," Aiden said half mockingly, which earned him getting punched on the shoulder.

"It's moonshine, love," Mary corrected. "You were sitting in the mud for hours before they found you. I don't want you getting an infection."

Ava gritted her teeth as Mary again dabbed at the stitches.

"Keep going, Kerstin," Ava said in spaced grunts.

"They got here about midday yesterday, and... well, I'd heard what battle with him sounded like when I was below deck on his ship in Gloran but... simply put, Jagger and his men turned the tide. They attacked Orenth's forces from the back before anyone knew what was going on. Jagger fought his way right through their lines and stood there at the gate waiting to be let in. Orenth was surrendering by then. Jagger said we should kill them all, but not even his own men were on board for that, so we sent terms of surrender."

"Which where?" Ava asked.

Mary pulled out a piece of paper. "I thought one of you might ask that." She handed it to Aiden to read out loud.

To the leading commanders of the invading Orienthian Army

This letter contains the full extent of our terms and conditions for your peaceful surrender.

Full Surrender : Your forces will be required to give over all weapons of any kind. From that point you will be given the promise of travel back to Orenth via the quickest means you possess. As well as the promise that so long as these conditions are not violated none of your soldiers shall be harmed further while doing so.

It went on to outline how they would surrender their weapons and return to Orenth along with who would be going with them. But Aiden stopped reading it partway through and Kerstin picked up where he'd left off describing what had happened.

"As soon as their letter agreeing to the terms was received, some of the soldiers and I went out into the Orenthian camp to find..." Kerstin trailed off.

"I'll take it from here," Mary said. She'd finished Ava's bandages a minute ago, tying the ends into neat knots.

"William? You were going to say William?" Aiden asked, the night begging to come back to him in full. Kerstin was already halfway out the door, however, doing as Mary had asked and leaving the conversation to her.

Mary's face had gone solemn as she shook her head and looked at Aiden. "He was dead before the fighting stopped and the men got to you."

Aiden didn't know what to say, only sat there looking at Mary.

Ava set her hand atop his. "So what now?" she asked slowly. Her voice was a little strained and a little croaky, whether from the injury or the news he didn't quite know.

Mary reached into her pocket and told them, "William asked me to get this to the right people after you left to go south." She pulled out a wax sealed letter and handed it to Aiden.

He held her stare for a heartbeat before looking down at the letter. Red wax, emblazoned with the seal of Anglen. It took him a moment of looking at it before he worked up the courage to break the wax.

*To Aiden Windren & Ava Corinth*

*At the eventual time of my death, which I imagine will come before this war is said and done, Mary was instructed to give this letter to the two of you. Enclosed are my final wishes for the Kingdom of Anglen and all assets and responsibilities there entrusted.*

*I leave all authority and power to the two of you, in the hopes that you will lead well, though I do not expect you want such a responsibility. I trust that you two will lead with the Kingdom's best interests. I hope that you will learn from both my mistakes and successes, that you will both keep our people happy and prosperous as I did, but also that you will keep us strong as I never could.*

*To my loyal servants I free you of your vows to me, and pray you keep your vows to this Kingdom.*

*To the children I never had, I love you.*

*Your Dear Friend,*
*William*

Ava let out a long sigh, leaning sideways against Aiden's shoulder, and sat there for a few long minutes. Mary muttered something about giving them some space before she walked out the door, bringing the tray with her.

Ava shifted her head to look up at him. "Thick and thin, kingdoms and... royalty?"

Aiden looked over his shoulder down to her, his lips parted in a wide gape. He closed his mouth and paused for a long moment, processing before answering. "And... whatever else."

# EPILOGUE

## *Five Weeks Later*

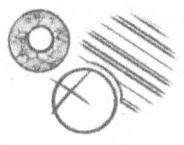

# RYDER & BRAN

"We'll have two more ales over here!"

"No... no!" Bran barked, beginning to slur his words. "I'm already... drunk enough to forget tonight. I... I don't need to wake up on the back of a horse who knows where tomorrow."

Ryder let out a laugh and slapped him on the back. "I didn't just run all over the damn country, screaming to the roof tops so that you could be an old fart for the celebration."

The barmaid brought the two tankards quickly. The woman had been making smiling trips to and from the barrels stacked behind the bar all night. Ryder wasn't the most reliable source of information at this point, but he was pretty sure the tavern was on its third barrel, although it could just as easily be on its fourth. Either way, among the few dozen people in the room, they'd drank more than enough to make a far larger town tipsy.

"So, are you going around being all high and mighty now that y-you've gone and met our King?" Bran teased, taking a large gulp from his own tankard.

Ryder gave a bow, working hard to hold his arm still so as not to spill his ale and only partially succeeding, not that the small puddle on the floor was out of place. The whole place had been growing progressively dirtier and dirtier since the two of them got there.

"A song!" shouted one of the men at a table beside them.

"Please, no!" Bran cried in mock sorrow. "M-my old ears can't take hear, hearing Ryder s-sing."

Bran's protest died before it was ever heard. A moment later the whole of the tavern was dancing in a circle that bent and bowed to allow people to get around the tables and chairs strewn around the room. They sang out the words of the song, many off tune, but in unison in triumphant voices.

Like love and life, rain and strife
Stand our home strong, oh stand our home long
Rain and shine and pointless rhyme
Our neighbor seek destroy our time,
But NO said one, and NO said two
And off to mountains grand they went...

Rain and shine and pointless rhyme
Oh how far the two did fall
Home they ran, as war drums blamed
And oh our enemy did come...

Through rain and shine and pointless rhyme
One and two, joined a few and off they flew,
In sails filled with wind,
Fear never their companion...

Through ruckus seas and wrathful men
Until then hope had been drear to them
But one or two grew and grew till power they did hold...

Home they came through rain and shine and pointless rhyme
Time and time the enemy committed crime
Bellows and wallows against our gate
But one and two lead the few

May our enemy feel wrath...

Through rain and shine and pointless rhyme
Our forces did prevail,

Time and loss, our King did fall...

But through rain and shine
One and Two did prevail.
King and queen of a simple dream
Only for their people do they kneeelll...!

The song ended in a collective roar that set the ceiling beams rattling dust upon them.

"I know the King...!" Ryder half sang.

"If the scar on your arm's any in-indication, you know the Queen too!"

Ryder spit out a little beer in outrage. "I thought we agreed," he said through his teeth, "to keep that between us..."

Bran let out a laugh. "That w-was before you h-hopped up on that high horse of yours."

Ryder looked around as though everyone in the tavern were listening in on them. No one was, of course.

"Now..." Brand started. "H-have I had enough ale for ya, or should I bring up some other s-stories, for the g-group...?"

Ryder had the old man up and out of the chair walking toward the door before Bran had the chance to say another word.

# ARLIN, ZACH & JAGGER

"What can we expect when we start coming to Barataria more frequently for trade runs?" Zach asked.

Jagger gave him a flat look.

Zach made a confused face. "Barataria isn't exactly welcoming of new trade partners so who else am I supposed to ask if I want to know?"

Arlin placed a hand on Zach's shoulder giving him a vaguely happy smile. "C'mon, the ceremony ended less than an hour ago and you're already back to this."

"Back to this? You're the one who's always trying to make deals with people."

"Not right after a coronation!" Arlin shouted, somewhat exasperated.

"Any questions you've got you can take up with the emissary I'll be leaving here," Jagger said, already turning to walk away, bored and disinterested in their conversation.

"Whatever…" Zach muttered.

"Where we should sail next though, that's a better question," Arlin rebuffed. He and Zach began walking to the nearby stable where their horses were tied. "I was thinking somewhere more south. Or maybe east."

Zach let out a scoff. "And we're going south for totally innocent non-trade-with-Barataria related reasons?"

"Well, I never said anything about that," Arlin replied while untying his horse.

"Are we not going to say goodbye before…"

Arlin cut Zach off. "They aren't letting our dirty sailor carcasses anywhere near them anymore, at least not in that shining pile of rock. I bet they're going to want their privacy for awhile anyway."

Zach unfastened his own horse and the two of them mounted their animals in smooth motions. Arlin took a quick peek in his saddle bags, a grossly poor equipment check, before digging his heels into the horse's sides and slipping into motion down the road.

"Is there anything we need before we set sail?" Zach asked.

"Nope, and if I had to guess, we're going to get called back to Gloran before too long to haul those two somewhere," Arlin chuckled. "I'm trying to get out of here before they get a chance to tell us we can't leave."

To his side, Zach flashed him a grin. Leaning forward on their mounts, they pushed their heels in further and spurred their horses into a canter out of the city.

# ALVA

"Are you sure you're well enough to be…" Mary trailed off as Alva pushed herself up off the bed.

"I am fine. I was nothing more than tired."

"Of course," Mary said with a nervous bow.

This… woman had fought on their side, but something about her still seemed to tell everyone that one wrong look would be all it would take for her compassion to run short.

"Is… is there anything I might get you before you depart? Food, at least, or something else?" Mary asked.

Avla considered the woman for a moment before replying, "That would be nice."

Behind them a growl sounded that made Mary jump.

Alva chuckled, "I think Zalve would like something as well if that's at all possible."

Mary took a small step forward, putting more space between herself and the wolf, which of course put her closer to Alva. "Of course, will the… I'm afraid I don't know how to refer to them, the snakes, be wanting anything?"

"I don't believe they will. Now that their debt is up, I'd imagine they're halfway to the far northeast by now."

"Debt?" Mary asked before she could stop herself, though she figured at this point she might as well commit to the question. "But Zalve is still… "

"Zalve is here because she is my friend. The snakes came because they owed me a favor and they knew it was easier for them to repay it than risk my wrath, nothing more."

This was all becoming a little too much for Mary between the gigantic wolf and the magical being. "I'll be back with food for both of you as soon as possible," she said breathlessly, already taking steps toward the door.

Alva didn't look in her direction as Mary walked out, shutting the door behind her. Zalve took a few steps lumbering toward her but still far more nimble than any normal wolf. She went to Alva's side and sat down. Even sitting, the wolf towered over Alva. Zalve's great fur coat was an impenetrable wall of white that reached up to her curious expression.

Alva let out a long sigh, stretching the span of a few seconds before looking up to the wolf's face. "I think it might be time for us to head home?"

The wolf turned its great head looking east, knowing through smell or some other unnatural sense the exact direction of Sylvanwood.

"No," Alva said, directing her gaze a little farther north.

The wolf glanced back confused at where Alva was facing.

"Our real home," she said, looking far off through the walls of the castle. Her gaze penetrated through mountains and across the sea to a place she hadn't thought of for a long time.

It took the wolf a moment to comprehend and a moment longer to lie down and rest its head against Alva's legs where she sat on the edge of the bed.

"I know," she muttered more to herself than the wolf as she stroked Zalve's head.

# HEATHER & ARCHER

Heather was walking half a step ahead of Archer, their hands clasped together in post ceremonial celebration. Archer had never seen the streets of Clystera before arriving with the army, but he had a feeling that it must not usually be like this. It couldn't be, not practically at least. A city could not keep up this state of... it was a hard feeling to describe. People weren't exactly happy, per se. They'd lost too much to be happy. It was more the feeling of having known that something bad was going to happen and having it be less bad that one expected. It was the temporary euphoria felt when months of stress and weeks of pain are finally lifted and one is left with less but still something.

Heather stopped to set a big bunch of flowers at a candlelight memorial. A sketch stood at the center of the small arrangement. It was not a particularly good one but still enough to get the gist of the man's features. There was a young woman, maybe nineteen, standing with a single yellow rose, facing the portrait a few paces away.

"Thank you..." she mumbled, sounding a little far off.

Heather paused for a beat. "Did... did you know him?"

The young woman didn't answer for a long moment, just stared at the picture like the face within was a million miles away.

"He was my brother," she said in that same far off voice.

"I'm sorry for your loss," Archer said seriously.

The young woman gave him a small, sad smile. "I know... I... I just... it feels more like it's everyone's loss, that they won't ever get to meet him now."

Archer didn't quite know what to say to that. Still, he asked, "He was a good brother then?"

The young woman repeated the sad smile. "He was."

"How are you holding up?" Heather asked.

"I'll be alright. He... he told me he likely wouldn't come back when he left."

Archer heard Heather suck in a breath. "I... I'm sorry to hear that."

The young woman took a deep breath before looking up, her sad smile had morphed to one slightly more optimistic. "Don't be, he wouldn't want that."

"Sorry?" Heather asked.

"He told me when we were young and again right before he left that if I ever did lose him he didn't want me to be sad. Right before he left to join the forces fighting at the walls, he told me that if it bought even a chance I'd be safe that he'd join a hundred times. He said I was the only person in the world he would do anything for..."

"It sounds like you had a wonderful brother," Archer offered.

Her smile grew a little more. "I did," she said and set the single yellow flower leaning on the drawing, giving it one last, not far off, but loving look, before turning away from the memorial.

"Good health to you...!" Heather offered as she walked away.

She gave them one last smile. "Death is scary, but not living is scarier." And with that, she disappeared into the night.

It was a minute before they began walking down the street again. Heather and Archer didn't speak much as they walked this time. They passed right through the city gates and out beyond them to wander through the fields for a while.

Heather stopped. Archer was a few steps past her still holding her hand before he realized she had.

"I want to get married," she said to Archer's surprise.

"What?" Archer asked, half laughing. "What do you mean?"

"I mean I want to get married."

"Why?"

"Because I love you and..." she paused.

Archer gave her a slightly concerned look.

"And because life is short. I want to promise to spend my life with you before it's over."

"Do you plan on dying sometime soon?"

"No, but if I do someday I want to have told you that... that I love you and I want to be yours."

A few moments passed in which they considered each other in the moonlight. She dropped his hand and took a small step back to face him fully. "So?"

"So what?" he asked.

"Gods damn, you're dumb! Will you marry me?"

Archer gave her a look and she was debating whether to smack him or walk away before she had a chance to cry when he answered.

"It would be the greatest honor of my life."

# AIDEN & AVA

Hours earlier…

"Do you swear before the people of the Kingdom of Anglen that you will do all in your power to serve them justly and fairly, that you will protect them from harm, and lead them to happiness?"

"I do," he said and the words were echoed beside him.

"Do you swear to do whatever it takes to protect this Kingdom?"

"I do."

Ava said the same.

"Then I crown you King and Queen of the Kingdom of Anglen, wardens of its lands, protectors of its realms, the speakers of our law, and those in whom we trust our fate."

The officiant set crowns on each of their heads. Behind him, Aiden felt the crowds that were packed all the way up the castle steps shift, then break out in cheers. This sound was different from the screams that still rang in his dreams. It was a bright noise that filled the world, the same holistic tune he remembered as a child back home playing with his friends, loud enough to drown out the distant whipping wind of winter, as the sun split the clouds raining down on the steps of the castle.

Ava pinched him.

"Ow, what?"

"Face your people, dumbass," she whispered through pursed lips.

He turned to face down the steps. They stood there smiling down at the crowd long enough that Aiden started to get a little uncomfortable just waving back.

Kerstin stepped up beside Aiden. "You two are allowed to go in the castle you know."

Aiden turned his head. Kerstin was sporting a faint bruise around his left eye. Aiden would ask about that later.

"Thank you," Aiden said quickly. He turned, not fast, but quickly enough that Ava pinched him again before following him in through the newly polished walnut doors. No one followed them in.

"Remember you have to be at the feast tonight!" Kerstin called after them before shutting the doors.

Aided looked back at Ava. "I don't think I've ever seen you wear a dress before," he reflected out loud.

She passed him, frowning. Her scars poked out the exposed sides and back of the dress, still pink and fresh on her right side. "Don't get used to it," she said.

He grinned. "Fair enough, how would you beat people up in bars?"

She chuckled. "Now I can have the guards beat them up."

"I don't think that's how justice works," Aiden said while looking around the hall. "Where are all the guards?"

Ava made a noncommittal noise.

He watched her out of the corner of his vision. "What did you do?"

"I convinced… Kerstin not to station guards around us."

"You beat up our general before you were even pronounced Queen?"

"I told him if he could punch me, he could station guards," she replied, smiling guiltily.

Another question occurred to Aiden just then. His thoughts were pulled away from the current conversation as he asked, "Did we just get married?"

Ava seemed taken aback. She blinked looking at him, then back at the door at the far end of the hall. "I don't... actually know? We should probably ask someone about that."

Aiden shrugged. "Later."

She laughed, her mouth gaping wide at his casualness, as they started up the steps. After a moment, she asked, "So what do you think our first action as King and Queen should be?"

Aiden considered for a moment. "We should put some of the common people on the council."

"Ok," she responded.

Aiden looked at her. "You really think so?"

She smiled. "We're King and Queen, we can do whatever we want." She then considered for a moment and added, "I think we should replace that old, fat guy with Kerstin as commanding general."

"I agree."

They came to the top of the staircase and started back down the hall to the front of the castle.

"I was talking with Archer," Ava began but stopped at the smile on Aiden's face.

"You two are finally getting along?"

She muttered something Aiden chose not to hear.

"I was talking with Archer," Ava began again, "and he said he convinced his dad to let him stay for a little while. He's hoping he might be able to forge some kind of alliance with us after everything."

They reached the far end of the hall and stepped out onto the balcony.

"After everything...If Barataria will have us as an ally, I think we should," Aiden agreed.

Ava nodded.

Aiden reached the edge of the balcony. The crowd at the steps was starting to disperse, though the cheers still rang through the city.

Aidens smile faded... "It's all on us now." He leaned against the railing of the balcony.

"Yep," Ava said and moved beside him. "Let's do better." And she turned to him, smiling faintly.

He smiled back. "Better."

# - Author's Note -

First and foremost thank you for taking the time to read my book.

This story was never written with the intention of someday being published, but... well, as with many things in life the intention differed from the outcome.

I suppose, I don't really have anything left to say at the moment... you read the book.

But a piece of advice.

To anyone who thinks they might be even the slightest bit interested in writing, try it. Having done it now, and looking back on it, I believe there are more than likely thousands, hundreds of thousands, of stories drafted only in our minds that people never took the time to write. The world has never been worse off for the sharing of knowledge. What's the worst that could happen? You waste someone's time?

And on that note, I am doing so to you right now, and so I will leave you with one final tidbit.

Give it a go, write down your day dream...


I did.

# - ACKNOWLEDGMENTS -

To Daniel Copeland,

I know you'll never get the chance to read this, and I know I always made you talk with me about skiing rather than doing my classwork. But that's of no consequence now. What I'm really trying to get at Cope, is that I'm thankful... More than I ever let you know, I'm thankful for your conversations. I'm thankful for your support. I'm thankful for the perspective you gave me on literature and on the importance of writing. I'm thankful for the perspective you gave me on the world, on people, on connections, on the way we work our way through life.

I'm thankful Cope, more than I could ever say, for your teaching, for your lessons, assigned and not, for your discourse, your joviality, your deep laugh and easy smile, your boisterous greetings every day in the halls, and your well wishes every day when I left. I'm thankful for the way you changed my life.

But most of all, I'm grateful for your friendship.

Peace love and powder turns,
Your friend still, Owen.

To Matt Siler,

For changing the way I see literature, language and most importantly storytelling, I am eternally grateful. For introducing me to English as I had never before seen it, and to

*To Kill a Mockingbird* (my favorite book for anyone wondering) for being my friend and my mentor, thank you.

All the best, climb hard,
Your friend Owen.


To Maya Brandewie

For being the person always willing to talk and brainstorm, you probably had the greatest influence on the actual creation of this book. As well as being the most versed, besides myself of course, in all the things that this book may have ended up being. For helping with the artwork and so much more, Thank you.

Call me if you ever need a ride,
Your brother Owen.


To Koren Nydick & Brad Brandewie

Little need or can be said here to encapsulate the influence the two of you have had on my writing. From the age of zero the two of you have been supporting me on my journey to today. Mom, thank you for agreeing to undertake the monumental task of editing my manuscript, a task that I understand was made incredibly difficult given my pitiful spelling and grammar, as well as always being willing to brainstorm, Thank you. Dad, thank you for reading the manuscript with all it's numerous faults and giving me recommendations for developmental edits. To both of you I love you and wish nothing but the best.

I'll make sure to call,
Your son Owen


To all the other people who have helped me along the way including Ali Burns, Ilah Reynar, Marsha Weaver, Sara Schmit, Susan Ryder, Zach Zehr, Gail Brandewie, and others. Thank you for helping me in whatever capacity you did to get me to where I am today. For that I am grateful and I wish nothing but the best for all of you.